Berger grabbed h[...] terminal. He starte[...] sign: EXCESS BAG[...] transfixed. EXCESS. The letters seized his consciousness. EXC.

The voices began yelling in his head.

The rage erupted so fast that Berger had no conscious reaction. He began screaming from the depths of his diaphragm and grabbed the shoulders of a dark-haired man who was standing nearby. Within seconds, the startled stranger was on his back on the floor, with Berger straddling him. Berger felt as if he were watching himself from a distance, seeing his body act on automatic pilot. He grabbed the man's hair and began slamming his head into the floor yelling, "Murderer! Killer!"

ALSO BY DON PASSMAN

The Visionary

All You Need to Know about
the Music Business (nonfiction)

DON
PASSMAN

MIRAGE

WARNER
VISION
BOOKS

An AOL Time Warner Company

WARNER BOOKS EDITION

Copyright © 2000 by Don Passman
All rights reserved. No part of this book may be reproduced in any form or by any electronic or mechanical means, including information storage and retrieval systems, without permission in writing from the publisher, except by a reviewer who may quote brief passages in a review.

Cover design by Jesse Sanchez
Cover photography by Image Bank/Pete Turner

Warner Vision is a registered trademark of Warner Books, Inc.

Warner Books, Inc.
1271 Avenue of the Americas
New York, NY 10020

Visit our Web site at
www.twbookmark.com.

For information on Time Warner Trade Publishing's online publishing program, visit www.ipublish.com.

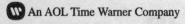 An AOL Time Warner Company

Printed in the United States of America

Originally published in hardcover by Warner Books
First Paperback Printing: November 2001

10 9 8 7 6 5 4 3 2 1

For Bea Shaw.
And
For Sam Passman.

MIRAGE

CHAPTER 1

Piedra Alta, Colorado

The patient known as Oliver was in the final stages.

Gamma observed him through a square hole in the thick metal door. Duty required the guard to keep watching, even though he knew he'd dream about it for weeks. He always did.

Inside the windowless cinder block room, Oliver's khaki pants were soaked with perspiration and other bodily excretions. He twisted against the leather straps that pinned him to the bed, clanking metal hooks against welded bolts, and chafing his wrists to the bleeding point. Oliver's raw eyes, depleted of tears, scanned in terror for unseen attackers. His neck muscles strained into tight cords as he screamed in guttural yells.

Kenneth Combs, Director of the Mirage project, elbowed the guard aside and peered through the small opening. Gamma could hear Oliver whimpering like a dog with a broken leg.

Combs ran his hand over his bald head. His face betrayed no emotion as he studied the scene, then said, "Dispose of him in the usual way."

As Combs turned to leave, the guard said, "Sir." His voice cracked slightly.

Combs spun back and lasered his obsidian eyes into the man. Gamma looked down as he continued. "Based on some of the others, there may be a chance this patient—"

"Did I ask your opinion?"

Gamma cleared his throat. "No sir."

"You're aware there's an inspection in two hours?"

"Yes sir."

Combs walked away and spoke without looking back. "Dispose of him in the usual way."

General James Weston sat in the back of a black Chevy sedan. His driver was dressed in civilian clothes so as not to attract attention. A snowstorm whipped the car, oblivious to the pitiful efforts of the windshield wipers, and the wind whistled through an invisible seam somewhere in front.

"I'm sorry, General," said the driver. "I can't see the turnoff in this weather. I'll swing back around."

Weston grunted, adjusted his large frame on the seat, and pulled off the heavy wool overcoat. The shirt of his uniform, now soaked with perspiration, clung to his skin.

He looked out the window and could hardly see the aspen trees' bare limbs through the hazy gauze of snow flurries. Focusing on his reflection in the window, Weston studied his features intently, hypnotized by the rhythmic squealing of the windshield wipers. It seemed to him that his wrinkles were even more deeply creased than usual, and he was surprised by the spiderwebs of red veins in his eyes. Having to deliver this news wasn't helping.

"Here it is, sir," said the driver. The general was thrown

against the door as the car turned sharply right. He could hear the chains on the tires crunch against the ice, and he felt the rear wheels fishtail.

About two miles down a rough road, Weston saw anti-tank barriers—giant piles of rusted metal girders sticking out of the ground like rifles stacked in a teepee formation. They surrounded the first of the checkpoints, which was a small booth with thick, bulletproof glass. Jutting across the road was a red and white striped pole, almost three feet in diameter.

A sentry approached the car. When the driver lowered the window, a cold gust assaulted Weston.

"Afternoon, General," said the sentry with a salute. His mustache was laced with ice.

"Afternoon."

"Sir, I'm sorry, but security doesn't allow your driver inside. We have a van to take you from here."

Weston hobbled out of the car, moving slowly to buy a little more time. The wind sounded like a huge bellows, and the sharp cold assaulted his skin as he climbed into the van. He dragged his overcoat behind him, leaving a rough trail in the snow.

They drove several miles in silence, clearing two more checkpoints. The road finally led into the mouth of a man-made cave. A six-story cavern that was an abandoned NORAD site, meant to withstand nuclear attack. Overkill for the current project, yet convenient enough for the re-quired secrecy.

The van stopped in an open area that was bathed in a wash of halogen lights. The rock walls, cold and damp as though weeping, did little to shelter the workers.

"This way, General," said a pleasant young woman in a heavy wool coat. Her breath was visible when she spoke. "I'm called Dorothy here."

He followed behind her, aware of the icy echoes of his footsteps.

Combs sat in his office, fighting to remain calm now that General Weston was on the premises. He ran his hand over his bald head, worrying whether the fuzz had grown visible since yesterday's shaving. Then he began pacing across one of the few carpets in the facility.

By reputation, Weston was a tough scrapper, which was necessary to champion a controversial project like Mirage. Maybe today's visit meant he'd gotten enough money to kick the research into high gear. Combs certainly hoped so. Their breakthrough in the last few days had opened a whole new range of possibilities. The chance to tell the General about it personally was an unexpected plum.

He stood ramrod straight and examined himself in the mirror. His right shoe was scuffed on the side. There was no time to polish it, so he'd stand with his left to the General. He straightened his tie an eighth of an inch and smoothed the sharp creases in his white shirt. Finally, he examined his beard, making sure it was evenly trimmed.

Dorothy arrived with the General, and Combs rushed to greet him. The General lowered himself slowly into an armchair that barely contained his girth.

"General, I'm told you like two sugars, no milk," said Combs, handing him a steaming coffee.

"Your spies informed you correctly," said Weston. He cupped his hands around the mug and blew across the top of the liquid. Then he sat back and took a sip.

After an awkward silence, Combs spoke. "Sir, I want to be respectful of your time. Shall we start the inspection?"

"Uh . . . not now."

Combs drummed his fingers behind his back. "Our

biggest frustration is that we can't discuss what we've achieved. I'm looking forward to telling you everything."

Combs thought the General looked as if he were sitting on something uncomfortable.

"Major Combs—" began the General.

Combs whispered. "Sir, I'm sorry, but here I'm only called the Director. Even in my own office. The security—"

"Yes, yes, sorry. Son, the problem is . . . well . . ." Weston grimaced, then took another sip of the coffee. "The problem is . . . I've got to shut you down."

It took a beat for the words to register. When they did, Combs felt as if he had been punched in the solar plexus. He leaned against his desk for support. "Shut us down?"

"I'm here to see that everything is dismantled by tomorrow at oh-eight-hundred. There'll be vans for the equipment, and buses for the personnel. All the documents have to be shredded by then."

"Sir, we've had some astounding breakthroughs. Have you seen the reports?"

"Of course I've seen the reports. The problem is Peterson, that bleeding-heart pinko senator from California. He got wind of what you're doing up here. You've got a Judas in your ranks, son. That's the only way he could've found out."

"We have a leak?"

"Yes sir. Peterson went to the Finance Committee and threatened to go public if the plug wasn't pulled in forty-eight hours."

Combs's belly felt like it was on fire. He mentally scanned the faces of his personnel, trying to divine the traitor. His voice was tight when he spoke. "There must be a way—"

"There isn't. It's over, son. You got to retreat when you're licked."

The room seemed to swirl around Combs. The only sound was the low hum of a floor heater.

Weston continued, "You still divided into three sectors?"

Combs nodded.

"Keep the divisions physically isolated. And only the top dogs do the shredding." Weston pushed himself up, using the arms of the chair to support his large frame. "I'll be here at oh-seven-hundred for a final walk-through."

"You mean we have to start now?"

"Right now."

Within an hour, the personnel had been ripped from their duties and assigned to packing. Combs walked the facility in a daze. The scene was like an animal carcass being picked apart by buzzards. His top men reduced to filling cardboard boxes with years of research. Others wrapping lab equipment in tissue paper. Vans and buses parked outside, waiting like hearses.

He almost lost it when they wheeled in the four shredders. One for each of his Section Chiefs. And one for Combs himself. The boxes of paperwork from each division were sent to three separate staging areas, where each Chief had to personally shred his own material. They wheeled Combs's shredder right into his office. Strangers! Waltzing right into his most private space!

Inconceivable.

Just after 9:00 P.M., Section Chief Delta sneaked away from his shredding and dialed the number. He knew that security prohibited outside calls, but since they were shutting everything down, fuck 'em.

"Honey, I've got to work late," he whispered. "I won't be able to make it."

"Oh, no," pouted Penny, the twenty-something ski instructor he'd met when he fell down her slope. "I'm leaving tomorrow for three weeks."

"Believe me, I'm sorry."

"I bought a short nightie and some jasmine oil that's supposed to heighten your sexual livid—or something like that. The store said it's better than the oil from India. You remember the Indian oil?"

He remembered all right. That Indian oil had lit up his balls like Christmas bulbs. "If there is *any* possible way, I will get there."

"It's going to be awfully cold if I'm alone tonight," she purred. "I'm lying on the bed and reaching my hand into my panties."

It took all of Delta's willpower to hang up and go back to the shredding. He had at least six more hours of ripping up this shit, by which time Penny would be ice cold and he'd have blue-balls.

How could they give a menial shredding job to someone of his rank? Hell, the way things were divided up, no one could make heads or tails out of this crap anyway. So why did it have to be him? Did he accidentally piss off Combs or something?

Combs sat with his companion, Jack Daniel's. Although he rarely drank, tonight he was halfway through the bottle and finally getting numb. It was the warmest he'd ever felt inside this Ali Baba cave.

The most confidential materials were locked in his office. Since Combs was the only one who had access, he was the only one who could shred them. It had been more than four hours since they'd brought in the shredder, yet he hadn't been able to start.

He poured himself another shot, and threw it down the back of his throat. Then he stood up and found himself wobbly. Combs stumbled over to the shredder, pushed the green button, and the machine whirred to life. After fishing out his three-sided key, he unlocked the file cabinet and took out the oldest folder.

As he walked toward the shredder, he felt as though he were about to violate a sacred oath. Combs stopped and looked through the file. The very first experiment. He smiled at the naïveté it reflected. Especially compared to where they were now.

The rage began to build again. He'd hoped the booze would lower the flames, yet his anger seared right through. Those sonsofbitches. They didn't even bother to find out where he was before they pulled the gallows trapdoor.

Combs stood in place a long while before putting the folder into the shredder. As it tore up the paper, he felt as though his skin was being flayed. He sat down for another shot of advice from Jack, who told him that he had to get through this. No one else could see the material.

Wait.

No one else could see the material. The germ of an idea took hold and started to grow. He was the only one with the whole picture. And while the research and data were voluminous, the conclusions were relatively simple. No one could shred what was in Combs's head, and once he destroyed these documents, no one could even get that.

He began to smile.

Combs grabbed an armload of files and whistled as he fed them into the shredder.

Delta's fingers were slick and greasy from shoveling printed pages into the machine. The image of Penny fondling herself kept replaying in his head, and the piles of documents didn't look any smaller. He was already cramming in such large batches that the shredder had jammed four times in the last half hour.

Shit. Make that five.

He cleared the machine's blades and walked into the hall to work off some of his frustration. Delta strode down the corridor in long steps, his fingers fidgeting for lack of a cigarette. The place was buzzing with people in white jumpsuits loading pallets of equipment. He glanced into the open door of a lab and saw Private Green neatly laying out his equipment on a workbench. The man handled each piece like it was a newborn infant. He remembered Green as one of those geeky types who always had his nose in a book. The kind that worked late even when there wasn't any overtime pay.

Delta stepped inside and sidled up next to Green. Green smiled, proud of his work. This guy would be perfect.

"Green, come with me a minute."

"Sir, I can't leave the lab."

"It's okay. I'm giving you an order."

Green glanced around the room, looking for a rescuer. "I'm not supposed—"

"I said I'm giving you an order."

"Yessir."

Green trailed reluctantly behind Delta to the shredding room.

Green stopped at the door. "This is a classified area. My clearance doesn't permit—"

Delta put his arm around Green's shoulder and dragged him along. "You're with me. And I'm giving you permission." Green resisted, like a stubborn horse being pulled from a barn.

"I'm redeploying you, Green. From now on, you shred these materials."

"I'm supposed to pack up the lab."

"You the only one in the lab?"

"No . . ."

"Then start shredding."

"I don't think I can do that without the Director's—"

"Fuck the Director. All the rules went out the window when they decided to shut down this Roach Motel."

"I still have two years to go in the Army, sir, and—"

Delta leaned in close. "Look, Private. Lemme give you a real-life lesson about the Army. You can refuse me, and I can put something in your record about insubordination. Or you can take care of this shredding and nobody will know but us." Delta was bluffing of course. He didn't even know Green's real name.

"Sir, with all respect—"

Delta whispered conspiratorially. "Kid, you gotta learn how to grab opportunities when they drop in your lap. Shredding is a helluva lot easier than packing up lab equipment. And a lot less dangerous than some of those chemicals."

Green hesitated. "I don't know . . ."

"I got a hundred dollar bill in my pocket that says you make the right decision. Think, kid. A hundred dollars, or a demerit."

"Colonel Delta, I don't think it's right to accept money. If this is important to you, I'll take care of it."

Delta grinned. What a sucker. "Atta boy. Now I owe you one. See how it works?"

Green tentatively picked up a handful of papers.

Delta pulled on his coat. "Don't you read any of this shit, you hear?" He slapped Green on the back, then left with his mind and groin already soaking in jasmine oil.

For the next two hours, Green fed papers into the ravenous shredder, which gnashed its teeth as if calling for more. Just to change the monotonous routine, he went to the opposite side of the room and grabbed a handful from the boxes stacked there. On his way back to the shredder, his eye caught the heading on one of the pages. He looked around to be sure no one was near, then closed the door and began reading.

Green found himself involuntarily shaking his head, as if to deny what was on the paper. Still stunned, he locked the door and continued reading through the files.

This was absurd. No one would really do this. It must be one of those diversionary operations, where they pretend something happened just to confuse the enemy.

But what enemy? We weren't at war.

Could human beings actually do something like this?

CHAPTER 2

Three Years Later
Los Angeles, California

For the last few days, John Berger couldn't shake the feeling that somebody was watching him. Mostly it was instinct, since he hadn't actually seen anyone. Or maybe he was just being paranoid.

His eyes watered from having stared at the computer screen almost fourteen straight hours. Berger leaned back in his desk chair, causing his vertebrae to crack. Then he yawned deeply while he untied and retied his curly black hair into a ponytail.

The clock on his computer screen said 11:36 P.M. Besides the security guard, he had been the only one working at EXC Labs for the last four hours. This was the fourth late-nighter he'd pulled in the last two weeks, and they weren't getting any easier. On the other hand, since he'd decided to go with EXC, he didn't have a lot of choice.

Berger had been fascinated with puzzles since he was a child. He'd never imagined that would cross his career path, as his Stanford Ph.D. was in computer science. However, just before finishing his dissertation on artificial intelligence, he attended a lecture by Dr. Alan Konheim, the preeminent authority on cryptography. That talk connected the circuit between Berger's passion for computers and unlocking secrets, and he'd decided on the spot to become a computer cryptographer. Being a very fast study, he gained a reputation in cryptography even before graduation, and received literally dozens of offers—including a chance to "go inside" and work for the government's National Security Agency. Berger turned them all down in favor of EXC.

EXC was a small incubator company with a solid track record of launching high-tech enterprises. Incubators put up capital to develop companies during the riskiest phase, then bring in investors to take them to the next level. They loved Berger's idea, and if the concept worked, he would be incredibly rich. In the meantime, he only got a small salary and a piece of paper that represented twenty percent ownership of his fledgling company. "Keep 'em starving" as a way to motivate people had seemed like a reasonable premise when Berger started out. Now that he was over a year into it, he wasn't so sure. Between a low salary, student loans, and some aggressive credit card spending, his finances now teetered on the verge of collapse. And with EXC's seed money almost gone, if he didn't get a breakthrough pretty quickly, the whole thing would collapse.

Berger rubbed his eyes, then typed in another set of instructions in C++.

Contrary to popular belief, only a small part of cryptography is used for spying or hiding government secrets. Most is used for bank transfers, cable TV scrambling, ATMs, and the like. Also contrary to popular belief, cryptography doesn't rely on a secret way to encode data. Instead, the secret is the "key" necessary to unlock the encrypted text. In computer cryptography, an algorithm—

a set of computer instructions—translates text into mathematical values, then manipulates those values by multiplying and dividing by a secret key, or password. To decode, you need the correct key to reverse the process.

Berger was working on a way to speed up RSA, the most secure encryption system on the planet. RSA is used mainly to exchange keys for DES and other systems, because it's too slow to carry lengthy messages. Berger was on the edge of manipulating RSA's algorithm to operate with a speed close to DES, yet that edge was proving harder to cross than he'd expected.

His eyes were now blurred, and he knew he'd hit the wall for the night. Surrendering with a long exhale, he turned off his computer and listened to it whirr down to silence. Fatigue gave him a slight stoop as he ambled into the perimeter hallway. In the dead quiet, that feeling of being watched crept back. He glanced quickly around the hallway, where the smell of floor polish hung heavily in the air, yet saw nothing.

As Berger crossed the parking lot, the only sound was the clicking of his boot heels against the asphalt. His paranoia, if that's what it was, made his back feel vulnerable, as if it were bare. He sucked in cool mist from the evening fog, and told himself forcefully that it was unlikely anyone was following. True, there was this gray Dodge that he'd seen several times over the last few days. But he couldn't be sure it had always been the same car. And who'd care about his comings and goings anyway?

Berger rubbed his eyes with his knuckles, then pulled on a white helmet and climbed astride his Harley-Davidson Softail. He surveyed the parking lot one last time before kicking the bike into first gear and curling the right handlebar toward himself. The engine surged like ripping canvas. He started for home, reassured by the Freudian implication of a 1340cc engine between his legs.

As he drove along Centinela, Berger leaned back against the tufted-leather sissy bar and dug his boots into the upper footrests. His muscles were tense, and he found himself checking his rearview mirror so often that he wasn't focusing on the road in front. He shook his head, as if to scold himself, and picked up speed.

Berger lived in Venice, a few blocks from the beach, on Indiana Street. When he killed the bike's engine, the roar of the wind still reverberated in his ears, and the contrasting quiet of his street was almost disorienting. He walked quickly toward the 1920s house he'd rented for the last two years. It was a vague attempt to knock off the California Craftsman style—a one-story, pitched-roof cottage, with symmetrical windows, redwood-slatted siding, and a sagging front porch. Somewhere along the line, the landlord had covered the windows and doors with thin iron bars that looked like you could bend them with your hands.

As he neared the front, his perimeter alarm, Max, began barking. He could also hear repeated thuds as Max flung himself against the door in an effort to maim the intruder. Berger took one last look around before opening the door. As soon as Max recognized him, he began panting on the edge of hyperventilation, and his tongue fell out the side of his mouth. Max tried to jump into Berger's arms, which was impossible for a tiny, short-legged Jack Russell terrier who was at least twice his normal body weight.

Berger's living room was decorated with furniture from Chez Recycler. There was a mismatched sofa and easy chair, whose innards had been dissected by Max; a dented footlocker, painted with the name *Susie,* that served as a coffee table; and an oak wine barrel with a lamp made out of a plastic parking meter. Berger hadn't cared about anything but functionality when he'd bought the stuff, and now he couldn't afford to redecorate.

After bolting and chaining the door, he clunked his helmet on the blond, plank wood floor. Berger scooped up Max and carried him like a football to the couch, where he stretched out with a long sigh. Max forced his nose under Berger's hand, and when Berger scratched his ears, he grunted ecstatically in an odd assortment of sounds.

Berger quickly fell into the twilight lull between heavy exhaustion and sleep, and his body vibrated with a light buzz. With the door secured, and Max standing sentry, this sense of being followed now seemed a bit silly. Maybe even arrogant. To presume he was the subject of some nefarious plot?

He drifted into a quiet slumber.

In the duplex across from Berger's house, a thin man sat on a canvas director's chair, which was the only piece of furniture. The room was dark, save the slashes of light from a street lamp that filtered through the curtains. He listened to Max's grunting, courtesy of a thin microphone sewn into Berger's carpet remnant.

Within a few minutes, the dog went quiet and Berger's soft snores floated into the plastic earpiece. The man slid back his sleeve to reveal the glow of his watch dial, then used a lighted pen to write in the log:

"12:27 A.M. Subject asleep."

CHAPTER 3

Paris, France

Kenneth Combs, former Director of the Mirage project, sat in a woven bamboo chair outside the café Les Deux Magots, at the corner of boulevard St.-Germain and rue de Rennes, on the Left Bank. It was a chilly November afternoon, overcast and gray, and the air was filled with the aroma of French cigarettes.

As was typical with street cafés in Paris, the chairs faced the sidewalk like theater seats, and Combs watched people with shopping bags and briefcases bustle back and forth. There really was something different about Europeans, he thought. Tight lips, ruddy complexions. Wearing overcoats on their shoulders without putting their arms in the sleeves. Waving their hands like monkeys while they babbled in that gibberish. Coddling poodles on their laps during lunch, and giving the little mongrels every other bite. Right in front of him, two men kissed each other on both cheeks. Combs wondered if he could catch an earlier plane.

He took a swallow of bitter espresso from a tiny cup, and reflected on the irony of meeting in the same café where Hemingway, Fitzgerald, and Miller hung out in the 1920s. In light of Combs's mission, he felt a camaraderie with those American expatriates. Even the name of the café was ironic. "Magot." It sounded like "maggot" but meant the "Magi" who brought gifts to Christ in the manger. Combs had some gifts to bring. Real different from frankincense and myrrh.

A waiter startled Combs, causing him to accidentally elbow a fat lady at the next table. She sputtered a stream of French and stabbed at him with her umbrella. He turned away from her and realized his hands were shaking. Probably the industrial-strength caffeine they use over here.

Where were the assholes he was supposed to meet?

The bells of a stone church across the way chimed softly. Combs looked at his watch. They were a half hour late, and he figured that was a tactic. Probably supposed to rattle him, which he didn't want to let them do. He looked at his watch again.

About ten minutes later, he spotted them. Two pale-skinned men in business suits walking on the opposite side of the street. They were discreetly stealing glances at him, and both they and Combs acted like they didn't see each other. In his peripheral vision, he watched them blend into the crowd, then reappear in the doorway of a bank. Two more men joined them and huddled conspiratorially. A not so subtle show of force. The original two dispersed to posts at each end of the block, while the new arrivals made their way toward Combs.

Both men appeared to be in their early thirties. The taller one had a faded scar above his lip, and one of his ears was misshapen. The smaller one had a protruding forehead and wore amber-tinted glasses.

"Many things are possible in our world," said the taller

man, in perfect Oxford English. The shorter man riveted his stare into Combs.

Combs gave the prearranged reply. "All the more if we bind together."

The shorter man nodded and the two of them sat down.

"I am Milos," said the taller man. "And this is Peter."

Neither extended their hand.

"You can call me Alpha," said Combs.

In front of them, a mime began to perform for the crowd. He was a scrawny man in a black and white diamond harlequin outfit. The crowd tittered as he followed an unsuspecting passerby, mimicking his gestures.

Milos toyed with a sugar cube. "If you are able to deliver the items you claim, Mr. Alpha, you shall be very wealthy."

"I can deliver, Mr. Milos."

The mime pretended to take a woman's baby from her carriage and throw it into traffic. The crowd laughed.

"When will the demonstration occur?"

"Monday. When do I get paid?"

"Fifty percent will be wired tomorrow, if we are satisfied with this meeting. You'll have the balance on Tuesday. If the demonstration is satisfactory."

The shorter man leaned forward and spoke for the first time. His voice sounded as though he were hoarse, and he spat out the words in heavily accented English. "We have reason to believe you are setting us up for a trap. If you don't convince me otherwise in the next few minutes, you are a dead man."

While Combs assumed that was a bluff, Peter had said it with such force that it nonetheless unnerved him. He told himself they wouldn't have shown up if they really believed it was a trap. This had to be their way of softening him up for the negotiations.

"You're misinformed," said Combs, hoping to sound calm. "Do I look stupid enough to play games with you? If you're worried about me, let's forget the whole thing. I have someone else who wants the deal." That of course was a total bluff.

The men whispered to each other in some babble as the harlequin mime approached with his bell-tipped hat. They waved him away. Combs fished out a twenty-franc bill and stuffed it in the hat. He didn't want the guy hanging around.

"We agree to the demonstration," said Milos. "Then we shall decide if we wish to continue."

"You'll see the results on Monday," said Combs, sitting back for the first time during the meeting. "I want an answer by Wednesday."

CHAPTER 4

Venice, California

Friday night, Berger sat on the tattered beige couch in his living room. Max was comfortably ensconced under his petting hand, and Berger's girlfriend, Linda, sat on the easy chair. Linda was almost six feet tall—the same height as Berger—with long blond hair and green cat eyes. She managed The House of Usher, an independent bookstore in Santa Monica, and they'd met about six months ago when Berger's pal Jason dragged him to a dreadful poetry reading in her store. They'd been dating steadily ever since, though she'd grown a little distant over the past couple of weeks. Berger had been trying to ignore that.

The conversation dwindled into silence. Linda clasped her hands between her knees and hunched forward. Berger watched her hair play in the light and debated whether to tell her. They'd been together long enough for him to open up, he thought. Worst that happens is she thinks he's nuts. And she might already be there.

"I've had this weird feeling for the last week or so," he finally said.

It took her a moment to react. "Oh?" Her voice sounded distracted.

"This feeling like someone was following me."

"Following you?"

"Yeah. You ever feel like that?"

A pause. "Not really."

Well, that makes me feel real special. He shifted in his seat.

"Did you call the police?" she asked, still not looking at him.

"No. It's just, you know, a feeling. You can't call the cops about a feeling, huh?" He forced a chuckle.

A long silence. Maybe telling her about this wasn't such a good idea.

"John, we need to discuss something."

Both Berger and Max looked over at her. Somehow, with her distant attitude, she looked even more stunning than usual. Probably echoes of the gorgeous girls in junior high who didn't notice that Berger existed.

She bit her lower lip. Berger thought overbites were sexy. Then she said, "I'm seeing somebody else."

The words settled down on Berger like a spinning coin coming to rest. They hit bottom in his abdomen, and suddenly that overbite wasn't quite so appealing.

The most intelligent reply he could muster was, "What?"

"I said I'm seeing somebody else. I think we should both date other people."

"That's a terrible idea. I dated other people for years. It sucked."

She still wasn't looking at him. "If we're right for each other, it will work out in the long run."

That's right out of Dear Abby's Book of Polite Blow-offs. Shit.

"Who are you seeing?" Somehow he felt compelled to

ask the standard question. He waited for her to say it was no one he knew, or it didn't matter, or whatever the usual comeback was.

Before she could answer, Max lifted his head, as if catching a scent in the air. His ears went up and he started growling.

She began, "Let's not make this any—"

Max's growl erupted into a bark as he flew off the couch, not quite landing on his feet. He recovered in a flurry of nails scratching on hardwood, then rushed to the doorway.

There was a loud knock. With Berger's emotions scraped raw by Linda's sneak attack, plus the week's feeling of being watched, he was startled so badly that his teeth chattered. He looked at Linda, then at the door.

"Are you expecting anyone?" she asked.

Berger shook his head and whispered, "Maybe they'll go away."

An even stronger set of knocks declared they weren't leaving. He could see the door shudder in its frame.

Berger's legs wobbled slightly as he crossed the room, feeling Linda's eyes on his back.

"Who's there?" he asked.

The answer was increased pounding, so powerful that he worried the door might splinter.

Then it stopped.

The cessation was just as discomforting, especially since Berger heard no footsteps to indicate they were leaving. Not that he could hear much over Max's barking.

"Who's there?" he repeated.

Berger unsuccessfully tried to shush Max as he latched the chain. Then, with icy hands, he opened the door to the chain's length.

CHAPTER 5

Los Angeles

Eric Mattson finished cleaning the central area and turned out the lights. He went into the hall to make sure the security guard was on the opposite side of the building, then slipped back inside. It took some practice to maneuver in the dark, but now that he'd worked at EXC for a few weeks, he had the layout memorized.

Mattson tucked the feather duster under his armpit and began quietly opening drawers. He probed through each one methodically, examining the contents with the penlight on his keychain. The trick was to take small things so people don't get too upset—batteries, stamps, loose change. It wasn't much, but it added up.

The squeal of shoe leather on the vinyl flooring caused him to freeze and douse the penlight. He lowered himself behind the desk and watched the guard's shadow pass in the hallway. After waiting until the sound faded away, he went back to work.

In the third desk, he found a pair of red and yellow wires dangling from a drawer. That probably meant batteries, so he decided to explore. The metal drawer screeched when he got it halfway open, so he stopped until he was sure the guard hadn't heard him. His fingers followed the wires into the drawer toward something metallic. It was a silver object that looked like a thick lipstick case with a push button on the end. He picked it up—

Suddenly the room lights went on. A loud voice boomed at Mattson. "So you're the sonofabitch who's been stealing around here."

Mattson reflexively slammed the drawer, which caught his thumb and pushed the button on the metal piece.

Edward Tripp returned to his booth at Alcon Industries, after finishing the 9:00 P.M. security round. He lowered his thick frame into the office chair, deftly skirting the baton, pepper spray, and cuffs dangling from his wide belt. After plugging the white plastic earphone into his ear, he tuned the transistor radio in his breast pocket. It hissed and squealed before he found the Larry Preston show.

"Tonight's guests," came Preston's smooth, deep voice, "are an adult movie star, Honey Dot Cum, who will be debating Reverend Archibald Sanders, the family values crusader whose television series is carried on over four hundred stations."

Tripp had been looking forward to this one all week, ever since they'd started advertising it. He'd even rented one of Honey's videos to get in the mood. Man. The woman coulda been a sword swallower.

Tripp could hear Preston's chair swivel. "Good evening, Honey."

"Hello, Larry." It sounded like her tongue came out to lick her lips after she finished the sentence.

Tripp got up and opened the window a crack—just enough to let in a little cool night air—then poured himself a cup of hot coffee. Propping his feet on the desk, he raised the cup to his lips.

"Now, Honey, why would a beautiful woman like you—"

A blinding white-yellow light streaked through the window, searing the room like a powerful flashbulb. Before Tripp could react, there was a thunderous rumble and the window glass shattered, spraying him with shards that splashed into his coffee. Pens, pencils, and paperclips were jolted off his desk, and the earplug popped out of his ear. Leaping from the chair, he spilled boiling coffee down the front of his shirt. Tripp screamed in panic and pawed at the burns on his chest.

His eyes caught the sight outside. Dark gray smoke was streaming out of the EXC building down the way. Massive clouds mushroomed through the roof and poured through ruptured windows. A shower of debris cascaded for hundreds of yards in all directions. Wood. Metal. Tarpaper. Insulation. Thousands of office papers, with their edges smoldering, fluttered like a ticker-tape parade.

EXC was quickly smothered in a tower of thick smoke. It raged outward, invading Tripp's window with the acrid smell of diesel fuel.

Tripp stood frozen, mesmerized; the burns on his chest forgotten.

CHAPTER 6

Orlando, Florida

On Monday morning, Herbert Simms whistled as he drove to work in Bessie, his 1962 Buick. He had bought her when she was new, and he kept her 'cause those new foreign gizmos were about as sturdy as tinfoil.

Simms shifted into neutral at the traffic light and looked around. Away from the touristy glitz, Orlando had a heart of mature magnolia trees that lolled around sleepy, Old South squares. The colonial buildings had the character and architecture of prewar tranquillity.

A while later, Simms came to a stop near Lake Lorna Doone Park. He watched the kids laughing while their mothers swung them on wooden seats attached to old-fashioned metal chains. A little black dog barked, wagging its tail as it chased one of the swinging children's arcs.

When the light changed, Simms gently slid Bessie into first gear. He was still mellow from the weekend's fishing, even though he hadn't caught anything over three inches long. Or at least he didn't think he had. The weekend was still kind of . . . what would you call it? Fuzzy? He shook

his head and worried if this was the start of being forget-
ful. Age sixty-seven sounded younger every day, though
he had to admit some of the original parts didn't work the
way they used to. Only seventeen more months until he
could retire at maximum pay, and he had already saved
enough for a down payment on that cottage near Johns
Lake, where the bass and bluegill practically crawl into
your lap.

He whistled a peppier tune, turned onto North Orange
Avenue, then drove into the parking lot. He gave his cus-
tomary salute to the parking lot attendant, Howard, an
African-American man in his eighties with tightly curled
white hair, before parking Bessie in her usual spot.

Rain or shine, Simms always walked the block and a
half to Ryan's Furniture Warehouse. He climbed the stairs
up to the second-floor offices. Simms's arthritis was kicking up in his neck, so he bent the rules and loosened his
tie just a titch.

"Morning, Mr. Simms," said Laurie, a cute little bug in
her twenties.

"Laurie, how was your weekend?"

"Very nice, sir. And yours?"

"Any time I can fish, it's a good weekend."

Laurie smiled politely.

As soon as he arrived at his desk, he knew something
wasn't right. Nothing big, mind you. Just that things were
out of order. The calendar wasn't square with the desk, and
the pencil holder was a few inches further away than he
liked to keep it. Had someone been there? He didn't have
anything valuable, but he didn't like the idea of anybody
rifling through his things. Now where was his plastic water
bottle with the sponge top?

He opened his desk drawer to see if anything was missing. The darn thing was stuck, and he had to work it back

and forth. He managed to clear a couple of inches, but that was as far as she went. Simms stuck his fingers inside and wiggled them around. Finally, he pushed something down and the drawer popped open. There was a twisted pair of red and yellow wires.

As soon as he saw them, he felt the rage ignite. And he knew what he had to do.

Los Angeles

The wind whipped into Berger's face as he rode his motorcycle down Washington Boulevard on Monday morning.

Something wasn't right. His hands were sweaty, so he took off a riding glove, held it in his teeth, and wiped his palm on the carpet he had attached to the cycle's teardrop gas tank. The nubby surface was for Max to dig in his nails when they took the corners.

He put the glove back on and tried to concentrate on the road. His memory of the weekend was a blur, and he couldn't get in touch with Linda. When he'd called her last night, he'd gotten her machine and she hadn't called back. Ditto this morning.

He shifted his position on the leather seat, and kicked into a higher gear. Could she have just run off with this other guy for good? The thought pissed him off. She had said "date others," which meant they'd keep seeing each other. Didn't it? He twisted the handle and accelerated, causing the wind to press his sunglasses against his eyebrows.

Berger tried to distract himself by thinking about the weekend. While his memory was sketchy, he knew he'd played in a chess tournament for the first time since college. He'd forgotten how exhausting it was to sit on your ass for hours beating up some nerd. Or had the nerd beaten him up? He wasn't quite sure. He remembered playing International Master Jeremy Silman, whom he hadn't seen in years. That was about all that was clear.

Why the hell had he entered a chess tournament? Berger hadn't been in a human chess game in ages, since none of his friends would play him. The reason was simple: With his mathematical skills, he could compute up to twenty moves ahead, and chess brought out his killer instincts. All of which meant he couldn't help squashing his opponents in the first thirty moves. When the last of the diehards gave up being his punching bag, he started playing computers that didn't complain. And after the invention of Pentium processors, which sped up the computers' skills, he'd finally gotten a reasonable challenge.

Berger turned off Centinela onto Teale and suddenly braked for a police barricade that wasn't supposed to be there. White sawhorses with blinking orange reflectors blocked the road, and off to the side was a black and white patrol car with its radio yapping loudly. Berger's cycle skidded to the side as he stopped a few feet from the barricades.

An officer came up to him. "I'm sorry, sir. The road is closed."

"I work up there," said Berger.

"Where do you work?"

"At EXC Labs."

"Not today. EXC is closed."

"Closed? Why?"

"Some kind of incident. You'll have to turn around."

"Incident? There's a lot of valuable data—"

"Sir, you'll have to turn around."

His encryption program. Two years of work.

Berger looked up the road, straining to see around the

bend. He could only see the pavement winding out of sight toward the industrial complex that housed EXC and a number of other businesses. The officer walked past him to a newly arrived car, and Berger considered running the barricade. It didn't seem worth the risk.

He swung his bike around and started west on Centinela, then onto Jefferson. A few miles ahead, he knew there was a dirt road into the industrial park, off Lincoln Boulevard. His heavy bike wasn't built for off-road, and he knew that if he turned it over, he couldn't lift it up without a crane. Which would cost over a hundred dollars that he didn't have, even assuming there was no fine for trespassing on the private road. Yet he worried about his programs. He was the only one who could preserve them if there was a problem.

The Cyclone gate that guarded the dirt road was held by a chain that had a little slack. With some bending and twisting of the fence, Berger finally managed to wedge the Harley through. Even though he took it slowly, the bike's suspension croaked against the rough path, and the thick tires kicked up a spray of dust that clouded his view. He rode over a crest and squeezed the brakes gently on the downslope, knowing too much tension would throw him over the handlebars. The hill was steeper than he'd thought, and his front wheel hit a pothole that slammed the bike into his kidneys.

At the bottom, he rounded a bend and saw EXC. The building was rimmed with yellow police tape on wooden stakes. The roof had collapsed in the middle, and rubble was strewn about. He felt as though he had discovered a friend lying injured in the road, and he shuddered back a sob. The possibility of his work surviving didn't look good.

Berger parked his bike behind a stand of large brush, then walked toward the building. He avoided the policemen guarding the perimeter and went toward the bobbing, bald head of Ernest Clifford, Berger's EXC liaison.

"What happened?" asked Berger.

"What are you doing here? The road's supposed to be closed."

"My program. It was—"

"Did you turn in the backup on Friday?"

"Well . . . I worked late." EXC's procedure was to make backup copies on Fridays and take them off-premises, as a precaution against exactly this kind of problem. Berger had gotten lost in his work and missed the Friday messenger, which meant his last week's work was gone. Truth be told, he hardly ever remembered to make copies for the messenger, which meant his archived material would be way out of date. It could take him months to get back where he was. Assuming he could do it at all.

Berger felt like he was sinking into quicksand. "What happened?"

Clifford turned to face him. "Arson. An explosion. A security guard and another man were killed."

"My God."

Smitty, the daytime security guard, walked up to them. Berger thought the little man was looking at him with an odd expression. That wasn't like Smitty. Maybe he was just shaken up by the explosion.

Smitty spoke to Clifford yet never took his eyes off Berger. "Mr. Clifford, I don't see nothin' else useful. Them arson officers said don't touch nothin' anyhow."

"You can go home, Smitty. There's nothing else here." Smitty walked off, rubbing his tiny hands against his wrinkled temples.

"Ernie, when do we reopen?" asked Berger.

"Who knows. A week? A month?"

"A month? What about my funding?"

"That will take some time to sort out. And as I recall, you were pretty much at the end of your seed money anyway."

Berger felt his temples flush. "I've still got some funding left."

"Well, we have to reconstruct our records. And you're not the only one in this boat. Call me in a few weeks."

"I need tomorrow's paycheck right away. Or at least a loan."

"Impossible." Clifford's mouth stretched into a crooked smile. "You didn't put away money for a rainy day, Berger? I always put ten percent of my paychecks into a savings account. I have enough to tide me over for at least six months."

"Yeah, well, my investment banker's in the Riviera, so I can't get to my bond portfolio for a few weeks. When can I get some money?"

Clifford looked as if he were suppressing an amusing thought. "Your guess is as good as mine."

CHAPTER 7

Sparky Scott, of the Bureau of Alcohol, Tobacco and Firearms, stepped over the yellow police tape. He walked into the remains of EXC's building, oblivious to the groans of the structure around him. Scott was one of the ATF's five Certified Explosive Specialists in Los Angeles. At six foot one, with an angular jaw and slight paunch, he resembled a retired linebacker. His face was decorated with scars that looked like faded highways on a roadmap, and he was an old-timer at age forty-three.

Scott was also a survivor of the days when performing an RSP—Render Safe Procedure—meant risking your life to disarm a bomb by hand. These days, bomb squads mostly used robots, and Sparky only investigated after the event. He missed having contact with live IEDs—Improvised Explosive Devices—although he supposed he should consider himself lucky to be doing anything at all. Well, it was more than just luck. He always carried a bomber's finger in a jar of formaldehyde, as a reminder to watch his ass.

The plywood subfloor creaked under his weight as he walked toward the blast seat. Along the way, he absorbed the surroundings into his consciousness. The walls were zippered with pockmarks, meaning the bomb had shrapnel. From the fragments, they looked like nails. He studied the desk in which it had been placed. Without shrapnel, the desk would have been opened up like a flower. Instead, it was riddled with holes. Shrapnel meant the bomber wanted to kill people, since his bomb would have done about the same damage to the building without it. That made it odd that the device went off in the middle of the night, when only two people were around. Probably an accidental early trigger. Or a late one.

Sparky had always loved the challenge of bombings. They were the most difficult crimes to solve because the bomber needn't be around when the explosion went off, and the detonation itself mutilated or destroyed the evidence. Based on the damage he saw today, he knew the device was powerful enough to obliterate most or all of the clues.

He arrived at the blast seat—the immediate area around the explosion. It was a four-foot oval rip in the plywood subfloor. Below it, the concrete slab had been pulverized into a fine mist that covered the immediate area like talcum powder. The cement foundation was severely cracked, but the explosive hadn't been powerful enough to crater it. The concrete's durability forced the blast upward, causing the ceiling to collapse. Nearby walls were buckled, and leaned at precarious angles.

"Whattaya got, Sparky?" came a voice that broke Scott's concentration.

He turned to see FBI Agent Whitey Timmons tentatively making his way through the debris. Timmons was a slight man, whose suit hung on him in perpetual wrinkles, and whose head stuck forward from his collar like a turtle held upright.

The division between the FBI's and ATF's jurisdiction was a blurry one, despite a Memorandum of Understanding they'd worked out several years ago. If this was a terrorist act, the FBI had jurisdiction. However, that was impossible to know from one incident. In Scott's book, the FBI hung around only if there was going to be a lot of publicity. Since this one looked pretty routine, he figured Timmons would do a quick fly-by, then be on his way. In fact, Scott was thinking about analyzing the scene and bowing out himself. LAPD could have the joy of chasing the bomber.

Timmons tiptoed forward, watching the walls as if they were about to attack him.

"Is it safe in here?" asked Timmons.

Scott shrugged his shoulders. Timmons froze in place.

"What have you got?" asked Timmons.

"Clearly an IED. No smell of gas, and the explosion was in the middle of the room where there aren't any pipes."

"Any idea what kind?"

"Not a low explosive. There's no smell of sulfur, no sooty residue, and no fire. Also, the crater is too small for a low-grade explosive to do this kind of structural damage. They'd have needed so much of it that we'd see a huge hole."

"So blasting agent?"

"Yeah. Probably sensitized ANFO. A witness said he smelled diesel fuel."

"Anything to indicate we've got terrorists?" Timmons took a step forward and the debris crunched under his foot.

"Not even the usual nuts taking credit. Unless we find something out of line when we go through this shit, I'm guessing it's your run-of-the-mill wacko."

The wall creaked and Timmons's head snapped up with a start. He began backing toward the door. "Well, call me if you think there's anything for us to do." Without waiting for an answer, he left at twice the speed he'd entered.

The most common home-brewed blasting agent was ANFO, which stood for Ammonium Nitrate Fuel Oil. It was the explosive used in the Oklahoma City bombing, and was made from easily obtainable ingredients: fertilizer from any garden shop, and either nitromethane, which is used for model racing cars, or diesel fuel from any gas station. If that's what it was, he'd hopefully find traces of nitrates or fuel oil in the debris. The booster was probably a pipe bomb or a stick of dynamite. Since he didn't see any metal or PVC fragments, he suspected the latter. If it was dynamite, there would be a blasting cap—a thin metal cylinder with attached wires. And a blasting cap would mean batteries nearby.

Scott walked out of the building and gathered the two other members of his team. Knowing that debris from an explosion this size can be thrown some distance, he turned to the shorter man and said, "Parsons, expand the crime scene perimeter as far as you can without pissing off the neighbors. Try to get me a couple of hundred yards. Then grid out the area and let's start shoveling. Leland, set up the sifters."

Parsons trotted off, and Leland took out the double-deck sifter. He attached legs to the three-foot-square aluminum-framed meshes, putting the one with larger holes on top, and the finer one on bottom. He then arranged several coffee cans to store recoveries.

Parsons returned just as Leland finished. Scott said, "Get the crowbars and power saw and let's cut open some walls. I think we've got ANFO with a dynamite booster, so look for blasting cap wires. Also a switch, timer springs, and batteries. Who wants to take the bodies?"

Both men averted their gaze. "I did it last time," said Leland.

"I've done three in the last two months," countered Parsons.

A normal explosion doesn't disfigure when it kills. It's simply a sonic wave of such magnitude that it collapses the lungs, and a body can look perfectly normal. With shrapnel, however, the corpses are pulverized beyond recognition. In either event, there are often pieces of the bomb embedded in the corpse, so ATF officers have to be present when they're retrieved.

Scott flipped a coin. "Call it."

Leland lost, grumbling as he walked away.

A man with a bullet-shaped head that melded into a thick neck came up to Scott. Buck Reynolds of LAPD's Criminal Conspiracy Section, one of the detectives who did follow-up after the ATF's site examinations, clapped a thick hand on Scott's shoulder.

"Anything you need?" asked Reynolds in his gravelly voice.

"Not yet. Too soon to tell much."

"I got the names of the employees. I'll start checking to see if they know anything."

Scott nodded and Reynolds ambled off. Scott grabbed the power saw, crowbar, and goggles, then headed into the building with Parsons. As he neared the bomb seat, his eye caught a nine-volt battery embedded in the wall.

"Battery!" he yelled to Parsons outside.

"Right on!" answered Parsons.

Scott felt a rush of excitement as he carefully pried the battery loose and slid it into a plastic evidence bag. Batteries are excellent trace evidence, as they have a date code and manufacturing information. He hoped that was a good sign for things to come.

*   *   *

Berger arrived at home, dusty from his off-road ride to EXC. Walking up to the porch, he could hear Max barking and flinging himself against the front door, and he remembered how Linda had once called him a "Jack Russell Terrorist."

He carried Max to the couch, then lay back and called Linda's work number.

"Ms. Miller isn't in today."

"Did she call in?"

"I'm sorry. We can't give out that information."

He called her house and left a fourth message on the machine.

Max nosed under Berger's hand, demanding a scalp massage. Berger next turned his attention to that little matter of losing his job. If EXC was in limbo, he was too. It could take months to round up another venture capitalist for his RSA system, and he wasn't sure whether EXC owned the idea legally. That could also take a while to sort out. In the meantime, he needed to eat.

Maybe he could pick up some part-time work. Berger called three of his friends in the crypto game, yet no one knew of any openings. He felt his chest deflate as he hung up the phone and stared into space.

Max flipped up his head, outraged that it had been almost ten seconds without a stroke. Berger absentmindedly scratched Max's ears. They sat for a long while in silence, until Max suddenly barked and ran to the front door. It startled Berger, who jumped up from the couch and let out a yelp. Whoa. What was that? He never screamed out loud.

Now a loud rap on the door, and Berger's heart thumped in rhythm. Knocking. The sound stirred some distant memories. What were they? He also had a vague recollection of being followed, yet that seemed so . . . so disconnected.

Berger went to the door and noticed its chain was missing. There were gashes in the wood where it had been. When did that happen? Had someone been here while he was gone?

He opened the door to see a small, broad man in a rumpled suit. The man had wide-set eyes under dark, bushy eyebrows, and a thick neck.

"Jonathan Berger?"

"Yes."

"I'm Buck Reynolds, LAPD." His stubby fingers flipped open a badge in a leather case. "Can I come in?"

"Yeah, sure. What's this about?"

Reynolds walked in and quickly surveyed the living room. He sat on the overstuffed chair without waiting for an invitation. Berger remained standing.

"You work at EXC?" asked Reynolds.

"Yes. Why?"

"You aware that somebody blew the place up?"

"Yes. I tried to go to work this morning."

"Over the last few days, did you see anything unusual around work?" Reynolds pulled out a spiral pad and a sawed-off pencil.

"No."

"Any strangers around the place?"

"Not that I noticed."

The man peered up at Berger, and his face seemed to say, *You're probably lying, and I'll enjoy frying your ass.* "Why do you think someone would blow up EXC?"

"I have no idea."

Reynolds mumbled "Uh-huh" under his breath as he scribbled. "Where were you this weekend?"

A feeling of guilt clutched at Berger's chest. That was odd. Why should he feel guilty? Maybe because his weekend memories were so fuzzy?

"I played in a chess tournament."

"Both days?"

"Yes." At least he thought so.

"Where?"

"L.A. Convention Center. Downtown."

"Any witnesses?"

"The people in the tournament, I guess. I'm sure the officials have the names of my opponents."

"Mmmmm," said Reynolds, writing without looking up. "How do you feel about EXC?"

"I'm happy there. Why?"

"You're not upset with them about anything?"

"No."

Reynolds droned on with a series of questions about Berger's background, employment history, time at EXC, and other scintillating inquiries. Finally, he closed his notepad.

"Did you know that the bomb was in your desk?"

Berger felt the blood drain from his face. "No. I . . . had no idea." Why did he feel he should have known that? Sort of like he knew it and had forgotten. That didn't make any sense. "Am I a . . . a . . . suspect?"

"Not now. Bombers don't usually leave things in their own space. But I thought you might know someone who'd want to take a shot at you when they did their thing."

Berger's mind raced through the possibilities. "I can't think of anyone."

Reynolds stood up with some effort. "Here's my card. If you think of anything, give me a call."

As he turned to leave, he said, "You gonna be in town for a while?"

CHAPTER 8

Washington, D.C.

The J. Edgar Hoover Building, on the corner of Ninth Street and Pennsylvania Avenue, was often compared to a fortress, which was an image Carl Davidson rather liked. Davidson, the Section Chief of the Domestic Terrorism Unit of the National Security Division, was in his early sixties and had been an FBI man since he graduated from Cardozo Law School at age twenty-five. He had a long face with rugged features that had withered from being indoors for the last twenty years. His black toupee, which didn't match his white fringe, was fastened so tightly that it moved when he wrinkled his forehead.

Davidson sat in his standard-sized office, which almost had a view of Ford's Theatre where Lincoln was shot. Outdoors, a nasty wind whipped the rain into a frenzy, slaughtering umbrellas like pigeons. Inside, he kept his lights low, and the furniture cast dim shadows.

Across from Davidson sat Peter Weldon, a young FBI agent with a military haircut and a square jaw.

"Make it quick," said Davidson. "We just got an airliner down over Nebraska, and two terrorist groups are fighting for the credit. I've got a jet waiting for me at Reagan."

"It's a weird one, sir. Man named Herbert Simms. Old geezer, near retirement." Davidson stared hard into Weldon, who shifted slightly in his seat. "This Simms guy worked in an Orlando furniture warehouse. He was a thirty-year employee, and a Korean War vet. This morning he walked into work and blew himself up. He and sixteen other people were killed. Twenty-two were injured. We got the call because he destroyed government property when an IRS office next door lost part of its wall."

Davidson walked over to Weldon and looked down at him. "You came to *me* with some chickenshit nutcase in Florida?"

Weldon cleared his throat. "Well, sir, last night an office building was blown up in Los Angeles. A company called EXC. They work in a lot of high-tech fields, including some computer security for the Federal Trade Commission. It looks like similar explosive material, so maybe there's a connection."

"What were the explosives?"

"Probably sensitized ANFO, with dynamite booster."

"ANFO? Shit, Weldon, my mother could make that in her kitchen. Were the bombs sophisticated?"

"Uh, no."

"Is anyone claiming responsibility?"

"Not so far."

Davidson scowled at Weldon, then looked at his watch. He pulled on his tweed sports coat as he spoke. "Sounds like a coincidence. Don't waste your time."

"Sir, we think the Los Angeles explosion might have been set off by accident, since it happened late at night. It could have been planned for the next day when a lot of

people were there. That would be about the same time as
the Simms incident, which could mean a synchronized statement. It's possible the explosives were intentionally crude,
just to divert suspicion. I have a hunch there's something
here. At least enough to look over the locals' shoulders."

Davidson buttoned his tan raincoat and tied the waist
belt in a knot. He turned up the collar, then drilled his eyes
into Weldon.

"All right. Don't spend a lot of time. And for God's
sake, don't put anyone important on it."

Los Angeles

FBI Agent Jill Landis was in the kitchen of her one-bedroom
apartment, trying out a new recipe for chicken Marsala.
She sautéed the chicken breasts on the stove while she
mixed flour and butter into a roux. Then she slowly combined the roux with chicken stock and Marsala wine.

Jill had learned gourmet cooking from her father, who
had been the owner and chef of Dijon, a restaurant for dis-
criminating palates that was totally misplaced in her home-
town of Carbon, Illinois. Dijon consequently went broke
within a year, and Dad went on to work as an insurance
salesman. Although his passion for cooking quickly faded,
her father had kindled a lifelong fire in Jill. She loved the
precision and comfort of knowing that, if you accurately
followed the steps, you always got a perfect result.

Jill's passion for cooking had also led to her being about
fifteen pounds overweight (well, maybe seventeen or eighteen), save the time she went on a crash diet before the FBI
physical performance tests. The extra pounds softened her
stunning symmetrical features, and at the same time made
her smooth skin voluptuous and sensual. She had convinced

herself that, in her profession, it was better to play down her looks, and she figured a few extra pounds helped.

Jill added the mushrooms and glanced over at Ted. He smiled from beneath the glass. She liked keeping his photo on the counter while she made dinner, since he had always loved her cooking.

"It's a new recipe, honey," she said aloud.

Ted continued to smile. He looked handsome in his tuxedo, with his arm around her. That white wedding dress with pink lace ribbons had flattered her figure.

She took the chicken off the stove and placed it on one of the two Lenox plates they'd received as a wedding gift. She added the whipped sweet potatoes and green beans with slivered almonds, noting that the colors coordinated with the china. Then she poured a new Chardonnay she'd found at Trader Joe's into a crystal wine glass, and lit the burgundy candles on her breakfast table. The silver cutlery sparkled against the white linen place mat.

Jill pulled out her barrette, and with it went the last vestige of her business persona. Her molasses-colored hair spilled across her shoulders, and she studied her reflection in the facets of the crystal. Then she let out a deep breath.

The first bite of a new recipe was always an adventure, like traveling to a new country. She cut a small piece of the chicken, placed it in her mouth, then closed her eyes and chewed slowly. The flavors orchestrated her tastebuds, first playfully, then in full crescendo. The soft texture of moist chicken; a tart hint of Marsala wine. The sensation was almost erotic. Excellent. This recipe was a keeper.

As she reached for a second bite, the phone jangled loudly. She considered letting it go, yet it persisted beyond four rings. Turning awkwardly, she was barely able to grab the receiver.

"Jill, it's Peter Weldon. I've got a case for you. Direct from Davidson."

Jill stood up, as if she had been called to attention. The cloth napkin slid off her lap onto the floor.

"Davidson? Really?" Maybe he had finally taken notice of her.

"Yup. Did you hear about the explosion at EXC last night?"

Berger sat alone in his living room. He hadn't gotten up to turn on the lights, even though it was now dark outside. He'd called Linda's apartment over a dozen times, and her machine was no longer accepting messages. Neither her employer nor any of her friends knew where she was. He wondered if this was her way of blowing him off. Maybe that speech about dating others was just a nod at being polite.

On top of that, he had no leads for a job. With his current credit card bills, that put his net worth in the negative category, and his cash reserves at "minimal."

Shit.

Max announced the fact that someone had dared to open a car door outside on the street. His bark grew louder in direct proportion to the approach of footsteps that Berger could hear nearing the house. He got up and looked out the window to see Reynolds, the detective who had been there earlier in the day, walking up the sidewalk. When Reynolds hit the porch, Max started slamming himself against the door, and almost flew out when Berger opened it before the policeman could knock.

"Hello, Mr. Berger. Buck Reynolds. I was here earlier? Can I come in?"

Berger thought the man was looking at him differently.

Max crouched in readiness to take out the man's ankle, growling like a dragster on the starting line.

Reynolds stepped inside and looked directly into Berger's eyes. "Lemme come right to the point. Except for a buncha junior high school kids in Garden Grove, there weren't any chess tournaments in L.A. this weekend. Not at the Convention Center. Not anywhere else. So how 'bout you tell me where you really were."

CHAPTER 9

Jill Landis walked through Parker Center, the LAPD head-quarters in downtown Los Angeles. She came up to Buck Reynolds's desk, which was jammed together with dozens of others in a large, raucous room where the sound of ring-ing phones punctuated high-volume conversations. Reynolds was engrossed in a telephone call and didn't seem to notice Jill. She stood there staring at him, shifting her weight back and forth. He kept talking and pulled at the knot of his tie. Finally, she knocked on his desk. He looked up and nodded, then continued his conversation for several more minutes.

When he hung up, Jill said, "You remember me, De-tective?"

"Pretty little thing like you? How could I forget."

That remark brought back all her memories of Reynolds. They'd once worked on a kidnapping case, where he'd re-peatedly called her "sweetie" and "honey." When she fi-nally exploded, he apologized with "I'm sorry, darlin'."

Reynolds half stood up to shake hands, then sat down again. "What'cha need?"

"EXC bombing. I thought I'd nose around a bit."

Reynolds's eyes narrowed. "FBI's interested in a little pop-gun incident like that? What gives?"

"I'll let you know after I've done some digging. Please tell me what you've got."

"You gonna take my case away from me? It must be juicy if the feds are here."

"What have you got, Detective?"

"I got dogshi—I don't got much. The guy whose desk had the bomb in it lied about where he was when the IED was planted. We haven't identified the bodies for sure, but it looks like the night security guard was one of 'em. They weren't recognizable after the blast." He handed her color photos of the bodies, and Jill figured he was looking for her to squirm. He came close to succeeding.

"Tell me about the liar," she said, pushing away the pictures.

Reynolds described Berger and his background, and how he'd lied about a chess tournament.

"His profile doesn't fit any bombers I've seen," said Jill. "And it's odd that he'd make up a story that was so obviously false." She also knew that the profile of Simms, who set off the bomb in Orlando, didn't fit a terrorist pattern either. She kept that to herself.

"I think he's dirty and I wanna squeeze him," said Reynolds. "I went back to his house, but he cut me off and asked for a lawyer. I'm trying to set up an interview."

"I'd like to watch when you do."

Reynolds smirked lecherously. "I'd love to have you watch."

Against her strongest will, she flushed.

Berger stepped into the public defender's office, which was located in a storefront on Venice Boulevard. The receptionist, behind a half-open, wavy-glass sliding panel, was a heavy Asian-American woman with wide gaps in her teeth that were accentuated every time she chewed her gum. She answered a ringing line while three others blinked for attention.

"I'm here to see Hugo Dorn," said Berger. His words were obscured by a crying baby in the waiting room.

"Your name?"

"John Berger."

She looked over a list and then told him to sit. All the chairs were full, so he stood in the corner. Half the occupants were old people with metal canes and hearing aids, who spoke to each other at high volume. Most of the others looked to be single mothers, whose children sat on the floor coloring and tearing pages out of magazines. The room grew more crowded as new arrivals came faster than the others emptied.

Over an hour later, Berger had secured a seat on the frayed couch and thumbed through a year-old issue of *Tropical Fish*. A small boy kept pulling the magazine out of his hands, throwing it on the floor, and running away giggling. His mother was oblivious, in deep conversation with an African-American man who touched her thigh each time she laughed at his jokes.

"Mr. Booger," called the receptionist.

She escorted him to Hugo Dorn's gray-paneled cubicle. A photo of a cat, inscribed "Minerva," hung next to Dorn's diploma from Norton Law School.

"Have a seat," said Dorn. He was a thin, bony man, probably in his thirties, dressed in a gray tweed suit. His frizzy brown hair flailed in several directions away from his head.

"You're not really eligible for a public defender," said

Dorn. "You're still employed and you earn more than our cutoff."

"I know, but my employer—"

"I saw that in your application. No sweat. I won't say anything. We should be okay unless someone upstairs goes on a crusade."

"Thanks."

"So why do you think the police are questioning you?"

Berger explained about the explosion, the bomb being in his desk, and the nonexistent chess tournament.

"Do we have to worry about what the cops might find?"

"*No!*" he shot back, louder than he intended.

Dorn looked up, raising his eyebrows. "No offense. It's just a routine question. Why did you tell them you went to a chess tournament that didn't exist?"

Berger started pacing. "I remember playing in that tournament. Maybe the cops made a mistake."

"Possible. Though unlikely."

Berger fidgeted with his star-shaped earring. "The whole weekend is a little foggy. But I remember specific people who were there."

"What are their names?"

Berger rattled them off for Dorn.

"Should I make a deal?" asked Dorn.

"What do you mean 'a deal'?"

"Try to plead a lesser offense."

"I didn't do anything."

"Well, you might have. By giving the cops a story that didn't check out, you might have an obstruction of justice problem if they want to squeeze you. Let's go over your story again in detail. And please tell me everything, because I can't afford to be surprised. Or let me put it another way: You can't afford to have me surprised."

*   *   *

Berger's neck was stiff from having sat in the interrogation room for almost two hours. It was a small, windowless cubicle, furnished only with a tiny table and a few folding chairs. Berger and Dorn were on one side of the table, and Detective Reynolds sat across from them, straddling a chair backward. Reynolds had made him repeat his weekend story three times in detail, and Berger's voice was now hoarse. It didn't help that the air conditioner was blowing frigid air directly into his face.

Despite Berger's initial worries, Dorn had proved adroit at keeping Reynolds's questions away from anything incriminating. Dorn had said he believed Berger, even though his story didn't make a lot of sense, and he had recommended total honesty. Berger wasn't sure whether that advice was a sign of support or abandonment.

Reynolds loosened his tie, took another sip of coffee from a white Styrofoam cup, then cleared his throat. "Mr. Berger, why do you keep insisting you went to a chess tournament that didn't exist?"

"I know it existed. I was there. Don't you think I'd just say I was home alone if I wanted to lie?"

Reynolds shook his head. The room seemed to be getting colder, and Berger rubbed his palms together for warmth.

"The other chess players you say were there. What if they don't back you up?"

Berger was worried that's exactly what would happen. He had already called the Convention Center and confirmed there hadn't been a tournament. He also knew that Dorn had contacted one of the players, only to discover the man had been in Cleveland. Berger had omitted giving that name to Reynolds, yet he remembered seeing him in L.A. None of this made any sense.

Berger replayed the weekend in his mind. He remembered using the Queen's Gambit, an aggressive tactic, and sacrificing a pawn to take control of the center. It was all so real, and at the same time foggy, as if he were viewing it through a gauze curtain. He was also getting the uncomfortable feeling that someone was setting him up, although he couldn't imagine why. Or how.

"Mr. Berger?"

He snapped back to the room. "Yes?"

"I just asked if you'd give us fingerprints. Mr. Dorn has agreed if it's okay with you."

"Yeah, sure," said Berger absently.

Jill sipped water from a sports bottle while she watched Berger through the two-way mirror. She knew from experience that some people were such accomplished liars that detection was almost impossible. Still, she liked to see if she could outguess suspects, and her favorite technique was something called Neuro Linguistic Programming. Most right-handed people's eyeballs went down and to the right when they were making things up, and they went up and to the right when they were remembering something that had actually happened. It was a reflexive action and had proven accurate over the years of her experience.

According to the NLP test, as well as her instincts, Berger was telling the truth. That made no logical sense, since he kept claiming he'd attended an event that didn't exist. If he was going to lie, something that could be disproved in a single phone call wasn't exactly a smart move. Which was also illogical, since this guy was a Stanford Ph.D.

Weird.

There also was something familiar about his demeanor. Something she couldn't quite place. Something she'd seen before, in other people.

What was it?

CHAPTER 10

Berger pounded on the door of Linda's apartment with the side of his fist. Each thud echoed through the crisp night air. He was there mostly because he couldn't shake the feeling that something had happened to her. Yet he was also there because he didn't want her to get off the hook just by hiding. If she wanted to dump him, she could do it to his face.

He pounded harder, and every blow seemed to bend the door as it rattled in the frame. He knew it was useless, as he had looked through the mail slot and seen a pile of mail on the floor. Still, he kept hammering. The edge of his palm grew numb, as if he'd gotten a shot of novocaine.

He felt a gentle hand on his shoulder, and he turned to see Kim, Linda's neighbor across the street.

Kim said softly, "I don't think she's home, John."

He cradled his hand, which throbbed as if he were still pounding the door. Kim was a tiny redhead. She had several crystal necklaces looped around her neck, and she was wearing a loose-fitting, blue floral dress.

"Have you seen her?" asked Berger.

"Not since Friday."

He stopped himself from pounding the door again.

"Did you guys break up or something?" asked Kim.

"No. Well . . . maybe. I don't know. I've been calling her for days. She hasn't been at work."

Kim looked quickly at Linda's door, then back at John. "Do you think we should call the police?"

"If she doesn't show up in the next day or so, we probably should."

Kim twisted her mouth. "Oh dear."

A long silence.

"Are you okay?" asked Kim. "You look a little stressed. You want some coffee or something?"

"No. I'm okay."

They walked down the sidewalk, toward Berger's motorcycle.

"Will you call me if she shows up?" he asked as he climbed on.

"Sure. And please do the same for me. I'm only here tonight and tomorrow. Bill and I are taking our son to northern California for a week. If you know someone who could water the plants and keep an eye on things, I'd pay them a few bucks."

"Possibly." He figured he'd need the money if a job didn't materialize soon.

Berger drove his motorcycle without a destination and found himself on the Pacific Coast Highway. The cold night whipped into his jacket, and he sucked in deep breaths of stinging salt air.

He knew he'd played in a chess tournament. He could see everything in his mind. The rows of tables, lined with vinyl chessboards. The slapping of time clocks. The players writing down their moves. The intense concentration you could feel radiating through the room.

Why did everyone keep saying it didn't exist?

He pushed his cycle harder, and leaned into the winding road along the palisades. His mind wandered back to the only person who routinely beat him in chess, and his mouth eased into a smile for the first time in recent days. Her name was Karla (or that was as close as he could get to pronouncing her name), and she attended the University of Texas at the same time Berger was doing his undergraduate work there. A tall woman, with black eyes and a willowy body, she came from some place near Macedonia, wherever that was. Berger was never very good at geography.

In his first game with Karla, he didn't play seriously, and she slaughtered him with the Dragon Variation of the Sicilian Defense. It was the first time he'd lost since being in college. Annoyed and embarrassed, he poured all of his concentration into the next game. So did Karla, and she pulled him into a draw using the Queen's Indian. For the rest of the night, and well into the morning, it was the Clash of the Titans as they wrestled victory back and forth.

The memories of Karla eased his tension, and he downshifted his motorcycle. The engine roared as he jolted to a slower speed, and he recalled how Karla had been another "first" in his life. The first woman he had ever seen naked. It happened in a dormitory called Goodal Wooton, across from the campus. He had borrowed a tie to hang on the door, which was the signal for his roommate to stay the hell out. They were playing a game of "strip chess," which had sounded like an exciting idea when she suggested it. Unfortunately, with their respective skills, it had taken over two hours to get her blouse and his shirt half unbuttoned.

Finally, he knocked over his king in surrender and came around to her side of the board. She didn't move away. The stereo was playing a New Age orchestra with recorded surf in the background, and his breathing accelerated as he nervously finished opening her blouse. He placed his hand on top of her bra, which felt like it had steel reinforcement in the cup. Then he struggled with the clasp until she took pity and opened it for him.

Berger took off his shirt and watched as she continued to undress herself. First she slipped out of her skirt, then she slid down her pink satin panties. She opened his fly and eased him out of his pants and underwear. He was embarrassed by the size of his excitement, which she handled gently, and he feared he would finish before they could do much more.

A loud banging on the door interrupted them. What the hell? Didn't his stupid roommate see the tie? He ignored the door and kissed Karla deeply. The hammering grew louder. He caressed her soft skin, moving his hand gently up her thigh, yet his mind was half on the intruder. As he cupped his hand between her legs, the door splintered open and the lights went on.

A small man stood in the doorway, tensed into a fighter's crouch. He was breathing heavily, baring his teeth, and the muscles in his neck strained in tight bands.

"Who the hell are you?" asked Berger.

"It's my brother," said Karla. She pulled her dress in front of herself. Her brother started yelling at her in some strange language, and she shouted back. The man crossed the room, roughly shoved Berger onto the floor, then dragged Karla toward the door by her wrist. Berger, no longer having to worry about the size of his excitement, tried to cover himself with his underwear. So much for his contribution to world relations.

Her brother spat on him. "You fucking bastard!" he shouted in broken English. "You touch her again and you are dead."

Berger, who was not very physical to begin with, froze in panic. The man jerked Karla, who was barely covering herself with her dress, into the doorway. Her eyes locked with Berger's, pleading. He finally broke his paralysis and got up to come after her, using one hand to hold his jockey shorts in front of himself. Her brother now had her in the hall, and Berger came out to an audience of students roused by the ruckus. The brother charged back at Berger, with fire in his eyes. Berger, with a great deal of self-will, stood his ground.

Suddenly, a campus policeman arrived, blocking the man's way.

"He's the one who broke the door," said a stringy-haired girl from across the hall. She looked at Berger's bare body, then looked away self-consciously.

Karla's brother turned and ran. The officer took off after him and caught up within a few steps. The man took a swing, which the officer ducked. Then the policeman slammed him into the wall and handcuffed him. As the officer dragged him down the hall, Karla started after her brother, then stopped. She looked back and forth between Berger and him several times.

"Stay with me," said Berger.

Her eyes flashed indecision for a split second. Then she followed her brother and didn't look back.

Berger never saw Karla again. He knew that her brother lost his student visa over the incident. When he was deported, Karla went home with him. He wrote her a number of letters, but never got a response.

Berger slowed his bike to a puttering idle at the traffic light on Point Dume Road.

He reflected how Karla was part of his life pattern. Just like Linda. The women he cared about always left him.

The light changed, yet he didn't move.

CHAPTER 11

Berger's flashlight scattered a dancing oval on the ground at 3:00 A.M. He hadn't been able to sleep, so he'd decided to visit the source of his insomnia.

The remains of EXC resembled a haunted house in the dim moonlight. The buckled walls cast strange shadows and created menacing nooks and crannies. His footsteps were the only sound to break the dead silence, save the scurrying of unseen creatures from one pile of rubble to another.

Berger had no idea what he expected to find at EXC. Only a compulsion to connect with whatever was there. He needed to see the remains of his computer, as if to accept the reality that it was truly dead. The end of two years' work that he might never replicate.

A bird chirped in the distance, and the flashlight beam shivered in rhythm with his hand. He ran his fingers over a section of what had been a wall, and his skin scraped against the rough scores of pockmarks left by the bomb's shrapnel. His heart now thudded in his chest and produced the only sound in the suddenly still night.

He headed toward the spot where his desk had been. Maybe something there could help with the situation in which he found himself. He reflected how it would feel to be a chess piece. Inside the game, you couldn't see the board or understand the strategy.

Suddenly he stumbled against something that screamed in terror. The piercing yell was immediately joined by Berger's, and he dropped his flashlight. His hands reflexively sprang up, as though someone had pulled a gun on him. He was afraid to run through the rubble in the dark, so he stood frozen.

The other screaming came from the ground. Berger's eyes, which weren't adjusted to the dark, desperately scoured the area. He finally discerned the figure of a man. Apparently someone had been sleeping in the debris. Berger fumbled for the flashlight and pointed it at the screams.

Below him was a man dressed in torn, grease-stained clothes, trying to get up. The man squinted and covered his yellow eyes. He had long matted hair, a beard with remnants of food from the day, and a skin condition that produced dark blotches on his face and hands. He also smelled of urine, which Berger hoped was caused only by the surprise.

"I only been here two nights," said the man shakily. "I didn't touch nothin'. Just lemme go. Please, mister."

Berger's hands and the flashlight oval were still trembling. "I'm not going to bust you. I'm not supposed to be here either."

The man didn't look convinced. He was picking up a pillowcase stuffed with lumpy possessions. Berger fished a dollar out of his pocket and handed it across. The man eyed the bill like it was a vicious animal. Berger laid it on the ground and stepped back. Finally, the man picked it up.

"God bless you," he said quietly.

With the future looking so bleak, especially here in EXC's graveyard, Berger was oddly comforted to see someone worse off than he.

The man stuffed the dollar into his pillowcase, and Berger turned away. In the debris, he saw the sign that had hung behind reception. EXC in large, block letters. Suddenly his teeth bared and his facial muscles tensed. He felt as though some remote control took over his body as he tightened his forearms and grabbed a fallen two-by-four. Berger screamed in a primal rage and began beating the EXC letters with the piece of wood.

The metallic letters clanged and dented with each blow, crumpling in retreat. The homeless man screamed in panic, then escaped into the night without his pillowcase of goods. Berger continued smashing the sign, yelling, "Bastard! Sonofabitch!" Or more accurately, those words escaped his mouth, as he no longer had control of his actions.

Berger's mind raced to catch up with his movements. What the hell was going on? Now he found himself swinging at walls, glancing impotently off one, then landing a solid blow on another. The attacked drywall sprayed a mist of powder that flickered in the moonlight.

His screams degenerated into croaking sounds, no longer words. His forehead was soaked in perspiration that seeped into his eyes. He knocked the support out from a crooked piece of ceiling that almost collapsed on him. Berger willed himself to stop, hoping to impose some control, and the involuntary actions slowly began to subside. Almost as if his limbs were regaining feeling after being asleep. A few minutes later, he was able to drop the two-by-four on the ground. He looked at his hands, which felt as if they didn't belong to him.

The returning control only heightened his panic. He

began shaking spastically, and almost lost his balance. This had to be his pent-up rage at EXC, for leaving him high and dry. Yet he'd never done anything remotely like this before. He wasn't a violent guy. He didn't even fight the grammar school bullies when he was cornered.

Hallucinating chess tournaments? Vandalizing the rubble at EXC? He feared he was going insane. And the cops probably thought he blew up the place, which could mean he'd go to jail. Or a mental facility. Either way, he'd be locked up in a small room. He shuddered at the thought of a confined space.

Berger looked up at the sky, through what had been the roof of EXC, and cried from the depths of his throat.

CHAPTER 12

Amsterdam, the Netherlands

Combs, the former Director of Mirage, ran a lemon peel wedge along the edge of his tiny cup of strong, black coffee. He sat in a sidewalk café on Leidestraat, just off the Prinsengracht. Combs reflected how the Serbians were café freaks, although he didn't blame them for wanting to meet in public places. That made Combs more comfortable too.

He was on his third cup of coffee and the caffeine wasn't mixing well with his anxiety over Berger's survival. Fortunately, the papers hadn't identified the bodies found at EXC, so he doubted that the Serbians knew Berger was still alive. And Combs had already arranged to fix that little problem.

Other than Berger, he couldn't have been more satisfied with the current state of affairs. Ed Baxter, his number two man, had organized the crew into a taut, disciplined unit, and every man had pulled off his duty perfectly. That was all Combs could control. How could he be responsible for some random hiccup?

He tore the end off a small paper tube and poured sugar into his coffee. Where were these assholes?

Combs had met Baxter in Miami, when they were both in grammar school. They formed a secret club called The Squad. Combs supplied the plans, and Baxter took care of the execution. The Squad never grew beyond seven kids, because Combs personally screened each boy before he was admitted—even before the kid knew he was being considered. He looked for the outsiders, the rebels. "Get me the broken toys," he'd tell Baxter. "We'll fix 'em." Combs only took the ones who had brains and conviction for something, whether it was music or drugs or women or whatever. He didn't really care about their cause, as long as they had a passion. With his natural ability to open people's heads and push the right buttons, he could easily rechannel their energy into The Squad's missions.

They started with small pranks, like turning off the PA system during the principal's morning announcements. The Squad members were perfectly happy with little stuff, yet Combs was just using that to hone their skills. Next came finance. Combs organized a punchboard game, where you could pay twenty-five cents to punch out a rolled-up piece of paper. You won whatever was on the paper, which was anywhere from nothing to five dollars. His crew sold punches to the kids at school, and Combs soon had a war chest of more than three hundred dollars. It never bothered him to keep selling punches after the five dollars had been won.

By high school, they'd graduated to the big leagues—

A waiter tapped Combs's shoulder, startling him. He waved off an offer for another of those mini-coffees and shifted in his seat, trying to get comfortable. The Serbians' habit of being late was really starting to piss him off.

He looked around for them, yet saw nothing. The street

was clogged with those European tin-can cars, mopeds, and old-fashioned bicycles with upright handlebars. All the bikes had their rear fenders painted white, like some cowardly streak down their backs. Across the way, he could see houseboats moored on the polluted canal. One had slatted wooden sidings, one had dozens of cats crawling all over it, and another was decorated with hundreds of white pinwheels. According to the yappy Dutch woman at the next table, people started living on boats during the housing shortage after World War II. He tried to ignore her, but she yammered on about how Amsterdam's row houses were narrow because they used to be taxed on their width, and that they had outside roof hooks to haul up furniture because the stairwells were too small. He finally told her to fuck off, which she seemed able to translate.

An electric trolley in front of him dinged, then pulled away to reveal the two Serbians he'd met in Paris. Peter and Paul, or whatever the hell they called themselves. He wondered how long they'd been watching him. Combs looked around and quickly spotted their two goons, stationed so they had him in a cross-watch. Smart.

The two men crossed the trolley tracks and sat down with Combs.

"How nice to see you again, Mr. Alpha," said the taller man pleasantly. "I am Milos, and you remember Peter. Would you please follow us?"

"Where to?"

"A more private environment."

"No. We meet in public. That was the deal."

"Someone quite important wishes to see you. For security reasons, he cannot be seen in public."

"We'll talk here. Then you deliver the message."

Milos never lost his smile. "I'm terribly sorry to inconvenience you, but I'm afraid I must insist. I promise this will be worth your while."

Combs hadn't brought any backup—they'd made it clear he had to be alone, and he knew that if they spotted anyone, they'd bolt. On the other hand, the idea of disappearing down some alley with a bunch of terrorists didn't seem like a smart play. He stood up and threw his napkin on the chair. "Then I don't think we have anything more to say to each other."

Milos remained seated. "Please do not be rash, sir. We have some mutually beneficial business to discuss. Very beneficial."

Combs knew his options were to blow it off or take the chance. And walk away from a potentially huge deal. Well, he figured, if they'd wanted him dead, they'd have probably already done it. May as well roll the dice.

"I got people expecting me back in thirty minutes," Combs bluffed. "If anything unfortunate should happen, it'll be you guys that are sorry."

"Of course. May we go now?"

A waiting Mercedes took them to Amsterdam's red-light district along the Oudezijds Voorburgwal. Milos walked Combs up the narrow street next to the canal, where even in the daytime bikini-clad prostitutes sat in bay windows. The ones with curtains closed were "entertaining." Combs figured these broads must look better at night, when they sat under black lights. He followed Milos past a fountain shaped like an upright penis that was constantly pissing, or something, into the air.

They crossed the canal on a bridge decorated with red light bulbs and went into a store that said "Coffee Shop" in English, which was the Amsterdam buzzword for a place to buy hashish and marijuana. The bearded man behind the counter was enthusiastically showing a small gray chunk of something to a young woman, and Combs overheard him saying, "This Super Bubble Head shit won last year's Hash Bash."

Milos led Combs through the kitchen to a flight of stairs so narrow that Combs's shoulders touched one wall or the other with every step. On the third floor they went down a dark corridor to a large man standing in front of a door. He glared at Combs, then cross-examined Milos for several minutes in some gibberish language. Finally, he patted down Combs for weapons and opened the door. Milos, Combs, and two goons that materialized out of nowhere went into a one-room apartment.

The windows were covered with heavy curtains that only allowed a dim light. A man who had been sitting on the bed stood up, and his dark eyes shot about quickly in a controlled surveillance. He was short, strongly built, with a loss of pigmentation on his neck that made him look like he'd spilled bleach on himself. Combs immediately recognized him as "Charlie," the world's most wanted terrorist.

Charlie was a freelancer, with a hard-on for the Western world, who flitted through the shadows to help anyone with anti-West causes. It was rumored that Charlie was the deep-cover mastermind of the Munich airport explosion, the London subway gassing, and the Lausanne airline disaster. In this case, he'd obviously tapped into the Serbians, who were probably still angry about the U.S.'s role in Kosovo.

These guys had to be very serious if Charlie was here.

The door closed and the goons took up posts beside it. Milos stood next to Charlie and waited for him to nod before sitting. Charlie and Combs looked at each other for several minutes without speaking. Combs figured this was some kind of intimidation game, so he sure as hell wasn't going first.

"Your demo was defective," said Charlie in heavily accented English. He stared hard into Combs.

Combs shuddered. They knew about Berger. He started to explain how he already had plans to take care of him, then caught himself. "What do you mean?"

"Someone survived in your Orlando. Los Angeles was for daytime, with many people. Bomb explode at night. We do not pay for sloppiness."

Combs exhaled his tension, he hoped invisibly. "Details. And inconsequential. The survivor in Orlando is in a coma, and even if she wakes up, she can't tell them any more than they already know. The Los Angeles thing, well, this is art as much as science. So we were off by a few hours. It was only a test. For the main event, we'll have backup and contingency plans that we can't afford at this stage."

Charlie snorted. "Can't afford? For the prices you ask?"

"If you don't want what I've got, there are plenty of others who do. Now that I've done the demo, I can think of at least three buyers who are ready, willing, and able."

Charlie continued staring at Combs. There was something in the eyes. Combs flashed on a lion stalking a zebra, just before taking it down. The image shoved into his gut like a dagger, and Combs suddenly felt isolated and vulnerable. He realized that this guy could simply tilt his head to signal some unseen hand to slit Combs's throat.

Milos spoke pleasantly: "We consider threats to be disrespectful, Mr. Alpha."

"I'm not threatening anything. I'm just trying to say there's no obligation past the demonstration."

Another silence followed. Charlie whispered to Milos in some foreign language. Milos turned back with a smile. "I believe we may continue our discussions. What would you require to proceed?"

Combs caught himself about to lower the price. The

bullshit these assholes were throwing at him, either on purpose or by instinct, was getting through. Pretend you're dealing with a fucking used car salesman, he told himself.

"One hundred million dollars."

The color drained from Milos, giving him an odd gray complexion. Combs thought he caught the curl of a smile flash quickly at the corners of Charlie's mouth.

"Absurd. Totally absurd." But Combs noticed that he didn't stand up. These guys weren't such hot negotiators after all, he thought.

"For what you want?" countered Combs. "Worldwide publicity for your cause? Six lethal strikes into the heart of the beast, or whatever you guys like to call these things. The fear and intimidation that follows? You'll spend more than what I'm asking on a bunch of little firecracker tricks that don't add up to ten percent of the impact this would have."

"If we are to negotiate in good faith, you must give us a more realistic price."

Good tactic, thought Combs. He wants me to lower my price before he even gives a counteroffer. Not a chance.

"How realistic must I be?"

They whispered again for a while. Combs smiled at one of the goons, who ignored him.

Milos finally spoke. "Fifty million. No more."

Not bad, thought Combs. He had hoped to end up in the fifty- to sixty-million range. Now he figured he was looking at seventy-five.

Combs stood up and said, "We're too far apart, gentlemen. No hard feelings." He didn't want to turn his back on them, so he backed toward the door.

The men whispered to themselves, and Milos held up his hand for Combs to stop. He kept walking until there was a second gesture, then he returned to the group. He didn't sit.

"Yeah?"

"Sixty. No more."

"Eighty. No less." If they were moving up this quickly, they were hooked. All he had to do was hang tough.

More whispering. "Sixty-five."

"Let's not waste time. Eighty. No less."

Charlie stood up. He thrust his face within inches of Combs, and Combs could smell his tobacco-stained breath.

"Seventy million," said Charlie. He spat while he spoke. "Final offer. You will not be happy if you walk away."

Combs figured there was another five million if he hung tough. Yet his instincts said to let them have this round. After fifty million, it was play money anyway. Since he didn't plan on paying any taxes, he doubted he could even spend it all in his lifetime, though he intended to give it a good try. Also, he didn't like that comment about not being "happy" if he walked.

Combs put out his hand. "We have a deal, Mr.—"

Charlie left Combs's hand dangling. He nodded curtly and turned back to Milos. The two goons escorted Combs out the door.

Los Angeles

Berger approached the Federal Building on Wilshire Boulevard in Westwood. It was a high-rise concrete structure; gray, uniform, nondescript. Typical government issue. Beside it was an expanse of lawn, with a semicircle of poles flying the American flag. The perimeter nearest Wilshire Boulevard was ringed with concrete posts that had been installed to thwart suicide car assaults.

He spotted Hugo Dorn, his public defender, by the front door. Berger dumped his keys into a plastic bowl and walked through a metal detector into the lobby. Dorn placed his briefcase on the X-ray machine's conveyor, and a guard studied the monitor like it was an engrossing TV show.

The elevator was crowded, which always made Berger a little nervous. Usually elevators didn't trigger his claustrophobia, although the anxiety over today's meeting, mixed with the noisy people who had jammed him into a back corner, started him sweating. By the time they reached the seventeenth floor, his collar and armpits had grown wet spots.

Berger walked a few steps behind Dorn across the gray industrial carpet, where they were buzzed through a pair of glass doors etched with the FBI logo. The waiting room had gray walls and framed reproductions of 1930s headlines in which G-men were besting Dillinger and Baby Face Nelson. A receptionist behind thick, bulletproof glass spoke to them through a slot in the bottom, like some clerk at a late night gas station. She directed them to a lumpy couch, where Berger watched a number of white-shirt-and-dark-tie men trundle back and forth with serious expressions.

After a half-hour wait, Jill Landis appeared and ushered them into a small, windowless interrogation room just off the lobby. Berger was immediately taken by her stunning looks. She had violet, doe-shaped eyes, flawless skin, and full, sensual lips. Berger also liked the fact that she was a few pounds overweight, as he had always been attracted to heavier women. He figured it was because his mother was on the chunky side.

Landis seemed oblivious to Berger's stares. He worried about shaking hands, because his nerves had turned down the thermostat on his extremities. As it happened, her handshake was a quick pump and release. At least she didn't wipe off her palm afterward.

The only furnishings were a wooden desk and three chairs. Jill sat in the desk chair with straight posture, keeping her shoulders a few inches from the chair back, and laid out a yellow pad and ballpoint pen. Berger stood for a few seconds, waiting for an invitation that didn't come, then sat. Dorn remained standing.

"Thank you for coming," she began. "I asked you here because the FBI is carefully watching the EXC investigation."

"Is that because you think it might be a terrorist act?" asked Dorn.

Jill's demeanor was unreadable as she ignored Dorn and looked directly at Berger. "I would like to ask you a few questions."

"Is he a suspect?" Dorn interjected.

Jill continued to look at Berger and said, "Not at this time."

"You're aware there's no evidence connecting him to this crime," Dorn pressed.

She finally turned to Dorn, keeping her posture rigid. "Is he going to answer the questions or not?"

"He's been more than cooperative with the authorities."

"Except for the part about attending a nonexistent chess tournament."

Dorn cleared his throat and quietly sat down.

Jill opened a desk drawer and took out a photograph. "Have you ever seen this man?" she asked, pushing the grainy image across to Berger.

Berger studied the picture. It was a man in his sixties, balding, with white hair. Heavily wrinkled face. Gray eyes. A smile like a grandfather. He did look familiar. Wait a minute . . .

"I think I saw his picture in the paper. Is this the guy that blew up a warehouse in Orlando?"

He felt like Jill was studying him for a reaction.

"That's correct. Have you ever met him?"

"Do you think these cases are connected?" asked Dorn.

"Do you know this man, Mr. Berger?"

Berger thought maybe he did. Which seemed impossible. Even more unlikely was that he had a mental image of the guy naked. What was going on?

"I don't think so," said Berger. He was sure his voice modulated to such a degree that she thought he was hiding something.

Her eyes gave away nothing as she asked, "You don't *think* so?"

"I don't remember him."

"You don't know him or you don't remember him?"

Dorn interjected. "If he doesn't remember him, how can he say if he knows him?"

"Did you go to work at EXC last Sunday?" asked Jill.

"No. I was at a chess— I mean, I think I was at a chess tournament. But I didn't go to work. I'd remember that. I'm just a little confused right now." Berger grimaced like a preschooler trying to explain why the toothpaste had been squeezed all over the bathroom. So far, he rated his story right down there with "Something big came out of the woods and did it."

"According to the security company that monitors EXC's alarm," said Jill, pulling out a perforated stack of computer paper, "your keycard deactivated the alarm on Sunday. The only other deactivation was Horatio Smith, the daytime security guard. How do you explain that?"

Dorn looked like his chin had been hit by an invisible punch. He grabbed Berger's arm, signaling him to shut up, then pulled Berger into the hall.

"Do you know anything about this?" whispered Dorn.

Berger shook his head vigorously. "No. I swear."

Dorn's voice grew louder. "I thought I was clear when I said that you can't afford to have me surprised."

"You were. Someone must have used my alarm card. Or made a phony one with my code on it."

"Have you ever given your card to anyone else?"

"No. But security isn't what lay people think it is. Anyone who really wants to get somebody's code can do it."

Dorn didn't look convinced. "I don't like where this is going."

"You think I'm having fun?"

Dorn furrowed his brow and stared at Berger for a few moments. "All right. Just tell her the truth."

They returned to the interrogation room.

"I wasn't there," said Berger. His voice modulated again, which was thoroughly annoying. He knew he hadn't done anything wrong. Why was he feeling like this?

"Then how do you explain the alarm records?" she asked.

"Someone must have used my alarm card. Or a duplicate."

"While you were off playing chess?"

CHAPTER 13

At the EXC bomb site, ATF Agent Leland dumped another
shovelful of debris through the wire mesh. Beads of sweat
trickled into his eyes, causing him to blink rapidly. He took
off his black ATF baseball cap and wiped the back of his
hand across his drenched forehead. Then he stood up and
leaned on the shovel. His lower back twinged on the verge
of spasm.

Thank God they were down to the last four grids and
he could move on to another investigation. Once the FBI
decided to horn in, ATF was relegated to the scutwork of
sifting through the shit and turning over the findings. He
thought about the miners in South Africa, who dig through
tons of ore to find a diamond, then hand it over to some
asshole in an air-conditioned office.

On the other hand, the way things were going here, it
didn't much matter. The only bomb parts they'd recovered
were a nine-volt battery and a twisted pair of yellow and
red wires that had belonged to an Atlas blasting cap. The
wires confirmed that dynamite was the booster, yet little
else—they were so common that there was no possibility

of a trace. The battery was sold at one of several hundred Rite Aid drugstores in Los Angeles. Also not a help.

Maybe they'd get something from the desk fragments. He'd already rubbed a few of them with distilled water, looking for nitrates, and some others with ammonia, hoping to find fuel oil, which wasn't water-soluble. The lab would tell him if he was on the right track. But even that wouldn't put them any closer to the bomber.

He took one last stretch, then heaved in another scoop of rubble. A dull silver piece of material caught his eye, and he dropped the shovel. He forgot his back pain as he realized it was a matted piece of duct tape. That was very good news. Duct tape often traps fingerprints between the layers. He rummaged through his evidence kit for a pair of tweezers, and gently put the tape into a plastic bag. Then he left his tools sitting there and drove directly to the ATF lab.

Berger pulled into the driveway of his Venice house shortly before ten in the morning. He took the key out of his bike's ignition, stomped down the kickstand, and pulled off his helmet. Then he rubbed his eyes hard enough to see tiny white spots behind the lids.

The idea of being home so early on a weekday, and the thought of having nothing to do, was disorienting him. So was the fact that he still couldn't find Linda. Or a job. And the fact that the cops and the FBI thought he was either a liar or a lunatic, or both. There was a very real chance they would try to lock him up. That would certainly do in whatever was left of his mind.

And where the hell was Linda? He pictured their first date at a revival movie theater, where they saw *Swept Away*. How he'd been too nervous to even hold her hand. He remembered their coffee afterward at an outdoor café on the

Third Street Promenade. The wonderful way her eyes danced when she laughed harder than his jokes deserved. The sensual way she stroked his face before their kiss good night.

Then the darker side. The memory of her sitting in his living room, telling him she was seeing someone else. And his worries about why she had disappeared. He couldn't shake the feeling that she was in trouble.

He forced himself back to the moment and unhooked the bungee cord holding his groceries to the back of his motorcycle. With both arms full, he started down the sidewalk toward his front door.

A few steps in front of the porch, he stopped.

Something was wrong. He didn't know what. Only that the house wasn't right.

He didn't see anything that shouldn't be there. Yet . . . wait. It was the opposite. Something wasn't there that should be. What?

He set down the groceries and took a few tentative steps toward the front door, conscious of keeping his bootsteps quiet against the concrete. When he got to the porch, he had it.

Max wasn't barking. By the time anyone hit the porch, Max was always flinging himself against the front door. But today the house was quiet. Berger slid his key into the lock and turned it, then stopped before opening the door. To his left, he saw that the shade was drawn. He never pulled down the shade. The realization crept up the back of his head in an electric tingle. Someone had been in his house. Or might still be there.

Berger backed slowly off the porch and moved to the side of the house. Because the cottage was built on an elevated foundation, he couldn't reach the windows to look in. At least he didn't see any broken windows or signs of a forced entry.

When he got to the back, he saw that someone had pulled down the shade on the back door's glass pane. Whatever was going on, they'd wanted privacy. He thought about calling Max, yet was worried he'd alert someone inside.

Berger squatted down and opened the old-fashioned milk door—a small passageway for milkmen to put bottles inside the house. It led to a tiny compartment, the depth of the exterior wall, and another door on the inside. He held his breath and slowly pushed open the inside door. It squealed loudly, and he froze; ready to run if any sounds came from the house. Nothing but his heart thudding in his ears. After a moment, he pushed again, and realized he was still holding his breath. He didn't let it out.

When the little milk door opened all the way, he tried to survey the room.

That was when he saw the object on the front door.

CHAPTER 14

Berger sat on the curb, which was so short that his knees were higher than his shoulders. He could feel people's stares as he hunched his head forward against his legs, waiting for the police to arrive.

He worried whether Max was lying dead inside. In his mind, he imagined what might have been Max's last moments. He pictured him attacking the intruders, only to be bludgeoned savagely. Hopefully he'd run away from them, the way he sometimes did just to annoy Berger.

His eyes searched the area and he whistled for Max, half expecting to see the little puppy he'd first brought home. He'd chosen this little Jack Russell out of the litter because Max was the only one who ran toward him. Berger remembered picking him up, watching his tiny legs waving in the air. How Max the puppy would proudly put his front paws on the newspaper while he peed on the carpet. How little Max tried to take on a rottweiler at the vet's. How Max licked Berger's dishes after dinner, as a "prewash" before the dishwasher.

The depression hunched his shoulders forward. Linda.

Max. His job and money gone. The police and FBI pressuring him like a criminal. Embarrassed to cry, even though he knew it would be a release, he sucked in a shuddering breath.

Berger realized someone was shaking his shoulder. He looked up, squinting into the sun, to see a hulking figure above him.

"I'm Sparky Scott of the ATF. You called about a bomb?"

"Yeah."

There was a moment of silence before Scott said, "So talk to me."

Berger stood slowly, knees creaking. He told Scott about the device he'd seen attached to his front door. Scott listened intently, then went to the rear of the house and looked through the milk door. Berger followed in a mild stupor, like a puppy waking from a nap.

Scott next went to the side of the house and pulled himself up to look through the window. "I can't see the back door, but I can tell the windows aren't rigged." He told Berger to move away from the house.

Berger wove back and forth on the sidewalk as he wandered away. His mouth hung slightly open, and his eyes defocused. He had no idea where he was going, yet he moved forward as if propelled by an unseen push.

The sight of an armed explosive still excited Scott as much as the first time he'd seen one. Every year his family in Stockton took him to the high school football field for the Fourth of July. He remembered the smell of cooking burgers and burning charcoal, and the sight of families on folding chairs with laughing children running circles around them. He remembered the sagging lines of clear bulbs that lit the area, which were turned off at nine when the fireworks began. But mostly he remembered the bursting flowers of fire in the air. The multicolored starfish that spread their fingers overhead. Scott dreamed of what it would be like to be on one of the rockets. To see the crowd below oohing at each explosion; the volume of the gasps growing with the intensity of the fireworks.

He remembered how he harassed his father into taking him early one year, so he could use the "little kid" trick to get backstage. They went past the NO SMOKING and KEEP OUT! signs to meet a white-haired Hispanic man with a thick mustache and a gentle face who gave him a tour of the dark cylinders that launched the fireworks. They looked to Sparky like small cannons, arranged in an array of wires and triggers that seemed both haphazard and precise. Like artillery, ready to attack the black skies. Sparky stared for the longest time, until they forced him out just before the show began. The man promised that the first one, a blue and gold shower of fire, would be just for Sparky.

Scott opened the trunk of his car and began to put on the thickly padded bomb suit. It was made of dense, black material that looked like quilted moving van blankets, and the heavy weight bowed his shoulders. He cinched up the suit and was reaching for the clear face mask when Jed Adams, an LAPD officer on the scene, grabbed his arm.

"You're not thinking of going in there," said Adams.

"No. I'm putting on the suit because I'm cold."

"Sparky, don't be an idiot. LAPD bomb squad is on the way with a robot. We're not even through evacuating."

"Those guys always fuck up the evidence. This one looks sophisticated and I want a close look. Then I'll get out."

"Look, Rambo, you'll fuck up more than the evidence if you set that thing off."

"I can handle it. I'm a CES."

"A CES who hasn't done a Render Safe Procedure for over ten years, as I recall."

"It's like riding a bike," said Scott. His words were muffled because he now had on the face mask.

"Scott, you stubborn sonofabitch . . ."

Scott's warm breath recirculated against his face as he pushed past Adams to the side of the house and climbed onto a wobbly orange crate. He smashed a glass pane on one of the windows and opened the latch. Because of the awkward suit, it took three tries before he could clumsily vault inside.

As he approached the device, he was aware of his accelerated breathing, which was beginning to fog the face mask. Scott stepped over a large, torn area of the carpet, then slowed his pace as he approached the front door. About four feet away, he froze and involuntarily stopped breathing.

The device had a mercury switch. Mercury switches were set off by vibrations, like the tilt button on a pinball machine. Seeing one in front of him meant he wasn't going any further, and that he was lucky to still be standing there. It also meant this device was more sophisticated than he'd thought.

The next observation was even more disturbing. From the milk door, the IED had looked like a simple set of pipe bombs. Now he could see it wasn't pipes; it was three bundles of cast boosters—melted-down RDX, the ingredients in military C-4—wrapped in silver duct tape. They were wired with a blasting cap detonator, and next to them was a three-gallon container of gasoline. There looked to be almost four pounds of explosive, which was enough to obliterate whoever came through the door, and a few of the neighbors as well. The gasoline assured a raging fire after the explosion.

Beads of perspiration sprouted on Scott's forehead, creating a terrarium inside the face mask. Moisture dribbled into his eyes, blurring his vision, yet he couldn't risk taking off the mask to wipe his face.

He saw a nine-volt battery power source, attached by wires to two magnetic alarm sensors on the door and frame. They were "normally closed" switches, which meant the explosive was activated when anyone opened the door and separated them. A second set of wires ran to the mercury switch and another battery. Whichever one got it first would set off the bomb. This was set by one nasty sonofabitch.

Scott became aware of his temples throbbing in rhythm to his heart. He inched backward, suddenly worried that the thumping of his heart might set off the mercury switch. He knew that was impossible, but the fact that he was even considering it meant he needed to get the hell out of there. He'd secretly hoped it would be a simple dismantle, so he'd have another grab at the ring. This was definitely one for the bomb squad, who would sandbag the area and use a robot to attempt a disarm. That was unlikely with the mercury switch, as any movement would set off the explosive. They would have to clear the block, and he sure as hell had to get out of the house.

He kept his eye on the mercury switch and took a tentative step backward. The floor creaked and the mercury seemed to slosh in the bulb. When he saw how sensitive it was, he realized he'd been fortunate not to trip it on the way in. Whoever set this thing knew exactly what he was doing. A lot of bombers blow themselves up with much cruder devices.

He stood still until the mercury stopped moving. Then he took another step back and felt his foot catch on something. The unexpected obstacle threw him off balance. He looked down in panic and saw that the rip in the carpet had snared his heel. Scott began flailing his arms, trying to regain his balance, and his mind processed the possibilities, almost in slow motion. His first hope was that he wouldn't fall. That much of a concussion would certainly set off the IED. His next thought was that he hoped they'd cleared the area.

For a moment, he teetered in seeming balance on one foot, like a tightrope walker recovering from a falter. With his breath locked tight, he wobbled awkwardly—head flung back, arms outstretched, and one foot stuck out straight in front of him. Making microscopic adjustments in his limbs, trying to keep the delicate equilibrium. He almost had it.

In the next instant, he knew he didn't. He began to fall backward and didn't want to hit head first, so he pulled his chin toward his chest. His instinct was to roll as he hit, hopefully spreading out the force of his fall and minimizing the jolt to the mercury switch. He doubted that the bulkiness of his suit would permit that kind of maneuver, and quickly discovered he was right.

Scott thudded flat on his back. Maybe it was his imagination, but he was sure he heard the switch trip. His first thought was the jar he kept with a bomber's finger, and he wondered whether someone might find his fingers and save them to warn young ATF agents. His next thought was that he was now fulfilling his childhood fantasy. Riding the fireworks into the sky. Looking down at the crowd. Their faces lit by the exploding rockets and blazing sprays of gold, sapphire, and topaz. The smell of burning gunpowder, and the sound of oohs and ahhs. The crowd's applause and the children's laughter.

CHAPTER 15

Jill got off the elevator on the fourteenth floor of the Federal Building, where the Domestic Terrorism Unit is housed. She slid her plastic FBI badge, emblazoned with a blue "L.A." over wavy red lines, into the reader and placed her feet on the painted footprints on the floor. When she heard the lock click open, she pushed the thick blue bars on the revolving metal door that resembled an overgrown amusement park exit.

She fell into her desk chair and turned on the computer. An "FBI Los Angeles" screen saver crawled across the screen. The walls of her gray cubicle were bare, and her desk had the outward appearance of neatness because she stuffed all the unsorted crap into drawers. The only items in sight were a few neat stacks of files and memos, a calendar, and one of those toys that hang ball bearings on a row of nylon threads so you can clack them against each other.

She was still numbed by the news of an explosion at Berger's house. Sparky Scott, the ATF agent killed in the blast, was the second friend she'd lost in her short career of law enforcement. The hurt seemed less the second time around. That bothered her as much as the loss itself.

The phone rang, jolting her. It was the needle-nosed woman at reception, who said Jill had a delivery. She ambled slowly up the stairs to the seventeenth floor, running her hand against the rough texture of the wall along the way. Needle-Nose handed her a sealed manila packet, which she opened while climbing back down the steps.

It contained a report on the piece of duct tape recovered at the EXC blast. Jill stopped in the stairwell and read that the lab had found a fingerprint trapped in the tape. Excited, she flipped to the next page. Her hopes dwindled just as rapidly. The print was only a partial and therefore not enough to put through AFIS, the Automated Fingerprint Identification System. Although four points— unique fingerprint characteristics—matched with Berger's thumbprint, they weren't unique enough to prove they were his. A decent suspicion, but diddly in court.

She continued walking down the stairs. Why would someone as bright as Berger make up such a stupid alibi? The chess story was so absurd that she'd quit trying to corroborate it after the first two phone calls. One of Berger's supposed opponents said he'd been in Switzerland, while the other had been at home.

Then someone plants a bomb at Berger's house. Could Berger have done that to divert suspicion onto others? Two bombs around him within a few days wasn't likely a coincidence. And now he'd gone AWOL. Apparently the guy just walked away from the blast scene in the confusion. Was he hiding? Or was he simply nuts? Suspects simply didn't act like this. Not dumb ones, not smart ones.

She returned to her desk and stuffed the report into a drawer that barely shut because of all the clutter inside. Jill couldn't shake the feeling that Berger was legit, although she worried it was because she had found him physically attractive. She knew better than to think that way about a suspect, so she had consciously buried her feelings. She hoped they weren't bleeding through to her thought processes, and told herself forcefully that they weren't. No. There was something else about Berger. Something she'd seen before. Where? What was it? She couldn't reel it in.

She wished Ted were here to bounce things off. His ability to pull theories out of scattered facts had captivated her right from the beginning. She took out the set of wedding pictures that she kept in her desk and began to thumb through them. Ted and Jill in front of the rabbi and priest who married them. Ted mushing cake into Jill's face. Ted and Jill with their parents, neither side looking happy. Apart from the religious differences, Jill's parents objected to Ted's being almost twenty years older. She remembered her mother's words when they'd started dating. "You know, dear, women live longer than men." Those words had been cruelly prophetic. She wondered if her mother remembered them when Ted shriveled from leukemia and was gone less than a year after their wedding.

Jill stroked Ted's face with her thumb, then phoned Carl Davidson, the head of the Anti-Terrorist Unit in Washington.

"That pissant EXC thing?" he barked. "Why are you calling me about that?"

Jill stood up and fiddled with the receiver cord. "Sir, I thought you personally asked me to get into this case."

"I did? Oh. Yeah, well, I guess. Look, I only got a minute. What do you want?"

She wasn't prepared to give a machine-gun delivery, and her tongue began to stumble on itself. "Well, sir, I wanted your opinion on the next move." She quickly ran down the situation with Berger.

"What do you think you should do?"

"We don't have enough to arrest him, so I thought maybe we should watch him."

"Haul his ass in. Keep him a couple of days and let him think you got something. Make him roll over on whoever's pulling his strings."

"Sir, we're not even sure if he's involved, much less if he's got conspirators."

"Does your gut tell you the Orlando thing's connected?"

"Well . . . it's hard to say—"

"Yes or no?"

"Uh . . . yes."

"Then someone's pulling his strings. Unless he cooked it up with the old fart in Florida, which I seriously doubt. Squeeze his nuts."

"You don't think we should first watch him a few days?"

"Am I stuttering?"

"Uh . . . no, sir."

"Don't call me again until you get a breakthrough."

The line went dead. Jill stared at the handset, as if it were the last remains of her stinging pride, then gently cradled it onto the receiver.

She couldn't disobey a direct order like that. Even if it went against her instincts. On the other hand, there was that pesky little problem that Berger had disappeared. She'd have to—

It clicked. She remembered why Berger's reaction was familiar. The Los Angeles airport hostages. A group of passengers held on an airplane for four days. She'd worked closely with the negotiators, and then debriefed the hostages after release. They had the same fear of authority that she saw in Berger's eyes. Some of them had hallucinated detailed experiences as a means of mental escape, and a few believed those experiences were real.

Could Berger's chess tournament have a similar origin? If so, what would cause him to do that?

CHAPTER 16

There were twenty-four people seated in the room, all hand-screened by Combs. Twenty-one from the former Mirage project, and three from The Squad, Combs's high school gang. The two other Mirage members who'd made the initial cut, then showed they didn't have the balls for the game, were no longer a problem.

Combs paced in front of the group, squealing his shoes on the slick white vinyl floor. Fluorescent lights buzzed overhead, throwing multiple shadows.

Ed Baxter, a five-foot-four man who had developed a forty-eight-inch chest through bodybuilding, stood to the side, studying the scene with his cobalt blue eyes. Baxter had been Combs's number two since grammar school. They'd drifted apart after high school, then gotten together ten years later, after Tony Beeson's funeral. Tony was a Squad member who'd been into PCP and eaten the barrel of a shotgun.

After a few drinks, Baxter told Combs he'd gone career army. He said he was in Psy Ops—Psychological Opera-tions—which meant they put out information to fuck with the enemy's morale. Baxter told him how they dropped leaflets on the Iraqi troops during the Gulf War, saying that Arab brothers shouldn't fight each other, and shit like that. And how the surrendering prisoners had said those flyers really got to them. Combs was fascinated with the concept, and kept Baxter up until 4:00 A.M. peppering him with questions. Within a week, Combs applied to officer candidate school. A little inside help from Baxter greased the wheels.

Combs showed such brilliance during his Psy Ops training that, within a year, they plucked him for the ultrasecret Mirage project. Two years later, he was running the entire operation. He earned the position with his extraordinary skills, but it didn't hurt that the former Director was fired for breaching security. It seemed the man was screwing this civilian nurse—a fact that Combs discovered and let Baxter make known to the brass.

Combs cleared his throat to quiet the group. The conversation halted immediately.

He started pacing again. "Gentlemen, we have a go."

Cheers and whistles.

"Yeah!"

"Right on!"

Combs allowed himself a rare smile, then waved them quiet.

"Orlando and Los Angeles were just pricks at the balloon. This will be The Show."

He paused for effect, then spoke quietly. "None of us will ever do anything more important in our lives. Ever. Yes, we'll all be wealthy when this is over. But that's only the frosting on the cake." His voice grew louder as he continued. "We have a power that people don't even dream exists. And those pussy bureaucrats, who left our asses dan-

gling when they shut down Mirage, will know in spades
what could have been theirs!"

The men were on their feet, yelling and shaking their
fists in the air.

Berger ambled leisurely down the boardwalk at Venice
Beach. An unseasonably hot November sun was melting
his soft-serve ice cream faster than he could lick it off the
cone, and the vanilla dribbled stickily between his fingers.

Because of the nice weather, the boardwalk was packed
with pedestrians, cyclists, jugglers, magicians, and mimes.
He took a deep breath of the salt air and listened for the
surf, which he couldn't hear over the music, scraping of
rollerblades, and entertainers shouting for an audience. The
crowd ebbed and flowed in both directions, and he allowed
it to carry him along, as if he were a cell in some large
organism.

Berger tossed the ice cream into an oil drum that had
been recycled into a trash can, then washed his fingers in
a water fountain. He stopped at Muscle Beach and watched
the men and women pumping iron. Their muscles bulged
and rippled under the heavy weights, all to the admiration
of the crowd. Berger unconsciously ran his hand over his
thin biceps.

A few minutes later, he rejoined the crowds and strolled
along the walkway. Berger had never cut school as a kid,
and he couldn't quite remember why he'd decided to take
off work today. He looked at his watch and was surprised
to see it was almost noon. He must have really unwound
to lose track of time like that. Had he been here all morning? He couldn't quite remember.

He got off the boardwalk and turned up Rose Avenue,
toward his house. As he left the beach behind, the orchestra of sounds subsided into a few soloists. A singing bird;

a kid on a bicycle whose gears whirred rhythmically; a car engine purring as it drove past. The relative quiet was calming.

When he turned off Hampton onto Indiana, he saw police cars with blue revolving lights and a group of people behind a barricade. There were always petty burglaries in his neighborhood, but this looked more serious. He moved cautiously ahead and saw fire trucks on his street. The air smelled of burning wood and was flickering with gray debris that fluttered like dark snowflakes.

This was definitely more serious. He elbowed his way into the crowd, trying to get a look at his house. Or more accurately, where his house had been.

His house had burned into a black rubble, and he realized that the snowflakes were settling ashes. His neighbors' houses were buckled and partially collapsed; one was also charred and still wet from the fire hoses. The windows of undamaged houses were shattered. His motorcycle had been flung into his neighbor's yard, crumpled like a discarded cigarette pack.

The memories hit him with such force that he felt like he'd been thrown into the blast of a jet engine. He backed away through the crowd and collapsed, sitting on the street. Now it was all back. The bomb on his front door. Max. The ATF guy. The explosion. Berger had read about people having a "disassociative reaction" to a trauma, where their minds simply disconnected. That's obviously what had happened when he took his stroll along the boardwalk.

He was sorry to be back.

With the flood of recall came the emptiness of reality. His house was gone. Everything he owned had been in there. Linda had deserted him. Max was missing or dead. His work was gone.

The sound of a car door opening caught his ear. He

looked up and saw the passenger's and driver's doors swing out from a blue car parked a couple of hundred yards away. The open doors made the vehicle look like a bird of prey unfolding its wings. Two men got out and were looking directly at Berger. One was tall and thin, and the other was compact and muscular, with a pencil mustache.

Instinctively, he knew they wanted him. It must be the EXC bombing. Now they probably thought he blew up his own house. He pictured himself locked in a cell. A space so small that he couldn't stretch his arms to his sides. He felt the walls squeezing in close. Tightening against his shoulders.

The men were moving rapidly toward him. Berger remembered when his cousin Matty used to come over for family dinners. Matty always played with his little cousin Johnny, to the smiling approval of the aunts and uncles. They never knew that Matty's idea of "play" was to lock Berger in a closet. They never knew because Matty told Berger he'd kill him if he ever told anyone; a threat so scary that, to this day, Berger had kept the secret. So Berger spent hours in various uncles' closets. Lit only by a crack of light under the door. Lying on the floor, tied up with neckties, breathing in the smell of mothballs and leather shoes. Berger couldn't even cry without risking that he'd be found and Matty would kill him. As soon as Matty moved on to younger cousins, Berger swore he'd never be locked in a closet again.

Before he realized it, Berger had begun to run. He stole a glance over his shoulder and saw that the two men were running after him. At least you're not paranoid, he thought to himself. They really were coming for you.

He picked up speed and stretched his hundred-yard lead by another thirty or forty. Then he began to feel sharp needles of pain in his chest and side. Berger was wholly out of shape, and he knew he couldn't run much further before slowing to a pace that any ten-year-old could beat. Which meant he had to outthink them.

He pushed his lungs to pump harder. Maybe this wasn't such a good idea, he thought. Maybe he should just turn around and get this over with. The idea of being locked in a small room sped him up.

He turned down Rose Avenue and headed back to Venice Beach, where he could hopefully disappear in the crowds. His face and body were sweating heavily, and he pretended it was oil that lubricated his machinery and moved him faster.

When he hit the boardwalk, he slowed down so he wouldn't attract attention. Not that any kind of weirdo would attract attention on Venice Beach. His breathing wheezed loudly as he pushed the tip of his index finger against a sharp pain in his ribs. Perspiration soaked his clothes and filled his nostrils.

Berger walked without looking back, despite an almost irresistible urge. He told himself that looking wouldn't change his pursuers' location, but it would give them a chance to see his face. At least no one had grabbed his shoulder. Yet.

After a block or so, he ducked into an open-air stall run by a wrinkled Korean woman with a round face and thick eyebrows that were angled so steeply that she looked like she was scowling. He grabbed a T-shirt with a picture of a donkey that said "Kiss My Ass," and a baseball cap with fake bird poop that said "I Hate Seagulls." Near the back, he found a pair of sunglasses with thick black Buddy Holly frames.

Berger got behind a heavily loaded table, peeled off his sopping denim shirt, and put on the donkey T-shirt. Next he tucked his ponytail under the baseball cap and punched the lenses out of the sunglasses. He had read that some movie stars use plain glasses to disguise themselves, since sunglasses look like you're hiding. He hoped the cops wouldn't get close enough to see there was no glass in them.

Berger ditched his denim shirt under the table and strolled back onto the boardwalk. His breathing had returned to normal, and for the first time he looked around for the two men. Neither one was in sight. He knew they'd still be there, probably split up in two directions. He went toward the skateboard obstacle course.

As he watched the skateboarders weave between trash cans and jump over ramps, he saw the tall, thin man making his way toward him. Berger didn't think he'd been spotted, since the man was still looking around and hadn't picked up his pace.

Berger walked casually in the opposite direction, worried that moving quickly would call attention to himself. Ahead on the right, he saw two jugglers barking up a crowd. Berger reasoned that a thick crowd of onlookers might shield him, so he made his way toward the front. He hoped these guys were talented enough to pull a lot of people.

The jugglers were an odd-looking pair. One was skinny, with shoulder-length red hair and a wiry beard that covered only the tip of his chin and ran halfway down his chest. The other was pudgy with deep-sunk eyes and a dark tan. The fat one started juggling bowling balls and flaming Indian clubs at the same time. The crowd thickened, and Berger stayed toward the front. He felt a little guilty when a short man behind him made sarcastic remarks about not being able to see, yet Berger stood his ground.

The crowd was a thick crescent by the time the fat guy finished juggling and bowed to uneven applause. The skinny man put on a purple stovepipe hat and asked for a volunteer. No hands went up. Berger looked over his shoulder to see if the men following him were around. He didn't see them. When he turned back, someone grabbed his wrist.

"Mule Man," said the skinny juggler, pointing to the donkey on Berger's shirt. "C'mon out."

Berger shook his head and pulled his hand loose.

"Awww. He's shy. Whaddaya say, folks? Don't you want to see Mule Man?" He began chanting, "Mu-ule . . . Mu-ule . . . Mu-ule . . ." The crowd picked it up.

Berger kept shaking his head and thought about running. That would be too suspicious. The chanting grew louder. Then people shoved him into the performing area. Probably the short asshole behind him who made the rude comments. He pulled back into the crowd, and said "No!" loudly. The crowd laughed and kept yelling, "Mu-ule."

Berger realized he was out of options. He stepped forward and the crowd roared its approval.

"What's your name?" asked the skinny juggler. Up close, Berger saw that the guy had an Adam's apple that stuck almost an inch away from his neck and bobbed up and down when he spoke.

"Jimmy."

"Give it up for Jimmy!" Applause. "Jimmy Hoffa? Jimi Hendrix? Jimmy Page?"

"Just . . . Jimmy."

"Okay, Just Jimmy. We're gonna throw some nice, two-foot machetes about six inches from your ear. Is that okay?"

The crowd laughed and Berger used the chance to look to his left. He saw the tall agent scanning the crowd. The man was moving through methodically, checking all the faces. His concentration seemed to be on the audience, not the show.

"Well?" asked the juggler.

"Huh?"

The crowd laughed. "I guess I wouldn't want to hear that either. I said we wanna throw some sharp knives around your face, and I asked if you minded."

"I really don't want—"

"Oh, I'm just kidding," he said with a wink. "We use rubber knives." He held up a knife and bent the blade into a U shape. Then he took a few steps back and his partner got behind Berger. They began throwing the rubber knives back and forth. Berger watched curiously as they whizzed by either side of him, about waist level.

"Don't step to the side unless you want to become Jewish," said the juggler.

Berger's eyes were on the agent, who was about a third of the way through his surveillance.

The rubber knives stopped.

"How was that, Jimmy?"

It took Berger a second to realize they were talking to him.

"Uh . . . fine."

"That was our warmup. Four knives. Now we're gonna use eight." The crowd started giggling. Berger had lost the agent when the juggler distracted him. He rapidly surveyed the left side and couldn't locate him. Then he turned to check out the right.

A hand grabbed his shoulder, and a voice from behind said sternly, "Don't move."

Berger's posture deflated. How'd the sonofabitch sneak up on him? He considered bolting, then realized he was blocked by the crowd. Not to mention that this guy could easily catch him without a head start. He turned to face the man head-on.

It wasn't the agent. It was the fat juggler, who was holding eight brightly polished steel knives. Berger realized that was why the crowd had snickered.

"I said, Don't move."

Berger turned back and the knives began flying. Oddly, he was relieved to feel that his only danger was the two-foot razor blades whipping about six inches away from his body. Concentrating on the rhythmic swish of the knives, he felt as if they were guarding him from the attackers. He began to smile.

After a few moments, the jugglers stopped and the crowd applauded. Adam's Apple said, "Isn't Jimmy a good sport? Give him a round."

The audience cheered and shouted "Yeah" and "Jimmy." Berger walked back to the crowd and looked for the agent. The man seemed to have moved on. Berger worked his way to the rear and looked up and down the board-walk. When he saw the back of the tall agent's head bobbing a few inches above everyone else, he turned and walked slowly in the other direction.

A few blocks later, the crowd and noises thinned as he passed a nearly deserted beach. He watched a seagull floating on an updraft, and Berger related to the sensation. Being carried by the whims of prevailing winds. In losing all his possessions and relationships, he had also lost his burdens and obligations. It gave him an odd sense of calm.

Berger went to a pay phone and called for a cab.

It was time to see Bert.

CHAPTER 17

"You lost him?!" Jill sputtered at the two men. She was standing over her desk, fists clenched, leaning forward on her knuckles.

Hastings, the taller of the two, stood with his shoulders hunched, his chin near his chest. His hands were clasped in front of him as if he were holding an imaginary hat over his groin.

Talbot stood erect, the veins in his neck bulging slightly. He answered her slowly and deliberately, yet his eyes didn't meet hers. "He disappeared into the crowds at Venice Beach. You know how many people—"

"How did he get to Venice Beach? You were supposed to pick him up at his house."

Talbot cleared his throat. "Well, we saw him approach the house, but when we started toward him, he cut and ran."

"Cut and ran? A wimp who couldn't win the hundred-yard dash in a Special Olympics?"

A long silence.

"Just go," she said, waving them away with the back of

her hand. "Put out a description and get on his family, friends, and anybody else he's ever smiled at. I'm holding you two personally responsible for delivering his ass to me."

The two men quickly turned and left. Jill's anger was subsiding, and her bravado along with it. Losing Berger meant Davidson would come down on her. If she got labeled a screwup, that would stay with her for years. She didn't need this while her career was still in its infancy.

What would Ted have done? She ached, longing for him. And feeling very alone. She opened the drawer to take out his pictures, then closed it again when she had an idea.

Jill called Buck Reynolds of the LAPD and asked for his help in picking up Berger.

Reynolds chuckled. "So the Bureau muscles in for the glory, then comes slinkin' back with its tail between its legs?"

"Thank you for your views on law enforcement cooperation. Now will you please put out his description?"

"Oh sure. We'll get him. I'll even wrap him in pretty little ribbons for you."

The prospect of the next call was even less inviting. She had to tell Davidson that she'd lost Berger. The same Davidson who said to call only when she had a breakthrough. The same Davidson who yelled at her for calling him instead of hauling in Berger on her own initiative.

She stared at the phone so hard that her vision blurred. Maybe she was hoping it would make the call for her, or offer some magical words of wisdom.

After several minutes, the phone rang loudly, causing her to rise up slightly in her seat. Her first thought was that it was Davidson, who already knew, and was calling to fire her. She let it ring three times before answering.

"This is Fredericks in Orlando. The survivor of the blast down here is waking up from her coma."

Jill felt like she'd just found a shiny quarter in the garbage. Maybe this was the breakthrough she needed. If she could call Davidson with some good news, it would soften the blow of losing Berger. Actually, she could put off calling Davidson until after she interviewed the survivor. He did say to call only when she had a breakthrough. Maybe she'd even have Berger by then.

"I'll be on the red-eye tonight," she told Fredericks.

In the late afternoon, Berger crouched behind a patchy row of hedges that separated the gas station from a shopping mall. He knew his backside was exposed to the mall's parking lot, but there was no place to fully hide and still see the street. So he sacrificed his rear flanks for a good vantage point.

He was looking for anything unusual before involving Bert. His ankles and calves ached from the sprint along the beach, and crouching behind hedges for the last hour hadn't helped. Maybe the desire to get out of this position was coloring his judgment, but things seemed clean. He hadn't seen any people or cars lingering, so either the cops were really skilled or he was ahead of them. Either way, he may as well get on with it.

He surveyed the street one more time, then looked over at the gas station. It was an old Mobil that hadn't been remodeled, on the corner of Overland and Jefferson, just a few blocks from where Berger had grown up. The antique pumps—probably the last in Los Angeles that didn't accept credit cards—had white wheels with black numbers, and were set on concrete islands painted fire engine red wherever they weren't peeled, scraped, or tire-treaded. Bert, who was running a credit card through a slide machine, was easy to spot. Five foot seven, two hundred and eighty pounds, with matted, short hair. Clenching an unlit cigar, which alarmed the motorists, in fingers that were roughened from years of work and grease.

The hedges scraped Berger's face as he wormed through and headed for the repair bay. He stood up straight and walked slowly. If anyone was watching, he wanted them to pick him up before he got Bert into any of this. One of the bay doors was open, while the other hung halfway at a strange angle. He kept his full attention on the open door, in hopes that concentrating on his goal would ensure arrival.

Berger felt like his peripheral vision was expanding, and every movement spooked him. He finally couldn't stand it and looked around.

Nothing unusual. People walking with shopping bags, kids on bicycles, cars turning into traffic.

He swung wide to avoid Bert, whose attention was on a customer, and walked into the garage bay.

The dark cool radiating from the concrete floor was a pleasant contrast to the afternoon sun. Raoul, a thin man with a muscular body and perpetual smile, stood in a short, two-foot-deep pit, underneath a Chevy raised on the lift. He was hanging a yellow-caged light bulb on the car's chassis and boogying to "Stayin' Alive," which was playing loudly on an oldies station.

"Raoul," whispered Berger.

He turned a ratchet in time to the music and didn't look up.

"Raoul," Berger said louder.

Raoul sang the chorus along with the Bee Gees.

Berger went to the radio and lowered the volume.

Raoul spun around in reaction. "Juanito!" he said with

a wide grin. As he leapt out of the pit, a crescent wrench fell from his blue overalls and clanked on the cement floor.

"Bert's been worried ever since you called, man," said Raoul. "Go sit over there." He pointed at a lopsided folding chair in the corner.

Raoul pulled a stained rag from his back pocket and wiped his hands. When Berger sat down, Raoul turned out the lights and pulled down the bay door with a metal hook on the end of a wooden pole. The door hit bottom with a crash that sounded like the glass had shattered.

"With the lights off in here," whispered Raoul, "we can see out, but nobody can see in. Just stay put and I'll get Bert." Raoul wheeled two red tool chests together, forming a screen in front of Berger's chair. Berger sat back and the broken seat angled his butt at two different levels. The smell of gasoline and grease hung heavily in his nostrils.

A few moments later, Bert rushed inside and grabbed Berger in a bear hug, pinning his arms to his sides.

"Johnny!" said Bert, kissing him fully on the lips.

"Hi, Mom."

CHAPTER 18

Berger, Bert, and Raoul sat in the dark garage bay, shielded by the tool chests. Now that Berger's eyes were accustomed to the low light, he could see that his mother was more worried than she was letting on.

"Mom, I don't want to stay here very long. In case someone comes looking—"

"Don't sweat it. No one can see you back here. And we don't get many people 'cause business sucks."

The silence hung for a moment before Berger said, "I feel really weird putting you in this position."

"I can take care of myself. I'm a big girl." Bert patted her stomach and laughed. Raoul giggled. "Did I tell you Raoul is converting?"

"Converting the station?"

"Nah, man." Raoul laughed. "I'm becoming Jewish."

"You're what?"

"You heard me. Bert wouldn't marry me unless I converted."

"You two are getting married? Whoa. This is all coming a little fast."

"After living together for three years, I told him to make me an honest woman or get his ass out. You'll get the invitation in a coupla months."

"Well . . . mazel tov."

"Gracias."

The ding of a car rolling over the sensor hose startled them. Raoul sprang out of his seat and put his hand on Berger's shoulder to stop him from getting up.

"Chrysler minivan full of kids," said Raoul on his way outside.

Bert whispered, "I don't suppose you want to tell me what the hell you're doing."

Berger explained about the explosions at EXC and his house, and about the weekend chess tournament.

"Are you sure about running away?" she asked.

"The idea of being locked up is—"

"If you didn't do anything wrong, they can't lock you up. We can get a heavyweight lawyer and fight it."

"I can't afford more than a public defender. And bail would be on top of that, if I could even get bail. Now that I've run, they might say it's too risky to let me out."

"I've got about eleven thou saved up."

"And I've got about two," said Raoul as he returned.

"That should be enough to cover you," Bert continued.

Berger felt tears filling his eyes. "I can't risk everything you've got. I don't even know how I'd begin to pay the money back. It's better if you stay out of this."

Bert reached over and wiped the tear that spilled onto Berger's cheek. Her rough hand against his face reminded him how she had brushed against his skin when she pulled the bedcovers over her little boy. He held her hand tightly.

She leaned in and kissed him on the forehead. "You got your daddy's brains, even if you seem to have temporarily lost 'em. So I guess we'll do it your way. If you change your mind, just call."

Berger nodded.

Bert handed him a bulging plastic grocery bag. "Here's the gear you wanted. Raoul built a secret passage to the bathroom after that guy blew his brains out and we couldn't get in. Go inside and throw the bolt to keep out customers. When you're done, come back the same way."

He took the plastic bag.

"Here's four hundred bucks," she continued. "It's all I could get out of my ATM and the cash box. Don't use a credit card. It just draws 'em a map to where you are. And stay away from here. They'll be watching me pretty soon if they haven't already started."

They went into the office and Raoul unscrewed a ply-wood panel leading to the rest room. Berger squeezed through and fumbled along the wall for a switch. When the lights came on, he latched the dead bolt and set the grocery bag on the toilet seat.

First he took out the peroxide bleach and scissors. Then he laid newspapers carefully on the floor. He held out his ponytail and sighed. It had taken two years to grow. He opened the scissors and placed the blades around it, feel-ing like an executioner whose victim was lying on the chop-ping block. Finally he closed his eyes and began to cut. It took several tries to finally sever the ponytail. He'd half expected it to hurt his scalp.

Berger carefully laid the hairs on the newspaper. With all these DNA tests, he knew that even a single strand could connect him to Bert. Next he took his father's electric razor and plugged it in. The last time he'd seen the black de-vice, it was lying next to the hospital bed of his uncon-scious father. He remembered how his mother had shaved his father daily, as if his looks would matter.

Berger turned it on and the murmuring whirr echoed in the small room. He got down close to the newspapers and trimmed the sides of his head into a rough, punk-looking tangle.

Next came the peroxide. Berger had no idea how to use this stuff. He'd forgotten to ask Bert, although it wasn't likely she'd know either. He was sure it should be diluted, so he clogged the sink drain with paper towels, filled the basin with warm water, and poured in what looked like a reasonable amount of the bleach. Then he cupped the mixture in his hands, hoping he wouldn't burn them, and ladled it onto his hair. He didn't know how long the bleach would take to do its thing, and the writing on the bottle was no help. He figured the longer the better, and if his hair fell out, it would be an even better disguise.

Berger heard the door rattle and he froze. It was quiet, then it rattled again and the knob turned. His eyes shot over to the escape route, yet he couldn't leave without gathering up his gear.

Outside, a child's voice said, "Mommy, it's locked."

"Wait your turn, dear."

Berger rinsed out the bleach, gathered up the newspapers with his ponytail and the casualties of his punk cut, then stuffed everything into the grocery bag. He thought about leaving the door bolted, yet felt wrong doing that to a kid. If he threw the lock quickly, maybe he could get out before the boy came in.

After putting the bag on the other side of the escape passage, he did a quick mental calculation of the distance to the door, then unlocked the bolt. He dove for the hatch, but before he could even get on all fours, he heard the door fly open. Outside was a very small boy, holding his crotch and dancing in place. The kid looked up at Berger with a flash of panic, and the mother's face said she was thinking about grabbing the boy and running. Berger realized that he must look pretty frightening. That was probably a good thing.

It would be too suspicious to go through the hatch with them watching, so he smiled at the boy and walked out the door. Making a tight circle around the station, he tried to act casual as he surveyed the area for anyone stalking him. A red-haired woman on the sidewalk was staring, and he hoped that was only because of his new looks. She appeared to lose interest after a few moments, so he figured it had been his punk do. Or else she was very good at undercover work.

He ducked into the office, then back into the garage bay.

"*Qué guapo,* Juanito," said Raoul, admiring his new looks.

"You shouldn't have gone outside," barked Bert. "You're gonna make a lousy fugitive."

"Thanks. You always do wonders for my confidence."

Berger started to explain about the little kid and the bathroom. He was interrupted by the dinging of the sensor. Outside were the two men who had been after him on the boardwalk in Venice.

"Oh, shit. It's the two guys from the beach."

"Get in the pit," said Bert. She pointed to the two-foot hole below the car lift.

"It's filthy down there. These are the only clothes—"

"Because it's filthy, men in suits won't crawl down to look for you. Get in."

"It's such a small area," said Berger as he edged toward it.

"Shut up and lay on your stomach."

Berger reluctantly got in and lay flat on his face. He could feel himself sticking to the floor, adhered by grease, oil, and God knows what other kind of gunk.

"Lower the car," said Bert.

"What!"

"Shut up."

He heard the hiss of compressed air escaping. The car on the rack dropped so low that he could feel metal against his back. Almost immediately, panic ripped through him. He couldn't move if he needed to. If the car slipped, he'd be crushed. His cousin Matty laughed somewhere in the echoes of his memory, locking the closet and leaving him gagged and bound. This was starting to feel worse than the possibility of prison.

"Raoul, stall them," Bert said in a loud whisper.

Berger spoke louder than he intended. His voice quavered. "Can you see me?"

"With the car down, they'd have to get underneath to see anything," answered Bert. "If they tell me to raise it, I'll say the lift's broken. More importantly, it's the only place I got to stash you."

Berger's perspiration was mixing with the grease. "Mom!" he yelled.

"Shut up!"

"The bag with my hair and the bleach. It's in the office."

"Oh, shit. I'll dunk it in the drum full of old oil. If they want it bad enough to reach in there, they can have it."

Berger thought of his father's razor coming to such an ignoble end, yet couldn't afford the luxury of sentiment. At least that got his mind off the concrete and metal coffin for a moment.

Raoul's attempts to stall the men weren't very effective, as within minutes they were standing just outside the bay. Their voices were muffled through the door, yet Berger could make out the conversation.

"Are you Bertha Berger?"

"Yes."

"When was the last time you saw your son?"

"About a week ago. He was over for dinner."

"How about you?"

"Yo no remember," answered Raoul in much worse English than he actually spoke.

A silence.

"I assume you're aware that obstructing justice is a crime?"

"Yes," replied Bert.

"It's important that we talk to him as soon as possible."

"Did you call his house?"

"If we'd been able to find him at home, we wouldn't be here asking you, now would we?"

"You mean he's disappeared? You think he's okay?"

"We don't really know. Do you have any idea where he might be?"

"No."

More silence. "Do you mind if we have a look around?"

"Not at all."

"Would you please open the door?"

Berger heard the garage door squealing open. He felt the cold concrete against his face and he pushed his cheek flat against whatever slime was on it. He thought he could feel the glop seeping into his pores. The throbbing of his heartbeat in his temple seemed to move his head up and down. He unsuccessfully tried to slow his breathing.

"Could you turn on the lights?"

"Some of 'em are broken."

The fluorescents in the other bay flickered to life. Berger closed his eyes and tried to control his shuddering breath. He felt footsteps reverberating through the concrete as they moved around. He could hear someone poking through junk, and the clanging and scraping of various objects. Then the sound of shoes scuffling in his direction. He took a deep breath and held it.

The following silence was more upsetting than the noises had been. Berger imagined that they were aware of him and signaling each other where he was. Trying not to let him know as their grasp tightened around his neck. He opened his eyes and tried to steal a glance without moving his head. Would the light reflect off the whites of his eyes? He couldn't see anything except the concrete side of the pit. He closed his eyes again and continued to hold his breath, even though his lungs were stinging.

More silence. He finally had to breathe and slowly let out the air. There was a tingling in his fingers, and he assumed his arms were going to sleep. His urge to stretch and shake them out was overwhelming, and he fought to control it. That was when he realized that it wasn't a tingle. There was something stabbing at the tip of his index finger. It felt like electricity. No. It felt like something . . . alive. Something nibbling at him with tiny, sharp teeth.

Footsteps near his head. The stretch and creak of someone squatting down for a closer look. Berger held his breath again. His body began to jitter and he tried to be still. The reality was that he was either visible or he wasn't, and he had no control over whether he was discovered. That was oddly comforting, since there was nothing more he could do.

That was when the critter bit sharply into his finger. A piercing pain shot through his arm into his heart. Berger pictured rabies flowing into his bloodstream and chewed his lip to keep from yelling. He involuntarily swiped at the animal, which gave a high-pitched shriek and scurried away.

"Whoa!" yelled a voice nearby.

"What?" answered the other man, as footsteps ran up. "It's a mouse, you idiot." One voice laughed.

Berger's finger throbbed and he felt with his thumb to see if it was bleeding. He couldn't distinguish blood from oil and grease. The voices seemed to be moving away from him as they rummaged through the bay, then went into the office. The lights went off after another several minutes and he allowed himself to breathe more easily. Yet he worried it could be a trick, so he was staying put until Bert or Raoul said it was okay to move. The panic of being trapped was returning, and he became aware that his body was covered in perspiration, lubricated like some automotive part.

Along with the panic came doubts. It seemed stupid that he'd bolted and run. He should have just come clean and tried to straighten things out. Now he was evading the authorities and obstructing justice, or whatever they called it, and he was really in trouble. Berger considered just calling out to the agents and getting this over with. He wriggled, as if in a trial run to see if he could move.

No. Finding him now meant they'd arrest Bert and Raoul for hiding him. If he was going to turn himself in, it would be far away from here. He was screwed either way. Bert and Raoul didn't have to be.

Now the car seemed to be lowering on his back, and he felt the air being crushed out of him as he lay there helplessly. Berger knew it was his imagination, yet that didn't help. The terror was very real, and he imagined his ribs on the brink of snapping under the weight.

Why was all this happening? Why would someone go to such an enormous effort just to frame him? He couldn't think of a single reason. He didn't even know how deeply the deck was stacked. Maybe the FBI was in on it, and that's why they were pushing so hard.

Finally, Berger heard a car drive away. He still didn't

move until he heard the pump lifting metal off his back. In the dark, Raoul and Bert pulled him out. His legs were weak and he leaned on Raoul for support.

"Juanito, amigo. It's time for you to get the fuck out of here."

"Don't call me," said Bert. "I expect those guys will be watching me, if not tapping the phone."

Berger nodded. He looked at his bitten finger and didn't see any blood. At least the little rodent hadn't broken the skin.

"I'll lock up," Bert continued. "Hang out here until you're sure it's clear, then take the bicycle out back. Here's the padlock key. Your clothes are history, so wear one of Raoul's jumpsuits. Dump yours in different places."

She gave him another bear hug, a full kiss on his greasy lips, then left with Raoul.

Berger slowly pulled off his clothes and sat in his underwear on the wobbly chair behind the tool chests. His body was still cold from having lain on the concrete, and his bare skin shivered. The dark silence seemed to close in on him.

Finally, he ventured into the garage and found a pair of Raoul's coveralls. They came halfway up his calves and arms, and were too tight to zip all the way up. At least they warmed the majority of his body. Thinking he must look absurd, he stepped outside and surveyed the area carefully. He didn't see anyone in the dark.

Berger found the bike, an old-fashioned contraption with upright handlebars and thick tires, padlocked with a rusty chain. He fiddled with the key in the dark and finally got the lock to open. Instead of going toward the street, he walked the bike through the hedge at the back. Something scraped metal to metal every time the wheel made a revolution. He continued to the parking lot of the shopping

center, then ambled along the perimeter, avoiding the overhead lights.

Berger came to a traffic signal at the opening onto Jefferson. He took one last look around, then climbed on the
bike and pedaled away.

CHAPTER 19

Combs sat in his den with Baxter, who was wearing one of his perfectly tailored suits and shirts with monogrammed cuffs. Combs had always thought Baxter's fancy clothes were an incredible waste of money.

Baxter handed over a thick stack of folders and said, "Here's the first cut of bios. The videos are over there." He waved toward a table stacked with videotapes.

"Stick around and make some notes for me."

Baxter stole a look at his watch. "Yeah, okay. How long you think it'll take?"

"However long it takes." Combs opened the top file. Angela Taylor. Thirty-five years old. Resident of Portland, Oregon. Housewife. Two children. Husband an architect. Politics: Republican, which was a plus. The more conservative the better, though he needed a cross section.

The only thing Combs wanted his subjects to have in common was for them to have nothing in common. He wanted old, young, white, black, yellow, and brown. Native born and foreign. An Equal Opportunity Employer. The prospects had been chosen randomly by the field teams.

They'd started with hundreds, and used surveillance to narrow the pool down to the thirty-five.

He flipped the page of Angela's résumé. She had a shoplifting charge as a teenager. A minus for that. He preferred squeaky clean.

Combs looked at her picture. Blond hair, sharp features, narrow chin. Nice ass and decent tits, not that it mattered. The next picture was her husband, who didn't look so tough.

"This Angela Taylor looks promising. Put on her tape."

Baxter stuck the video into the machine. Angela Taylor at the supermarket, loading groceries into the back of a blue station wagon. Tipping the bag boy who had helped her carry them. Cut to her coming out the front door in a bathrobe. Picking up the paper without looking around. Good sign; not a paranoid. When she straightened up, her robe came apart and he got a good look at her bra-less tits inside the nightgown. Not bad at all.

Cut to a picture of her front door.

"Here comes the wire," said Baxter. A man in a brown business suit knocked on the door.

She opened the door a crack and studied him.

"I'm sorry to bother you, ma'am," said the man warmly.

"Who are you?"

"Bad sign," said Combs. "Her voice sounds too strong."

"My car broke down," the man continued, "and I wondered if I could use your phone."

"I'm really busy right now. There's a pay phone about a block away." She closed the door.

"Pass," said Combs, feeding her folder into a shredder.

He grabbed the next file. Lenny Seal. Seventy-four years old. World War II vet. Lives in Flushing, New York, with wife of forty-eight years. Before retiring, worked forty years for the Tax Assessor's office. Good sign. Bureaucrats had no problem letting others make decisions for them.

"Play the tape."

Seal was a thin man, with a balding head. He walked arthritically, although he managed to get around. That might be a problem, though it could be a plus because no one stares at someone with a handicap. The tape showed him slowly moving up the stairs to his apartment, clutching the handrail. Cut to him walking a small black dog in a park. The dog was trying to rush ahead, keeping the leash taut. Cut to a man going up to Seal's door and asking to use the phone.

Seal opened the door wide. "Sure, young fella. C'mon in."

Excellent, thought Combs.

"The phone's over there," said Seal. "Cynthia? Bring some lemonade for this gentleman."

Combs drew a star on the tab of Seal's file.

About eight that night, Berger pedaled north on Overland, riding the antique bicycle from Bert's gas station. There were no gears, and he panted to get up even a moderate speed. Some piece of metal scraped with every stroke, grating in his ears. Riding the old bike, with its upright handlebars, made him feel like the wicked witch from *The Wizard of Oz,* carrying off Toto in a basket.

He'd decided to go to Linda's neighborhood. While it seemed obvious they'd be watching if they knew about her, he remembered her neighbor Kim saying she was going away for a week. He doubted anyone would think to look across the street, so he should have Kim's place to himself. Unless she'd found someone to house-sit.

Berger turned on Westminster in Palms, a block behind Tabor where Linda lived. He walked his bike in the shadows, since his grease-stained body and jumpsuit made him look like someone about to dismantle parked cars for their parts. He cut down a driveway to the alley that ran behind Kim's house, found her yard, and climbed over the fence. He lost his footing on the way down and landed with a thud, slightly twisting his ankle. He lay still on the ground and watched Kim's dark house. No lights came on, either in her place or the neighbors', and the only sounds were buzzing insects. He made a tactical decision to stay low, so he crawled across the yard on all fours.

The house was dark. Berger climbed onto the back porch and picked up the rubber doormat, hoping for a key. Nothing. He used the mat to shield his fist and broke the glass window on the back door. The tinkling crash was less noisy than he'd expected, yet he still crouched in the shadows for several minutes, waiting for any reactions. When nothing happened, he reached carefully through the shards and opened the door.

Berger didn't turn on any lights, since he assumed the neighbors knew Kim was gone and might call the cops if her house lit up. He tiptoed to the living room and looked out the front window. There were a few parked cars, and it was too dark to tell if anyone was inside them. He thought he saw a shadow move in a Ford, which startled him enough to step back from the window.

Walking into the bedroom, he peeled off the jumpsuit and sank into a sitting position against the wall. His body was pulsating with aches from running and cycling, which had been more exercise than he'd had in the last five years combined. He leaned his head heavily against the wall, and his consciousness blurred on the edge of heavy sleep.

Berger didn't want to get on Kim's bed without her permission, despite the irony of having just broken into her house. He pulled up his knees and rested his head against them, figuring he could sleep in a handstand at this point. That proved to be wrong, so he stretched out on the floor. It was hard and cold, and he worried that maybe he shouldn't be sleeping in any event. He realized he was too exhausted to have any choice.

As he curled on his side in a semicomfortable position, he remembered once reading that hope makes a lousy dinner but a good breakfast.

He certainly hoped that was true.

CHAPTER 20

It was 7:30 A.M. when Jill was awakened by the stewardess. The only flight she could get had been a red-eye from L.A. to Miami, then a propeller plane to Orlando. As she walked down the old-fashioned portable stairs, she yawned so deeply that tears squeezed out the corners of her eyes. Jill could never sleep much on planes, and she didn't function very well without sleep. The overall feeling was like walking through soft sand.

She was met at the gate by a freshly scrubbed FBI agent named Dean Fredericks. He appeared to be in his late twenties, with black hair that was combed straight back and still wet at the ends. Taking her flight bag with an energetic sweep, he explained that his chipped front tooth was from a scuffle the week before. Then he went into an exposition about the Miami Bureau Office in a singsongy voice. She hoped he'd cut the chatter on the way to the hospital, as her head was already starting to throb.

Her hopes were in vain. Fredericks moved into a steady narrative about the history of Florida, pointing out sights with animated gestures. She didn't dare mention the pictures of his children that were placed strategically around the dashboard, for fear of triggering a lecture about four generations of Frederickses.

"Did you get me an interview with the bomber's family?" she asked, interrupting a description of the Orlando tangelo, some kind of local fruit.

"No can do. Herbert Simms was an old geezer, but the youngest in his family. So we got no brothers, sisters, or parents. He and the missus had no rug rats, and she's been missing since the bombing."

That was disappointing. She'd really hoped to get some insight into this guy. A decorated war veteran blows up himself and his co-workers? It's possible he just snapped, yet . . .

"Did you say his wife was missing?" she asked.

"Yep. No one's seen her since the Friday before he did his Bombs Away."

Jill remembered that Berger had said his girlfriend was missing. And that she disappeared on Friday. Was that a coincidence?

"Have you talked to the woman in the coma?"

"No one has, except the doctors. She's only conscious for short periods, so you'll have to wait till her train gets to the station. And the docs said only one person at a time. Since you were flying in, I told the Orlando cops it had to be you."

"Thanks." The locals must have loved that, she thought. She imagined they weren't real happy to see her moving in on their case in the first place.

Our Lady of Mercy Hospital was built of red brick, and from the architecture, Jill guessed it was constructed sometime in the 1930s. She didn't dare ask Fredericks. Inside, tall ceilings towered above black and white checkered floor tiles. The lobby was lit by white, acorn-shaped lamps hung from the ceiling on long white cords. The only decorations were crucifixes, and the hallways smelled of antiseptic.

The nurse at the third-floor station was a plump lady with gray hair tied neatly into a knot.

"Miss Jenkins is in room 305," she said pleasantly, adjusting her crisp nursing cap. "I'm afraid she's in and out of consciousness rather unpredictably. After what happened to her, the poor thing is lucky to be alive."

"How did she survive?"

Fredericks answered. "She got under a heavy desk, and most of the shrapnel didn't go in her direction. She was the only one who made it."

"How seriously was she injured?"

"Concussion and fractured skull," the nurse replied. "She lost her left eye, and most of her left arm. She only regained partial consciousness yesterday, but we let the police know right away."

"Thank you for that. It's important that we work closely together."

The nurse straightened up in her chair, empowered by the authority. "The doctor says you can have five minutes with her, whenever she regains consciousness."

"Where may I wait?"

"There's a waiting room over there. Or you could take a folding chair into the hall outside her room."

An African-American orderly handed the nurse a clipboard, which she studied intently. Shaking her head, she made a few scribbling corrections, then signed her name. The orderly looked Jill up and down, then trotted off down the hall.

"Could I wait in Ms. Jenkins's room?" asked Jill.

"Oh, I'm afraid I can't do that . . ."

"May I speak to the doctor?"

"She's not in until later."

The phone rang and the nurse answered. She uttered a series of "Uh-huhs," then said, "His blood pressure is really high. You want me to take a TO for clonidine?"

When she hung up the phone, she opened a red three-ring binder and made notes.

"I'd really like to wait in the room," Jill pressed. "If I'm sitting next to Ms. Jenkins, I'd know the second she wakes up. That way I'd be out of there much faster. And I wouldn't miss any of her short period of consciousness."

The nurse wrinkled her forehead. "I'm sorry."

Jill leaned in and whispered. "I can see you have a lot of authority here. Please. This will be best for everyone."

An Asian woman appeared at the station and started to ask a question. The nurse held up her hand to silence her, then spoke quietly to Jill. "I could get in trouble for this."

"If I get caught, you don't know anything about me."

Jill sat in a folding chair, watching Ellie Jenkins's chest move slowly up and down. Ellie's head and left eye were covered with a bandage that made her look almost mummified, and the portions of her skin that showed were black and varicose blue. A tube ran into her neck, and an IV was taped to her right arm. She had no left arm below a stub that dangled from her shoulder.

Ellie's working eye had been closed for the last two hours, and Jill's eyes were starting to close as well. A short woman with snow-white hair arrived and introduced herself as Ellie's mother. She sat by the bed, holding Ellie's right hand and stroking the back of it. Every once in a while, she looked up at Jill and smiled self-consciously.

Jill looked at her watch for the fifth time in the last ten minutes, and yawned deeply. She wished she'd brought something to read. Every fifteen minutes, a nurse stuck in her head, and Jill began to look forward to her appearance. She worried that a doctor would show up and throw her out, although that would at least create some drama.

Around two in the afternoon, Jill heard an "Oh!" and immediately sat up. The elder Mrs. Jenkins was standing, still holding her daughter's hand and looking around the room anxiously.

"She's awake," she whispered.

Jill moved quickly to the bed. Ellie's uncovered eye was open, though it stared unfocused into space. Her face was flaccid, expressionless.

"Mrs. Jenkins? Can you hear me?" asked Jill.

Ellie groaned indecipherably. Her mother let out a quiet squeal of excitement.

"I'm Agent Jill Landis of the FBI. May I ask you a couple of questions?"

"FBI," mumbled Ellie. A small amount of spittle ran out of her dry, cracked lips.

"Can you understand me?"

Ellie's eye surveyed the surroundings. Her head turned slowly toward Jill and she nodded. Mrs. Jenkins began to cry.

"I'm truly sorry to bother you. I promise I'll be very brief."

"Is okay," said Ellie. Her voice was regaining strength, and her eye seemed to focus on Jill. She even managed a slight smile.

"Do you know what happened to you?"

The smile drained away. "Mr. Simms. Blew us up."

"What do you remember?" Jill pulled out a palm-sized tape recorder and held it near Ellie's mouth.

"At work. He came in. Sat at his desk. Across the room from mine. He . . ."

Ellie's eye filled with tears. She awkwardly tried to wipe it, causing the IV to clank the bottle against its rack.

". . . He had this box. And some wires. Then he said something."

"Do you remember what he said?"

"Something like 'Your country will bring you pain.'"

What? thought Jill. This was a decorated war veteran. Could Ellie be hallucinating?

"Are you sure that's what he said?"

"Not sure. Something about 'country' and 'pain.' He scared me. The box and wires. They looked like a bomb. I got under my desk. It's a big oak one. Then I heard this really loud noise. That's all I remember."

Her mother had been stroking her hand the last few minutes. Ellie suddenly seemed to notice.

"Mom?" she said.

"Yes, dear."

"Are the biscuits ready yet?"

"Biscuits?" asked her mother, looking up at Jill with a flash of panic in her eyes.

"My assignment for Home Ec," Ellie replied, somewhat impatiently.

"Oh. Yes, dear. They're almost done."

Jill clicked off the recorder and stepped into the hall, suddenly feeling like an intruder. She walked down the corridor and tried to process the bits and pieces. It was possible that Simms just flipped out, and the business about "country" and "pain" sounded like pretty good evidence that he was a few fries short of a Happy Meal. Yet something must have triggered his actions. What? Without anyone around who knew him, that would be difficult to find.

It was also possible that Ellie was the one who'd flipped out, which was understandable after a trauma like this. Maybe Simms hadn't said anything at all, and Ellie had just imagined it. Jill didn't think so, but she couldn't be sure.

What about the idea that Orlando was connected to the EXC incident? Maybe they weren't related at all, and maybe everything looked so weird because she was trying to connect them. Maybe.

The image of Ellie, lying in bed drooling, replayed in Jill's head. She remembered Ellie asking about the biscuits. Disorientation. Jill's mind wandered back to the freed hostages she'd interrogated. They were also disoriented. Berger had acted sort of like that.

Her gut said there was something there.

CHAPTER 21

Combs's ears ached from the adenoidal country singer and the steel guitar. He was huddled against the bar, assaulted by the sounds of clanking beer bottles, watching a line of sweaty people dressed in jeans, boots, and cowboy hats line-dancing more or less in step with each other. Tom Curtis, his personal bodyguard, stood by the door. Between the two of them, they could see the entire room.

The humidity from sweaty bodies made the air so thick that Combs couldn't take a full breath. He walked away from the bar and leaned against a bale of hay. Curtis shifted his stance, watching carefully.

Combs was so bored that he was counting the cycles of a neon Lone Star Beer sign on which the Texas flag went up a pole and waved in the breeze. He wished Leeds would show up so he could get the hell outta here.

About ten minutes and three loud songs later, Leeds appeared in the doorway. He was a lanky man, wearing a Hawaiian shirt. This guy had no sense of how to look inconspicuous, and Combs thought about leaving. Yet he needed to hear what happened.

Leeds finally spotted him, raised his eyebrows in recognition, and worked his way over. Curtis inched closer.

"Gimme some good news," yelled Combs.

Leeds put his mouth next to Combs's ear and took his time before he spoke. "We missed him."

Combs recoiled. If the cops linked Berger to him, his plans were history. If the Serbians found out that Berger was alive, Combs was history. He grabbed Leeds by the shoulders and gripped so tightly that he felt the man's bones. Then he stuck his mouth against Leeds's ear.

"You dumb fuck!"

Leeds unsuccessfully tried to wriggle loose. "Hey. I set a sophisticated bomb that did what it was supposed to. Shit, I took out a guy in a bomb suit. The way I see it, Berger was tipped off and sent in the cops. Maybe we got a leak."

"I got no leaks. Just weak links, like you." He threw Leeds against the hay bale. Curtis moved forward, and Combs stopped him with an almost imperceptible shake of his head.

Leeds clumsily recovered his balance, then brushed strands of hay off his arms.

Combs relaxed his face. He put his arm around Leeds's shoulder and spoke calmly. "I'm sorry I got a little hot. I didn't mean that. You did the best you could."

Combs told Leeds to wait twenty minutes before leaving. As Combs went out to the parking lot, his ears were still vibrating from the noise. The night chill stung his face, feeding on his perspiration from that human sauna. Curtis walked a half-step behind.

"Looks like we'll be twenty-three instead of twenty-four," said Combs.

Curtis didn't need to answer.

"I'd like you to personally handle Berger. And no more *Mission: Impossible* bullshit. Just put a bullet in his brain."

Berger had been on the floor of Kim's apartment, in more or less the same position, for almost eighteen hours. The sleep he'd gotten was fitful, and he kept dreaming about Linda. He saw her being strangled, with her eyes bulging in terror. A thin black band tightening around her neck. The image was so vivid that he woke up screaming. Even awake, remembering the dream caused his heart to race.

It was getting dark and he knew he couldn't turn on the lights. He ran his hand over the stubble on his face, then rubbed his eyes. The image of Linda being strangled continued to haunt him. He tried to calm himself with a memory of the first time they'd made love.

Berger had planned a romantic evening, with soft music and scented candles. Things hadn't started well, since the candles' aroma set off Linda's allergies and he had to quickly douse the flames. It took her almost an hour to recover from the sneezing. When she had finally wheezed out, they got into some serious caressing on the couch. He then took her hand to lead her to the bedroom, and discovered that Max had appointed himself as Berger's personal chastity belt. Max leapt in front of them, growling to keep Linda at bay. They laughed at first, yet Max didn't think it was funny and went for her ankle. A few minutes later, Max was in the bathroom, where he spent the night.

A car horn jolted him back to the moment. He suppressed his urge to look out the window, since he was across the street from Linda's place and, if anyone was watching, he didn't want to be seen.

Where the hell was Linda? Berger at first had assumed that she was hiding from him. Maybe off with her new boyfriend. Yet something told him she wasn't just running away. He had this uneasy feeling that she was injured or in trouble. Maybe it was the dream. Berger also felt he was responsible for Linda's disappearance, though he couldn't think of any reason why.

He tried to stretch out his arms and legs. His only food in the last twenty-four hours had been a can of sardines that he'd found in the pantry, and the look of mutilated fish had stopped him from finishing it. He'd felt sorry for them, trapped in a net and then jammed into some can without their heads.

Another honk. He had to look. When he crawled across the floor and pulled himself up slowly to the window ledge, he saw a kid run giggling to an open car door.

After the car drove off, Berger scanned the street. There were three parked cars. He couldn't see anyone inside, and he couldn't remember if they were the same cars from last night. His eyes moved to Linda's place, and he was disappointed to find it dark, even though he'd known it would be. He sat back on the floor, suddenly feeling like he'd never see her again.

Berger glanced at the television he hadn't dared watch, and wondered if there were any stories about him. He doubted he was a fugitive worthy of TV coverage, or at least he hoped he wasn't. Running from the law seemed pretty stupid in retrospect. It only made him look guilty. He should have just turned himself in.

"You must keep running," said a deep voice.

Berger reflexively yelped and spun around. He couldn't see anyone in the dark.

"Who's there?" he asked.

Laughter. Now it sounded like two gravelly voices in unison. They were different tones, as if harmonizing, yet out of key. One voice was a man's; he wasn't sure about the other.

"You're a killer, Berger. You deserve to die."

"I'm not a killer. Who are you? Where are you?"

"You're a killer. You'll die, and so will everyone around you."

"Stop it!"

Laughter.

"Where are you?"

"You know where we are."

And he did. The idea of hearing voices had always been laughable to Berger. Until now. He was certain it must be a trick. Someone had been watching him all along, and now they were toying with his mind.

"We're the ones who told you to run from the police. We said it quietly, so you'd think it was your own idea."

"Leave me alone."

"You're going to die, Berger."

Berger ran into the child's bedroom and collapsed onto his knees. He clamped his hands over his ears.

"You're going to die," came the chorus at the same volume, undiminished by his hands. He stood up and began pounding his head against the wall. Maybe the physical pain would drive them away.

They laughed again.

Berger looked around the room and saw toys scattered all over the floor. A pistol caught his eye. He picked it up and felt the rough plastic handle scrape against his palm. Then he put his finger on the trigger, aimed at the window, and pretended to squeeze off a few rounds. He wanted to put bullets into the source of the voices. Now he found himself putting the barrel into his mouth and closing his lips around the slick plastic.

Losing his mind was the only explanation for everything

happening to him. It all seemed so clear now. But why? There was no history of mental illness in his family. At least that he knew of. And loony or not, somebody was still framing him. Why?

He felt tears on his cheek and forced himself to pull the toy gun out of his mouth. As he looked at the black revolver, it reminded him of Smitty—the security guard at EXC, who carried a similar weapon. Jill Landis, the FBI agent, had said that Smitty was the only other person at EXC on the weekend. Whoever planted the bomb must have done it on the weekend. Maybe Smitty knew something.

Berger went into the shower and soaked for a full twenty minutes. As soon as his skin got used to the heat, he turned the water hotter. As if purging himself by fire.

Mercifully, the voices had gone quiet. He got out and wrapped a towel around his head like a turban. His skin was red and raw from the shower's fiery needles, and now he was fully awake.

Without turning on the lights, he went into Kim's bedroom and found some of her husband's clothes. He couldn't quite see what he was putting on in the dark, though it was clearly pants and a shirt, and they had to be a lot more presentable than Raoul's jumpsuit.

He was halfway through buttoning the shirt when he heard a key in the front door. Berger's head snapped toward the sound, and he froze. His next calculations took less than three seconds. Since they were at the front door, he had to get out the back. It was likely to be Kim returning from her trip, or someone checking the house for her, or the cops. In any case, there was no upside to hanging around.

He grabbed Raoul's overalls, the only thing that could connect him to his mother, and ran as quietly as he could toward the back door. He was within a foot of grabbing the handle when he heard the front door swing open. Worried they'd hear him go out the back, he stopped by the refrigerator and pressed himself against the wall. His heart slammed against his chest, and he hoped his heavy breathing wasn't audible.

The lights came on in the living room, and he prayed he hadn't disturbed anything they'd notice. At least not right away.

"Someone's been here," came a woman's voice. She sounded scared.

"Huh?" said a man.

"Get out of here," shouted the voices in his head.

This time, Berger agreed with them. He pushed off from the wall, wrenched open the back door, and ran like hell.

CHAPTER 22

Bert wiped her hands with the oily rag she used for dipsticks, then walked away from the pump, twirling the unlit cigar in her fingers. She went into the office and plopped into the oversized chair she'd finally found to fit her.

Raoul came in from the garage. "He's okay," said Raoul.

"I suppose."

"Our guardian angels just left." He motioned with his head toward the gray Ford pulling out of a parking spot into the traffic on Overland.

"Change in shift."

"I don't think so. I think they decided we're too boring." He took hold of her hand. She looked into his eyes and forced a smile.

Raoul continued, "Whattaya say we close early and go home for a little humpty-dumpty?"

The sensor dinged, announcing another customer.

Bert forced another smile and got up. She saw a late-model, silver Lincoln, with tinted windows in the back, pulling up to the full service pump. Nice wax job, she thought, as she walked around to the driver's side.

The driver got out. He was over six feet, with huge shoulders and a thick neck. His massive eyebrows met in the middle.

"Are you Bertha Berger?" he asked in a warm, smooth voice.

"Who are you?"

"Can we talk for a minute?"

Another man got out of the passenger side. He was equally large, with a crooked nose that he probably wasn't born with.

"Can we step inside and talk privately?" He grabbed her elbow and squeezed just above the joint. A sharp pain radiated up her arm.

"Hey! Get your hands off me."

The man used the pain to guide her toward the office. The other man looked around to make sure no one was watching.

Fortunately for Berger, there was only one Horatio Alger Smith in the Los Angeles area. And even more fortunately, he had a listed phone number and address.

It had taken Berger three bus transfers to get to Smitty's place on Chandler Boulevard in North Hollywood. The address turned out to be a trailer park straddled by steel towers that supported buzzing power lines.

Berger looked for a directory of residents. No such luck. He wandered between the trailers and was startled by a mother who stuck her head out the window and yelled for Arnold to get inside. The head disappeared before he could ask for Smitty. Berger then approached an old man with long hair who was sitting on a milk crate beside a yellowish trailer, and got a curt "No." Finally, a little kid pointed out Smitty's place and offered the editorial opinion that Smitty was an asshole.

Berger worked his way down the rows to a metal Airstream trailer that was bashed in several places, like some aluminum can on its way to the recycler. The lights were on inside.

He banged on the screen door a few times until Smitty answered. The man looked a lot like Walter Brennan and was dressed in old trousers and a ribbed undershirt with thin shoulder straps. When he saw Berger, his white eyebrows escalated in surprise.

"Who're you?"

"It's me, Smitty. John Berger."

Smitty looked him up and down. "Shee-it. That's some getup. What the hell're you doin' here?"

"I came to see you, Smitty."

Smitty looked around, as if to check whether anyone was watching. Then he pushed open the screen door and motioned for Berger to move quickly. When Berger stepped in, Smitty closed and locked the door.

Smitty's left cheek began to twitch as he asked, "What do you want?"

"I want to talk to you."

Smitty's eyes, which had milky circles around the irises, peered at Berger over small, frameless glasses. "I ain't said nothin' to nobody," he whispered.

"Huh?"

"I said I ain't told nobody nothin'."

"About what?"

"You know what."

"No, I don't. What are you talking about?"

Smitty stepped back. "What do you think I'm talkin' about? About Sunday."

"Sunday?"

"Yeah, Sunday."

"What happened on Sunday?"

He looked skeptically at Berger. "Is this some kinda joke?"

"No. I swear. I don't know what you mean."

Smitty reached under his bed and dialed the combination on a small lock box. He took out a crisp hundred dollar bill and handed it to Berger.

"Here. I don't want no money. Just take it and get outta here."

"Smitty, have you lost your marbles?"

"It's the same bill. I couldn't spend it after that bomb went off. You didn't say nothin' about no bomb, John. Some people got killed, for Chrissake."

"What the hell are you talking about?"

"Oh. I get it. This is some kinda mindfuck game, huh? Well I don't want no part of it. Just take your money and stay the hell away from me."

Smitty was starting to shake, and he looked like he was going to cry. Berger took him by the shoulders and spoke forcefully. "Smitty, I swear to you. I don't know what you're talking about."

"I'm talking about this here hundred dollars you give me on Sunday."

"What? I didn't give you any hundred dollars." Berger hadn't seen Smitty between Friday and Monday morning at the bomb site. He couldn't have given him anything on Sunday. Not to mention that a hundred dollars would have been almost ten percent of Berger's liquid assets.

"I don't want no part of no bombing. Whatever you're up to, you leave me out, you hear? I won't tell nobody nothin'. Hell, you done got me into this shit, so if I talk, I'm fryin' my ass too. 'Course that was probably your plan all along, huh? I guess I'm a real sap."

"Smitty, I didn't give you the hundred and I don't know what you're talking about."

"Then you got a twin brother who did," he snapped sarcastically.

"No, I don't have a brother. Tell me what happened."

Smitty stared at him for several moments. "You really don't know?"

"No. I really don't. Everything's been very weird for the last few days. Please. Tell me what happened."

"This ain't no mindfuck?"

"No. I'm just as upset as you are. Please. Tell me."

Smitty didn't look convinced, and his expression said he was debating whether to answer. Finally, he sat down on the edge of his bed. Despite being a skinny man, his gut bulged into his undershirt.

"If you're shittin' me, I'll kick your ass."

"I'm not shittin' you."

He studied Berger a few more minutes before continuing. "All right. I'm doing my usual rounds on Sunday. Everything's deader than Kelsey's nuts. Not a soul in sight. Not even a football game on the radio. So I'm strollin' round about three o'clock and you show up."

"It wasn't me. I think I'm being framed for this bombing."

"Well, if it weren't you, it was somebody who knew me and looked just like you."

"Go on."

"So you, or your twin or whoever, has this package under your arm, and you say, 'Smitty, here's a hundred bucks and you didn't see me today.' I says you don't need to gimme nothin', 'cause we're pals and all that, and you say I should take it anyhow. I says you really don't have to, and you keep on insistin', so I figure it means something to you if I take the dough, and so I take it. Then you go in toward your desk and tell me to get on with my rounds, and I don't see you no more."

"How big was the package?"

"I dunno. About the size of a breadbox. Anyway, after that explosion, I figgered you bein' there didn't have nothing to do with it, so I kinda forgot to mention you to the cops. I ain't proud of that, but I figgered if you was involved, you sorta made me an accomplice and I couldn't squeal. I didn't think you was no killer, John. Why'd you do something like that? And why'd you have to drag me into it?" Smitty's eyes glistened in the light.

"I wasn't there, Smitty, I swear. There's some incredibly elaborate scam going down, and I'm being set up as the fall guy. I'd never do anything to hurt you. We're pals."

"Yeah. I always thought we was. You always gimme a pint at Christmas, huh?" The silence hung for a moment. "You in trouble, John?"

"Looks like it. I'll get out of here, so nobody sees me and gets you in trouble. I'm sorry you got pulled into this."

"I'd have swore it was you. If he was a fake, he was a helluva fake."

Somewhere, deep inside, a feeling was starting to grow. A feeling that Berger might somehow be involved in the bombing. Could he have actually been there on Sunday? If so, why didn't he remember it? The answer might be that he was losing his marbles, which was a terrifying thought. Especially for someone who makes his living with his brain. Is this what it was like to slowly go nuts?

The voices in his head began to laugh at him. "You're going to die," they said in unison.

CHAPTER 23

The tall man from the Lincoln, still gripping Bert's arm, steered her into the office of the Mobil station. The other man pulled down the shades over the plate glass windows.

"I'm sorry to inconvenience you, ma'am," said the tall man pleasantly.

"Let go of me." She wrenched her elbow loose and began massaging it.

Raoul heard the commotion and came into the office from the garage. The second man grabbed him and twisted his arm into a hammerlock.

"What the fuck is this?" Raoul barked, now struggling to keep his balance under the hold.

"We won't be long if you cooperate," said the first man. His voice was so melodious that it sounded like he was putting a child to bed. "We're looking for your son."

"I don't know where he is," said Bert. She looked over at Raoul. "And he doesn't know anything."

"Ah. You've told me two important things. One is that you do know something, as I read people's voices and body language quite well. The other is that this gentleman is important to you, which I will be forced to bear in mind. Now I ask you again, where is your son?"

"I don't know. Get out of here."

"Oh, I think you do. Ian, go turn out the station lights." The tall man opened his suit jacket to reveal a large handgun stuck halfway into his waistband. "It would not be smart of you to try any heroics."

Ian rummaged around until he found the switches, then turned off the outside lights. The tall man pulled a thick twine out of his jacket and tied Bert to her chair, while Ian tied Raoul's hands behind him.

"Now go move the car and lay down the trail," ordered the tall man.

Ian trotted outside and Bert heard the Lincoln start, then drive around back. Next she heard a sloshing sound, and she was afraid she knew what it was.

Ian opened the door and the strong odor of gasoline assaulted her. He was pouring a line of gasoline from a red can as he walked through the office. He continued the trail up to Bert's feet, where he stopped and looked at the tall man.

"This gasoline runs out to your tanks. It would be a shame to have an accident." He lit a short candle, which sputtered as he balanced it on the floor, atop the gasoline by her feet. "The candle will burn for about ten minutes, and by then we will be quite gone. If you give us the information we need, we will happily take the candle with us."

It was probably her imagination, but Bert thought she could feel the heat of the candle's flame against her ankles. She knew very well what a fire could do to a gas station, and the thought terrified her. On the other hand, she doubted they would leave without blowing them up either way, so fuck 'em.

"I told you. I don't know where he is."

He walked over and put his face about six inches from hers. He smelled like expensive cologne mixed with tobacco. "That's not the right answer." With a slight smile, he slapped her face with enormous force. "Try once more, please."

The blow snapped her head to the side, and she felt her neck muscles tear sharply. The sting from his hand spread like a blaze across her cheek.

"Fuck you!" she yelled.

His smile didn't waver. "Ian, raise the auto lift in the garage."

Ian went into the garage and she heard the lift going up.

"You'll want to see this," said the tall man. He rolled her chair over to the door of the repair bay, and she could see the hydraulic had lifted a Volkswagen about two feet in the air. Ian grabbed Raoul and dragged him over to the lift. Raoul began screaming curses in Spanish, which the two men ignored. Together, they wrestled him to the ground and put his head under the edge of the lift. Ian held him in place while the tall man came back to Bert.

"Am I making myself clear? I really don't have lot of time. Now where is your son?"

Bert began to sob, which made her even angrier. She didn't want to show any weakness. "Raoul didn't do anything. Let him go. Then I'll talk to you."

"First you talk, then we let him go."

Bert stared at him. "No. Let him go first."

The tall man went over to the switch and opened it with a hissing sound. The hydraulic lift descended slowly.

Raoul's swearing came to an abrupt halt when the metal rack hit the side of his head.

"Stop!" yelled Bert. "John's in Claremont. About sixty miles east of here. He's staying in a dormitory at Harvey Mudd College."

The man stopped the lift. Raoul was pinned, but obviously alive because the curses started again.

"Which dormitory?"

"Raoul, you okay?"

"I'm okay," came the muffled reply.

"Which dormitory?"

"Let him out."

"Which dormitory?"

"He didn't say."

The man went back to the switch and put his hand on it.

"Okay, okay. It's called Randall House. He's in room 127."

The tall man came back to Bert. "What's the phone number?"

"There's no phone."

The man walked over to the front window and took out a cellular. He first got the area code for Claremont, then the number for the college. When he called the school's main number, she could hear that he got a recording.

"It appears I cannot verify your information just now. I'm going to leave you both tied up and locked in the rest room, where I already know there is no telephone. We are going directly to Claremont. If what you said is not the truth, I will return here, and it will not be a pleasant experience. If what you said is correct, we will let you out tomorrow. In case you want to modify anything, now would be the appropriate time to do so."

Bert looked over at Raoul and weighed the options. They'd know she was lying within a couple of hours. Even though there was a secret passage from the rest room, these men wouldn't have much trouble tracking them down. So either way, they were goners. She made a snap decision.

Bert shifted her weight forward enough to balance herself on her feet. Then she hunched forward, lifting the chair off the floor as if she were wearing a backpack, and screamed like a kamikaze pilot as she ran head first into the tall man's stomach.

It happened so quickly that she caught him off guard. She hurled him backward into the plate glass window, shattering it and sending him halfway through. His eyes stared at her in shock, then looked down at the glass dagger that protruded upward through his stomach. He began to retch blood as he groped feebly for his gun.

Now Ian was racing toward her from the garage. Even with the awkward chair on her back, she managed to step aside, like a matador clumsily avoiding a bull. Raoul, who had pulled his head free, ran into the office with his hands still tied behind him. Ian recovered from his first miss and began another charge. Raoul and Bert started toward him.

What happened next wasn't too clear. The bottom line was that one of them kicked over the candle. All three froze in place, and watched it ignite the gasoline.

Berger awoke with a start. He would later think he'd heard the tanks go off at Bert's, yet that was impossible because he was ten miles away.

He sat up in bed at the Cozy Court Motel, on Sepulveda Boulevard in Van Nuys, where twenty-eight dollars had bought him a lumpy bed and a lamp bolted to the bedside table. He listened to the staccato of gunshots from the neighboring streets and knew he wasn't going back to sleep for a while.

Berger put his head between the two foam rubber pillows and closed his eyes.

Maybe things would look better in the morning.

Although that's what he'd hoped when he went to bed last night.

CHAPTER 24

Berger awoke the next day, unsure where he was. He looked up at the ceiling fixture, which resembled a large Tums tablet, and ran his fingers over the knobby, wool-like bedspread. Oh yes. The motel.

Bright sunlight splintered through the window, searing his eyes. He shielded them with his hand and squinted at the clock radio. Almost noon. Then he lay back and pulled a pillow over his face. His tongue felt thick, and the appeal of staying put was powerful. His mind knew that wasn't a good idea, even if his body felt otherwise.

He climbed into the shower-bath combination and stood under a drizzle of alternating boiling and freezing water. At least the adventure of dodging in and out of the stream was waking him up. He towel-dried his punkish, bleached hair, which still startled him when he looked in the mirror, and felt a glowing tingle in his scalp.

Berger pulled on the blue jeans and tan oxford shirt that he'd bought yesterday in a thrift shop, and the feel of freshly laundered clothes energized him. As his mind continued to clear, he suddenly felt foolish for having run.

Did he really think he could get away with it? Was he going to start life over in another city, like some disappearing husband? It now seemed absurd. He should stand up and face his problems. However elaborate this frame was, he had the truth on his side. And maybe insanity as a defense.

He gathered all of his belongings into a white plastic grocery bag and went outside. The day was crisp, cool and sunny, with a virtually cloudless sky. He took a deep breath of fresh air and began to walk briskly.

Jill stood outside the smoldering remains of Bert's Mobil station. The odor of burning wood and fuel still lingered in the air, and the metal flying horse had been melted into an obscene parody of itself, like the monster in some cheap horror film. A small Bobcat tractor, with a fingered trough in front, chugged out black smoke as it scooped up debris and flung it into a Dumpster. The way that the tractor hacked up the remains only rubbed in the fact that there was no evidence left.

Phil Churning, of LAPD Arson, ambled toward Jill. He was a heavy man, with several chins and droopy eyes, and his belly shifted left and right when he walked.

"Morning," he said with a voice that sounded like his mouth was full of mashed potatoes.

"What have you got, Phil?"

"Intentional fire. Source was a candle, of all things. We found melted wax and pieces of a wick."

"A candle? Was it an accident?"

"Nope. Residue shows that a line of gasoline was poured from the office to the tanks, and a wick was dangled down into the fuel. Lucky thing the tanks were almost full. If they'd been near empty, there'd have been enough oxygen for an explosion instead of just a fire.

Also, we found a guy pushed through a plate glass window, with chunks of glass stickin' through his gizzard. That's always a telltale sign that there's been a struggle."

"You ID him?"

"Not yet. He's pretty barbecued."

"Any survivors?"

"Three we know of. According to witnesses, one guy got away clean. The other two were the owner and a man who worked here. They're both in the hospital."

"Are they conscious?"

"Don't know."

Jill walked back to her car, crunching rubble under her feet as she stepped. Torching Bertha Berger's station was no coincidence. And Berger wouldn't do this to his mother, unless he was psychotic. Which was possible. More likely is that someone came here looking for him. Which meant he knew something they didn't want anyone else to know.

Berger stood at the corner of Motor and Pico, by a stand-up pay phone. He'd been there almost ten minutes, debating whether to make the call. Finally, he took the plunge and dialed.

Jill answered on the second ring. "Agent Landis."

"It's John Berger."

"I'm glad to hear from you." He could hear her voice rise in excitement, despite her trying to project indifference.

"I assume you can easily ID where I'm calling from. I'm at a pay phone and I'll be gone in a few seconds." His words were macho. His tone was wobbly, like his legs.

"You shouldn't run."

He shifted the phone from one ear to the other. "I'm being framed for this. I got scared."

"Let me help you prove that."

"How?"

"I have a theory of what's going on. If you come in, I'll tell you about it."

"Will you arrest me if I come in?" Berger wiped his moist palms on his pants.

"I'll do everything to keep from—"

"That's not enough."

"It was a lot less complicated before you started running. And we're not the only ones looking for you."

A large truck barreled by, deafening Berger and rattling him in a wake of an air concussion.

"What do you mean?"

"I mean what happened to your mother."

He felt his breath suspend. "What happened?"

"You don't know?"

"No. What happened?" He looked around, almost as if he expected to see Bert.

"There was a fire at her gas station. A man was killed. She and another man who worked there are in the hospital."

His eyes teared and he couldn't speak for a moment. When he did, his voice broke. "How are they?"

"Critical, I'm afraid."

"Where are they?"

"I can't say. LAPD is protecting them. Come in, John. I'll try to help you. I'll take you to your mother."

He realized he was staying on the phone too long. "I . . . I have to think about it." Then he hung up, missing the hook on the first try.

Jill held the phone limply in her hand, as if it were an animal that had just died. When she became conscious of it, she slammed it down.

This guy is an idiot. She'd thought he was smarter than this, and that he'd start acting rationally when he calmed down. You can't help someone who won't help themselves. Screw him.

She went over to Calhoun's desk.

"I just heard from Berger."

"Yeah? He comin' in?"

"No. But I think he'll go see his mother. She's at Bendix Memorial Hospital. Go keep an eye on her."

"You got it," he said, reaching for his coat.

Berger's mind was hijacked by the news about Bert. He unconsciously wandered west along Pico, past Fox Studios, toward the shopping area. How seriously hurt was Bert? Could she be close to dying? Might he lose her before he got to say goodbye? Had he caused this by going to see her? He unsuccessfully fought back tears and picked up his pace.

"Berger!" came a voice.

He spun around like a cornered animal, forced to attack. There was no one there.

"Berger!" it said again. He spun the other way before realizing it was the voice in his head. He forced himself to start walking again.

"You really fucked up," it said.

"Shut up," he said out loud, startling an elderly woman who was walking past him.

"You almost killed your mother. You deserve to die." More laughter.

Berger broke into a run, weaving between the pedestrians. The physical exercise seemed to help. He had to train himself to ignore the voices. It's all in my head, he repeated like a mantra.

A half mile or so later, lungs aching, he slowed his

pace and went into a restaurant called Papa's. It was decorated in Early American Helping Hands at Home, with little chintz curtains on cute rods and pictures of dogs on the wall. His chest still heaved from running, and the woman behind the cash register eyed him like he had just snatched some old lady's purse. Oh yeah. The punk look. He changed several bills into coins and went to the phone book hanging next to a wall phone. Turning in the Yellow Pages to "Hospitals," he cradled the receiver against his shoulder and he began calling.

Fortunately, Bendix Memorial was at the beginning of the alphabet, so he found her after only three calls. Yes, they had a Bertha Berger, but visiting was immediate family only. He knew better than to admit that, or even to show up during visiting hours, which ended at 9:00 P.M.

Berger curled up in a booth at Papa's, ordered a cup of coffee, and waited for nine o'clock, or until they threw him out, whichever came first.

Papa didn't bother him, so at 9:15 he took a cab to Bendix Memorial. Bendix was a small hospital, located on Venice Boulevard in Culver City, and within a mile or so of Bert's gas station.

When Berger arrived at 9:30, he found the front door locked. He tried several other doors, with no luck. Near a side door, he saw a maintenance man mopping the floor, and Berger knocked on the glass. The man, whose name tag said "Willy," looked up, and Berger tried his best "Please let me in" puppy-dog look. Willy just shook his head.

At least the security was pretty good.

Then Berger remembered that emergency rooms are always open. He went around to the emergency waiting room, where he saw a crowd of people in varying degrees of pain. One barrel-chested man, who was pacing and holding his stomach, kept yelling, "Man, this is bogus!"

The security guard studied Berger suspiciously. Berger smiled at him. The guard nodded, then went back to his magazine. Berger sat down and watched the activity. He quickly saw that the way into the hospital was through a pair of large doors remotely controlled by the security guard. Only people with passes were allowed to enter, but people coming out apparently pushed a button on the other side to spring them open. Berger pretended to read a *Family* magazine as he watched for a chance to slip through.

The surroundings began to seep into his consciousness. Scrubbed linoleum floors. The smell of antiseptic. Doctors and nurses in white uniforms. Bringing back vivid images.

Berger's father, gaunt and colorless; lying in a crank-up hospital bed. The rhythmic beeping of a heart monitor, ticking away his life like some primordial clock. Berger would sit with him for hours, lamenting the imprisonment of his sharp mind in that frail body.

After the stroke, his father could only communicate by squeezing Berger's hand. Berger remembered holding the cold, bony flesh. One squeeze for yes, two for no. Squeezes that grew progressively harder to detect.

"Can I get you anything, Dad?"

Two squeezes.

"Want me to read for you?"

A slight squeeze. He took out the *Odyssey,* which they were halfway through. Berger had decided on Homer, in a not-so-subtle tactic of inspiring the heroic determination of Odysseus. He read of raging seas and sorceresses, of gods and goddesses, of Calypso and Cyclops, stopping only to wipe a tear from his father's face. And when he was out of Dad's sight line, from his own.

In the end, his father had summoned the last of his fading energy to pull out the tubes that dripped bland nourishment into his body. That set off alarms and brought nurses running. In a wrenching decision, Berger sent them away. His father's eyes said he was grateful, as the light in them dimmed.

The casket was so light that only four people were needed to carry it. They laid him to rest on a sunny day, at the top of a gentle green slope in Hillside Cemetery. A short cantor, with a full beard and deep baritone, sang *Esa Einai*, "I Lift Up My Eyes Unto the Hills." Beneath his voice were the songs of birds and the steady drone of cars on the San Diego Freeway. Berger had found the bustling life nearby comforting.

He stayed until the grave had been filled, despite the cemetery's attempts to make him leave. And right before the little tractor bulldozed in the final scoop of soil, Berger threw in a white carnation. Just like the ones his dad had always worn in his lapel.

A woman wailing in pain brought him back to the emergency room. She had just come in, holding a bleeding wound on her stomach. The security guard came around to help her, and at the same time, two doctors in green surgical gowns walked out the double doors leading to the hospital. With the guard distracted, Berger was able to spring up and dash inside.

The doors closed behind with a sucking sound and it was suddenly quiet. Berger had no idea where he was. There were too many patient rooms to just start checking, and most of the doors were closed. He couldn't open them without looking suspicious.

He needed to find an information desk and get his mother's room number. After visiting hours, that might not be so simple. Not to mention that he had no idea where an information desk might be.

Meandering through the hallways, he hoped he looked like he knew where he was going. Finally, he wound his way to the front entrance and found the information desk. It was closed and dark. He went behind the counter to see if there was a directory, or if they'd left their computer turned on.

Nope.

Two halls branched off from the information area. He picked the left one and started down it. Dead end. He came back and tried the right hall, which led to an open area. There, an orderly in a starched white uniform sat behind a desk with a computer. This looked promising.

Berger reasoned that he couldn't just ask for his mother. For one thing, the cops might have told the staff to alert them if anyone came calling. In fact, it occurred to him, they might even be watching her room, which would mean he'd have to abort the whole plan. That thought depressed him.

He had an idea.

"You know a maintenance man named Willy?" asked Berger, remembering the name tag of the man he'd seen mopping the floor.

"Yeah," answered the orderly.

"He said to tell you he needs you. He said it's an emergency."

"He needs *me?*"

Berger looked at the name tag. "Aren't you Steve?"

"Yeah."

"Then it's you. He's down that way." Berger pointed in the opposite direction of where he'd seen Willy.

"Willy knows I can't leave my desk."

"I'll keep an eye on it, if you want. Or not. Whatever. He seemed pretty upset and told me to hurry."

"I dunno . . ." said Steve, standing partway up.

"He said something about biohazards."

Now Steve was standing up straight. "Biohazards! You'll watch my desk?"

"Yeah. Sure. Just don't be too long, okay?"

"Okay. Thanks." Steve took off in a run.

Berger knew he had only a couple of minutes before Steve found Willy and came back very pissed. He sat down at the computer. Fortunately, Steve had logged in, so Berger didn't have to get past the security. The current page was "Physician Directory."

He got back to the main menu, and then selected "Patient Information." A little flashing hourglass appeared and the old computer creaked and groaned, sluggish as hell.

Berger thought he heard a noise down the hall. He looked up and saw nothing. When he looked back, the screen said "Patient Information." He found "Search" and typed in "Berger." Another round of whirring, and a flashing message "Searching."

Finally, up came several Bergers. He scrolled to "Berger, Bertha." It listed her address, next of kin, and other information. No room number. Shit.

He moved to the next page, then the next, until the screen said "No More Pages." He went back to the main menu and checked the options. One said "Hospital Directory" and he clicked on it.

Footsteps echoed from the hall. The same direction Steve had taken. They weren't moving quickly, and he hoped it wasn't Steve. Whoever was coming, he needed to finish and get the screen back to the way he found it.

Under "Hospital Directory," he typed in Bertha's name and a few moments later, he had a hit: Room 453.

Yes!

The footsteps were moving faster. He exited the "Hospital Directory" and was in the "Main Directory." The footsteps were very near and accelerating. He didn't have time to pull up the "Physician Directory" that had been on the screen when he sat down. He'd have to leave it on "Main Directory" and hope Steve didn't remember. Or if Steve did remember, that he wouldn't connect any of this to Bert.

Berger got up from the desk and rushed down the hall, away from the footsteps. The steps seemed to follow him. He ducked into a stairwell, and before closing the door all the way, made sure it opened from the stairway side. After waiting until he caught his breath, he began a climb to the fourth floor.

The door to the fourth floor creaked at a high pitch when he opened it. He peered around the edge and didn't see anyone in the hall. He was across from room 420, so he started toward the higher numbers. He passed an old woman inching along the handrail, with an IV on rollers trailing behind her. He smiled at her and she frowned at him.

Berger came to a corner. He looked around it cautiously, worried there might be a guard in front of Bert's room. He didn't see anyone, so he turned onto her corridor. From the opposite direction came a balding orderly who stared at Berger. Maybe it was his imagination, but he thought the man seemed to recognize him before looking away. Berger turned his eyes downward, and the orderly walked past.

The door to room 453 was closed. Berger took another look up and down the hall. No one around. He found it disconcerting that they'd leave her room unguarded. And even suspicious. Was this a trap for him? He considered turning to leave, yet he didn't want to miss seeing his mother. Depending on circumstances, there might not be that many chances.

He quietly pushed the door inward. The room was dark, and he assumed Bert was sleeping. He slid inside and was about to close the door behind him when he saw that no one was in the bed. Shit! It was a trap. He quickly spun around to leave when a figure in the bedside chair switched on a reading lamp. Berger turned to see the torso of a man in a dark suit, whose face remained in darkness.

"Your mother's not here, son," said a deep voice. Berger stood still. Maybe it was because he wanted to know what happened to Bert. Maybe it was because he was tired of running.

The figure stood and walked toward him. "Let go of the door and I'll tell you where she is."

Berger complied, and the automatic door sealed the two of them in. He suddenly felt exhausted. And relieved to finally let go.

The man turned on the room lights. He was about six foot, with close-cut black hair and an angular jaw. "I'm with the FBI," he said. "I'm sorry, Mr. Berger. Your mother is dead."

The words hit him like a tazer in the chest. So much that he physically jolted backward, slamming into the door and cracking the back of his head against it.

Bert was dead? He would never see her again? He was an orphan. His mind replayed images of his mother when he was a child. Bringing him a birthday cake full of candles that lit her beaming smile. Singing to him in bed at night. He remembered toddling around the gas station behind her, trying to clean tires with paper towels.

Without thinking, Berger began banging the back of his head against the door. After a few blows, he became aware of the door pushing against him. Someone was trying to get in. Berger stepped away from the door, and the balding orderly he'd seen in the hallway came in carrying a clipboard.

"Who are you?" asked the orderly, looking at the FBI man.

"FBI. You'll need to leave."

"Take your hand slowly out of your coat," said the orderly.

The FBI man glared at him and didn't move his hand. "Didn't you hear what I said? I'm FBI and you have to leave. Now."

Berger looked back and forth at the surreal volley.

The orderly snapped back, "You're not FBI because *I'm* FBI. Now take your hand out slowly."

What happened in the next few seconds seemed to Berger like a slow-motion movie. He saw the man in the suit pull a gun from his coat. The orderly dropped the clipboard to reveal a gun as he flexed into a shooting stance. Berger instinctively hit the floor and the sound of two gunshots reverberated loudly in his ears. Then an eerie silence and the unmistakable thud of two bodies. A woman screamed from a nearby room, and some kind of high-low toned alarm sounded.

Berger grabbed the clipboard and scrambled to his feet. He stepped into the hall and forced himself to walk slowly, hoping the clipboard would make him look like he belonged. He passed a nurse's station, where almost all the rooms had lit up their call buttons. Coming toward him, like the waters of a flash flood, were a flurry of doctors and nurses heading toward room 453. None of them seemed to notice Berger as they jostled past.

He went down the stairs to the empty lobby. Walking across it slowly, he moved to a side door, then stepped out into the black night. His legs reeled, near the point of collapse.

Berger threw the clipboard as far as he could into the bushes, then extended his arms all the way out to his sides. He turned slowly in a circle, looking up at the randomly strewn stars and constellations he could not name. Then he wept out loud, no longer caring who might hear.

CHAPTER 25

Jill walked into the hospital room of Calhoun, the FBI agent who had been shot the night before. The early morning sun spilled through the window blinds, creating slats of shadows across the room.

She gently laid a stack of magazines on his stomach. "Here's *Field & Stream, Soldier of Fortune,* and *Playboy.* I figured you macho types like this kind of stuff."

He smiled, which caused him to wince and grab his bandaged shoulder. "Ah, shit. I was hoping for *Bride and Gown.*"

Jill sat down in a vinyl chair that wobbled under her weight. "How're you doing?"

"At least I was in a hospital when I got shot, so I didn't get a chance to bleed much. The doc says I'll be back in action in a few weeks."

"And the other guy?"

"He's off explaining why he was impersonating an officer and taking a shot at a real one. Explaining it to the Lord, that is."

Neither of them spoke for a few minutes.

"How's the investigation?" he asked, taking a sip of water through a bent plastic straw.

"I'm running down the body they found at Bert's Mobil station. He was burned too badly to identify without dental records, but the gun near him had fingerprints all over it. Assuming it was his gun, then his name was Tom Curtis." Jill pulled out a thin folder.

Calhoun squinted at the meager dossier. "Not much of a bad-ass, huh?"

"Not really. His whole life filled up a whopping two pages. Greco-Roman wrestler at the University of Montana. Then a stint in the army, followed by a career listed as 'chauffeur.' No criminal record, although the gun wasn't registered. After he's through being dead, maybe we'll prosecute him for that."

They chatted small talk for a while, then Jill kissed him on the cheek. She left the hospital, climbed into her car, and sat deeply in thought before starting the engine. It obviously wasn't Calhoun's fault, yet it really pissed her off that Berger had slipped away again. The fact that he showed up at the hospital meant he was a real amateur, and that he'd been lucky to stay out of sight this long. Luck could only take him so far, so she figured she'd have him pretty soon. If the other guys didn't get there first.

She rolled down the window, and a cool breeze blew through the car, ruffling her hair. She decided to read the report on Curtis one more time. The sun glared harshly off the paper, and she forced herself to concentrate.

Nothing leapt out at her.

She finished the first page, leaned her head back, and opened her mouth as she looked at the roof of the car. Her eyes defocused, making the roof look like a pool of tan paint. Where was the thread that pulled it all together? Her instincts knew it had to be here somewhere.

She started the second page and her eye caught something she'd missed before. The dates in the file showed that Curtis had been in the army for a period of two years. Yet his discharge came almost fourteen months after those two years ended. Which meant fourteen months were missing from his record. Was that significant?

She started the car and headed toward her office.

Berger slept past eleven in the morning. He pulled himself out of bed at the Cozy Court, where another twenty-eight dollars had bought him a second night's "sleep." He looked at himself in the mirror and saw his face had become deeply lined, with dark circles under his eyes. After dousing his face with water that wasn't quite hot and wasn't quite cold, he tried to dry himself with a nonabsorbent towel that was about twice the size of his palm.

He sat on the side of the bed in underwear he hadn't changed for two days. With his feet still on the floor, he lay back on the bed and closed his eyes. He saw visions of riding on Bert's back like a horsey. Her running around the living room, whinnying and bucking, while he laughed and giggled. His father sitting in an easy chair, absorbed in one of his mathematics books, periodically wincing from a particularly loud scream. Berger remembered rolling around on the floor as Bert tickled him, every once in a while nudging his father to join in. His father would look up from the book, manage to force a smile, then dive back into the academic waters.

Now they were both gone.

"You killed them," came the voices. He sat up and

opened his eyes. Reflexively, he looked around the room. "You deserve to die," they continued. This time it was both voices, speaking in that disharmony. "Kill yourself and save everyone the trouble."

Berger backed into a corner of the room. The solid walls gave him comfort that no one was behind him. He bit his lower lip with enough force that he almost felt his teeth touch.

"You're going to die," they chanted louder and louder.

"Fuck you!" he screamed. He started banging his head roughly against the wall, as if he could somehow dislodge the voices.

They only laughed.

The office runner, a scrawny kid with a few wisps of hair he probably considered a mustache, handed Jill the information on Robert Winston, the man who shot Calhoun in the hospital. No prior criminal record. Grew up in Bismarck, North Dakota. High school football player, junior varsity. Stint in the army. Worked as a—

Her eye went back. Army. She flipped the page and saw that he was in G Company, 2nd Battalion, 16th Infantry. And there were nine months missing from his record. She grabbed the file on Tom Curtis, the man killed at the Mobil station. Curtis had also been in G Company, and he had fourteen months missing.

Jill ran into the hallway and grabbed the runner again. She made him stand there while she filled out a pink requisition slip for the rest of the soldiers in this G Company, 2nd Battalion, 16th Infantry. Then she told him to ship it immediately to the Federal Records Center in St. Louis.

*   *   *

Berger sat in a taxi that smelled of incense from a little wicker hanging basket. The driver sang along with some atonal Middle Eastern music as they pulled up to Los Angeles airport. Berger grabbed his small carry-on bag and went inside the Delta terminal.

It took twenty minutes to get through the line to the ticket desk, where a smiling blond woman with emerald eyes looked up at him. Her name tag said "Tiffany."

"I'd like to buy a ticket to Dallas," said Berger.

"Do you have a reservation?"

"Yes. Manny Gomez."

She typed with her index fingers and then looked up. "That'll be two hundred eighty-nine dollars, Mr. Gomez."

Berger pulled out the money in twenties and smaller denominations. She counted the crinkled bills, laying them in sorted stacks.

"Thank you, Mr. Gomez. Now I need to see a picture ID."

Shit. Berger had forgotten that, since the Unabomber, they always asked for ID. He reached for his back pocket, then feigned shock. "Oh, dear. I left it at home."

Tiffany's face molded into a sympathetic apology. "I'm so sorry, but they won't let you board without a security stamp. And I need to see an ID to give you one."

"I don't have time to go home and back before the plane leaves. Please. It's really important for me to get there. My father is sick."

"I would love to bend the rules for you, Mr. Gomez, but I just can't. Would you like me to call my supervisor?"

Berger quickly calculated that the fewer people who saw him, the better.

"No. Just give me back my money."

Tiffany handed over his cash with a pleasant smile, and he wandered along the counter.

Now what?

He thought about taking a bus to Barstow or some other small town. Or he could go to Alvarado and Wilshire, a rough neighborhood where he'd heard you can buy picture IDs for fifty dollars, including the photo. That would open up his options. Assuming no one slit his throat in the process.

He started toward the street when his eye caught a sign that read EXCESS BAGGAGE.

He froze, transfixed. EXCESS. The letters seized his consciousness. EXC. The name of the company where he had worked. The voices began yelling in his head. "It's him! It's him!"

The rage erupted so fast that Berger had no conscious reaction. He began screaming from the depths of his diaphragm and grabbed the shoulders of a dark-haired man who was standing nearby. Within seconds, the startled stranger was on his back on the floor, with Berger straddling him. Berger felt as if he were watching himself from a distance, seeing his body act on automatic pilot. He grabbed the man's hair and began slamming his head into the floor, yelling, "Killer! Killer!"

A crowd quickly formed around them.

"Murderer! Killer!"

The helpless man looked shocked and terrified. His eyes asked Berger, "Why?" Berger was asking himself the same question, yet his body had wrested control from his mind and he couldn't stop.

Suddenly, Berger felt a baton across his throat. An airport security guard wrenched him off the man by jerking hard enough to choke him. He felt his eyes bulge, and his chest tighten, burning from lack of air. His arms flailed in impotent rage. Now he was being shoved face down onto the floor, and someone was handcuffing him so roughly that he could feel the skin scraping off his wrists.

Two men pulled him up by the armpits and forced him away.

CHAPTER 26

Combs's wheels crunched over the oyster shell parking lot of Maxine's Place in Le Fontaine, Louisiana. He turned off the motor and sat for several minutes before exhaling a long breath and climbing out of the rented Toyota. The sky was growing dark, and a roll of thunder tumbled overhead.

Combs tightened his collar against a chilly gust that flapped red-checked window curtains in the white clapboard house that had been converted to a roadside diner. He hurried inside and sat in one of the two booths, happy to be the only customer. A radio in the kitchen played zydeco music, and the place smelled of frying chicken. Near the unplugged jukebox, a chalkboard advertised a "Bucket o' Crayfish and Bottle of Beer" lunch special.

A gaunt middle-aged woman, with teased hair and several inches of makeup, wiped off a plastic-covered menu before handing it over. Combs ordered black coffee and pushed the menu to the other side of the table.

Playing with the glass sugar container, to watch the metal flap open and close, he wondered if he'd recognize him this time. Even though it had only been a couple of years, it seemed that the man faded more and more with each meeting.

The waitress brought the coffee and Combs stirred in sugar with a knife, since she'd forgotten the spoon. He checked his watch again.

His father was twenty minutes late. Bad enough that Combs had to drag his ass out to this Cajun backwater, where Harold lived in a shack he'd inherited from Combs's grandmother. On top of that, he had to sit around and wait. Wait for a man who had nothing to do.

Combs watched the ceiling fan spin erratically. It was just like the ones at the Dade County Recorder's Office, where young Kenneth sometimes went to work with his dad. Harold always made him comb his hair and put on clean clothes before they went. *You have to make a good impression, Kenny.* When they got there, Combs got to go through a special door. Behind the big counter, where only Authorized Personnel were allowed. He'd sit on Harold's lap for hours, hitting rubber stamps on soft ink pads, and splattering papers with words like *Recorded, Confidential,* and someone's personal stamp of a happy face. He remembered the smell of ink, and the blue smears on his hands. The ringing of phones and the clanking of big metal stamps he wasn't allowed to use. He remembered Mr. Thornton grunting as he hefted the big books with gray canvas covers. And uniformed sheriffs, with real guns, handling blue-backed documents like they were fragile.

It all ended when Combs was ten. The County Recorder let his father go in something called a "restructuring." That sent the old man looking for a job he never found. The family lived on his mother's salary as a receptionist, plus his dad's few temp jobs as a handyman—a skill

Harold Combs just didn't have. Combs remembered
Harold coming home at night, with his hands cut from
trying to use a hammer or a chisel, looking as tired and
wrinkled as his clothes.

Within six months after his father was fired, Combs
formed The Squad—his grammar school gang. He spent
years whipping them into shape with small-time pranks.
Then, when they were in high school, he squared things
up.

Combs tapped Baxter and two trusted Squad members
for an elite team. He spent weeks educating them how
the government fucked with people's lives. How guys like
them were held down by the cops, so the ones with power
could stay that way. And how most people were too chickenshit to do anything about it.

When he knew they'd bought into all this, he told the
trio that they needed to fight for people too weak to protect themselves. He said they had to make a symbolic
strike at the authorities. Something that would make all
the newspapers and television shows. How else would
people like them ever be able to do something important?

Combs gradually led them to understand that the
County Recorder was the symbolic heart of local government. It was where they kept records that the government needed to manipulate people. Combs was never sure
whether they actually believed him, or were just humor-
ing him. He didn't really care.

Using *The Anarchist's Cookbook,* which he bought from
a Jamaican drug dealer, Combs made an incendiary device from a glass bottle, gasoline, and a rag. He drilled
the team in his backyard for a week. When he decided
they were ready, he chose a Friday night. A night when
Combs could be seen socializing with the chaperones at
a high school dance.

The hours of practice paid off. Baxter and the two Squad members first shattered the County Recorder's windows with rocks. Then they lobbed in the incendiary. They were gone in thirteen seconds, according to the sweep hand on Baxter's watch. The Recorder's office was almost totally destroyed, and many of the records were lost forever.

The crime was never solved.

The Squad's reward was the promised headlines and TV news stories. And four teenage prostitutes for the three of them, courtesy of the Squad's war chest.

Combs heard footsteps near the table, and looked up from his coffee.

"Hello, Kenny."

He saw his father grimace with arthritis as he slid into the seat. They shook hands, and Combs felt how Harold's palm had shriveled with age. He wanted to pull back, but forced himself to finish the shake. His dad's face and body were almost skeletal, draped with dangling flesh. Harold's smile seemed to take considerable effort, and the strain soon gave way to a melancholy droop.

Combs forced himself to smile back, hoping Harold would buy it. They chatted about nothing for several minutes.

"You heard from Mom?" asked Combs.

His father shook his head. "Not for a year or so. She's still upset about the back alimony, I'm afraid. You should call her."

The zydeco music in the kitchen changed to a comic, telling jokes to canned laughter.

"You hungry, Dad?"

"Starved."

Harold ordered a heaping plate of crayfish. They barely

spoke as he pried out the flesh with his bent fingers, then sucked the heads. Combs sipped his coffee, and found his eyes wandering away from his father. Outside, the sky had turned a blackish gray and the incandescent lights made Harold glow, as if he were under a low flame.

"Here's a few bucks." Combs slid over a thick envelope.

"Oh, no, Kenny. I can't take that."

It was the standard dance. They always went back and forth a few times before the old man said, "Well, maybe just this once."

Today was no different.

Combs knew this was the only money his father lived on. Harold had never found that job, and now he was too feeble to work. Combs increased the amount in the envelope each time, as it had to last until they saw each other again. Those periods had increased as well.

"Have you seen the doctor, Dad?"

"Oh, well, when I really need to," said Harold, jimmying the envelope into his shirt.

"You know you can't—"

Harold waved off the conversation. "Doc Gosland's all the way over in Metairie. I'm fine, just fine."

A snap of lightning, followed by rumbling thunder, floated through the open window with a rush of moist air. The rain quickly made good on its threat, pelting the wooden house in a thick staccato.

"I have to go away for a while," said Combs.

His father looked up. "Oh? More of your hush-hush government stuff?"

"Yeah. I'll send you some money when I can. At the general delivery."

"You don't have to do that."

A burst of thunder jolted the small house. "There may

be some people looking for me. Just tell them the truth. That you don't know where I am."

Harold nodded, long resigned to his son's odd doings.

They sat in silence while Harold finished the last of the crayfish, then sat back with a sigh.

"Guess I have to get going now," said Combs.

"All right."

When they got up, it looked like Harold wanted to hug him. Maybe it was Combs's imagination. That move wasn't in either of their repertoires. It passed quickly, if it had been there at all.

Another feeble handshake. "Stay in touch, son."

Combs watched his father hobble out the door into the heavy rain.

Carl Davidson, head of the Anti-Terrorist Unit, walked down the corridor of the FBI Building in Washington toward the Secure Room. The agent accompanying him inserted his key at the same time as Davidson's, and they turned simultaneously. Then, on the two keypads that were shielded from the other's sight, they each punched in their eight-digit codes.

The twelve-inch-thick door buzzed loudly as it opened, and Davidson went alone into the windowless cubicle. The door closed with the sound of a vacuum seal, almost popping his ears, and it was perfectly quiet. The air smelled stale and dusty, which was not surprising since cleaning crews were only allowed in once a month.

It was almost 7:00 P.M. in Tel Aviv, which meant Moshe would be calling any minute. Davidson knew he wouldn't have to wait around for the call, since Moshe was an "on-time airline."

The call came precisely on the hour, and Davidson answered before the first ring finished.

"Shalom, Carl," said Moshe in his thick Southern accent. Moshe was born in Israel, but had lived in Mobile, Alabama, as a small child, while his parents attended college and grad school. Davidson was always amused to hear one of Israel's top security officers speak English like he'd never left the farm.

"Howdy, partner," answered Davidson.

They exchanged pleasantries for a few minutes. "Ol' buddy," said Moshe, "I wanted you to hear what I'm gettin'. The Serbian fellas are plannin' somethin' on a big scale in the U-nited States, right around Thanksgiving. I hear the chimes are gonna ring in a buncha your cities, all at the same time."

Davidson clutched the handset tightly. That was less than two weeks away. "Do you have anything more specific?"

"Unfortunately, no more than what I just gave ya. And even that cost one of our boys his life. If it's true, it's under real deep cover. We're still digging, and I'll keep you up on what we find, if you'd be kind enough to do the same for me."

"You got it. Have you told the CIA?"

A short silence. "I'm afraid we had a bad experience with those folks recently, so I thought I'd go through my buddy Carl. We got our own troubles with the Serbian folks, and if they found out we even got a hint of this, it could be, shall we say, 'expensive.'"

"I won't bust you. Thanks for the tip."

When Davidson hung up, he sat for a long while. It was dicey to leave out the CIA, yet domestic terrorism was the FBI's domain. And he wouldn't break his word to Moshe in any event. What was more disturbing was that he hadn't heard any of these rumblings. Either this was a false alarm, or it was way underground. Moshe was rarely wrong, but it seemed unlikely that something this big wouldn't produce a ripple in Davidson's pond.

He thought about calling Gregg Harrison, his top domestic terrorism agent. But Harrison was working on an airline bombing, and that investigation would be seriously delayed if Davidson pulled him off. Which could cause all kinds of political problems—especially if Moshe's information proved to be just smoke.

Davidson decided to spread out a few discreet tentacles before he committed any significant manpower.

Berger awoke on a narrow, metal bed to find his mouth filled with a rubber gag. The front of his neck was raw and tender, and he suddenly remembered being choked with a baton. His body felt caked and dusty, and he wondered if he'd soiled his pants while he slept, since the room smelled like urine.

He tried to sit up, which caused the mattress springs to creak. That was when he found that he was strapped down with wide leather belts. The best he could do was raise his head toward his chest, to see that he was in a dark gray room with a metal, riveted door. Sunshine through a barred porthole told him it was daytime outside. He studied the room until the strain of holding up his head became too much, then he collapsed back on the mattress.

As he gathered his bearings, he realized how small the room felt. The walls seemed to be moving closer, and maybe the ceiling was lowering too. The idea that he couldn't move increased the sensation that he was in a tight, confined space. Like being buried alive in a coffin. What if there was a fire? With this rubber thing in his mouth, he couldn't even scream for help. What if the ventilation system stopped working and there was no oxygen? His chest heaved, as if to gasp enough air to see him through the possibility.

Berger began to wrench his body against the restraints, making the bed inch toward the wall. The exertion made him slippery from perspiration, yet he couldn't loosen the shackles. Finally, he lay back in resignation and tried to calm himself.

He had a vague recollection of being restrained not too long ago. Where did that come from? There was no conscious memory. It was foggy, like a dream. He remembered needles going into his skin, as if he were a voodoo doll. He could feel their stings, radiating pain through his body. What was that all about?

As a mental escape, he tried to imagine himself elsewhere. It took some doing, yet he finally drifted into a meditative state. Berger saw himself soaring like a seagull, lolling on an updraft of salty air, listening to the rhythmic surf below. His breathing slowed, and he felt himself relaxing.

The jangling of a key snapped Berger back to reality. The loud thunk of a thrown bolt was followed by the squeal of a door swinging open. He strained his neck toward his chest to see who was there.

Jill Landis walked in with Hugo Dorn, Berger's public defender. The guard took off Berger's gag, and he could taste cool air circulating in his mouth. He moved his jaw in circles, savoring the freedom.

"Where am I?" he asked.

"The prison ward of L.A. County Psychiatric Hospital," answered Jill. "Mr. Berger, you have the right to remain silent . . ." She finished explaining his rights.

"Thank you, Agent Landis," said Dorn. "I'm now advising him not to say anything. Would you excuse us so I can talk to Mr. Berger privately?"

"Can I get these restraints off?" asked Berger.

The guard shook his head. "You're a potential danger to yourself and others until a psychiatrist says otherwise."

"It's humiliating and dehumanizing," said Berger.

"Too bad," said the guard.

"Will you excuse us?" repeated Dorn.

Jill and the guard went outside and closed the door.

"Are these restraints legal?" asked Berger.

"Technically, they can only do it when you're having visitors. If they do more than that, I'll get a court order."

"I woke up like this."

"I'll get on it. Mr. Berger, why did you run from the FBI?"

"I panicked. I know it was stupid. I didn't want to be locked up. They're trying to frame me for the EXC explosion. And I think someone else is chasing me too."

"Who?"

"I don't know."

"Why do you think someone's chasing you?"

Berger explained about the explosions in his house and at Bert's station.

"And you don't know anything about these bombings?"

"Nothing."

Dorn let out a long sigh and shook his head as he spoke. "The arrows all point to you. Your security card was used at EXC the day before the blast. Fingerprints resembling yours were found on duct tape at EXC. You told a false story about a chess tournament, then you disappeared. I'm on your side, Mr. Berger, but you're not making it easy. This is a serious situation. You have to level with me."

And you should hear Smitty's story about my showing up at EXC on Sunday. "I am leveling with you. I didn't do it."

"Do you know who did?"

"No."

"And you still don't remember your whereabouts on the weekend before the EXC blast?"

"I know it's crazy. I'm just so . . . confused about what I remember."

Dorn began pacing. "We could plead insanity. Temporary or otherwise. I think I could get you off lightly, maybe—"

"I won't plead to something I didn't do. And if you don't believe my story, I want another lawyer."

Dorn put up his hands in surrender. "Okay, okay. I only give advice. We'll play it any way you want. If you're innocent, then we should cooperate fully. Do you want to talk to Agent Landis?"

"I guess so. I don't remember much, but I can tell her what I do."

"Tell me first."

Berger ran through his story, leaving out the part about the voices and Smitty. Dorn seemed satisfied.

When Jill returned, her stunning looks once again struck Berger. He worried that her presence, like the last time, would make him tongue-tied because he wanted so badly to make a good impression. On the other hand, he wasn't likely to impress her very well in his current state. He somehow doubted she was into filthy, tied-down fugitives who smelled of urine.

Jill spoke crisply. "Mr. Berger, I'm having a hard time believing that you've told us everything you know. This is a very serious crime. We have several people dead. If you're connected to it, hiding information will make things a lot rougher on you when I get the truth."

"I know it looks bad. If I were you, I'd have the same doubts. Why did this guy run if he was innocent? Why can't he explain his whereabouts? And who else is chasing him if he doesn't know something they want silenced?"

Jill cocked her head to the side. "Those are the right questions, Mr. Berger. You're pretty smart. I assume your technique is to disarm me by expressing sympathy for my position. To diffuse suspicious circumstances by calling attention to them."

"I'm not trying to manipulate you. If I was doing that, I'd have come up with a credible lie to explain everything in the first place. The truth is that I'm just as confused by all this as you are."

Jill stared at him a few moments without talking. Dorn looked back and forth between the two of them.

She finally spoke. "So you don't have anything new to tell me?"

Berger realized he'd been keeping all this information to himself, and that hadn't worked out very well. He made a decision to unload everything.

"If you'll unstrap me, I'll tell you the rest of what I know."

The guard shook his head. "Nossir. We can't do that."

"Are you about to say anything we haven't discussed?" asked Dorn.

Berger ignored him and spoke directly to Jill. "If I know something helpful, I want you to have it. Just treat me like a human."

"You viciously attacked a man in the airport," said Jill. "You haven't been evaluated psychologically. I don't see how—"

"You trust me, I'll trust you."

Jill looked at him intently for a few minutes, then turned to the guard. "Unstrap him."

"That's not a good idea, Ms. Landis," said the guard.

"I'll take the responsibility," she answered. "Let him loose."

"I don't have the authority."

"You do. I just gave it to you. Let him loose."

"Don't talk, Mr. Berger," said Dorn. "We have to discuss this first. You could be putting yourself in jeopardy."

"I'm willing to trust her."

The guard still hadn't moved. Jill snapped at him, "Unstrap him. Now." When he still didn't act, Jill went over and started unbuckling the thick straps around Berger's legs. She had to strain because the stiff leather had no slack in it. The guard reluctantly undid the straps on his arms.

When they finished, Jill, Dorn, and the guard took a step back, as if they'd just let a wounded animal out of a trap. Berger sat up and rubbed his arms, which were numb from having been pinned. The circulation returned with a prickly feeling, and he waved his arms slowly in large circles. He cautiously stood up, and his legs only half cooperated. The guard's eyes never left him, and his hand stayed on his baton.

"What have you got, Mr. Berger?" asked Jill.

"I can't promise it'll make any sense, but here it is. When you showed me a picture of an old man in your office, I thought he looked familiar."

Dorn threw up his hands in exasperation. "Mr. Berger, you should not be talking about matters we haven't discussed."

Berger waved him away. "I don't think I've met the guy, but I feel like I've seen him. And I remember seeing him naked, which makes even less sense."

"Naked?"

"Yes."

"Go on."

"A few nights ago, I went back to the rubble at EXC. While I was walking around, I saw the letters 'EXC' and went nuts. I felt, like, this rage build up, and I started beating the walls with a two-by-four. At the airport, I saw the letters 'EXC' in a sign, and I attacked a perfect stranger. I still don't know why. This anger just took over. Then, the other day, I started hearing voices in my head. Telling me I'm going to die. They're getting more frequent."

"What else?"

"There's a guard named Smitty."

Dorn interrupted. "Mr. Berger, for heaven's sake, shut up. I can't protect you when you act like this."

"I want her to know everything." He explained how he'd gone to see Smitty, and what he'd said. Dorn paced nervously in tighter and tighter circles.

"Anything more?" asked Jill.

"That's about it. I realize I sound like I'm nuts. Maybe I am." Berger felt a cathartic release from opening up. It was immediately followed by the anxiety that he had just punched a nonstop ticket to the loony bin.

Jill had been listening intently, her forehead furrowed in concentration. "I can't say any of this makes much sense, but I think you're being honest for the first time. Would you agree to see a psychiatrist?"

Dorn chimed in. "If we agree, I want a stipulation that anything he says to the psychiatrist can't be used against him."

"We'll discuss that later," said Jill. "How about it, Mr. Berger?"

"Yeah. Sure."

"You shouldn't be doing this," said Dorn, wagging a finger at Berger.

Jill nodded militarily, then stood up and shook his hand.

The warmth of her touch moved through him, and he had an almost overwhelming desire to pull himself against her, like a small child taking refuge in his mother's embrace. That didn't seem like a good idea under the circumstances.

Dorn stayed behind after Jill and the guard left. "You realize you've now given an admissible confession, and led her to a witness who can place you at the crime scene with a package the day before the blast?"

"It's the truth. It would have come out anyway. I have to believe the truth will be on my side when it's all said and done."

"I'm not so sure anymore."

A long silence. Berger massaged the wound on his throat.

"Look," Dorn continued, "the only damage control we have left is to keep you away from their shrink. I think that would be a terrible mistake."

Dorn spent a half hour trying to talk Berger out of seeing the government's psychiatrist, but Berger held his ground. Dorn finally left in a sulk.

When Berger was alone, the cell felt emptier than before. He paced back and forth over the few steps that it permitted, until the door clanked open and the guard stepped in. Two large men in white jackets stood just outside.

"Time to get strapped in again, Mr. Berger," said the guard with a slight smile. The two men simultaneously crossed their arms across their chests, like soldiers moving in lockstep.

"Am I having more visitors?"

"Nope. Just tucking you in for beddy-bye."

"My lawyer says you can only do that if I'm having visitors."

"Well, your lawyer's not here now, is he?"

The two large men moved forward. Berger quickly retreated, lay down on the bed, and closed his eyes.

Jill stood in her kitchen, watching a small TV on the counter. She was preparing angel hair pasta with a marinara sauce. Since the day had been exhausting, she was sticking with an old, familiar recipe rather than anything adventurous.

After stirring in the tomato paste and Italian herbs, she tasted the sauce on the tip of a wooden spoon. It needed a little red wine.

Channel 28, the Los Angeles public television station, was running a documentary called *The Quest for Bridey Murphy*. A woman in the 1950s was regressed under hypnosis, first to her childhood, then to a former life. In that state, she spoke with a thick Irish brogue and said her name was Bridey Murphy. She also claimed to have lived two centuries earlier. The incident spawned enormous notoriety, despite the fact that no one could prove whether Bridey Murphy really existed.

Jill got so absorbed in the program that the marinara sauce burned on the bottom of the pan. She scraped the remains into the disposal before throwing a frozen yuppie dinner in the microwave. While she waited the required five minutes, she lay down on the couch and draped a damp washcloth over her forehead.

Berger's mental state reminded her of the hostages. Now that he was opening up, the connection was even more pronounced. The flashback images. The jumbling of thoughts and memories. Even the voices.

Voices. Bridey Murphy spoke in a different voice. Hypnotism. Connecting experiences with other lives. Hostages. All these ideas stirred in Jill's head.

When it hit her, she sat up so quickly that the washcloth sailed across the couch. Of course. He was exhibiting the classic symptoms of someone who had been brainwashed, or whatever the politically correct term for brainwashing was these days.

She didn't need a shrink. She needed an expert on mind control.

CHAPTER 27

Berger awoke late at night in the cell. It was dark outside and he was still strapped to the bed. Since he'd been dozing throughout the day, he figured he'd be awake for a while. His back was stiff, yet he couldn't shift his position to get comfortable.

"Don't look up," ordered a voice somewhere north of his head.

At first, Berger thought it was one of those voices that had been taunting him for the last several days. Then he realized it wasn't. This one was deep and resonant, with a controlled strength.

"Who are you?" asked Berger.

"Your fairy fucking godmother."

"How did you get in here?"

"I got ways."

"What do you want?"

"This ain't twenty questions, asshole. Just shut up and listen."

Berger surreptitiously tried to look at the speaker. The

position strained his neck muscles to the verge of snapping into spasm.

"Keep your eyes on the ceiling. I'm not gonna warn you again."

Berger relaxed back to his original position. He couldn't see the ceiling in the dark.

"You talked too much today," the voice continued.

"She said it didn't make sense."

"That's not for you to decide. You got no idea what you're into."

"What am I into?"

"If you wanta see the sun come up for a while, then shut the fuck up. You got it?"

Berger didn't answer.

"I'm gonna be watchin' to make sure."

The emotions of the last few days cascaded at once. Everything in his life gone. Voices in his head. Strapped down like some sick dog. Enough.

"Who are you?" he screamed, wrenching his neck around to look at the voice.

The room was empty.

In the late morning, Agent Russ Harley sat across from Jill in her cubicle. Harley was in his early thirties, with blondish hair and a thin scar above his lip. His crew cut was seeping perspiration, and Jill thought it made him look like a porcupine caught in the rain.

"Mind control these days focuses on cults," said Harley, "and there's a few big names in the field. The most prominent was Dr. Jolly West at UCLA, but he passed away recently. Margaret Thaler Singer in the Bay Area is also top notch, but she's on sabbatical in China for the next six months. Leon Nesson in Boston is deprogramming a senator's son who just came out of a cult. Our best bet is

Chuck Durham. He's a relative newcomer, but pretty well respected. Wrote a couple of books on mind control, and lectures about cults. I spoke to Durham this morning. He took my call right away and was fascinated by the case. He said he could see you tomorrow, but he's giving a seminar and you'd have to go to Arizona. If you want him to come here, it'll have to be Wednesday."

"I'll see him tomorrow in Arizona."

Jill drove the rented white Taurus along Scottsdale Road in Phoenix, heading north toward Cave Creek. The city peeled away slowly until she found herself in open desert, where the only signs of civilization were an occasional Arabian horse ranch and a pockmarked metal sign that said NO SHOOTING. Tall saguaro cacti, with their arms reaching upward in graceful L shapes, stood like sentries over clusters of desert scrub.

The car's air conditioner blasted a loud stream of air that fought the heat reasonably well, while mirages of water appeared and disappeared on the road. Up ahead was a mountain that looked like a pile of large, craggy boulders, silhouetted against a crisp blue sky. The scene reminded her so much of Western movies that she was surprised to hear rock music instead of country when she turned on the radio.

She turned left onto Long Rifle Road, then onto Stage Coach, and finally Cave Creek Road, past signs that promised she was near the Tonto National Forest. At the corner of Cave Creek and Spur Cross, she saw the faded red pickup truck parked off to the side. A short man in a cowboy hat was leaning against it, with the sole of one boot against the door. He pushed off when she pulled up.

"I'm Buddy," he said, extending a weathered hand into her car. Durham had told her that he no longer gave out directions, since he'd found himself rescuing almost every guest. Now he routinely sent an escort.

"Jill Landis." A gust of sand made her cough.

"Follow me up the road. Wouldn't want to lose a pretty miss like you."

Jill debated giving him one of several lectures, but instead opted for rolling up the window. She stayed close behind the truck, using its bashed taillight like a homing beacon through the clouds of dust.

According to Jill's odometer, they wound for almost four miles through stark desert terrain. The last two miles were dirt roads with no signs, and she hadn't seen a house for over fifteen minutes. They stopped at a cattle guard with a padlocked gate made out of pipes. Buddy left his motor running while he opened the gate, then he drove through and waited for Jill before relocking it. They continued up a hill for several miles to a long, tan stucco wall that stretched in both directions beyond the sight lines. Buddy drove to a heavy wooden door and punched in a code. When the door rolled off to the side, Buddy drove through and Jill followed the white taillight.

Inside the wall, in radical contrast to the parched desert, was a manicured lawn, scores of date palms, and an elaborate cactus garden. She parked her car and followed Buddy past a statue of a cowboy riding a horse that stood on its hind legs. The cowboy held a canteen aloft, with water trickling out to create a fountain. Beyond the fountain was a large, peach-colored Spanish hacienda, with semiround red tiles on the roof. Along the front wall was a redwood lattice, covered with magenta, hot pink, coral, and white bougainvillea.

A thin, wiry man with graying black hair came out of the house toward her. He wore blue jeans, a thick stitched leather belt with an oval silver buckle, and boots that looked like they were made from some kind of reptile. His face was deeply creased from years in the sun, and he had a warm, open smile.

"Welcome, Ms. Landis. I'm Chuck Durham." He spoke with authority, and no trace of the Western accent she expected from his appearance. He looked directly into her eyes and shook hands with a strong grip. He held on to her hand for a moment afterward.

"Your home is lovely," she said, taking back her hand and breaking the gaze.

"Thanks. Please don't mind the security. I've had to beef things up since one of the cults stuck a Gila monster in my mailbox. Did you know that Gilas are North America's only poisonous lizard?"

"No, I didn't."

"There's a lot about the desert you don't get at first glance." He put his hand gently against her upper arm and guided her toward the open front door. She had the feeling he was studying her body as they walked. "Come on in and rest up for a minute. What'll you have to drink? Soft? Hard?"

"Just water, thanks."

"It comes from our own well, and it tastes a lot better than the designer water they sell for three dollars a bottle."

He walked her into a large, spacious living room, decorated in Navajo blanket designs. There was Western art on the walls, and a large picture window that displayed views of the desert and boulders.

"This area was an ocean floor, millions of years ago. It's a young desert, so we don't have sand yet. Just decomposing granite."

Buddy appeared with a glass of water. Jill sipped it and was impressed. Clear, pure, and sweet. Durham gestured for her to sit in a tan overstuffed chair, and he sat on the couch. The blanket draped over the chair's armrest made Jill's skin itch, so she awkwardly tried to keep her hands in her lap.

Durham leaned toward her. His knee lightly touched hers.

"Now tell me about your man. This sounds fascinating."

Jill relayed the information she had on Berger. She started to talk about Simms in Orlando, then held off. She could give him that later if she decided to use him. While she spoke, his eyes bored into her with such intensity that she periodically had to look away.

"I thought he might have been subjected to some kind of mind control," Jill continued. "Does it sound like that to you?"

"Maybe. I need to know more."

"Is it possible he was brainwashed and doesn't remember it?"

"Not with standard cult techniques. Those folks manipulate people while they're fully conscious, and the members know everything that's happened."

"So it's not possible?"

"Hypnosis can block out memories. And there's always new methods coming along. Maybe somebody found a way to do what you're describing. Maybe some variation of the cult techniques. Do you know how those work?"

"Not really."

"Come with me."

He stood up and started toward the back door. She followed a few paces behind. They went outside to a wooden building, and Durham went into a room attached to a stable. After a moment, he came out holding a pair of blue jeans and a work shirt.

"These look about your size. Throw them on in here." He gestured toward the door with his head.

"What?"

"Put on these clothes. We're gonna take a horseback ride."

"I'm really pressed for time—"

"I want to show you something. I promise it'll be valuable."

"I really—"

He pushed the clothes into her hands. "It's a fifteen-minute ride and scenic as hell. We'll talk on the way."

"Why can't we talk here?"

A horse whinnied in the background. "There's something there you need to see. If you don't think it's worth it, you can kick right here when we get back." He pointed to his rear end.

"I don't know anything about horses."

"I used to break them for a living. You can ride Lady, who's so gentle you'll think she's asleep. What size shoe do you wear?"

Jill hesitantly took the clothes and went into a small room with pegs on which she hung her skirt and blouse. She pulled on the jeans, which were a bit baggy, and buttoned the shirt, which was tight and pulled around her breasts. She wondered if he'd done that on purpose.

Durham knocked on the door and a hand reached in holding a pair of cowboy boots. When she took them, the hand gave an "Okay" sign and withdrew.

She came out and squinted from the sun. She wasn't quite balanced in the boots. In front of her was a magnificent golden horse, as tall as Jill at the shoulder. Durham rested his foot on a sawed-off oil drum next to the horse.

"Good fit," he said, nodding at her clothes.

She looked down shyly.

Durham took her hand with a firm grasp and helped her stand on the drum. She placed her left foot in the stirrup, then heaved her right leg over the saddle. To her relief, the horse stood perfectly still. Durham adjusted the length of the stirrups, gently handling her legs in the process.

The vantage point from up high was invigorating and a little unnerving at the same time. She hadn't been on a horse since the ponies she rode in grade school. Jill reached down and patted Lady's neck. Lady nodded, as if in appreciation.

Durham appeared on a chestnut and white pinto that was taller than Lady. He pulled up next to her and said, "Stay close."

He needn't worry about that, she thought. They rode almost a mile before Durham pulled out a garage door remote and opened a gate in his stucco wall. Within a short distance after leaving his property, the dirt path narrowed and forced them to ride single file.

Durham, in front, turned around in the saddle as he spoke. "Those round balls are called barrel cactus. They're also called a compass cactus, because the tops of them always lean south. Over there's one of the three native trees to this area. It's a paloverde, and its roots go down over a hundred feet. The paloverde has the world's smallest leaves, and its trunk and branches are green because they also do the photosynthesis."

He swung around to the other side of the saddle. "That there's a saguaro cactus. It's the state plant, and its picture's on our license plate. Saguaros can live over two hundred years, and can grow to over sixty feet, but the roots are only eighteen to twenty-four inches."

Jill's legs were beginning to chafe from the saddle, and the armpits of her blouse were dampening.

Durham continued talking. "Stay far away from these

cute little fellas." He pointed to a plant with barb-covered
balls about the size of plums. "Those are chollas and their
needles can go through cowboy boots. If you get one in
your leg, and you grab it with your fingers, you staple two
body parts together. They pull your skin out six inches before they come loose. When hypodermics were developed,
the scientists studied chollas to see how they worked. Native Americans put them on sticks and used them as spears.
If your horse gets up against one, it'll be one helluva ride,
and you'll only be on for part of it."

Jill began to feel like the path was getting narrower, and
that the chollas were reaching toward her. She hugged her
legs against Lady more tightly.

"What are we supposed to be seeing out here?" she
asked.

"Just a few more minutes."

Something rustled between the cactuses. "What was
that?" said Jill, quickly bolting upright.

"Probably a javelina. They call 'em wild pigs but they're
really rodents. We also got quail. Mule deer. Cottontail rab-
bits."

She was just as happy she hadn't seen the javelina. "I
get the feeling you're leaving out some of the less friendly
inhabitants."

Durham chuckled. "I forgot you're FBI. Yeah. We got
tarantulas, but they don't have much venom. We also got
scorpions, which is why I keep chickens. Did you know
that chickens eat scorpions? And of course we've got Gila
monsters and rattlesnakes."

Jill was sorry she'd asked.

"These critters don't bother you unless you do something to them. This is beautiful country, once you get into
its rhythm, but almost everything has a barb or a fang or
a stinger."

Jill had no desire to bother the critters. She ducked under a low-hanging tree branch that brushed across her back. Thankfully, it was barb-free.

Now they were going uphill and the vegetation began to thin. They rounded a corner to a clearing, where Durham climbed off his horse. He came over and helped Jill down, holding her waist in the process. She was self-conscious of her love handles under his grip.

"Have a seat on the rock here. I'll tie up the horses."

She walked awkwardly, with slightly bowed legs, watching where she stepped. Then she examined the rock for anything that moved before slowly sitting down.

Durham went over to Lady and began walking her. Suddenly, the horse bolted off.

"Lady, dammit!" he shouted, running after her. Lady disappeared around the corner in a whirlwind of dust.

Durham shouted back to Jill, "Stay here. Don't touch anything, and don't move. I'll be back as soon as I catch her."

"But . . . I . . ."

Durham jumped on the pinto and galloped after Lady. She watched until he was out of sight, then turned her attention back to the surroundings.

Where was she? What if Durham didn't come back right away? She didn't even know which way to walk back. He wouldn't leave her here. Would he? She didn't know very much about this guy. No. He wouldn't do that.

What the hell was she doing out here? She should have insisted on interviewing this guy back at his house.

Idiot.

Berger had lost all sense of time. He had no watch, and he hadn't been able to move because of the restraints. Throughout the day, he had dozed in and out of a twilight sleep. His body ached from lying still, and he felt as though he was losing his strength. He thought of people who developed bedsores, and wondered how long it took.

As he fell into another light sleep, he dreamed of Linda, lying naked on his bed. Linda, the horrendous cook, making him an inedible vegetarian lasagna. Linda smiling as he unwrapped the books she'd given him: Ferlinghetti, Burroughs, Kerouac. Six-foot Linda at the beach, stopping traffic in a dental-floss bikini. Linda slipping away, her fingers sliding out of his hand.

Now a skier, shushing through powdered snow on a bright, crisp day. Sun glaring sharply off the snow. The man smoothly cutting across the mountain, leaving a virgin trail. He skied closer, and Berger saw that the man was wearing a black ski mask. His smile was visible through the mouth's opening. The skier stopped next to Berger, spraying him with snow, then quickly threw a plastic bag over Berger's head. Berger's vision blurred, and the plastic clung to his nostrils, choking off his breath. He felt a burning pain in his chest, and tore at the plastic, as if he were clawing off his own skin.

He shouted as he awoke, dizzy, light-headed, and covered in perspiration. His chest heaved as he gasped the air that now seemed so precious. Berger worried that being in this place was a self-fulfilling prophecy: a cage for the insane, driving him to insanity.

The door to his cell opened, and in came Dorn, the public defender, with the guard from the day before. The guard, who wasn't smiling, began to unstrap him.

"I got a court order to take off the restraints," said Dorn, waving a blue-backed piece of paper.

Berger sat up unsteadily and rubbed his arms. The numbness reluctantly receded. "Thank you."

The guard left without looking at Berger.

Dorn took hold of Berger's shoulders and looked down at him squarely. He focused on Berger's eyes and spoke firmly. "I want you to see our own shrink. I think we have to use an insanity defense."

Berger wrenched out of his grip. "I'm not crazy." He was trying to sound more convincing than he was feeling.

"We're talking legal insanity. It's just a technical concept."

"That doesn't go on my record?"

"Well . . . yes, of course it does. But so does being guilty of blowing up a building and evading arrest."

"The FBI agent said she wanted me to see a shrink. Won't that do?"

Dorn started pacing and shook his head vigorously. "No, no, no. That's the government's expert. We need someone that we're paying. So we can, you know, guide them."

"Is that legal?"

"It's standard practice. Psychiatry is as much art as science."

"I don't have any money to hire a shrink."

Dorn sat on the edge of the bed beside Berger. "I'll get someone through the public defender's office. It might take a little while."

"How long?"

"A few weeks."

"Weeks? I'm not sitting here for weeks. Can't we see if the government guy's opinion is good for me?"

"We won't know that until it's too late. And I don't want you to talk to him anyway. If you tell him something incriminating, the damage is done and we're sunk. Then you'll be sitting here a lot longer than a few weeks."

Berger got up and crossed the room, away from Dorn. "I haven't done anything incriminating. And I already told her I'd talk to a government psychiatrist."

"I'm advising you not to do it."

"But I said—"

Dorn interrupted, like a teacher with no patience for a slow student. "Look. My job is to get you out of here and back into your own bed. If that's what you want, you should take my advice."

Berger reflected how he didn't have a bed anymore. In fact, he didn't have much of anything else either. No mother. No Linda. No Max. No job. Still, he couldn't see waiting around for weeks if he could clear this up right away with the government shrink. And who knew how the FBI would react if he stopped cooperating. He had faith that he'd be vindicated when everything got sorted out.

"I said I would see their psychiatrist and I will. Maybe it will help me."

"Their purpose isn't to help you. It's to string you up by your balls. You are not obligated just because you said you'd do it. I can say you were mentally incapacitated when you agreed."

"No. I wasn't incapacitated. I want to cooperate."

Dorn gestured broadly with his arms. "What's the point of having a lawyer if you aren't going to listen?"

Berger smiled. "You got the straps off me, didn't you?"

Jill had been sitting on the rock for almost a half hour, still afraid to move and risk agitating some desert predator. She shivered in the encroaching night air, and the surrounding animal noises seemed to be growing louder. As she crossed her hands across her chest and began rubbing the upper part of her arms, the tight blouse made her feel confined, trapped. This man's disappearance was not funny.

Finally, Durham rounded the corner on foot. A thoroughly delightful sight. She stood up and wanted to run toward him, then decided she shouldn't navigate this terrain alone.

"What happened to the horses?"

"Lady got spooked and took off. I chased her until Devil threw me off on a tight corner. It would've taken too long to go back, and I didn't want you to worry. I also didn't want you out here alone after dark."

"Thank you. Can we get back before dark?"

"It'll be close if we hustle. Just stay with me."

"Don't worry."

They walked about fifty feet when Durham held up his hand and stopped.

"What?" she asked.

"Shhhh."

They stood in silence. She didn't hear anything.

"What?" she whispered.

"It's a wolf."

"A wolf?"

"Shhh."

"You didn't mention wolves," she whispered.

"Get down on all fours," he said, doing that.

"What about the snakes and—"

"Get down and don't argue."

She got on all fours. The rough decaying granite, or whatever he'd called it, pitted into her hands and knees.

"Now move your right hand followed by your right knee, and then vice versa. Most people move their right hand and left knee. Don't do that."

It was counterintuitive, but Jill wasn't about to argue. She followed him. They moved a few yards when Durham stopped. So did Jill.

"Stay down and turn around in place," he whispered.

"What?"

"Dammit, just do it."

Jill started a clockwise circle on all fours.

"All the way around."

When she came back to the original direction, she saw Durham's boots in front of her face. He was standing up.

"Okay," he said in a normal voice. "You can get up now."

"What?"

He held out his hand and helped her up. She brushed off her palms against her pant legs. "Is it safe?"

"Oh yeah. We don't have any wolves around here."

"What!" she sputtered. "If this is your idea of a joke, I don't find it the least bit amusing."

"It's not a joke."

He whistled using his fingers in his mouth, and the horses came around the corner. He patted Devil on the neck.

"You're sick," she said, spitting the words at him.

"No, ma'am. You said you wanted to learn about mind control. We just had a lesson. You see, mind control is all about disrupting someone's information-processing system, then reprogramming them. The cults destroy a person's self-confidence, then regress them to a childlike state. Where they're subordinate to authority. That's when the charismatic leader, together with peer pressure, installs a new set of beliefs. It mimics the parent-child relationship."

"What you did was despicable. And degrading."

"Correct. I put you in a foreign environment, and made you feel vulnerable. You were cut off from everything familiar. Then I told you to do things you'd never do under other circumstances, and you followed me because I acted like I had the answers. Most people think they'd never be susceptible to a cult, and that's just not true. When you're in a controlled surrounding, like a camp in the country, you're away from your normal life and you feel unsettled.

Which intensifies your need to fit into a group. That's when the cult invites you to be like them, and you do it because you want to feel safe."

He helped her back onto Lady, and she felt the security of being on the horse. While still humiliated, she realized he was right. She would have never thought herself susceptible to something like this.

Durham climbed on Devil and they started back. The horses' hooves clip-clopped rhythmically. He spun around to face her while he rode, and explained how cults talk in a jargon that only the members understand. So the recruit feels like they have to copy group behavior and lingo to be accepted. He described another technique called "love bombing," where the group tells recruits how wonderful they are when they conform to the cult beliefs.

"I've heard they sometimes do things to change your physical state," said Jill.

"Yes. Group singing or monotonous chanting. Keeping you awake for a long time so you're physically and mentally fatigued. Radical changes in diet. These things are incredibly powerful. A buddy of mine, who has a Ph.D. in psychology, went to a cult weekend so he could write an article on the experience. He came out at the end of the weekend, but just barely, and had to check himself into a mental hospital for three days just to deal with what they did to his head."

An hour earlier Jill would have scoffed at that. "What about my witness, who doesn't remember anything?"

"The only thing that could do that is hypnosis."

"Hypnosis is that powerful?"

"With the right subject, people can have surgery using hypnosis instead of anesthesia. It's like soldiers who don't feel pain in the heat of battle."

"Do cults use hypnosis?"

"They don't use formal hypnosis, although some cults create a hypnotic state just by demanding intense concentration. The problem is that hypnosis can't force someone to kill others or themselves. It can't override deep moral codes or the instinct to survive."

"What if it was supplemented with drugs?"

"There's nothing we know of that could do it."

"So it probably isn't hypnosis. Do his symptoms suggest anything else?"

"He sounds real similar to people coming out of cults. Those folks can get false and flashback memories. Fear of losing control or dying. Voices in their heads. On the other hand, if he's telling the truth about not remembering anything, that doesn't fit. It's a puzzler. I'd have to interview him before I could give you a more educated guess."

"Could we learn anything by having him hypnotized?"

"If he's a good enough subject, we might be able to recover some of the missing memories."

They arrived at the stable, and he helped her off the horse. His arms felt strong and firm around her. Was that the aftermath of her disorienting experience? She looked at him, and he winked at her. Jill wondered if his charisma was similar to that of the cult leaders he dogged.

They walked back to the house, as twilight draped across the hills. Her legs were sore and bowed, and she felt filthy.

"Plop down there and I'll get you some more well water," he said, waving her toward the overstuffed chair. When he saw her hesitation, he said, "I get dust on the furniture all the time. You can shower and change later."

She sank back into the soft chair. When he returned with a glass of water, she gulped it down and felt the cold liquid sliding toward her stomach.

"Have you had much experience with hypnosis?" asked Jill.

He went to the bookshelf and handed her a book he had written on the subject. His picture on the back cover smiled at her, and she felt his intensity even in the photograph. He sat down on the couch, and their knees touched again. She left hers there for a moment before shifting her legs to the other side.

"I'd need to get on this right away," she said.

"I can be in Los Angeles tomorrow."

She studied him for a few moments before speaking. "All right. Let's try it."

CHAPTER 28

Berger sat on the edge of the bed in his cell, swinging his feet. The relative freedom of being unstrapped had invigorated him, and for the first time he'd slept through the night. He had also regained enough sense of time to know it was late morning, and he looked forward to meeting the psychiatrist.

At the sound of approaching footsteps, he went to the small portal in his door and saw Jill approach with a man who looked like a graying Marlboro cowboy. When they came into his cell, she introduced him as Dr. Durham. He had a pleasant smile, and his wiry frame radiated a coiled energy on the verge of springing loose.

"Mr. Berger," said Durham, "I've arranged for an office where we can visit. Let's get you out of this animal cage."

Berger wasted no time leaving the cell. The guard's eyes never left him as they went down several corridors to an unmarked room. Jill left them, and Durham sat down behind a desk. He motioned for Berger to sit in a large brown easy chair. The soft cushions seemed to embrace him, and he leaned back his head to savor the cool, smooth fabric against his neck.

"Would you like something to drink?" asked Durham.

"Yes. Anything besides water."

Durham asked the guard to bring in two Dr Peppers. Being treated like a waiter seemed to annoy the guard, which delighted Berger. Berger opened the can with a noisy pop, then poured a long, bubbly sip down his throat. He could already feel the sugar and caffeine coursing through his system.

Durham switched on a tape recorder and explained that he'd been hired by the FBI, and that everything Berger said was admissible in court. Berger said he understood.

"Are you okay proceeding on this basis?" asked Durham.

"Yes."

"All right. First off, let me say that I believe the story you told Agent Landis. And I believe that you're confused about what's happening to you. I thought maybe we'd try to figure things out together."

"You really believe me? Or are you just trying to get me off guard?"

"That's a fair question. So here's a straight answer. I do believe you, but I'd be lying if I didn't say that I was hanging on to some skepticism."

"At least you're honest."

Durham leaned back and clunked his booted feet on top of the desk. "So tell me what's going on."

Berger relayed the recent events, from Linda's disappearance, to his memories of the chess tournament. The explosions at work and his house. His visit to Smitty's trailer. And his mother's death. He talked about his fragmented memories and the voices. About beating the walls at the EXC site, and attacking the man at the airport.

Durham listened intently, then said, "Mr. Berger, I think we could get some more information if you were hypnotized. How'd you feel about that?"

"I don't know. I've never done it."

"Actually, you have. You just don't know it. When you're on the highway, and suddenly you've gone ten miles and don't remember it. When you're about to fall asleep, and you have those sort of half dreams. Those are forms of hypnosis. It's just an altered state of consciousness, with very focused attention. When someone hypnotizes you, they guide your focus into parts of the mind that you don't normally access."

"I'm not sure I want to be out of control."

"You don't lose control. See, I can't really hypnotize anybody. All I can do is help people hypnotize themselves. You'll be fully conscious of everything that's happening."

"Okay, so I'm conscious. But would I be in control?"

"You won't do anything you don't want to. I leave the 'clucking like a chicken' crap to nightclub hypnotists."

"What if we start and I don't like it?"

"Then you say so, and we stop."

Berger wasn't sure he wanted someone probing around in his mind. He wasn't sure whether it was the invasion of privacy, or the worry of what might be buried. On the other hand, he hated stumbling around like some miswired robot. And he hated being locked up even more than that.

"Well . . . I guess."

"Remember, I can't do this unless you want to. Or more accurately, unless you're willing to hypnotize yourself. If you fight me, even in your subconscious, it won't happen. And I may not be able to hypnotize you even if you want it. Not everybody is a good subject."

"All right. I'll try."

Durham told Berger to settle comfortably in the chair. He told him to visualize himself on a slowly descending escalator, and to grow more relaxed as he went down. Then Durham suggested that his eyelids were too heavy to keep open. Berger felt them droop. He was awake and conscious, although his body felt heavy, and he had no desire to move. Now Durham's calm voice was offering pleasant suggestions of lying in a boat in a quiet pond, watching an azure sky and fluffy white clouds. Birds were singing, and water gently lapped against the boat. A warm breeze blew across his face. Berger let his mind flow with the images, and felt himself drifting in a pleasant, tingly numbness.

After several minutes, Durham suggested that Berger couldn't raise his arm. Berger thought that was silly until he tried to move his arm and couldn't. Sonofabitch. That was weird. He wasn't panicked; just oddly amused.

Durham gently worked through a series of general questions. What were his favorite foods? His favorite colors? Where did he like to travel? What education did he have?

Then he moved to the hotter topics.

"Mr. Berger, may I call you John?"

"Sure."

"John, did you work at a company called EXC?"

"Yes."

"I want you to relax and go deeper to sleep. In a moment, I'm going to show you something. I want you to tell me whatever comes into your mind about it, but I don't want you to get up or act anything out. In fact, you'll find your body is too heavy to move. You can try to get up if you want, but you'll find you can't."

Berger didn't even feel like trying.

"Relax deeper now. John, when you open your eyes, but not before, you're going to see a large sign with the letters 'EXC' on it. Ready? Open your eyes and tell me what you feel."

Berger opened his eyes and saw a six-foot, red-lettered EXC sign. His impulse was to vault out of the chair and annihilate Durham. Yet he couldn't budge. Straining against his leaden body, his muscles tensed as he shouted, "You fucking bastard! You killed her, you sonofabitch! I'll tear your eyes out of your head. I'll . . ."

Berger's words jumbled into heavy sobs.

Durham spoke calmly. "John, the sign's gone now. You're relaxed again. Everything's fine. You're here with me. Close your eyes and go deeper to sleep."

Berger's body complied without any conscious thought.

"When did you last see an EXC sign?"

"At the airport. An Excess Baggage sign."

"And before that?"

"At the company, after it was blown up."

"And before that?"

"At . . . at . . . I can't remember. I know it was something."

"John, go deeper to sleep."

Berger felt his body slump in the chair, and his head slid onto his shoulder.

"Deeper still. I want to take you back in your memory. Something happened with EXC that upset you. Can you remember what it was?"

Berger spoke in such relaxed tones that his words slurred. "I can't tell you. It's . . . locked."

"Locked?"

"Yes. It's locked."

"Where's the key?"

"I don't have it."

"Who does?"

A long pause.

"I don't know."

Jill was pacing the hallway when Durham came out. "Well?"

"Something's been done to this man," said Durham. "I don't know what. It seems like a posthypnotic suggestion, but that should have been accessible through hypnosis. Especially since he's a very good subject. He says he can't remember anything because the memory is 'locked.'"

"Locked? What does that mean?"

"I don't know. Whatever's buried in there is as dangerous as a land mine. It could go off at any time and do some serious damage to him or others."

She began clicking her ballpoint pen. "So we should keep him here?"

"Definitely. But I have an idea."

"What?"

"Whatever is supposed to trigger him is connected to EXC. You said the explosives were in his desk. If you made a mock-up of his office and desk, and put a dummy of the explosive in it, we could send him there and see if that unlocks the memory."

Jill stopped clicking the pen and scrunched her forehead in surprise. "That's bizarre."

"It's the best I've got. I'm afraid this one is off the charts."

"All right. Let me see if I can find the money for it. Our Washington lab sometimes duplicates rooms to practice hostage rescue."

"I've got a buddy at Warner Brothers who'd probably

donate some props and a soundstage. Can you find out what Berger's work area looked like?"

"I'll get right on it."

Late that night, a clanking noise startled Berger in his cell. He reflexively tried to sit up, and realized he'd been strapped down again. They must have done it while he was sleeping. All the muscles in his body tightened. Court orders obviously didn't mean shit to that sadistic guard.

He craned his neck toward the noise and saw a large man. Panic ripped through him as the man pressed a knife against Berger's throat. He felt the cold blade draw a warm trickle of blood across his neck.

A deep voice blasted foul breath into Berger's face. "Move and you're dead."

The man took the knife away from Berger's throat and lumbered around the bed. Berger felt the blood seeping down the sides of his neck as he strained his eyes to see in the low light. All he could make out was a hulking figure. The man laid his knife on the metal bed frame with a metallic clunk, then began to unzip Berger's pants. Berger had the absurd worry that his penis might catch in the zipper.

When he was fully exposed, his body began to shudder in the cold. The man grabbed hold of his exposed member, stretching it toward the ceiling, then raised the knife to slash.

Berger screamed. A primal howl from the depths of his body cavity, scraping his chest and lungs as it escaped.

The guard banged on his cell and shined in a flashlight.

"What the fuck is the matter with you?"

Berger sat up.

Sat up? He wasn't tied to the bed, and his pants were

zipped. He looked around, and saw he was alone in the cell.

"Sorry," he said to the guard. His voice was raspy. "Bad dream."

The guard grumbled as he left. Berger lay back on the bed.

He hoped that when his mind finally went, he wouldn't be conscious of it.

CHAPTER 29

Combs handed the files to Baxter. "Here's the top ten winners."

"I thought we only needed six."

"I want a margin for error. Suppose a couple of them take unexpected vacations. Or have a gun club meeting at their house when we show up? We can always lose the extras down the road."

"Got it."

"How's Blue Team doing with the airports?"

"Surveillance is twenty-four/seven. We'll have full schedules and routines tomorrow, and they'll update them every three hours."

"And the equipment?"

"Fertilizer and diesel oil are easy. We're getting them from unrelated sources and shipping everything to the ranch from scattered drop points. Dynamite is trickier, since the sales are regulated. We're exploring theft or buying from an accommodating user. For the big cities, we've got C-4 vests."

"And the drugs?"

"We won't order them until the last minute."

When Baxter left, Combs sat alone. He replayed the plan in his mind yet again. There were no loose ends. Everything was covered and backed up.

After the show, Combs knew he'd have more offers for his wares than he dared imagine. And the seventy million for this job wouldn't even be the down payment for the next one. He found himself smiling at the prospects, then checked himself. Too soon to be dreaming about the future. And besides. Maybe he'd chuck all those opportunities when the time came. Move to a nonextraditing country and roll around in the money with some big-titted women. Those were decisions to make when he had the cash in his pocket.

As he started to get up, the one loose end tugged at his sleeve. Berger. A gnat flitting around his head, avoiding the swats. A gnat that somebody might figure out how to use.

Time to end that game.

The skinny runner arrived at Jill's cubicle with a stack of files so tall that his eyes were almost covered. He laid them on her desk with an "Uumph."

"What's this?" she asked.

He used his sleeve to wipe off beads of perspiration that speckled his forehead. "The army records you wanted. I've got three more trips."

When he finished, Jill had a wall of paper around the perimeter of her desk, blocking her view. She pulled a file from the middle of a stack, just to avoid the depressing feeling of having to start at the top.

Six hours later, it was dark outside and she was the only one left on the fourteenth floor of the Federal Building.

She had read over a hundred files, and had found three people whose army records were missing periods from seven to fourteen months.

She walked down the hall and made herself another cup of coffee. The caffeine quickly kicked in, yet her vision was still blurry. At least her eyes opened wider. She dug into the next file and began checking the dates.

By four in the morning, her pace had accelerated and she'd made it through all but the last twelve inches of paper. She told herself she was moving faster because she was becoming more efficient, not because she was skipping material. She now had six people with gaps in their service.

Her will to continue was strong, but her eyes were raw and blitzed. She stood up and felt light-headed. Although the lure of her bed was overwhelming, she didn't trust herself to drive home in this condition. So she went into the ladies' room and lay down on the couch. It was about a foot too short, and the air-conditioning blasted cold air directly on her face.

She was asleep in less than a minute.

Jill's neck was stiff from having slept at an odd angle. She rubbed it with the palm of her hand as she looked in the ladies' room mirror at her wrinkled clothes and disheveled hair. She really ought to go home and freshen up, she thought. On the other hand, she wanted to know where the hell these six guys had been during the gaps in their service.

She compromised by washing her face and brushing her hair. A few people seemed to look at her oddly as she walked to her desk. She sat down with a strong cup of coffee, took out her list, and started making calls.

The first man was dead. The second, Charles Shaw, lived in Idaho. She dialed his number.

"Mr. Shaw?"

"Yeah."

"Jill Landis, FBI."

"Yeah?"

"Were you in the G Company, 2nd Battalion, 16th Infantry?"

"Yeah."

"We're doing a routine personnel check and found that our records are a bit sketchy for an eleven-month period of your service." She read off the dates. "Can you help fill in the blanks?"

"What do you mean?"

"What were your activities during those eleven months?"

"I don't remember."

"You don't remember?"

"I don't remember." He hung up.

Jill hated being hung up on. Maybe it was a junior high school thing. She slammed the phone down in response, waited until she calmed down, then called Shaw back. No one answered.

The next man had moved to Canada and left no forwarding information. The third, Julian Tibbs of Billings, Montana, sounded very nervous.

"Why are you asking?"

"It's just routine."

"Bullshit. Nobody does routine checks on stuff like this. What's it about?"

"We do periodic reviews—"

"If you want to talk to me, get a court order." He hung up. Jill slammed the phone down again. She decided not to waste time calling this bastard back. But she put a black check next to his name, thinking she might take him up on that court order.

Next was a Robert Kelly in Boston.

"Mr. Kelly?"

"Yes. How can I help you?" He spoke with a thick Boston accent, and Jill imagined a red-haired, ruddy-faced Irishman, cuddling a Guinness.

"Jill Landis of the FBI. We're doing a routine review of your military service and found a twelve-month period with no record of your activities. I was wondering if you could help me fill in the gap."

There was a long silence, and then an audible exhale. "I always figured I'd get this call."

CHAPTER 30

Within two minutes after her call to Robert Kelly, Jill briefed Davidson on the Mirage project that Kelly had described. Davidson seemed both impressed and skeptical, and said he'd research this Mirage thing right away. An hour and a half later, she was on an airplane to Boston.

She managed to sleep fitfully on the flight, and wondered if that made her even more groggy when she arrived at 9:00 P.M. East Coast time. Once she stepped outside, the debate was academic because the twenty-degree air woke her up fully. She pulled her light Los Angeles coat around her and climbed into a taxi that took her from Logan Airport over Storrow Drive.

They drove along the Charles River, which coldly reflected the lights of buildings that lined it. After crossing Memorial Bridge into Harvard Square, she rolled down the window. An icy breeze stung her face, and with it came the amplified sound of Peruvian street singers and shouts of men hawking newspapers to help the homeless. The wrought iron gates that guarded Harvard's reputation looked down disdainfully on the raucous activities.

They continued up Massachusetts Avenue, or "Mass Ave" as Kelly had called it, past an old church graveyard and a park, which he'd called a "commons." Finally, they turned onto Beech, a residential street lined with older houses and apartments.

Kelly lived in a three-story Victorian, with a round turret and gingerbread filigree. The outside stairs, which appeared to have been added when the home was converted to apartments, swayed and creaked as Jill climbed them. She knocked on the door, curious to see if her image of Kelly as a ruddy-faced redhead was correct. When he opened the door, she saw an almond-skinned African-American in his late twenties. He was slightly taller than Jill, so she pegged him at about five eight. He had kind, doe eyes, and closely trimmed hair, parted with a small ridge cut down one side of his scalp. His clothes were neatly pressed, and he smelled of Ivory soap.

Kelly's apartment was a single room with a kitchen. The walls had no decoration other than quarter-inch-thick peeling paint. Jill sat on a frayed blue couch that apparently converted to a bed, since she didn't see one elsewhere. When Kelly sat on a metal folding chair, his pant legs hiked up and she saw that his left leg was made of aluminum. She guessed he still had his knee, since his walk appeared normal.

"Auto accident," he said.

"Excuse me?"

"I'm used to people looking at my leg, so I satisfy their curiosity right away."

"I didn't mean to stare."

"You didn't. A truck backed over me. And yes, the leg sometimes still itches, even though it isn't there."

Jill looked down and pawed through her purse. "I'm sorry."

"No, no. It was a gift from God. I'd never appreciated the blessings in my life until then. Are you a religious person?"

She opened up her notepad. "Not really."

"Religion gives us a way to take pleasure in the things we have, rather than worry about what we lack. God has showered me with gifts. I'm alive. I can talk. I can see the sunshine and feel the wind."

"Mr. Kelly, I'm sorry, but I'm on a limited schedule. Do you mind if I record our conversation?" She laid a small tape recorder on the chipped coffee table.

"I used to always be in a hurry myself."

Jill started with the preliminaries of his background, then worked toward their conversation on the phone.

"Now about the army," she began.

"Are you hungry? Would you like some coffee?"

"No. I'm fine."

"Tea? Soft drink?"

"The army, Mr. Kelly?"

"Yes." He looked around the room, as if he were being watched. Then he leaned forward and spoke quietly. "As I told you, the project was code-named Mirage. I was called Private Green. I'm a biochemist—I had a master's at the time—and my work was pretty limited. I had no idea what we were doing until the end. Delta, one of the section directors, asked me to shred some documents. I wasn't supposed to read them, but the material caught my eye and I just couldn't help it. I was really shocked by what I saw."

Kelly appeared to be fighting tears. "I swear I had no idea what they were doing until then. I would have come forward sooner, but I thought this was all shut down and forgotten."

"That's understandable."

"Thank you." He tensed his lips and then continued. "All I did was some biochemistry. I had no idea why, I swear. They had me altering Ketamine by adding a nitrogen atom. 'Neo-Ketamine' they called it. Do you know what Ketamine is?"

"No."

Kelly walked over to the window and peered outside. Then he adjusted the curtain to cover the glass before continuing. "Ketamine was developed as an anesthetic. It looked like a breakthrough, because it didn't depress the cardiovascular or breathing functions. Then they found that it caused hallucinations while wearing off. So the medical community stopped using it. Now it's a street drug, called Greens or Special K. It's used by people who *want* to hallucinate."

"And Neo-Ketamine?"

"Neo-Ketamine takes the effects to a whole other level. The documents I shredded said that it was an extremely powerful way to alter consciousness. The Mirage project was using it to control people."

"How?"

He shook his head. "I swear. I never knew what they were doing until the end."

"I believe you."

"I wouldn't have done it if I had."

"I know. How did they use Neo-Ketamine?"

Kelly surveyed the room once more, as if to make sure no one had sneaked in. "They'd put someone with a group of stooges to create peer pressure, similar to the way cults operate. For example, if they wanted to know your secrets, they'd put you in a group of people who were supposedly spilling their guts. The twist was that they enhanced the experience with Neo-Ketamine, which made the suggestions virtually irresistible."

Kelly went on to explain how they were able to induce almost any kind of response. He told her that they took a government agent and pumped him for highly classified information.

"The Director once bragged he could even switch someone's sexual preference."

"Who was the Director?" asked Jill.

"No one used their real names. He was simply called 'Director.'"

"What did he look like?"

"About six feet. In his early forties. Bald head. Beard. I don't remember much about him. I only saw him once or twice."

"Have you ever seen this man?" She showed him an Army picture of Tom Curtis, the man killed in Bert's gas station explosion.

"Yes. He was there. I don't remember his code name. He worked closely with the Director."

Jill pushed the tape recorder closer to Kelly. "Did you ever see any of the mind control sessions?"

"No. Just a lot of test tubes. I only knew about the sessions because of what I read. I swear."

"Was there a way to retrieve what had been programmed into the subjects?"

"I'm not aware of any. They were obviously worried about that. No one wanted the subjects deprogrammed by an enemy."

"Hypnosis couldn't get it out?"

"No. They had a way of . . . what did they call it . . . 'locking' the memories."

Jill realized, with a chill, that "locked" was the word Berger had used to describe his memories. "What about using drugs to deprogram a subject?"

"None that I'm aware of."

"What about a mock-up of the situation they were programmed to encounter?"

"Definitely not that. That sent them straight into the psychosis."

Jill tried not to show any reaction to Kelly's statement as

she made a note to call off the mock-up of Berger's desk. "What do you mean 'the psychosis'?"

"That was the major flaw of the program. Putting aside the moral aspects, of course. The problem was that about eighty percent of the subjects had mental breakdowns within a few weeks after being programmed."

"What kind of breakdowns?"

Kelly described how the subjects became catatonic, lost control of their bowels, and couldn't even feed themselves. "If the idea was to turn a spy and leave him in the field, it wouldn't be much help if he became a vegetable within a week or so. We were working on an antidote to the psychosis, but to my knowledge, we didn't find one."

"You said 'we'? You were working on this?"

Kelly shifted in his seat and looked away from Jill. "They told me it was a separate program. That the Army was experimenting with ways to help people who had breakdowns in the line of duty. I didn't know Mirage was actually causing these breakdowns until I read those documents."

Jill saw his eyes pleading for absolution. "They took advantage of you, Mr. Kelly. By talking to me, you're helping to right that wrong."

He nodded, eyes moist.

"What are the symptoms leading up to the breakdown?" asked Jill, looking at her notes to give him privacy.

It took him a moment to answer. "Hallucinations. Hearing voices. Increasing paranoia. Flashbacks of the programming, usually in disjointed snatches of memory."

Jill realized that Berger was experiencing all of these. "If the subjects showed these symptoms, did they always end up catatonic?"

"Yes." Kelly studied her intensely. "You've got someone in that state, huh?"

"I'm not at liberty to discuss our investigation."

"I understand. From what I saw, when they start the hallucinations, they've only got a few weeks left. And they slide pretty fast. If it helps you, some of the subjects responded to amitriptyline hydrochloride, which is a common prescription drug known as Elavil. Elavil can cause hallucinations in normal people, but it produced a paradoxical effect in some of these subjects and masked their symptoms. Unfortunately, it only bought a few more days of coherence. If your person didn't start hallucinating within a few days after the programming, they should be okay. If they did, you've got two or three weeks, tops."

"I haven't said there was such a person."

"I'm afraid your body language did. Don't worry. I wouldn't be telling you this if I meant you any harm. And you certainly know I can keep a secret. I've been sitting on this one for three years."

Jill felt a pang for Berger. Now she was convinced he'd been manipulated in whatever this scheme was. The plan was obviously for him to have blown himself up like the Orlando guy. That would have neatly solved the problem of "the psychosis." On the other hand, in a week or two, it wouldn't make much difference whether Berger was alive or not. He deserved to know what was happening to him. If he'd be able to understand it by the time she got back.

Jill continued the interview past 1:00 A.M. Kelly insisted on driving her to the Holiday Inn on Mass Ave. When they arrived, he came around to open her door.

Shivering in her light outfit, she said, "Mr. Kelly, I appreciate your coming forward like this."

"If I think of anything else, I'll call you." He got back in the car.

"Any time of the day or night."

Kelly started to roll up his window. "Remember what I

said earlier. Take time to appreciate the blessings in your life."

"At the moment, you're one of them."

Jill's room smelled like stale cigarette smoke. She pulled off her clothes and almost fell asleep standing up in the shower. Afer getting in bed, she reluctantly asked for a 7:00 A.M. wake-up call and turned out the lights.

Kelly's words reverberated in her head. Appreciate your blessings. Like the ability to think and reason, which was slipping away from Berger faster than he could comprehend. She imagined him as a deaf child, playing on a railroad track. Unable to hear the approaching train.

CHAPTER 31

Jill swiped her credit card through the airplane phone and called Durham, the cult specialist.

"What do you know about Elavil?" she asked.

"I'm afraid I'm a Ph.D. in psychology, not a medical doctor. I've heard of Elavil, but I don't know more than the name. I can call a friend who's a psychiatrist."

"Don't bother." If Berger was a goner in a few days, she figured Elavil couldn't hurt him. It'd be faster to get a Los Angeles shrink to see him and write a prescription on the spot.

"Why do you ask?"

"I can't really say," she replied.

"Fair enough. By the way, I'm going to be in Los Angeles in the next day or so. Would you like to have dinner?"

She shifted in the airline seat. "Uh, you mean to discuss Mr. Berger?"

"No. I mean I'm hitting on you."

Her voice fluttered. "Oh, well," *cough,* "I don't really think I'd have the time . . ."

He chuckled. "No pressure. Just a thought. I'll call you when I'm there and we'll leave it loose."

She hung up and reflected on that last turn of events. She had to admit that she'd found Durham attractive, though a social life was the furthest thing from her mind right now. And it wasn't like she had any spare time. On the other hand . . .

Whatever. She'd deal with it later.

Jill called her friend Dave Greenberg, a forensic shrink. After explaining the situation cryptically, since she was on a radio phone and worried about security, she asked, "Can you meet with him before I land?"

"When's that?"

"Two hours."

He laughed. "Oh, sure, just let me cancel some of my insecure patients. They love rejection."

"Dave, I need this."

"That bad, huh?"

"You have no idea."

He let out an exasperated sigh. "How soon can you get him here?"

"Well . . . see . . . I kinda need you to go to him. He's a little locked up. In County."

Jill held the phone away from her ear for the explosion. When he finished, she said, "I'll owe you one."

"You already owe me five or six."

Jill sat in a patient interview room at County, stifling a yawn. Across from her was Berger, with his public defender, and Dave Greenberg, the psychiatrist. Two nights of minimal sleep, not to mention airline food, were taking their toll. Her eyes were dry and raw, and her hair felt like little crawly things were creeping through her scalp.

In a hoarse voice, she related what Kelly had told her about the mental breakdown, and the possibility that Elavil could help.

Berger looked at Jill with a half smile and said, "At least you know I'm not a liar. Even if I'm about to become the psycho you suspected."

She found his self-effacement so charming that she almost returned the smile. Instead, she looked down at the floor.

"Can this Elavil do me any harm?" Berger asked.

Greenberg answered. "Possible side effects are orthostatic hypotension, paresthesia, and disorientation."

"In English, Dave," said Jill.

"You could get dizzy or faint if you stand up too fast. Or you might have tingling in your nerves. Or a feeling of confusion."

"Sounds like an improvement from where I am now."

Dorn got up and paced. "I don't think Mr. Berger has the mental capacity to make a decision like this. If you want to give him medication, you'll need a court order."

Berger grabbed Dorn's forearm. "My mental capacity is working just fine, and I understand the decision perfectly. I'm on my way to becoming a veggie in the next few days if I do nothing. If I take these pills, it might add a little time. So I want the Elavil."

Dorn waved his arms in exasperation. "You haven't listened to one thing I've advised you to do. I don't see any reason to continue as your lawyer."

"Thanks for your help, Mr. Dorn. Have them send someone else from your office. And based on what Agent Landis just told us, I suggest they hurry."

Dorn stared at him, blinking. "Shit. There isn't any time to get a new lawyer without prejudicing your case."

He sat down again, with an expression that looked like he'd stuck his head in a dark cloud.

"Because of the critical timing," said Greenberg, "I took the liberty of picking up some Elavil on the way here." He handed Berger a bottle of tiny red pills and a glass of water.

"How long have I got?" he asked as he swallowed one.

"I'm afraid nobody knows," answered Jill. "We're getting you out of here and into a safe house tomorrow afternoon. You're a victim, not a criminal."

"Thank you," he said softly. His eyes glistened and he took hold of her hand. She found his touch warm, and she squeezed his hand before she realized what she was doing. He locked eyes with her, and she felt a connection surge between them. In that instant, she understood his struggle.

And her troubles seemed trivial.

Dorn walked several blocks away from the jail, intentionally zigzagging his path. He continually glanced over his shoulder to see if anyone followed. When he felt certain he was clear, he stopped at a pay phone in front of a red and yellow storefront that promised *Money Wired Anywhere in the World!*

"Yeah?" answered a voice on the other end.

"They're giving him something called Elavil. I tried to stop it, but this asshole's stubborn."

Combs hissed through the phone. "That could make him lucid enough to cause some trouble. How the hell'd they know about Elavil?"

"I couldn't find out without looking suspicious. The FBI dragon lady is moving him to a safe house tomorrow."

"Where?"

"I couldn't get that either."

"Shit. What time are they moving him?"

"In the afternoon."

CHAPTER 32

Jill sat in her office, trying to sort out the pieces. Her brain was numb from lack of sleep, yet she had to get this together. And quickly, if Berger was to be part of it.

Kelly was credible, and Berger's symptoms matched his description of the Mirage subjects. Men connected with this project had hunted Berger at Bert's gas station, which made the link between Berger and Mirage a virtual certainty. But why hunt him? Were they afraid he knew something that could be pried out? She certainly hoped so.

In the bigger picture, what was all this about? Terrorism for hire was the only logical answer. Someone involved in the Mirage project had decided to profit from the knowledge. According to Kelly, only the Director had the full picture. He was most likely the guy, although one of his close lieutenants could have figured it out.

Her concentration was punctured by a tap on the shoulder. She jumped several inches off her seat before realizing it was Larkin, a paunchy agent with bug eyes.

"Sorry. Didn't mean to startle you. Lunch today?"

Her heart was still tap-dancing. "Not today. Thanks."

"You hear about the big one that's coming?"

"What? Another earthquake?"

"No. The rumor that Davidson's working on the biggest terrorist plot in U.S. history. It's been buzzing around for the last few days."

"I haven't heard anything." That sonofabitch Davidson. How could he hold back something like this?

Larkin shrugged. "Want me to get you a sandwich?"

Jill waved him off and called Davidson. Before she could say anything, he barked, "Landis, there's no record of this Mirage project ever existing."

"I'm not surprised, based on what it was." She explained in detail what Kelly had told her.

"Pretty bizarre. And far-fetched. You sure you're not being had?"

She cradled the phone between her ear and shoulder, then began drawing circles on a notepad. "I don't think so. Somebody's in the terrorist-programming business. It's the perfect crime. The perps blow themselves and all the evidence to kingdom come. And to top it off, they're normal citizens who can't be connected to the source."

Davidson "Mmmm'd."

Jill got up and paced away from her desk. "If the Mirage records existed, where would they be?"

"There's a secret Military Archives in Salt Lake City. I already tried to get access, but no dice. They want a court order before they'll even tell me if they have anything, and that'll take a couple of days."

She paced to the end of the phone line and it almost jerked the receiver out of her hand. "We don't have much time. Whoever's behind this is worried that Berger has something useful in him, so we have to assume he does. And we've only got a few days before he loses his mental faculties and it's gone. Isn't there any way to speed up the courts?"

"I'm already trying."

Jill shifted the phone to her other ear and hesitated before asking the next question. "Is it true that you're looking into the possibility of a large-scale terrorist attack?"

A long silence, then a controlled tone in his answer. "Why do you ask?"

"I heard a rumor. Don't you see that this could be connected? Berger and the Orlando guy could have been free home trials for this new product. Is it true?"

A beat. "Yes. It's true."

Maybe it was her exhaustion. Maybe it was her frustration. Maybe it was even her sympathy for Berger. Whatever it was, both barrels unloaded on Davidson. "How dare you keep something like that from me. I'm busting my ass to bring this case home, and you leave me hanging in the dark? We have so little time that we can't afford to waste even a minute of it. I don't know what— Dammit. When you decide to play it straight, call me back. Otherwise, go work this case yourself."

She slammed down the phone. The rush of anger flared like a blowtorch against her temples, and her chest heaved with gasping breaths. She paced away from her cubicle, like a bull scraping his feet before goring the matador. It took several trips around the floor before the tide of emotions retreated, leaving only the empty feeling that she'd just blown her FBI career.

Later that night, Jill stood in her kitchen. Anxiety about the confrontation with Davidson still hung in the air. She was trying to dilute the gloom by cooking, and had decided to make a Caesar salad dressing. Her emotions were souring the recipe.

She absentmindedly mashed anchovy paste into olive oil and lemon juice. Her temper hadn't gotten the better of her in years, and Davidson wasn't the place she should have let it explode.

Jill read the next part of the recipe and reached for the garlic. That was when it hit her.

Ingredients. Mixtures. Maybe . . .

She looked at her watch. Almost 9:00 P.M. Almost midnight on the East Coast. This was too important to worry about ceremony. She grabbed the phone.

"Mr. Kelly? Did I wake you?"

"No." He chuckled sleepily. "I had to get up to answer the phone."

"I'm very sorry. You said you made Neo-Ketamine for this Mirage project?"

"Yes."

"How difficult is that to do?"

"It's not simple. You need a research cyclotron that can add a radioactive form of nitrogen to the molecule."

"Are cyclotrons common?"

"You can find regular cyclotrons at most medical research centers. Ours had to be altered to accommodate radioactive nitrogen isotopes, and I doubt there are a lot of places with the equipment and expertise to do that."

"Would you need some kind of license?"

"Anything producing radioactive energy is controlled by the government. The old Atomic Energy Commission, as I recall."

Jill hung up the phone, riding the crest of possibilities. Whoever was behind this would need Neo-Ketamine. Maybe she could trace everyone with these machines and work up the food chain.

She thought about calling Davidson, but didn't have his home phone number. And waking him up at midnight didn't exactly seem like a smart move under the present circumstances.

At least she'd have something in her defense tomorrow morning.

If she still had a job.

CHAPTER 33

"I'm sorry," said Baxter. He laid the obituary clipping on the table, then stepped back as if it were capable of attacking him.

"Just go." Combs was well into a bottle of Maker's Mark whiskey.

Baxter nodded, then closed the door behind him.

Alone, Combs allowed his eyes to moisten. There was something final about losing your father. Something that made you unmistakably an adult. Even though he hadn't depended on Harold for years. Even though he hardly ever talked to him. It was different to know that he couldn't.

Ever.

Combs snorted back a sob, which came out louder than he would have liked.

He thought about calling his mother. Not that she'd care much about Harold, who she'd divorced twenty years ago. Nah. Forget it. She hadn't spoken to Combs in years. Besides, it could be risky right now. Who knows who might be watching or listening in?

Maybe later.

He took another shot of whiskey, which seared its way down his numbing throat.

Combs thought about the bastards in the County Recorder's office. The ones who crushed Harold with their fucking "restructuring." Why, Dad? Why'd you just sit there and take the shit they fed you?

And the final memory of Harold, broken and hobbling, stepping out of Maxine's diner into the heavy rain.

Combs allowed himself one more shot, then tightly stuffed the cork back into the whiskey bottle. After wiping his eyes dry, he tossed the remains into the trash.

He didn't have time for mourning.

Berger awoke after a good night's sleep and realized he didn't have anything to pack for the move. He splashed cold water on his face and sat on the edge of the bed, whose springs squealed under his weight. Although the tiny cell had come to feel like a safe haven, he couldn't wait to get out.

He dressed in a pair of blue jeans and a tan oxford shirt. It was odd to wear civilian clothes. As he combed his hair, Berger felt a new surge of energy and wondered if it was the Elavil. He was familiar with the placebo effect—people who got better by taking a sugar pill—and wondered if his euphoria was a result of that. Whatever it was, he was glad that his mood was up and his spacey-ness was gone.

He picked up the magazine that Jill had brought him. She had looked incredibly attractive yesterday while she was explaining his condition. Her forehead wrinkling with intense concentration. Her violet eyes staring into his. She seemed so much more interested in him now that she knew he was innocent. Or at least he hoped so.

Linda seemed more distant now. After all, she'd wanted

to date other people, hadn't she? There was no harm in fantasizing about another woman.

Abruptly, he flashed on a disturbing mental image. Linda's eyes bulging in terror. Pleading for him to help. Her mouth was gasping open, yet she was unable to scream. Berger felt lost, powerless. Wanting to run to her, yet frozen in place.

He shuddered and swallowed back a bitter taste in his mouth, then paced around the cell until the image broke apart in his head. Finally, he chucked the magazine onto the floor and lay stiffly on the bed.

Jill arrived at work at 8:00 A.M. sharp. The phone was already ringing.

"Landis? Davidson."

A sting of anxiety played down her abdominals. Was this the ax?

"From now on," said Davidson, "you work directly with me. I've already got a U.S. Attorney subpoenaing the Mirage records. Word is that they're going to argue national security, which means a minimum ten-day delay. It also means the friggin' records exist or they wouldn't be trying to hide 'em. My sources tell me the terrorist extravaganza is scheduled for the day before Thanksgiving, which means we've got six days."

"Those files are the key," Jill shot back. "They'll have the name of the Director and his cohorts."

"I'm trying to pull some strings behind the scenes."

"I had an idea last night." She explained her thoughts about tracing the Neo-Ketamine.

"That's good. Whatever manpower you need, you've got it."

"I need someone to find out who has the right kind of cyclotron."

"Armstrong will call you in ten minutes. For however long it takes, he's dedicated to you."

Jill hung up the phone and broke into a broad smile. "All right!" she said out loud.

By noon, Jill knew that there were thirty-seven labs in the U.S. capable of manufacturing Neo-Ketamine. And there were fifty-one outside the U.S. She hadn't considered that these people might use a foreign company. The necessary quantities were small enough to smuggle in easily, which wasn't a comforting thought. And the time difference meant they wouldn't get any information before late tonight for the European and Middle Eastern countries.

Jill had Armstrong set up a phone bank of six agents, two of them multilingual, calling every company that was awake. She paced back and forth, listening to their ends of the calls, and had the unhappy realization that the chemical could be made illegally. Her instincts said they'd go for quality, because of the meticulous character of the original project, yet she knew that might be wishful thinking.

By mid-afternoon, they'd had no hits. She shuffled back to her desk and found the phone ringing.

"Ms. Landis? Dr. Durham."

She felt an adolescent flush. "Oh. How are you?"

"I'm fine. And I'm gonna be in L.A. today as promised. How about that dinner?"

"Oh. Well, I'm . . . I'm unfortunately really busy right now."

"With that same case?"

"Yes."

"I wouldn't mind a little shop talk. And maybe I can help. So if we went out, it'd be like working."

"I'm dealing with a couple of crises. I don't even know if I'll get out of here until late tonight."

"So let's leave it loose. I'm staying at the Sunset Marquis if you break free." He gave her the phone number.

"I don't really think I'll have any time."

"No pressure. If not dinner, maybe a quick drink."

"Let's see how things shape up. But today really doesn't look good."

After hanging up, she toyed with the pad on which she'd written his phone number. A few hours' escape might be good medicine. Yet she only had six days. And her mind would be on this Mirage thing. Maybe she'd give herself the luxury of a break when Mirage was over.

Jill tore off the sheet with the hotel number and stuffed it in her pocket. Then she called Armstrong about the chemical plants, and he patiently explained that not much had happened in the last five minutes. She looked at her watch. She wanted to wait around for the results, but she had to move Berger to the safe house. He was still a key witness, even if that wasn't exactly the word.

She patted her SIG Sauer 226 9mm semiautomatic against her rib cage, then put on her jacket and adjusted the collar. She really hadn't considered whether she might be in danger moving Berger, and the thought barged into her consciousness like an uninvited guest. These terrorists were clearly ruthless, although she doubted they'd go after a federal agent. She tried to shake off the idea and started toward the door.

One thing was for sure. She'd feel better when Berger was in the safe house.

"I said four guards!" barked Jill.

"Ma'am, I'm sorry but we only have two that can leave

their posts right now." The squat prison official spoke in a Southern drawl.

"When are the others available?"

"I got three boys out sick. We're just plain shorthanded."

"How soon can I get four?"

"Tomorrow."

"No. No. This is a key federal witness. His life may be in danger."

"Lookit, he only has to be outside a coupla seconds."

"Outside?! Are you nuts? He can't go outside!"

"The only other way is through the basement, and it's all tore up from the construction. We can't get a car down there for another two weeks."

"This is ridiculous."

"Ma'am, we've been shuffling prisoners across the sidewalk for the last two months, without no problems at all. You just pull your car up to the curb, and we'll skedaddle him down the steps before you even see him coming."

"Who's your boss?"

"The Great State of California."

"Don't get smart with me."

"No offense. I just meant to say I'm the only one in charge here today."

She looked around the room, as if hoping an army would waltz by. "Will you help guard him?"

"I wouldn't be much help unless he needs some pencils pushed around a desk." He clapped his hands on his belly, and the thumping resonated in her ears.

"Just . . . give me a phone." Jill called the Bureau and told them to get two agents over immediately. It would cost a half hour, yet she didn't want to take any chances.

As she sat down to wait, she had another idea. Quickly leaving the jail, she drove off to buy the materials.

*   *   *

It was almost 3:45 when Jill and the two FBI agents convened in Berger's cell.

"Mr. Berger," she began, "this may seem silly, but I don't want to take any chances with you. Would you please put this on your face and hands?"

"What is it?"

"Black makeup."

"Black makeup?"

"Yes. We have to be outside for a few seconds, and I don't want you recognizable."

"Are you serious?"

"Yes. If I'm right, this saves your life. If I'm wrong, you feel silly for a little while."

Berger looked skeptical as he took the makeup and put a little on his finger. He sniffed it, then tentatively smeared a line on his cheek. Within a few minutes, he'd covered his face and hands.

Jill handed him a bandanna to put over his hair, and a pair of sunglasses. When he put them on, she stood back, as if admiring him. "You may like this look so much that you decide to keep it after we're done."

He smiled at her and she averted his glance. She had to keep her concentration on getting him into the car.

Jill went out front to make sure the bulletproof car was waiting. Bullet-resistant was more like it, she thought. She'd asked for a Chevy instead of a Lincoln—the less ostentatious the better—but all they had was a black Lincoln that looked like it belonged in a funeral procession. She checked to be sure the car doors unlocked with her radio remote, then made certain the car was empty. Before leaving, she looked behind and underneath it.

All clear.

*   *   *

The smell of oily makeup filled Berger's cell. He felt incredibly self-conscious, and wanted out of this getup as soon as possible.

All these precautions were making him nervous. Was Jill just paranoid, or did he really have to worry? He looked in the mirror and didn't recognize his face.

Jill returned with the goons, then assembled the entourage. Berger in the middle, prison guards front and rear, and FBI agents on either side. Jill went first as they walked through the halls, smoothing out the coordination of moving as a cluster. The FBI men's eyes constantly searched the area. The prison guards looked bored.

"I feel like a wrestler on his way to the ring," said Berger.

No one laughed.

They came through prison security, where the agents were given back their weapons. Then they marched downstairs and through a long empty hall. When they arrived at the front door, Jill held up her hand and the troops halted. She looked outside through the chicken-wired glass, then turned toward them.

"We're going to move very rapidly to the car. Mr. Berger goes in the back seat." She turned to the prison guards. "Stay alert until the car is out of sight. Clear?"

Everyone nodded.

"On my signal." She held her hand in the air. *"Go!"*

She dropped her hand.

Berger almost stumbled as the man behind shoved into him. The cluster loosened on the stairs, then regrouped as they hit the sidewalk. The guards' jitters were contagious, and Berger felt his breathing accelerate. He looked down at the sidewalk and broke into a fast jog.

Berger saw a black Lincoln parked at the curb. Jill pushed a remote control button, and he heard the car doors click as they unlocked. She grabbed the back door handle and started to open it. Then she froze.

Berger heard the sound of an exhaust backfire. Or at least that's what he thought it was, until he felt the warm liquid splatter on him. He turned to look at the FBI agent on his left and saw that the man was falling. The agent's head had exploded, and Berger was covered with blood, bits of bone, and gray matter. One of the eyes that had so rapidly searched the area lay on top of Berger's shoe.

There was dead silence, followed by a chaotic eruption of panicked shouts. Berger had never seen another human mutilated, much less been splattered by one. The scene was surreal. This was not the movies. The man was dead, or mortally wounded. And it was actually happening right in front of Berger. He started to retch.

In the next moment, Jill was on top of him, slamming him to the ground. Less than a foot from his face, a bullet hit the sidewalk so loudly that his ears rang, and flecks of powdered concrete sprayed into his eyes. A split second later, he felt Jill drag him upright and stuff him into the back seat like a rag doll.

Berger peered out the window and saw the living guards and agent spinning in place, returning fire. They didn't seem to agree on a direction. One of the prison guards fell down, clutching his chest. Jill slammed into the front seat and turned the ignition. The starter screamed with the sound of scraping metal, as she apparently held the key after the engine caught. Tires squealed and bullets ricocheted off the glass and doors as they pulled into traffic, almost colliding with a bus.

Jill was already on the radio, ordering backup and ambulances. Her voice sounded like it was a full octave above her normal tone.

They rounded the corner, and she went into a series of

evasive maneuvers that threw Berger left and right. Finally, she sped along a residential street.

Jill dropped the radio and asked, "You all right?" without looking back.

"I can't tell if I'm hit or not. There's too much blood."

"Just hang on."

CHAPTER 34

"What happened with Berger?" barked Combs.

"No report," said Baxter. He shifted his weight between his feet.

"You're lying. What happened?"

"I don't have a final—"

Combs stood up and towered over Baxter. "Give me a straight fucking answer."

"The preliminary indication is that they . . . missed him."

Combs slammed his fist against the wall. "Son of a fucking— You told me they were the best there is. Now he's in a safe house, and we can't get anywhere near him?"

"I . . . I . . ."

Combs grabbed a gun and jammed it into Baxter's mouth. "I ought to blow the back of your head all over your fucking Armani suit, you incompetent asshole. Do you have any idea what kind of risk this Berger is?"

"I . . . I . . ." The words were now muffled and Baxter was trembling so hard that he made the gun shake.

Combs pulled the gun out roughly, scraping it against Baxter's teeth. "Just get the fuck out of here."

Baxter quickly complied.

Shit. This Berger was fucking charmed. And if the Serbians got word of his being alive, Combs would be the one needing a charmed life.

The Serbians had insisted on using Berger, claiming they'd picked his name "at random." They said they wanted proof that the Mirage techniques could work on anyone—not some rigged stooge that Combs supplied. Combs's gut knew there was more to the story, and with a little digging, he found the truth. Charlie, the terrorist that Combs met in Amsterdam, had been deported after a college fight with Berger. Apparently because Berger tried to fuck Charlie's sister. She must have been some piece of ass to set Charlie off like that.

Still, Combs had gone along with using Berger. Even though he'd felt from the start that Berger wasn't a great candidate. He cursed his arrogance for agreeing.

Combs threw the gun down and felt a shudder through his chest. Now Berger was in a safe house. And the FBI knew about Elavil. What else did they know? What could they get out of Berger?

Jill took a circuitous route to avoid being followed. Berger had scraped his thigh when he fell, and it felt as if he'd been scalded with boiling water. He took a few deep breaths and tried to concentrate away from the injury. Watching kids playing on the street. Palm trees zipping by like fence posts. The pain burrowed through into his consciousness.

Remembering Durham's words about controlling yourself with suggestions, he tried closing his eyes and relaxing. Berger imagined gently swabbing his leg with a soothing balm. Then he visualized applying a clean, soft bandage.

Sonofabitch. It made him feel better.

Almost two hours later—Jill's evasive measures having stretched out what should have been a thirty-minute drive—the car pulled up to the safe house. They were in an industrial area of Gardena, surrounded by manufacturing plants with semis parked at loading docks. Berger saw a sign that said AMERICAN LAUNDRY SYSTEMS in front of a two-story, concrete tilt-up building. Jill drove to the twelve-foot wrought iron gate and spoke briefly into the intercom. The enormous panel lurched to the side, propelled by a whining electric motor and an oversize bicycle chain.

"This is a legit business," she explained. "They own washing machines in apartment buildings. Because they collect and count the coins here, they have tight security and it doesn't raise any eyebrows. We rent some space upstairs and supplement the security for our section."

Jill pulled around to the back of the building. She and Berger walked quickly to a heavy metal door, where she punched in a security code. Only then did a voice respond and, after identifying her, buzz the door open. They went up a steep stairwell to another metal door. A guard eyed them through a thick window that distorted his face.

"You're now locked between the two doors," Jill explained. "If your ID doesn't check out, the guard releases a sedative gas before he cuffs you."

"Can I get a little if I have trouble sleeping?"

She started to smile, then checked it. Jill passed her FBI ID through a slot under glass, and Berger thought her hand was shaking. The guard verified her through a computer, then buzzed them in.

Down the hall, through still another metal door, was a

nicely furnished one-bedroom apartment. The walls were a soft beige, with posters of Paris, Rome, and Amsterdam. There were shelves sagging with books, a stereo, television, VCR, and stacks of videotapes. Berger pulled open the floor-to-ceiling curtains, anxious for sunshine and fresh air. What he found was a blank wall and the realization that there were no windows in the apartment.

"If you need anything that isn't here," said Jill, "use the telephone. It only goes to the guard, I'm afraid, since we can't allow outside calls."

"Do I have to tip the guard?"

"That's not necessary," she replied, missing the joke.

Berger sat on the tweed Herculon couch, asking, "How can you be so calm after what we just went through?"

"Same way as you. Shock."

"I'm trying to put on a brave facade to impress you," he said. Then he stood up and gently took hold of her shoulders. She didn't resist as he'd worried. "I owe you my life."

She shrugged out of his grasp. "You're the key to something very big."

"What do you mean?"

Jill turned red. "I shouldn't have said that. I can't discuss it."

"You can't just drop it like that."

"I have to. I'm sorry."

"Look. I'm obviously the target of something. Being shot at is one of those telltale signs. See, I only have this one life, and however limited the mental part of it might be, I'm still pretty fond of it. I've been totally open with you. The least you can do is tell me what's going on."

"I just can't."

"Let me put it another way. Based on our last conversation, I won't be able to tell anybody a few days from now. And maybe, just maybe, I can help you. I do have a rather large stake in the outcome of all this. Perhaps even more than you do."

He thought the words might be seeping through the crevices of her resistance.

"And finally," said Berger, "who the hell am I gonna tell here on Island Washateria?"

She actually laughed. Jill motioned toward the bathroom with her head. "Go clean yourself up. With your half-black face you look like a Holstein cow."

Jill sat on the couch. Through the bathroom door, she could hear the shower and Berger's off-key singing.

Should she tell him about Mirage? She had no doubt the Bureau wouldn't come near approving. On the other hand, they were down to a few days before endangering tens of thousands of lives. They needed a long pass or a Hail Mary or whatever those football jocks said when things got desperate.

She looked down and for the first time noticed that she had blood on her dress. The adrenaline pump from the shooting was draining, and her body was beginning to ache. So much for the idea that these people wouldn't take out a federal agent. How the hell did they know when and where Berger would be? It had to be an inside job. She'd be up the kazoos of everyone who'd known the time and place of his transfer. But even with that, how did they recognize Berger in disguise? She had the unhappy thought that they'd recognized her, and therefore knew he was the one being escorted.

Her body started to quiver. Small trembles at first, then violent spasms. When she had to accept that she'd lost control, she buried her face in a pillow on the couch, so that Berger wouldn't hear. Comforted by the muffling velour against her mouth and eyes, she sobbed without inhibition.

When she finished crying, she realized that the shower water had stopped. She looked up and saw Berger standing there, with a towel wrapped around his waist. His body glistened with beads of moisture.

"I envy your ability to let things out like that," he said.

She sniffled and reflexively wiped her eye with an index finger. "That was inappropriate of me. I apologize."

"I promise that every book on etiquette permits a breakdown after being shot at."

She smiled and found her eyes searching his body again. The hair on his chest and legs was feathered with water.

He sat down on a chair causing the towel to split and reveal most of his thigh.

"I think you should get dressed," she said.

"In what?"

"Oh. Yes, well, we'll get you some clothes." She pulled a pad from her purse, wrote "clothes," and found her handwriting was wobbly. When she looked up, she saw a crimson spot growing through the towel around him.

"You're bleeding," she said.

He pulled back the towel and she saw a large abrasion on his thigh that had begun to seep blood.

"You should put something on that," said Jill. She went to the bathroom cabinet, found an antiseptic, and dabbed it on. He winced from the touch. She was conscious of leaning into him as she worked, and felt her breasts against his arm. He was probably looking into her eyes, although she concentrated on dressing the wound. She finished, patted the bandage gently, then clumsily tried to replace the top on the antiseptic.

"Well done, madame. Now tell me about this 'big thing'

I'm involved in." Berger walked into the kitchen as he spoke. "And do stay for dinner. We're having . . ." He opened an upper cabinet and looked in. ". . . Pop-Tarts."

She laughed out loud and it made her realize how much she'd needed the release.

"Okay. I'll cook," said Jill.

Jill rummaged through the kitchen and managed to make a reasonable dinner from the available supplies. During the course of preparing it, she wrote out a lengthy grocery list.

They sat down at the Formica breakfast table.

"Delicious," he pronounced after the first bite. She involuntarily blushed. He took another bite and said, "So tell me what's going on."

"I really shouldn't be doing this."

"There are lots of things I shouldn't be doing either. Tell me."

"Well . . ."

He opened his eyes expectantly, like a dog waiting for a treat.

"We've discovered a secret project, code-named Mirage." Jill explained about the mind control techniques, and the reports of a major terrorist act just before Thanksgiving. She laid out her suspicions that Berger and the man in Orlando had been trial runs.

"We can't identify the Director or his top people because we can't get access to the records."

"Why not?" he asked.

"The Military Records people are arguing national security and stalling. By the time we drag them through court, it'll be after Thanksgiving."

He stared at her for a moment, then leaned forward. "Where are the records?"

"Salt Lake City."

"Are they on a computer?"

"I would think so. Why?"

"I might be able to get them for you."

"How?"

"That's what I do. I set up computer security systems. If you can get me to the computer, I'll try to get what you need."

Jill laid down her fork. "That's illegal."

"So's blowing up a lot of Thanksgiving turkeys."

She shook her head. "I can't authorize something illegal."

"So don't authorize it. Just drop me at the corner and come back after school."

"That's way too risky. If you got caught, we'd all be toast." She sat for a moment in thought. "What if you weren't there? Could you do it over a modem?"

"No. Too much security on phone lines, for obvious reasons. If I had unlimited computer power and about fifty years, I could get in via modem. Since I assume you're on a tighter schedule than that, I'll have to go there."

"After today's incident, I don't think it's safe for you to leave here."

"You'd be amazed how risk aversion melts when you've only got a few days left."

Jill drove home without turning on the radio, constantly checking her rearview mirror. She realized she'd forgotten to call Durham back, who'd invited her to dinner. Something about him excited her from the neck down, which she hadn't felt in quite a while. She shook it off and decided she'd call him in Arizona when things lightened up.

Come to think of it, something about Berger excited her as well. She sure could pick 'em. A man her father's age, and a brainwashed computer geek who was turning into a vegetable.

She parked the car and approached her apartment cautiously. Her hearing was heightened, and her mind turned every sound into an attacker. She walked hurriedly up the concrete steps, aware of the clicking of her heels. Then she stood beside the door of her apartment before quickly throwing it open.

The door banged against the inside wall.

Then everything was quiet.

She peered around the jamb and saw nothing. Jill went inside, checked all the rooms, then drew the drapes before undressing. Her answering machine was blinking, and she was reaching for the message button when the phone rang. The noise made her scream and jump back. Embarrassed, she looked around the apartment, as if to make sure no one had heard her. Then she picked up the phone.

"Ms. Landis? Chuck Durham."

Her heart was still thumping. "Oh. Yes. Hello."

"I'm at the hotel and thought I'd try you again. I know it's late for dinner, but I also know you just got in because I've been calling. You up for a drink?"

She sat down, took off her shoes and began massaging her feet. "I'm afraid I'm too exhausted."

"Big day?"

"You have no idea."

"You sure you don't want some decompression time? I'm a great listener."

"It's tempting, Dr. Durham—"

"Chuck."

"Chuck. But I'm really fried. Some other time maybe."

"Well, I suppose that's better than a 'get lost.' If I stay over tomorrow night, how about then?"

"Well . . . I have to leave it loose. I'm really tied up."

"Loose it is. I'll check with you tomorrow."

Jill hung up the phone and rested her head on the back of the chair. There was something magnetic about Durham. He'd certainly tried to be helpful with Berger. Maybe she would go out with him if he called again. The possibility of a relationship was appealing, if she could clear the decks long enough to deal with it. And if she could clear the decks of Ted. She felt Ted's eyes on her, staring from the photo in the kitchen.

She got up and hit the button on the answering machine.

"Jill? Armstrong. I heard about the shooting. You okay? Purdy took out one of the snipers, but the rest got away. On the other front, we caught a break. There's a small chemical firm in Kenosha, Wisconsin, that delivered Neo-Ketamine about a week before the Orlando and EXC bombings. A courier picked it up at the plant. They were contacted by e-mail and paid in cash. Now get this. They got another order a few days ago, and it's being picked up tomorrow. A big one. The courier is due there at 2:00 P.M. They'll cooperate with us, but think it'd be suspicious to delay the order. So I've got the Milwaukee Bureau office mobilized. Our techies are checking the e-mail and wire transfers. Call me however late you get in."

She called Armstrong, who said the Milwaukee office was already wiring the factory for surveillance and setting up observation points. Next, she called Davidson, even though it was almost 11:30 in D.C. It took five rings before his groggy voice answered.

"Sorry to call so late, but we're short on time and I've got some news." She recounted the day's shooting, Berger's delivery to the safe house, and Armstrong's info on the Neo-Ketamine.

"You okay?" he asked, his voice now clear.

"Yeah."

"Good work. Maybe we can follow the chemicals home."

"What do you think about using Rover?" Rover was a system of tracking that didn't require a transmitter on the target. Most devices have to home in on a transmitted signal, which means a power source and easy discovery by anyone looking for bugs. In theory, Rover would be impossible to detect.

"It's still got glitches. But I guess this is as good a time as any for a field trial. Set it up."

"I have something else." She explained Berger's offer to retrieve the computer information.

"You brought a civilian into the case? Why would you do that without authority?"

"This isn't just any civilian. His life is on the line because of all this, and he's under lock and key. He can't even make a phone call. Look, I made a decision to trust him under these conditions, and I don't think he could screw us even if he wanted to. If he goes into the Military Records facility in Salt Lake City, he could do it as a private citizen and insulate us."

"He was almost killed today and you want to put him out in the open? You're pretty reckless, Landis."

"And we're running out of time. Gimme a 'yes,' a 'no,' or 'I don't want to know about it.'"

After a long silence, he said, "If I pick 'Don't tell me,' and this thing blows up, your ass would be hanging out there all by its lonesome."

"Right. So which is it?"

Another silence. "You sure got balls, or whatever the female equivalent of that is."

She was within a millimeter of telling him to shove

his chauvinism through his anal canal. She settled for, "What's it gonna be?"

"It's gonna be yes. My ass goes with yours. So keep 'em both covered."

CHAPTER 35

Armstrong met Jill in her cubicle the next morning. He had a short, military haircut and wide shoulders that strained against his shirt. He also had one eye that didn't quite move with the other, which Jill had always found unsettling because she couldn't tell if he was looking at her.

"I got a general description of the guy who picked up the chemicals last time," he said. "My guess is that it won't be the same man tomorrow. Chet Warren, the Milwaukee field agent, will have men out front in a street repair van. They'll be wired into the receptionist."

"I should be there."

"In an ideal world. On the other hand, if they recognize you, there goes our cover. Learn to delegate, Landis."

"I guess. I got some stuff to do here anyway." She had already called about getting blueprints of the Military Records facility in Salt Lake City.

"I'll be in continuous contact with Warren," Armstrong continued.

"He knows how sophisticated these guys are?"

"Yep. And we have Rover as a backup."

"How did you set it up?" she asked.

"We couldn't alter the Neo-Ketamine without damaging the drug, so we made bottles with radio-reflective material in the glass. The lab will put the Neo-Ketamine in them. We tested the bottles, and they gave off a distinctive fingerprint when they zapped 'em with Rover's satellite signal. So far, we've been able to follow the bottles from our lab to the chemical company, but we're still getting a few gaps. They said it's a problem in the atmosphere, or sunspots, or something like that."

"I hate relying on experimental gadgets."

"Rover's only a backup to Warren, who's first-rate. We were classmates at the Academy. He won't lose the courier."

"From your lips to God's ears."

Chet Warren sat in the command van, about a block from Wendel Chemicals. Wendel was near the corner of 51st Street and 51st Avenue in downtown Kenosha, a small town on Lake Michigan.

The air was freezing, and the chill was intensified by a strong wind off the lake. The sky was in the midst of dumping a predicted two feet of snow on the downtown area of low rises and empty stores. A truck chugged slowly along 51st Street, with its large blade curling snow in front, while a spinning fan in the back spread sand on the road. Warren had worried that the roads might screw up the courier's access, so he'd arranged to clear 51st as a priority.

From the outside, Warren's van looked like a teenager's alternative to a motel room: tinted windows, a painted scene of a sunglassed skier cutting through spraying powder, and script lettering that read "Let It Flow." The van was on a slight incline that afforded a wide view of the chemical plant, its parking lot, and the street.

Warren's attention was fixed through a pair of high-powered binoculars. Per his instructions, the employees had parked so that the visitor was left two spaces near the door. He moved his gaze over to the gas company repair truck, which was surrounded by orange traffic cones. A large yellow hose snaked from an air pump into an open manhole, and two men in thick parkas with fur collars seemed to busy themselves with various wrenches and meters. Warren checked in with them through their earpieces, and they each responded discreetly.

At 1:45, a sky-blue Saturn approached. Warren read the license plate to the other agent, who typed it into the computer, hooked via cellular to the FBI database. The Saturn ignored the spaces near the front door and parked on the perimeter, as Warren had predicted.

"Got him," said the woman at the computer. "Rental car from Milwaukee Airport. Name of Hiram Cullens. Drop-off at Chicago O'Hare."

"O'Hare? Shit. Get Chicago revved up. I want driver intercepts along the Interstate. Lipscomb and Shannon can't follow him that far alone."

"You got it."

The man climbed out of the Saturn, looked around, then started toward the front door. He was dark-haired, with an egg-shaped head, wearing a gray suit under an open black overcoat.

"Check out Cullens. If that's his real name, dinner's on me."

"No bet. Already working. Here it comes."

"And the winner is . . ."

"Why it's a miracle, Chet. Mr. Cullens has risen from the dead."

Warren spoke into the radio. "Passenger on board."

"Check," replied one of the street workers. "Male Cauc.

Approximately thirty years old. Black hair, medium build. Five foot seven, hundred and sixty pounds. Flat nose. Got a nice Polaroid of him."

"I'm plugging you into the receptionist's wire," Warren said to the workers.

"May I help you?" came a woman's voice over the radio.

"I'm here to pick up the Bonita Harvey order." The man's voice sounded pleasant, melodious.

"Certainly. Just a moment."

The squeak of a chair moving back. The sound of papers shuffling.

"Here you are. Please sign here."

"You have a nice day," he said.

Warren switched frequencies. "Wake up, Lipscomb, Shannon."

"Wide awake," said Lipscomb.

"Present," said Shannon.

"Gentlemen, start your engines."

Agent Terry Lipscomb sat in his car across from Wendel Chemicals. Ice was forming on his window glass and the cold thumbed its nose at the pitiful attempts of his car's heater. His teeth chattered as he watched Cullens walk out of the plant holding a cardboard box about the size of a football. Lipscomb rubbed the side window with his leather glove. It squealed as he etched a ragged porthole in the frost.

Cullens got into the blue Saturn and pulled out of the parking lot, skidding slightly on the icy road. Obviously not used to driving in this weather, thought Lipscomb, which should make him easier to follow. Lipscomb pulled out his radio and said, "Shannon, I'll take him first, then

lag back. You take the lead when he gets on the Interstate."

"Roger."

The Saturn drove at the speed limit, directly toward the
Interstate for the first few miles. Then it turned off into a
cul-de-sac. Lipscomb drove past and saw Shannon stop to
wait for Cullens to emerge and reverse his direction. They
alternated in the same way through U-turns and driveway
reversals for almost twenty minutes as Cullens worked his
way toward the freeway.

After Cullens got onto I-94 south, Lipscomb sipped a
lukewarm coffee as he blended into traffic. Lipscomb and
Shannon had worked together so long that they could read
each other's movements even without radio contact and
they alternated proximity to the Saturn, minimizing the
chance that he'd notice the same car near him. Knowing
they were headed to Chicago, Lipscomb settled in for the
ride.

When they turned onto I-90, the radio crackled with
Chet Warren's voice from the command van. "Lipscomb,
Shannon. Get ready to peel off. We've got fresh vehicles
about four miles ahead. Wait for my signal."

"Roger."

Good. Lipscomb's kids were away for the weekend, and
his wife had promised him an evening of snuggling by the
fire. If he got home in the afternoon, he could surprise
her.

About a mile later, the Saturn abruptly slashed across
four lanes of traffic to an exit, causing motorists to brake
and skid. A yellow Volkswagen Beetle almost went off the
road. Lipscomb immediately slowed, but couldn't follow
without endangering the other motorists. Shannon had already passed the exit.

Lipscomb grabbed his radio. "Chet, we got a change-up. The bird moved onto I-55 and I missed the turn."

"What? I-55 doesn't go to O'Hare. This another diversion?"

"Can't tell. I'm swinging around to chase."

Warren responded, "I'm leaving the other cars on I-90 in case he turns around."

Lipscomb got off the freeway and ran a red light to get back on in the other direction. A woman in a blue dented Toyota gave him the finger. Despite the slippery road, he almost hit eighty-five as he screeched back onto I-90. Then he took I-55 and cut in and out of cars as he tried to find the Saturn.

Fortunately, the Saturn was going the speed limit and Lipscomb caught a glimpse of him several cars ahead.

"I see him," said Lipscomb into the radio. He slowed down to about five miles over the Saturn's speed. "It'll take me a minute to catch up. Send the other cars over here."

"You heard the man," said Warren. The other cars acknowledged. "Where the hell's he going?"

Shannon whizzed past Lipscomb, then fell in behind the Saturn. Lipscomb dropped back, but kept the Saturn in sight. They drove quietly for several more miles, when the Saturn abruptly swerved across traffic and got off the Interstate.

"He's heading south on Cicero," said Shannon. "I think he's going to Midway." Midway was the smaller airport in Chicago.

"Shit," barked Warren. "Either he's fucking with us again, or the airport on the rental agreement was a decoy. All of you. Get your asses to Midway."

"Shannon's on him. I'm not that far behind," answered Lipscomb.

"Get closer!"

Lipscomb accelerated, cutting off a truck. The driver blasted him with an air horn that rattled his window.

Shannon broke in. "He's turning into the airport. He's about six hundred yards from me, going into short-term parking. There's a fence on the island between us. If I go around, I'll lose him."

"Shannon, keep him in sight and report," growled Warren. "Lipscomb, take the terminal."

Lipscomb sped into the airport at seventy. "Almost there."

"He's out of the car," said Shannon. "Terry, you're gonna hit a lot of traffic at the departure curb."

Lipscomb saw a sea of red taillights jammed into an irregular pattern in front of him. He skidded to a halt within inches of a Ford. Nothing was moving, and a light snow was beginning to fall.

Shannon reported, "He's walking toward the Northwest Airlines entrance. You got him, Terry?"

Lipscomb didn't see him. "Chet, you pay for the ticket," he radioed before abandoning his car and running toward the terminal. About twenty yards in, his foot slipped on a patch of ice. He fell hard to the ground, skinning his hand. His handheld radio slid across the sidewalk, twirling in circles as it went. Lipscomb scooped up the radio and broke into a hard run, accidentally slamming into a man with a backpack. The loss of a few seconds, and the thick crowd of people, made it impossible to see where this asshole had gone.

"He's inside now," said Shannon. "Northwest door number two." At least the radio worked after being dropped, thought Lipscomb. He accelerated his stride, weaving through the crowd like a tight end evading tacklers. His lungs stung from sucking in deep breaths of cold air laced with car exhaust fumes.

The Northwest Airlines door, about two hundred feet ahead, was jammed with passengers and bags. His open parka flapped behind him as the snow began collecting on his eyelashes.

Inside the door, the air was saturated with the crowd's perspiration. Lipscomb's heart was pumping from the run, and he was breaking into a sweat. He quickly looked up and down the aisles, then roughly shoved in the radio's talk button.

"I've lost him. We'll need people to check the gates. Chet, send in Shannon."

Shannon answered. "He's outside, Terry. Heading for the rental car."

"What?" said Lipscomb and Warren simultaneously.

"You think he's going to O'Hare?" asked Lipscomb.

"He's having trouble finding the car," said Shannon.

Warren answered, "How could he have trouble finding a car he parked five minutes ago?"

"I dunno. Maybe all these rental cars look alike."

"Maybe."

"I'm coming out for him," said Lipscomb, running toward the door.

"He's in the car," reported Shannon as Lipscomb burst outside into the cold. The wind whipped the snow, reducing his visibility.

Warren said, "Stay on him, Shannon."

"Got him," answered Shannon. "Wait a minute, Chet."

"What?"

"Shit."

"Shit what?"

"He went into the terminal with a package, but he came out without one."

"Shit! Get back in there, Lipscomb. I'm faxing the Polaroid of Cullens to airport security. See if somebody saw where this bastard stuffed the package. Shannon, don't lose him."

A few minutes later, Lipscomb found the head of airport security in an office behind an unmarked door. He was a trim, white-haired man with a constant smile and the improbable name of Harry Belafonte.

Harry and Lipscomb took the Polaroid of Cullens to each of the baggage personnel, then to all of the people working the ticket counters. No one had seen him. The last person they checked was a bleach-blonde in her fifties whose winged pin said her name was Doris.

"Sorry," said Doris.

"Do people here sometimes shift around and work the gates?" asked Lipscomb.

"Yes."

"Today?"

"I'm sure."

"C'mon," said Lipscomb. He dragged Belafonte to each of the gates, again with no results. At gate 46, he showed the picture to a young man in an American Eagle uniform whose face sprouted several large pimples.

"Yeah, I saw him. He asked me where he could find a phone."

"Do you remember where you sent him?"

"Right over there." He pointed to a bank of pay phones.

"You mean you saw him here? At the gates?"

"Yes."

"How long ago?"

"About a half hour ago."

That wasn't possible. Lipscomb had watched Cullens

leave almost forty-five minutes ago. He pulled out his radio. "Chet, do you still have a visual on the Saturn?"

"Roger. He's on the Interstate toward Chicago."

"This Cullens guy isn't just dead. He's a ghost. Or a— Fuck me!"

"How's that?" asked Warren.

Lipscomb turned to the gate attendant.

"Was he carrying a cardboard box?"

"Yes, I think he was."

Lipscomb slapped the counter loudly, stinging his hand and startling the gate attendant. He barked at the attendant, "Did he say where he was going?"

"No."

"How many flights left from this area in the last thirty minutes?"

"Maybe five or six. This is the commuter area."

"Can I get a list of them?"

"Sure. But a few of them are short hops. They'll be landing in the next few minutes."

Lipscomb pushed the button on his radio. "Chet, we got a problem."

"Twins?!" sputtered Jill.

"They were on top of it. You can't fault the agents," said Armstrong.

"Then why were they so far behind him that they missed the switch?"

Armstrong shifted his weight, as if the floor was rolling like a boat deck. "I . . . I . . . I'm sure it was the evasive maneuvers."

"Evasive maneuvers my ass."

"Nobody expected twins. You can't blame the agents. These Mirage guys are smarter than we figured."

"No shit. And now they've got everything they need,

while we only have five days left. We have to put the field offices on full alert."

"Activate Rover?"

Jill looked out the window at the rolling green lawn and symmetrical concrete markers of the Westwood Veterans Cemetery. "Yes. And pray it works."

CHAPTER 36

Jill sat across from Berger in the safe house living room.

"Here's the souped-up laptop," she said. "And the other junk you wanted."

"Please, Agent Landis. Not *junk*. High-precision surgical instruments."

Berger examined the multimeter, line tester, and inductive amplifier. Then he checked the CAT 5 Ethernet modular cables with RJ45 connectors, the coax with BNC connectors, and the Token Ring. They'd also brought him an assortment of patch cables and plugs that should match almost any network.

"They installed the software you wanted," Jill continued. "PC Dump, Telnet, and the others. Plus the chess program."

"Thanks. Playing chess against the computer will be several steps up from watching these videos. *Barney Versus Godzilla* was the most gripping."

"Here's the blueprints of the Military Records facility. And here's a white jumpsuit and badge that identifies you as a telephone repairman. We've got a way to blow out one of their phone lines, and we'll intercept the repair call if they're efficient enough to make one. If not, we'll keep blowing lines until they do. You go in right after they close, at 5:00."

"The file server will most likely be in a secure room that's locked at the end of the day. Can you get a key?"

"Sorry. I couldn't get any keys."

"Some systems disconnect from the server after hours, to keep people from doing exactly what I want to do. If this one does, and I don't have the key, we're out of business."

"We can only do what we can do. You leave in two hours from John Wayne Airport in Orange County."

"John Wayne sounds appropriate, in view of my mission to single-handedly take out the bad guys."

"You'll be on an FBI jet."

"Cool."

"It sounds more glamorous than it is. The jet's a noisy little plane, and it's so short that you can't stand up inside."

"Is there an in-flight movie?"

"*Barney Versus Godzilla II.* If you're caught, you're on your own. We'll deny any knowledge of you, and your safe house status is over. We won't be able to touch you."

"For the third time, I get it."

"Now are . . ."

Berger finished the rest of her sentence in unison, ". . . you sure you want to do this? Yes, I'm sure. Let me get the stuff organized and play a quick game of chess before Mr. Wayne and I head out of town."

A little after four o'clock, Berger walked down the jet's stairs onto the tarmac of Salt Lake City International Airport. The cold air was crisp and sharp. He looked at the jagged beauty of the surrounding snow-covered mountains, trying to imagine the reaction of Brigham Young and his followers when they first arrived. Escape from persecution into paradise.

A strong wind blew through his overalls as he ducked into the white telephone company van. It was warm inside, yet he continued shivering.

The driver, an enormous man with sunglasses and a square jaw, said, "Welcome to Salt Lake City. I'm Jack Leon." His voice was high and squeaky, so totally out of character with his huge build that Berger almost started to laugh. "The records facility is near Fort Douglas, all the way across town."

"Will there be a tour of major sights along the way?"

The man furrowed his brow, apparently turning the question over in his mind. "Not really."

They swung onto I-215, then I-80, and continued across town on Fourth Street, past the University of Utah, onto Foothill Drive.

Despite the van's lack of suspension, Berger was able to concentrate on the records facility floor plan. The data was stored in a room near the telephone equipment, yet it was far enough away that he couldn't be found there without blowing his cover. Jill had explained that the facility had a state-of-the-art security system, not just for the computers, but for the building itself. That was mostly because the data concerned national security, and partly because the records center had been selected to test security products before rolling them into other government buildings. Great.

The van jerked to a halt and Leon motioned his head toward a one-story concrete building with no windows. "They're expecting you."

Berger stepped out of the van, and the cold wind stabbed through him again. Leon handed him the red metal toolbox that had been modified to conceal his laptop and other materials. Berger slowly started forward. He knew he was a lousy liar, and not a particularly good actor. The sooner he got to the computer, which wouldn't give a damn about either skill, the happier he'd be.

Berger pulled open a heavy glass door and walked up to a squat security guard, who sat behind a desk. He pointed his thick index finger at Berger like a gun. "Yeah?"

"I'm from the phone company." Berger worried that his voice was quivering.

"I don't know anything about the phone company comin' out." This guy looked like he had less sense of humor than Leon. The guard peered out the window at the van, then used his frankfurter finger to dial an extension. As it rang, he studied Berger up and down. Then he listened and grunted into the phone.

"Down the hall to your left."

Berger already knew that, yet remembered he wasn't supposed to. "Can you show me where exactly?"

The man shook his head impatiently. "I can't leave my desk to lead you down there by the nose. Just go down the damn hall and look for a room marked 'Telephone Equipment.' And don't wander around. I'll be watching you on closed circuit to make sure you get there."

Ooops. Berger hadn't meant to draw that kind of attention. He decided to match the guard's belligerence. "I haven't got time to wander around. Find someone to show me."

The guard glared at him, and then punched in another number. A few minutes later, a young blond woman appeared. She had a constant smile and wore her hair in pigtails, which made her look twelve years old. Berger followed little Heidi to the telephone room, which was ex-

actly where the blueprint said it was. When he thanked the
woman, he half expected her to curtsy.

Pigtails left, and Berger decided he should make his
move right away. He assumed the guard would periodically
watch the cameras, but that he'd probably look away after
seeing Berger arrive at the phone room. So Berger pretended to work in the telephone room for a few minutes
before stepping around the corner and slipping into the unmarked computer room.

He could hear his heartbeat as he closed the door behind him. He locked it from the inside and surveyed the
layout. The room was large and government gray, jammed
with desks and monitors. One wall was lined with banks
of computers, and the system was connected by a multi-
wired cable. He selected a desk furthest from the door, then
turned on the computer. It beeped and whirred to life.

A buzzer went off at the front desk. The squat guard sat
up and looked at the panel, which was blinking "Current
Surge." In the computer room. Nothing should be going
on down there. He radioed one of the guards on rounds.

Berger first checked desk drawers, then looked underneath desks for Post-its. He knew that high-security systems required gibberish passwords, and that most people
were more worried about convenience than security, so he
hoped to find a password written down. No luck.

He then took out his laptop and reached for the multimeter. That was when he heard the doorknob rattle, followed
by the sound of a key going in the lock. Berger froze and
looked over to see the knob turning. He grabbed the toolbox and laptop, quickly searching for a place to hide. He
heard the lock turn over. His heart thumped against his
jugular, and he didn't see anything to get behind. Now the

door was opening, and someone was coming in. His eye caught the well beneath a nearby desk, and he squeezed himself, the laptop, and the toolkit into the tiny space.

The footsteps sounded like they were pacing off the perimeter. He figured the next round would bring them closer. Beads of perspiration sprouted on his forehead, and he slowly moved the back of his hand to wipe them. The footsteps came closer, and were moving slowly, cautiously. The sweat seeped into Berger's eyes, stinging them. That was when his laptop beeped.

The footsteps stopped. It was probably his imagination, but he thought he could hear the guard's head snap around to look for the source.

The sound of radio static broke the silence. "Whatcha got, Rod?"

Rod spoke. "Nothing so far. Still checking. Some dumb sonofabitch locked the door, so it took me a minute to get in."

The footsteps started moving again. Berger imagined Rod with his hand on his revolver, getting ready to flush out his prey and pulverize it. The perspiration now soaked Berger's shirt, and he worried the moisture would get into the laptop clutched between his thighs and chest. That would be the end of the operation. He eased the computer away from his body and banged the desk with the metal case. The footsteps stopped, then moved toward him, squeaking against the vinyl floor. He held his breath.

Dead silence. Not having any sensory input was worse than the sounds. The claustrophobic feeling he thought he'd left in jail started to return. Memories of the closet and his cousin Matty. The metal walls of the desk well now seemed to be squeezing in on him, tightening with every breath. The way a boa constrictor suffocates its dinner. Not by crushing, but by keeping your chest from expanding. Waiting patiently until you exhale. Knowing you won't get another breath.

Berger began to shake, and he was now holding the laptop in an awkward position that strained his muscles. He worried he'd rattle the desk. The footsteps started again, and suddenly Berger saw two heavy-shoed feet stop next to him. Pointing directly at him. Berger, who ached from holding his breath, let out a little air. It was a trick he used to stay underwater longer when he was a kid.

Berger heard a scraping noise above his head. Rod apparently picking up something on the desk. Had Berger left anything there? He didn't think so. His lungs were now screaming for air and he felt light-headed. His shaking was becoming more pronounced. The desk well squeezed as if he were in a vise.

A radio crackle startled him, and he almost gasped in a breath.

"Talk to me, Rod. What caused the power surge?"

Power surge, Berger realized. When he turned on the computer. So that was it.

"I don't see anything, Luke. Must be a malfunction. I'm outta here."

The feet turned and footsteps padded across the floor. Berger waited for the door to close before letting out his breath.

It occurred to him that it could be a trick. That Rod could still be in the room, waiting to see if anyone came out. He waited several minutes before quietly unfolding himself onto the floor, then he lay there for some time before peering over the desk.

No one there.

His knees creaked as he awkwardly stood up, using the desk for support.

He couldn't lock the door, since Rod had noticed it and

would certainly remember he didn't lock up when he left.
Berger didn't know how long the rounds were, or whether
Rod would poke his head in every few minutes, just on
general principles. Either way, there wouldn't be much time.

Locating the file server was the first order of business.
He cut off the jack from a desk computer's network
connection and used his multimeter to see if any of the
wires were in use. A red one was, which meant the server
wasn't physically disconnected from the desk units. That
was a good break. He found a yellow wire that had no signal and attached a tone generator to it. Then he moved an
inductive amplifier along the cable, tracing it back to the
server.

The trail led to the next room, which was locked with
a retinal scanner entry system. No chance of getting through
that. It was common to have a server under the tightest security, since hacking was easiest if you had direct access
to the console. He'd have to work from the outside, which
also meant he'd have to stay in the room where Rod might
try his Dirty Harry routine.

Berger reattached the jack near the workstation and
hooked the line into his laptop. Then he sat on the floor,
in case he had to climb back into the desk well, and loaded
the Telnet program. A few moments later, he connected to
the server.

The prompt showed a "%," which told him it was a
UNIX system. Berger rebooted the server and entered the
keystrokes to force it into "debug" mode. At the cursor, he
typed "list," which caused a core dump and scrolled the
server's memory. On the server itself, the data wasn't encrypted, and by using a core dump, he was bypassing the
login password system.

A warning flashed on the screen: "12 minutes to hub
disconnect." Shit. That meant he would be physically sev-

ered from the server in twelve minutes. He had to get his
ass in gear.

Berger had just located the checksum when he heard a
noise and his head snapped up. He couldn't see anything.
Was it his imagination? He divided his attention between
the screen and the room as he went through the next steps.

Berger put the checksum through an algorithm to cal-
culate the offset, which allowed him to find the root directory. The address to the left of the root directory was
the main directory of the system, which listed all of the
other directories. He looked through and found one named
"Mirage." His pulse quickened as he added the offset to
the Mirage address, which took him to the Mirage directory.

"9 minutes to hub disconnect" flashed on the screen.

Berger started copying the contents when the unmistakable sound of a turning doorknob sent him into the desk
well. He shut off the laptop, so it wouldn't make any noise,
even though he'd have to start over. The footsteps again
walked through the room, then stopped near his desk. He
wondered if Rod had seen the wires leading under the desk,
or if he understood that they would lead him right to Berger.
Either way, there wasn't much Berger could do now.

Radio static again. "Rod, you want anything from the
donut guy?"

"What's he got?"

"Hell, I don't know. If you want something, get down
here."

Rod grumbled under his breath and left the room.

Berger climbed out and repeated the procedure.

"5 minutes to hub disconnect."

He started copying the files in the Mirage directory onto
the laptop's hard drive. As they scrolled past, he noticed
that one of the files had been deleted.

Berger stopped the copying and examined the deleted file. It was the information on the Director of the project, which was what Jill wanted the most. This guy must be pretty well connected if he could delete a file from a secure facility.

"4 minutes to hub disconnect."

Computers don't immediately delete data; they simply tell the operating system that it's okay to overwrite them when it needs the space. If this was done recently, Berger might be able to recover it. He went to the "Mirage.log" file and found that the deletion had been done only in the last month. Fortunately, the hacker wasn't that good. Their technique left a trail, which Berger followed to the location of the file. He then used his Utilities program to restore what was left of the data.

Within a few moments he had it, although the data had been partially overwritten.

"?e??h C??s."

There was also a birth date of "May ???."

He started to copy it when the system announced "Hub Disconnect" and the screen went blank. He hadn't had time to copy the deleted data, so he tried to sear it into his memory. Hopefully those pieces would be enough to match whatever data they could find through nonclassified sources.

Berger unhooked the cables, closed the laptop, and put everything in the tool case. He left the workstation computer on, in case turning it off triggered another alert, then stood by the door and listened. When he didn't hear anything for several minutes, he stepped into the hallway.

Berger realized he was sweating, and hoped that wouldn't look suspicious. He forced himself to walk at a normal pace as he went toward the hallway with the telephone equipment closet. Turning the corner, he let out a long breath.

In front of the closet, he saw the squat guard from the front desk, standing with his arms folded across his chest. A scowl crumpled his loose forehead.

"Where the hell have you been?" snarled the guard.

"I, uh, well, I had to use the bathroom."

"Bathroom's the other way."

"I, uh, got lost I guess."

"I told you not to wander around."

"Sorry. I had to piss really bad." Berger was sure that he wasn't very convincing. Apart from his clothes being soaked, his voice was quavering and his leg was starting to shake.

The guard pulled his nightstick out of his belt and slapped the palm of his hand. "Open up that toolkit, son."

"I . . . I'm not allowed . . . it's against regulations . . . I—"

The guard grabbed the radio microphone pinned to his shoulder and spoke into it. "Rod, get over to the telephone closet on the double."

Berger considered running for the front door, though he didn't think he could outrun even this porker. Especially with Rod on the way. The guard reached for the toolbox without taking his eyes off Berger.

"Don't!" shouted Berger, for want of anything more intelligent to say.

Rod came up behind him. He stood close to Berger's back, crowding him. "Give him the toolkit. Now."

At that moment, Leon, the driver of the van, came trotting down the hall. Berger and the two guards looked up. Leon was wearing his sunglasses indoors.

"FBI," said Leon, flashing his ID. "We got a bomb threat, and we have to evacuate the facility. You work here?"

"Yeah," the squat guard said tentatively.

"Good. Call your cohorts and have them get everyone outside. Bomb squad is on the way."

Leon pointed at Berger. "You. Come with me."

Rod stepped between them. "We have to detain this man. He was acting suspiciously and—"

"I'll take him from here," said Leon, grabbing the toolkit.

"But—"

"Sir, we have no time for arguments. The tip we received said five"—he looked at his watch—"make that four minutes." Leon reached over and pulled the fire alarm lever, breaking the small glass rod. A high-pitched *hee-haw* blared in their ears.

The short guard looked back and forth between Leon and Berger. A third guard arrived.

"What's going on?" she asked.

The squat guard continued studying Berger and the driver. A moment later, he said, "We gotta clear the building. Bomb threat."

The woman looked panicked. She and Rod took off down one corridor, while Tubby grumbled off down another. Leon grabbed Berger's arm and rushed him toward the front door.

Berger whispered, "How'd you know to—"

"Outside."

They climbed in the van and drove quickly out of the parking lot. Fire engines rushed by them from the other direction.

"How'd you know to come in for me?" asked Berger.

"Ms. Landis had a wire on you. She told me to grab you if you got in trouble."

"You thought I was in trouble?"

Leon pulled the sunglasses down on his nose and looked

over them at Berger. "With all due respect, sir, you should not take up acting as a career."

Berger laughed. "Why didn't you tell me I was wired?"

"We thought it best not to make you any more self-conscious than necessary."

That was pretty insulting, thought Berger. Especially since they were right. "Where's the bug?"

"Your telephone company ID."

Berger looked down and saw that the ID was too thick for a piece of paper. The miracle of electronics.

"Thanks," said Berger.

Leon nodded.

Lenny Seal ice-skated every winter afternoon. At age seventy-four, that meant he'd skated every winter for seventy-two years. His arthritis disappeared when he pulled on the skates and glided across the frozen pond in Kissena Park.

It was a particularly cold day in Flushing, New York, and he was happy to be warming up after the first two laps. There were lots of little kids around, which was typical since they'd discovered that Seal kept peppermints in his pocket. One if you asked him nicely. Two if you fell down and were crying.

Smoothly turning to skate backward, he doled out candies to a gaggle of five- and six-year-olds who clustered around him. Once their hands and mouths were filled, Seal spun forward and leaned into the long strokes, picking up a little speed. He could no longer do the jumps and spins of his youth, and in fact he'd moved to hockey skates about fifteen years ago. But he could still keep pace with people forty years his junior.

Seal finished a few more laps, then coasted over to the fire that burned illegally in an old trash can. The smell of burning wood filled his nostrils, making his eyes water as he watched the small embers drifting upward in the draft. Seal took off his woolen mittens and stretched out his fingers, warming himself. Studying his hands, he marveled how you never see yourself aging. Not in the mirror. Not in the liver- spotted hands silhouetted against the flames.

"You're a good skater," came a pleasant voice.

Seal turned to see a man in his thirties with dark brown hair and a high forehead. He was wearing a camel hair overcoat.

"Thanks, young fella."

"Are you Mr. Seal?"

"Sure am. And who might you be?"

"Your neighbor, Mrs. Alter, said I might find you here. I'm sorry to have to tell you this, sir, but your wife's had an accident. She's in the Queens Medical Center."

Seal's face drained. At age seventy-four, the idea of being mortal is pretty close. But not that close. Not him. Not Cynthia. Life without Cynthia wasn't . . .

His skates slipped out from under him, and his tailbone hit the ground with a crack. The young man gently helped him up.

"What happened to Cynthia?" asked Seal.

"I'm sorry, I don't know. Mrs. Alter didn't give me any more information. Would you like a ride to the hospital?"

He looked up gratefully. "That would be very kind of you, son."

Seal got to his feet and found that his back hurt pretty badly from the fall. He sat on a nearby bench and let the young man take off his skates and tie his shoes. Then he put his arm around the man's shoulder and hobbled to a maroon minivan.

"Sit here in the back, Mr. Seal. It's more comfortable than the front." He slid the door open and helped Seal up

the step. Then the man closed the door and Seal sat back
into the plush seat. As he heard the engine start, he remembered that he'd forgotten his mittens by the fire. Surely
this nice young man would go fetch them.

Seal tried the sliding door. It was locked and wouldn't
open. Must be some child safety thing. Then he tried the
other side. Same thing. He leaned forward to yell at the
driver and found there was a wooden panel behind the curtains that separated him from the front seat. Seal pounded
on the partition, but no one responded. He pounded a little harder. The side of his fist stung. Finally, he sat back
in the seat. The driver probably couldn't hear him over the
motor.

Too bad. He'd had those mittens for twenty years. Cynthia had knitted them.

CHAPTER 37

As soon as Berger was airborne out of Utah, Jill got his call on a scrambled line. Sixty seconds later, she had Armstrong searching the Army records for a "?e??h C??s," with a birthday in May of some year, who'd been in the service around the time of Mirage. She had a hit within an hour.

"Kenneth Combs," reported Armstrong. "That's the good news. The bad news is that he doesn't exist anymore."

"No one erases their name from a database if they don't exist."

"He's deep underground. No record of him for almost three years. No property, no activity on his Social Security number, no utilities. He's obviously using an assumed name. We're going after relatives and Army buddies, and we're putting his fingerprints through AFIS to see if they match somebody else who's surfaced."

"My orders are real simple: 'Find Him Now.'"

"Got it."

Jill sighed. "At least we know that Kelly is credible. And that we're on the right track, even if it's a dead end. How's Rover doing with the chemicals?"

"So-so. We know they're in an area of Montana, but the sunspots are keeping us from pinpointing exactly where. The sunspot activity is supposed to slack off in the next few days, and hopefully we'll have the exact location."

"Hopefully? We only *have* a few days before this attack. Do you understand that tens of thousands of lives are at stake?"

"Of course I do. But Rover's all we've got. And we can't be sure we're tracking anything besides the containers themselves. If the chemicals got separated from them, kiss your butt goodbye."

She twisted the phone cord tightly around her palm, then let out a rough breath in an attempt to calm herself. "What about tracing the e-mail order for Neo-Ketamine?"

"Another dead end. Came through a bulletin board in Jamaica, via Hong Kong. They used something called I.P. Spoofing, and the cybersleuths ran out of rope before they could find the sender."

"Berger said he copied most of the Mirage data on a disk. His jet gets in from Utah in the next few minutes. Have someone get the disk and see if there's anything useful on it."

Seal had been in the van for almost fifteen minutes. He tried banging on the wooden driver partition again. Still no response. The park was only about ten minutes from the hospital, and he didn't recognize the scenery he saw through the tinted window. Until he saw the sign pointing to La Guardia Airport.

A few minutes later, the van stopped abruptly and rocked back and forth from the momentum. The sliding door opened and Seal saw the young man standing there.

"Son, what are we doing here? You said we were going to the hosp—"

Seal froze. Parked next to them was another van, and Cynthia was getting out.

"Cynthia! You okay?" He tried to get up and his lower back went into a sharp spasm that stopped him midway.

Cynthia cried out, "Lenny! They said you were—"

The man took Seal's arm to help him out. "We'll explain everything on the airplane, Mr. Seal," he said gently.

"Airplane? What are you talking about? I have to feed my dogs in an hour."

"We'll take care of that."

"You lied about my wife."

"I'm sorry, sir. Please. Let me help you to the plane."

That evening, Jill stood in the kitchen of the safe house, stirring a pot of chicken soup. Several brown paper grocery bags stood in parade formation along the counter.

Berger was next to her, dropping ice cubes into tall glasses with yellow squiggles on the sides.

"So give it to me straight," he said. "Was any of the stuff I got helpful?"

"You led us to the name of the Director, Kenneth Combs. He's under deep cover, but we're looking for him. You also got a list of most everyone in the project, which could be very useful. We know Combs is using some of these people in his operation, so we're tracking them down. Maybe we can turn someone."

"In other words, I didn't do much."

"I didn't say that. Your information may prove very helpful."

"May prove helpful. That sounds like something you say to kids who warm the bench during baseball games."

"Let me rephrase that. You did the most phenomenal job of computer hacking known to humankind, and because of you we solved the case and I've been promoted to Director of the entire Bureau."

"That's more like it." Berger picked up a glass of ice cubes. "I did play a rather good James Bond, didn't I?" He shook the ice cubes and continued in a horrid English accent, "Shaken, not stirred."

She took the glass out of his hands and put it on the counter. "Stick to computers."

"Nice talk for someone who laid down his hard drive for you. Where are you with the other leads?"

Jill explained about the courier and the e-mail. "Do you think you could trace the e-mail?"

"No. If your computer guys say the chain's broken, I'm sure I can't do any better."

They sat down to dinner at the wobbly Formica breakfast table. Jill had brought a wine that Berger found tasty, even though he didn't particularly like wine. The first few sips gave him a light buzz.

"You know," he said, "while I was curled up inside that desk well, the only thing I thought about was seeing you again."

"Oh yeah?" she said skeptically.

"Well, not really. I was scared to death and worried about getting my ass out in one piece. But that sounded more romantic, didn't it?"

She threw her napkin at him playfully. "Are you naturally this weird, or is it the Elavil?"

"In real life, I'm pretty shy. Figuring I've only got a few more days of coherence makes me so incredibly bold that I feel like some alien took over my body. I'm usually tongue-tied when I'm with attractive women."

Jill flushed a lovely shade of crimson. "And here I figured you were a Casanova who broke long lines of ladies' hearts."

Ladies' hearts. The words sent Berger's mind directly to Linda, his missing girlfriend. His light mood vanished and the wine buzz turned into a jackhammer. He realized that he hadn't thought about Linda for several days. Now the memories twisted in his stomach, as he felt that he would never see her again. And sitting here with Jill, at an intimate dinner, he had the feeling that he was cheating on Linda.

"Are you okay?" asked Jill.

His throat closed, and he couldn't speak. Without looking up, he waved her off.

It was almost midnight, and Berger hadn't stopped thinking about Linda. And the way he'd rejected Jill and sent her home. Why was Linda intruding after all of this? He felt something had happened to her, and that he was responsible, yet he couldn't remember anything specific. The vague sensation was like an itch he couldn't reach.

Despite his body's exhaustion, around two in the morning it became obvious he couldn't sleep. He stopped pacing the apartment and loaded a chess program into his computer. Even though stimulating his mind would keep him awake, he needed to change the mental scenery.

Playing chess against computers was different from playing against humans. Computers were tougher because they didn't make calculation errors, but they had a weakness that people didn't: Computers were trained to grab the opponent's pieces, and to protect their own at all costs. Berger's strategy was to preoccupy the computer's attention with one or the other of those needs, while sliding his own attack through the side door.

Tonight he felt like a quieter game, so he used the English Opening of pawn to c3. Not many people studied the English, so he figured the programmers hadn't either.

About twenty moves into the game, he saw the opportunity to sacrifice a pawn in exchange for moving his knight to a central position. The computer went for it.

That's when it hit him. A sacrifice. This was either a really stupid or a brilliant idea. It also scared the shit out of him, which of late had become something he was getting used to.

Propelled by a shot of adrenaline, he called the guard, who was his only contact with the outside world, and told him to get Jill on the phone.

"This better be important," said Jill when she arrived at 3:00 A.M. She hadn't buttoned her blouse all the way up, which was distracting Berger.

"Do you trust this guy Kelly?" asked Berger.

"So far, his story's been one hundred percent. Why?"

He handed her a cup of coffee and she blew gently across the top.

"I have an idea that would require his cooperation," said Berger.

"I'm listening."

"Here's how I see the situation. You may or may not find Combs before Thanksgiving. And if he's as smart as he seems to be, I'd bet against it."

"I'm hoping we'll trace—"

"Obviously you keep doing what you're doing. Here's my idea. There's a chess tactic called a sacrifice, where you give up a piece to draw out your opponent. I think we might be able to draw out Combs and bring him to us."

"Go on." She sipped the coffee.

"The newspapers thought the EXC bomber was killed in the explosion. Presumably so did Combs. If we put a story in the paper that says I'm alive, and hint that maybe I know something, that could make him nervous."

"We have to assume Combs knows you're alive. He's the one who shot at you and blew up your house."

"Good point." *Like, I'm an idiot to have missed it,* Berger thought. *I must really be tired.* "Okay. So he knows I'm alive. But whoever is sponsoring this terrorist attack may not know I'm still breathing. If they think I could point the way to Combs, and he could lead to them, maybe they'd pressure him to find me. Or maybe they'd back out of the deal. Making everybody nervous can only be to our advantage."

"This already sounds too dangerous."

"You won't like the rest any better. We have Kelly send an e-mail to the address they used to buy chemicals. We can't trace it, but they'll probably pick up the message. The e-mail says that Kelly knows what they're up to and that he's got me. He'll deliver me for a million dollars or something. Then you intercept them when they make the exchange."

"That would be incredibly reckless. We'd be endangering two civilians, and based on how they eluded us with the courier, there's a high probability they could grab you right out from under our noses. Then you and Kelly are dead, and we don't even have Combs."

"For all intents and purposes, I'm dead in a few days anyway. And Kelly doesn't even have to be there. He could just tell them to wire him the money. Who cares if they stiff him?"

"It's too dangerous. We can't risk it."

"You got something better?"

Jill arrived home and called Davidson at 7:30 A.M. East Coast time.

"Absolutely insane," pronounced Davidson.

"Agreed. On the other hand, the Wednesday before

Thanksgiving is four days away and we're running out of rope."

"I don't see how we can endanger civilians like that."

"How many civilians are in danger if we don't find Combs?"

A beat of silence. "I have to talk to the Chief about this one."

CHAPTER 38

Within an hour after hanging up with Davidson, Jill had a green light for Berger's plan to draw out Combs. She called Kelly, who endorsed the idea and insisted on personally delivering Berger.

"That's far too risky."

"God has blessed me with many gifts. They are useless if I don't use them to help others."

"These people will not appreciate your gifts. They may well kill you just to avoid the ransom."

"The first thing I'll tell them is that a reporter has been instructed to open an envelope describing the entire story if I'm not back within a few hours."

"You're watching too many B movies. They might call your bluff."

"They might. But I can be quite convincing. You see, I majored in drama at Tufts. And the fact that I show the courage to walk into their hands will speak volumes."

"If they pick up our coverage, you're dead. Really, Mr. Kelly. You'd be just as effective behind the scenes."

"I'm the only one you've got who's seen the Director.

I can insist on meeting him face-to-face, and that way you know you're on to the right person. Otherwise, you'll be dealing with middlemen."

"If something happened, I'm not sure I could live with it."

"Will it be easier to live with what happens if you choose another course?"

Jill got in bed early that night, hoping she'd made the right decision about Kelly. She reflected how the biggest decisions are always made on incomplete information. It was art as much as science, which was both reassuring and discomforting.

She had always wanted to be in the big leagues, yet had never fully appreciated a simple truth. When you play hardball, you can get killed by one that's a few inches off course. And the bigger the stakes of the game, the more intense your competitors.

Rolling over on her side, she slowly let out a long breath and fell into a restless sleep.

The next morning, Jill sat in the safe house with Berger. Kelly arrived from the airport a few minutes later, and she saw Berger steal a look at his artificial leg. Kelly seemed poised and quietly confident as he looked Jill in the eye and clasped her hand with both of his. Although his face and demeanor were relaxed, his hands were cold.

Kelly and Berger fell quickly into conversation, leaning toward each other with body language that suggested they were reunited childhood friends.

"The fuse is lit," she said, handing the morning *Los Angeles Times* to Berger. Kelly edged in close and they read the story together.

Jill continued, "The article says 'undisclosed sources'

revealed that John Berger, who was thought to have been killed in the EXC blast, was alive and in hiding. They report rumors that he'd been brainwashed, and through the use of drugs, the FBI is close to having the identity of the perpetrators. The same rumors say this may be connected to a highly secret government project code-named Mirage. I added the name to get their attention and hopefully create paranoia about their own people."

"That should make the Director's day," said Berger, handing the newspaper over to Kelly. "What happened with your tracking down the other people in Mirage?"

"We've interviewed roughly eighty percent of them. The four who were willing to talk had no information beyond their narrow section. The majority pretended not to know anything. About twenty have totally disappeared. I wonder where they could be?"

Berger chuckled. "The Kenneth Combs Home for Wayward Minds, if I had to guess."

"We're seeing if any of them were careless enough to leave a trail."

"I've got Mr. Kelly's e-mail message ready," said Berger. "We're sending it to the address of the Neo-Ketamine confirmation, and we've set up a return address they can't trace. I'll get the reply here, thanks to your supplying me an umbilical connection to the Internet."

"It comes out right after you use it. The safe house people went nuts."

"I couldn't help injecting a touch of irony. I set up an e-mail account for your dummy corporation with the same Hong Kong bulletin board that they used."

"Don't get too cute."

"What will I be saying in this e-mail?" asked Kelly, laying down the newspaper.

Berger read the message aloud. "'Dear Mr. Combs, or

shall I say "Director." I was also involved in the Mirage project, and I'm fully aware of your role there. I see that the newspapers have made the same connection.

"'I am happy to see you profit where bureaucrats have been so shortsighted. What you do is of no consequence to me, although I feel I should profit as well. And for that, I am prepared to deliver Mr. Berger to you.

"'If you are interested, I suggest you move quickly. My sources tell me that he is close to supplying the FBI with information you would prefer they not receive. The price is One Million, U.S. Cash on delivery, bills with random serial numbers. I assume it is a fraction of the compensation you are receiving from your clients, and the price is not negotiable.

"'Respond to this e-mail address. The offer and the address are good for twenty-four hours only. Signed, A Fan.'"

"I've never been quite so eloquent," said Kelly.

"Send it?" asked Berger.

Jill looked back and forth at the two of them. Their expressions reminded her of children waiting for a parent's decision about which punishment to mete out.

Finally, she nodded.

Combs's phone rang at 4:00 A.M. He fumbled for the damn thing, which ended up in two pieces on the floor. He could already hear the screaming before he got the handset to his ear.

"Whoever you are," Combs grunted, "you're not supposed to have this number."

"You fucking bastard! You knew this all along. I'll string you up by your testicles." The speaker's English was deteriorating with each sentence, in inverse proportion to the escalating rage.

"And good morning to you. Who the hell is this?" He

knew exactly who it was. He was just trying to buy time to gather his wits.

"If you withhold information like this, we cannot trust each other. The agreement is off. You will have instructions on how to return the deposit within an hour."

"What are you talking about?"

"Don't play coy with us. The wire services are carrying the story."

"I'm not playing coy. What are you talking about?"

"I'm talking about this Berger asshole."

Combs bolted upright. "What about him?"

Exasperated sigh. "He's alive, goddamn it, and you know it. We are out. He is now your problem. If you even hint toward implicating us, you are a dead man."

Combs stood up, cradling the phone against his shoulder. How the hell did they know Berger was alive? It's in the newspapers? Shit.

"I swear to you," answered Combs, "I know nothing about this. If he really is alive, which I seriously doubt, he doesn't know anything. You're well insulated from us, even if there were any problems. The plan is a solid go. We have the subjects assembled, and we have the materials ready."

"No. You have compromised us and our cause. We want an immediate refund."

Slight problem. Combs had spent most of the deposit on preparation. "Tell you what. I'm going to lower your price by ten million until one of two things happens. One, I take care of Mr. Berger permanently, or two, your event goes down without a hitch. And you can hold the ten million for thirty days after the event to be sure."

The hesitation told Combs he was getting through.

"Twenty million and we will consider it."

Forever the used car salesman. "Fifteen."

"I will call you in an hour. Whatever we decide, if anyone even points in our direction, you will not wake up the next morning. Goodbye, Mr. *Combs,* or whatever you now call yourself." The line went dead.

Combs felt a cold sting in his chest. They knew his name. They had his ultraprivate number. Berger was on Elavil, and it was now public knowledge that he was alive. Combs knew there was a way to extract what Berger knew, although the FBI probably hadn't found it. He hoped.

He went into the kitchen and made a pot of strong coffee. Then he started the phone calls.

Berger awoke with the knife against his throat. He looked up and saw a man in a ski mask, holding a huge blade tightly across Berger's windpipe.

"Make a sound and you'll bleed like a skinned deer," the voice said. It sounded vaguely familiar.

Berger tried to blink away the sleep.

"Get up," ordered the man.

Berger stood. "Walk." The point of the knife pushed between Berger's shoulder blades, propelling him forward.

How the hell did anyone get into the safe house? Was someone bought off? What is this? And how did he know the voice?

"You're going to die," said two voices, speaking in unison, then laughing.

Now Berger remembered. The voices in his head. The ones that had been chased away by the Elavil. The ones that had attacked him in prison.

This had to mean the Elavil was wearing off. He was heading into the final round. He felt like a terminal patient being told the experimental treatment wasn't working. Having some doctor feign sympathy, while he told Berger to get his affairs in order.

"Fuck you," said Berger. "Go ahead and cut my throat if you want. Otherwise, I'm tired and I'm going back to sleep." He spun around to face his attacker, and saw that the room was empty.

CHAPTER 39

Dawn crept into Combs's kitchen, where he was working on his second pot of coffee and the Berger problem. The coffee was cold, and so was his strategy. At least he hadn't heard back from the Serbians, which he took as a good sign.

Shortly after 6:00 A.M., the door buzzer startled him. He wasn't expecting anyone. Combs took out his Glock before pushing the intercom button.

"Who's there?"

"Baxter. It's important."

Combs tucked the Glock into the belt of his bathrobe and checked the security cameras to see if Baxter had been followed. When he was satisfied Baxter was alone, he cautiously opened the door.

They went into the kitchen, where Baxter handed Combs a computer printout, then poured himself a cup of coffee. Combs read the e-mail from Kelly, offering up Berger for a million dollars.

"What do you make of this?" asked Combs.

"You must really be rattled if you're asking what I think," said Baxter without a trace of humor.

"You have an opinion or not?"

"Well, the e-mail could be legit. This guy seems to know about Mirage. On the other hand—"

Combs waved off Baxter's words. "Pretty coincidental that this thing shows up right now, isn't it? The e-mail and the newspaper story, one right after the other. Sure would make nice bait for a trap."

"Yeah. It sure would."

"On the other hand, even if it's a trap, they might really produce Berger. How safely could we set things up?"

"You're thinking about going for this?"

"Our operation's in jeopardy because some meddler set off Berger's bomb a few hours early. The shooters didn't get him when he left the mental ward, and now he's locked up tighter than a frog's ass. Since Berger is a loose cannon who could fuck things up to a fare-thee-well, I can't pass up any chances to get him."

"But it's almost certainly a trap. You'd be risking everything."

"Oh, so now Mr. On the Other Hand thinks it's a trap?" Combs shook his head in exasperation. "Of course it's a trap. I asked you whether we can steal the fucking cheese."

Baxter thought for several moments. "We could meet Berger and this blackmailer at a remote site, then take them both out. I'd use a freelancer who doesn't know who he's working for."

"No. We'd have to be sure it was Berger, and not some look-alike. And anyone this smart would have a contingency plan to keep us from doing exactly that."

"Second best would be to use some of our sidewinders. They've evaded surveillance by the CIA. The twins are particularly good. Downside is they could be connected to us if it doesn't work."

Combs sipped the cold, bitter coffee, which puckered his mouth as he swallowed. "Better. Come up with a detailed plan for me to review within the hour. Set up hoops and hurdles, and get them to me without company. Do whatever you want to the blackmailer, but bring in Berger alive."

Baxter nodded.

Combs poured the rest of his coffee into the drain. "This would be a good time to use Berger's girlfriend, don't you think?"

"They're going to cut me?" asked Berger.

Jill answered. "Just a small flap on your leg."

He shifted in his seat. "If someone's going to handle my thighs, I'd hoped it would be you."

"Trust me. You don't want me slicing into your leg."

"I've done kinkier things on first dates."

The light banter was distracting Berger from the e-mail printout that lay on the breakfast table. The reply had been curt. "Interested in proposition. Supply terms at once." His eyes kept sneaking glances whenever Jill looked away. He felt sure she had caught him.

"How's Kelly doing?" asked Berger.

"Extremely well. He's either very brave or an excellent actor. Or both."

"I'll be a better performer this time. Since I don't have to talk."

"Right. Don't miss any chances to shut up."

"I took a shot at the reply." He handed her a typed page. "Basically, it says to meet in a public place, and that the Director must be there personally. I suggest the Santa Monica Pier or the Century City Shopping Mall. Kelly will bring me and expect the money in cash."

"Looks fine," said Jill, laying down the paper. "Now let me show you a few self-defense moves, just in case." Jill moved a chair and coffee table out of the way, clearing an area of the safe house living room. She had Berger put her into a hammerlock. He was so enthralled with the smooth feel of her skin that he missed how she got out of it. She impatiently repeated the procedure, showing him how to jump and spin to get loose. He tried it and spun the wrong way, wrenching his wrist and arm.

"Sorry," he said. "I should have warned you. I'm a major schlemiel. That means someone—"

"I understand Yiddish."

Berger smiled with enlightenment. "Oh? A nice Jewish girl in the FBI? Hoover must be spinning in his grave."

"Try the hammerlock again."

He spun the wrong way a second time. "Jill, forget it. I'm not particularly physical, and I'm certainly not coordinated. That's why I don't make a living with my body."

She slid the coffee table back onto its indentations in the carpet. "I'm not sure we should go through with this."

"I don't have to fight Mike Tyson. I just have to look pretty. Or, more accurately, look pissed that I'm being delivered by Kelly."

"I don't know if we can adequately protect you."

"I'm toast in a couple of days anyhow. Last night I had another hallucination."

Jill's eyes betrayed that she was stung. "You had what?"

"I heard voices. Telling me I deserve to die. That means I'm down to the last few gallons, huh?"

Jill's silence answered his question.

"Then we better hurry," he said as he went to the computer and typed in the e-mail response. Jill stood over his shoulder until he pushed "Enter" and sent the message.

He moved to the couch and patted for her to sit beside him. She hesitated, then sat a cushion away, keeping her knees tightly together, and her back ramrod straight. She looked ahead, not at Berger.

"With the marbles dropping out of my brain, I feel like I'm about to move out of town or something," he said. "I'm going to miss you."

Her eyes glistened. She turned to him, and one of them spilled over. "I'll miss you too. I don't know if I can let you do this in good conscience. You should spend your last hours doing something—"

"Productive? Helpful to others? I think that's what we're talking about."

She looked away. Berger's hands grew cold, in fear of his next move. He forced himself to do it anyway, and his heart pounded as he reached across and took her hand. Hers was cold as well. She didn't pull back her hand, yet she didn't look at him either. He slid across the couch and sat with his side touching hers. She didn't move away. And he didn't know what to do next.

After several moments of being frozen in place, he caressed her cheek and turned her face toward him. She was so beautiful, soft and caring. The tears gave her a surrealistic look of fantasy, as though she were glistening after a gentle rain. He moved his lips to hers, and he closed his eyes as soon as he saw that she had closed hers.

They kissed deeply for a long while. He wanted to savor the moment, to make it last. To burn it into his memory, deeply enough to survive what lay ahead. Their breathing and passion grew, and his arms embraced her fully. She turned toward him and their bodies moved against each other. Slowly, he unbuttoned her blouse and she lay back on the couch. He continued to undress her, and she insisted on getting up to turn out the light.

In the semidarkness, he saw her pull her blouse across her midriff, apparently self-conscious about the few extra pounds. He found that so endearing. As he kissed her neck and moved down across her breasts, she responded intensely. He then kissed her stomach and moved between her legs.

Finally, she pulled the blouse off her abdomen. He slid on top of her, and the touch of her skin bathed him in an erotic glow. They began slowly, escalating to an intense coupling that exhausted them in a cascade of perspiration.

Afterward, they moved to the bed and lay tenderly side by side. He toyed with the ends of her hair, and she fell asleep with a light smile across her lips.

Berger tried to stay awake. He didn't want to miss any of his remaining hours.

CHAPTER 40

Jill slipped out of the bed and saw that it was almost 5:00 A.M. She knew she'd have to sign out with the safe house guard, and hopefully no one would question why she and Berger were working so late.

She collected her clothes from several spots around the living room. Her mood was up, buoyed. A welcome contrast to the last few weeks. She hadn't slept with a man for almost two years, since Ted had gotten sick. At least the skills had come right back. Like riding a bicycle, she thought. A bicycle with an exceptional seat.

To her delight, she hadn't felt any pangs of cheating on Ted. She felt light on her feet, as though she were floating. Ted would want her to get on with her life. He'd want her to find an intimate relationship and move on to a new chapter.

Jill gathered her purse and debated whether to say goodbye. She decided on a light kiss that wouldn't wake him, since she doubted he'd let her leave without a protest. Or maybe another round, which would cost what little sleep she hoped to grab.

She took a pad and scribbled, "See you in the morning," then drew a little heart at the bottom. As an afterthought, she drew an arrow through it.

After placing the note quietly on the pillow, she kissed him on the cheek. It caused him to stir and smile. She watched him a few more moments, yawned, and left.

Berger hummed softly as he stirred the scrambled eggs in a pan. He was listening to a CD of 1960s music, probably selected by the father of the kid who picked the safe house videotapes, and moved the plastic spatula in rhythm to Jimi Hendrix's "Foxey Lady."

He'd been disappointed to find a note instead of Jill next to him in the morning, yet he knew she'd be there shortly. He had lain in bed for a long while, rereading the note over and over. In fact, he even smelled it, and was disappointed that the only aroma was pencil graphite. He'd tried rubbing it against his cheek with similar disappointment.

The heavy metal door opened and Jill came in. She was scowling as she walked past him without a greeting.

"What's wrong?" he asked.

"Sit down, please." She wasn't looking at him.

Shit.

His mind replayed Cheryl Kravitz. Cheryl, who had the largest boobs in the tenth grade at Culver City High. Cheryl, who never gave him the time of day until he was the only person she knew at a beach party. A party where she was more than a little drunk, and they had done more than a little kissing. Cheryl, who the next day at school and forever thereafter pretended she didn't know him.

"Why are you acting so formally?" asked Berger, afraid of the answer. "I carry the ultimate guarantee not to kiss and tell. I'm isolated from the world until I lose the ability to remember."

She wasn't smiling.

"Jill, what's wrong?"

"We can't do this."

"Last night wasn't some casual one-night stand. I—"

"No, I'm not talking about that. I mean we can't go on with this Mirage plan."

He was relieved she wasn't dumping him. But he was also confused. "Why not?"

"Sit down please."

He definitely didn't like the sound of that. His eyes never left hers as he felt for the couch behind him and fumbled his way down.

Jill sat next to him, a cushion away. "Your girlfriend, Linda. We found her body this morning."

The news hit Berger hard, physically propelling him backward into the seat. He felt the sting of tears in his eyes, and hoped Jill wasn't offended.

"What happened?" he asked.

"Her body was left . . . at the rubble of your old house. She's been dead since about the time you were programmed."

"How did she die?" His anger swirled into eddies as his eyes filled with warm tears.

"Best we can tell, she was strangled with some kind of cord. The body was . . . wasn't in great shape."

Berger had a graphic image of her being strangled. Her eyes bulging, pleading for his help. Trying to scream without the air to even gasp. Her face turning blue.

Snorting back a sob, Berger felt light-headed. His stomach soured as he realized this was more than an image. It was almost a memory, buried in the deep muck that fogged his mind. He was afraid of trying to retrieve it.

"It's obviously a warning," Jill continued. "To show that these guys play hardball. That they're on to us, and setting a countertrap. John, this has become too risky. I'm aborting the plan."

He slid next to her on the couch and took her hand. She pulled away and said, "Please don't do that. I'm stopping this operation. There's no discussion."

"You can't stop it. It's your only chance to find these bastards in time. What have I got to be afraid of? You know what's going to happen to me in a few days."

"They could torture you. Mutilate you. Who knows what else."

"This was my idea. I'm standing by it."

"No."

"Yes. You know you don't have anything else. Please. I need to do this."

She sat for several minutes in silence. "If, and I'm only saying if, we went forward, then we'd have to forget about last night."

"What? What's that got to do with it?"

"I'd have to run this operation as a detached professional. I couldn't think clearly if we were involved with each other."

"You mean the prisoner doesn't get any last requests?"

"This isn't a joke."

"You can just turn your emotions off like a spigot?"

"No. It wouldn't be easy. But I couldn't live with myself afterward unless I did. Especially if something went wrong."

Now Berger was feeling like the one-night stand. The crush of her withdrawal slammed him hard. Was she doing this just to make him abort the operation? If so, that was shitty.

"Fine," he spat out. "Last night never happened. This is business from now on, and maybe it's better if I deal with another agent. In fact, you shouldn't be here alone with me. Come back later this morning when the doctor's here."

Berger saw that her eyes were wet, and he worried he'd hit her too hard. He almost reached for her.

"All right," she said quietly. She got up and left without saying goodbye.

He ran to the door and watched her go down the hall. From the movement of her elbow, she seemed to be wiping her eyes.

Berger stomped back inside. Everyone around him was dead. His mother and father. Linda. Probably Max. He desperately needed someone's touch, yet had just shoved away Jill.

He turned off Jimi Hendrix and scraped the burnt eggs into the trash. Then he threw away the pan as well.

The doctor arrived later that morning, and Berger was disappointed that Jill hadn't come back with him. The doctor looked like he was about thirteen years old, with an unlined face, a gold-stud earring, and straight black hair with a part on the left. He told Berger to drop his trousers and lie down on the couch.

The plan assumed that Combs's people would search Berger thoroughly for wires. Accordingly, the doctor was implanting a homing device under Berger's skin.

"I don't normally make house calls," said the doctor with a wink.

"I'm flattered." Berger picked up the transmitter, which was about half the size of a playing card. "Will I be able to get *I Love Lucy* on this thing?"

"I'm afraid we no longer offer that channel. You can choose between Fishing or Home Shopping."

"Fishing. It'll be too frustrating if I can't call in for the porcelain carousels that play 'Somewhere My Love.' *Owww! That hurts!*"

"Sorry. That's the worst of it. Take a look."

Berger sat up and saw a thin incision on his thigh. He couldn't see the device underneath, and when he ran his hand over his leg, he couldn't feel it either.

"Nice job, Doc."

"Thanks. I also do hemorrhoids."

"What about breast enlargements?"

"Only after hours."

Berger sat up. "Is this a bug?"

"No. The feds won't be able to hear you, but it puts out a signal that lets them track you. The batteries last about three days, and it's on a microwave frequency that's not in the range of anything they're likely to have. If they can't feel it or hear it, they won't know about it. In theory."

"Thanks for adding that 'in theory.'"

"No problem. You'll get a full refund if it doesn't work."

Berger's thigh was throbbing from the incision when Kelly arrived at two in the afternoon. Kelly was putting on a stoic facade, yet Berger noticed a slight tic in his eye. Or maybe Berger was just projecting his own anxieties, which were growing exponentially as they neared the 8:00 P.M. rendezvous. As time ticked by, this whole thing was sounding less and less appealing. Maybe Jill was right after all. Wherever the hell she was.

He and Kelly made awkward small talk until Jill arrived. She gave each of them a curt greeting, then sat in the chair furthest from Berger. So far, she hadn't looked him in the eye.

Some guy named Armstrong came in right after her. He looked like a high school football captain except for the fact that his eyes didn't work in coordination with each other.

"Here's a map of the Century City Shopping Mall," said Jill. She unrolled a large page. "The meet is here, in front of the AMC Theaters. We have agents covering every angle, and the ones on the roofs have binoculars and parabolic microphones. We've also bugged the motel room where Mr. Berger will be waiting. Mr. Kelly, here's the gold lapel pin you're supposed to wear. They'll probably accuse you of notifying the FBI, which you should deny. Combs is supposed to be there personally, but I wouldn't hold my breath. My guess is they'll say he's waiting for you somewhere else."

"What do I do if they say that?" asked Kelly.

"You make the call. If you decide to abort, just walk away, and there's no hard feelings. If you're willing to try it, use the 'reporter has the story' ploy."

They ran through the routine several times, until the conversation dwindled into silence. Berger wanted to reach out to Jill. He wanted to take her hand. He wanted to hug and kiss her, right there in front of the others. He wanted to carry her into the bedroom and make passionate love to her.

His thoughts were punctured by Jill's words. "Last chance to abort, gentlemen. This is the fail-safe point." For the first time she looked directly at Berger. Her eyes moved rapidly back and forth while she stared, as if they were shivering.

"I'm in," said Kelly. He bowed his head and began to pray quietly.

Berger and Jill held each other's gaze. He wondered if she'd stay with him if he pulled out of this, and he tried to read her thoughts. He felt certain she would, although it wasn't right to take her love when he could only be there a short while. He only had one choice. He had to go down swinging.

"I'm in," said Berger.

Jill looked away.

Kelly continued praying.

CHAPTER 41

Kelly stood in the International Market Place, an assortment of food booths jammed around a raucous indoor area of the Century City Shopping Mall. He watched a tiny woman, dressed in black with a veil over her face, herd several children toward a pizza stand. A huge lady at a nearby table acted like every bite of her salad was bad-tasting medicine.

At eight precisely, Kelly strolled out to the open-air mall. For an East Coaster, an outdoor mall was an amusing and thoroughly California phenomenon. The weather simply didn't allow this kind of thing in Boston, especially in November. He walked toward the AMC Theater Complex, where huge lines led to a multiwindowed box office. The crowd seemed to be crushing each other forward, despite the SOLD OUT signs over most of the movies. His eyes searched the mob of people, trying to guess who might be his contact. Other than a few smiles from young ladies, no one seemed to notice him.

Eight-fifteen. His stomach was doing flips, and he worried that Combs had decided to abort. He didn't want to look for the FBI surveillance, although he hadn't noticed it. He hoped Combs's people hadn't either.

Eight-twenty. He had the absurd thought that this was rude to keep him waiting. Like they really cared about his feelings. They were probably just trying to rattle him. He didn't want to show that they were beginning to.

Eight-twenty-five. A tap on his shoulder. He turned around quickly and saw a homeless man, in filthy pants, holding out his hand. Kelly handed him a quarter, and the man said, "Thank you, Mr. Kelly."

Kelly's eyes widened. How the hell did they know his name?

"Try the men's department at Macy's," said the man before shuffling away.

Kelly walked over to Macy's, his pace quickening along with his heartbeat. He went into the men's clothing area, where a young salesman with dark eyes handed him a pair of pants.

"Try these on, Mr. Kelly. Back here."

He escorted Kelly to a changing room and closed the louvered door. Kelly stood there holding the pants, with no intention of putting them on. Being half out of his pants was way too vulnerable.

A voice spoke through the mirror. "Where's Berger?"

"Where's Combs? And where's the money?"

"When you supply Berger, you get the money."

"And Combs?"

"He's busy."

"Then so am I," said Kelly. He walked out and slammed the door, rattling the flimsy wall. Throwing the pants at the salesman, he said, "These don't fit."

Suddenly two men came up on either side of Kelly. They were both over six feet. One was an African-American with dreadlocks, and the other was a blond with a barrel chest and deep blue eyes.

"You shouldn't walk out on your host," said the blond.

"You shouldn't have kept me waiting for a half hour. Was that supposed to be some junior high intimidation technique? The deal was that I talk to Combs."

"Why do you care about Combs?"

"I have a proposal I want to make to him personally. Are we on or off?"

"We're on. But Combs isn't here. We'll take you to him when we have Berger."

"Uh-uh. You get Berger when I get the money and see Combs."

"We seem to have a standoff then, don't we?" The dreadlocked man crowded Kelly, forcing him into the blond. It caused him to lose balance on his prosthetic leg, and he grabbed the blond's shirt to keep from falling. The man roughly shoved Kelly's hand away and smoothed out the wrinkles where he'd grabbed.

"This routine is amateurish," said Kelly. "You must know that I trust you even less than you trust me. This deal only goes down one way. Everybody lays their cards on the table before anybody picks up their share of the pot. You produce Combs and the money. Then I produce Berger." It was a lot easier to act like a tough guy when FBI agents were waiting in the bushes.

The two men looked at each other quickly. Kelly read from their expressions that they didn't have much authority and weren't sure how to handle the situation. Good. He pressed on.

"Combs must know that I took out insurance against you dumping me in some garbage can. A reporter friend of mine has a sealed envelope. That might sound like some B movie, but let me assure you it works. If I don't show up in person by tomorrow morning, he opens it and has time to get the story on the afternoon news. The envelope's got the whole story of Mirage, a picture of Combs, and Berger's location for an in-person interview. Now you've wasted a half hour by keeping me waiting."

The men exchanged glances, then the blond moved Kelly against a wall and stood inches in front of him. Kelly could smell tobacco on his breath and tried to move away, but the man was too large. Dreadlocks took off and returned a few minutes later.

"Okay," said Dreads. "The money's in the mall parking garage. We'll show it to you now, then you take us to Berger. If he's there, you can either take the money and leave, or we'll take you to Combs with Berger. If I were you, I'd catch a plane to the Caribbean."

"You're not me."

They went down the escalator two levels to the lower parking garage. The men stayed on either side of Kelly, giving him the distinct feeling that he was a prisoner walking the Last Mile to the chair. They led him to a late-model black Jeep Cherokee and carefully surveyed the area before approaching the car. Once satisfied they weren't being watched, the African-American opened the tailgate.

Inside was a tan canvas satchel. Kelly opened the case and saw it was full of fifty and hundred dollar bills, banded into neat stacks. He picked one at random and fanned through to see if they were real. They were, and the smell of fresh money was exquisite. Then he picked up another and did the same.

The blond man took the packet out of Kelly's hand and tossed it back in the case.

"Let's go," he said.

"My car," said Kelly.

"No chance."

"No deal."

The blond and Kelly stood looking at each other in silence, like two Old West gunslingers waiting for the other to draw.

"Want to call your handler again?" asked Kelly.

The veins stood out in the neck of the blond, whose complexion was beginning to redden. "I'll go with you. He follows in this car."

"Fine. But the money goes with us," said Kelly.

Kelly drove the FBI's Ford Contour out of the parking lot, with Attila the Hun riding shotgun and the canvas suitcase locked in the trunk. The Jeep followed closely behind. He turned onto Little Santa Monica Boulevard, then cut over to Big Santa Monica, where he turned west. A few blocks away, he pulled into the parking lot of a tiny, one-story motel called Holiday Out.

They parked the cars and convened outside the Jeep. Kelly said, "I'm going to check you for guns that I assume you have and should therefore put away before I take them. Then you get a look at Berger, but you don't get near him until I see Combs. I don't want him having any unfortunate accidents. At least while I'm around."

"How do we know it's him?"

"Please. You must have pictures."

"First we check you."

Kelly held out his arms, and they patted him down. If they were surprised by his artificial leg, they didn't show it. Kelly was glad the FBI was using parabolic mikes instead of a wire, because these guys were probing him more thoroughly than his last physical exam. When they finished, the men went to the Jeep, surreptitiously dumped whatever arsenal they had, and returned. Kelly checked them for weapons just as Jill had shown him, hoping he wasn't missing anything.

His good leg felt wobbly as he took them to the window of room 6.

"Look through the small opening in the curtains."

The two large men crowded around a four-inch gap between the fabric. Kelly opened the door, reached inside, and turned on the light. Berger was tied up in a chair, with duct tape over his mouth and a terrified expression in his eyes. After a few seconds, Kelly turned out the lights and closed the door.

"Now let's see Combs," said Kelly.

"Sure," said the blond.

Kelly didn't even feel the blow before he blacked out.

Jill sat in the command van, parked on Century Park East. Armstrong was next to her, together with a techie who was working the equipment.

The black and white video was crude, yet it told the story. The agent on the motel roof was already whispering into the radio. "They knocked out Kelly and they've got Berger. They're putting bags over their heads. Do we take them?"

She held up the microphone, her thumb on the button. Her mouth was open, yet she didn't speak. She was transfixed by the grainy video image of two men throwing Kelly and Berger into the Jeep.

Finally, she pressed the button. "Let them go and follow them."

"You sure?"

"No. Do it."

CHAPTER 42

When the Jeep carrying Kelly and Berger drove off the video monitor, Jill felt as though she was physically rocking, like a car dangling halfway off a cliff. She clutched the arms of her seat in the control van, praying she'd made the right call to let them go.

Bernie called in from the single-engine Cessna that was circling three thousand feet above the scene. "Got 'em on infrared. Heading east on Santa Monica, now south on Avenue of the Stars."

Jill picked up the microphone. "Timmons, stay close."

"Got it."

"Wait," said Bernie. "They're turning into the garage of a high rise. Somebody get over there."

"Moving," called Timmons. The roar of his motor almost drowned out his voice.

Jill realized she was closer than Timmons. "Get us over there," she barked at the driver.

The van started with a lunge that almost threw Jill off her seat. She held on to the seat back as they cornered sharply.

"Shit," said the driver. "The metal garage door just rolled down behind them."

The techie in the van spoke in a deep bass voice. "I've lost Berger's tracer. The signal can't get through the concrete walls of the underground parking."

Jill said "Shit" under her breath. She threw open the van's sliding panel and jumped out.

"What are you doing?" called Armstrong.

"What does it look like? I'm going after them."

"If you go in, you blow the cover and the operation's dead."

"If I don't, Kelly and Berger are dead."

"Maybe, maybe not. We can still follow them. Let it play out."

"It's too risky."

Armstrong was worrying her. Was her judgment affected by her feelings for Berger? She had convinced herself that she could handle all that, and now he was rattling her. No. She was doing the right thing. She couldn't endanger civilians like this. She should have stopped this stupid plan when Berger first suggested it.

Armstrong ran out and grabbed her arm. "Jill, they knowingly took the risk. This is our only chance at Combs. Cut the line and the fish is gone."

"I'm making the call, and I say we go in."

Armstrong sighed. "At least stay in the van and let me go inside. We'll need you here to coordinate things."

"We'll both go. There won't be anything to coordinate if we don't get in there."

The techie threw them each a walkie-talkie. Jill and Armstrong ran to the front door of the high rise. A security guard sat sleepily by the elevators, watching a sitcom on TV. Jill banged the door with her shoe heel until the gray-haired man finally looked up and ambled toward them. She pressed her FBI badge against the glass door with one hand, and gestured for him to hurry with the other.

She turned to Armstrong. "You take even-numbered parking levels, and I'll take the odd-. Starting with the upper ones first."

Jill next spoke into the walkie-talkie. "Get as many agents here as you can. Put someone on the garage exit and all back doors and fire exits. Have the rest start checking the upper floors, from the bottom up, and from the top down."

The guard jangled a large ring of keys as he opened the door. Jill and Armstrong ran past the befuddled man toward the garage elevators. Their footsteps echoed off the terrazzo floor against the marble walls.

Inside the elevator, Jill pushed "P1" and "P2," then repeatedly hit the "Door Close" button. The doors closed slowly, and they descended in silence, save their labored breathing.

"P1" lit up and dinged as the doors slid open.

"Your floor," said Armstrong. He winked as she stepped out.

"Stay in touch," she retorted.

When the doors closed behind her, there was an eerie quiet. The garage was poured concrete with numerous pillars, but only about twenty cars at this hour. The recessed lights were placed far apart, blotting the area with dark pools of shadow.

One of the cars was a green Jeep, which could have been the one she'd seen on the monitor. Unfortunately, the monitor was black and white, and she didn't know if the color was right. Jill started toward the car, and her footsteps echoed so loudly that she took off her shoes. As she tried to move in the shadows, she felt the floor's oil and grease seep through the feet of her pantyhose. She placed her hand on her gun.

Jill stooped over as she approached the Jeep, to avoid anyone inside seeing her. She first looked underneath and didn't see the feet of anyone waiting on the other side. Then she gently pressed her body against the side panel and slowly raised her head to the window level. The car's interior was dark and appeared empty. She inched her hand toward the door handle.

Over her right shoulder came an electrical whirr. She spun toward the noise, reflexively pulling her SIG Sauer and crouching into a shooter's stance. Adrenaline pumped her heart, and she sucked in a deep breath.

In her sights was a security guard, riding in a golf cart with a spinning red light. His hands were already over his head.

"FBI," she shouted. "Keep your hands up."

He didn't look like there was any chance of not complying. Still, she approached him slowly and checked his identification.

"You see anyone on this floor in the last ten minutes?" Jill asked.

"No, ma'am. But I just started work."

"Have you seen a Jeep with four men in the garage?"

"No. Just a few businesspeople leavin' late."

"Where?"

"P2 and P3."

Jill pushed the talk button on her walkie-talkie. "Armstrong. Anything?"

"Negative on P2. I'm heading for P4."

Jill's walkie-talkie crackled. "Uh-oh," came Bernie's voice from the surveillance airplane.

"What?"

"There's a helicopter about to make an illegal landing on the roof of your building."

"Armstrong! Meet me on the roof." Jill ran to the elevator and banged her fist against the call button. She quickly seesawed her shoes back on.

"You in an elevator?" she asked.

"Affirmative," reported Armstrong.

"Hurry."

After several moments, Armstrong said, "Passing the fourteenth floor."

"Touchdown," said Bernie. "Blades still turning. Four people running into it. Two being dragged."

"Eighteenth floor," said Armstrong.

Jill's elevator still hadn't come. Shit. Shit. "Follow them, Bernie."

"They've lifted off. I'm on 'em. They're heading west."

"I'm not getting Berger's signal," reported the techie. "It's probably the height. I've only tested this device on a ground plane, and—"

"Stay on him Bernie," said Jill.

"He's an easy target."

Jill hesitated. They might not have anticipated the FBI having a plane in the air. But an easy target? That didn't seem right for people this smart.

"Stay at the building exits," she said. "The helicopter could be a decoy."

"Two cars coming out," reported Townsend, one of the agents who had just arrived outside. "First is a blue station wagon. Dark-haired female, mid-forties, driving. Second is a Range Rover. African-American male in his twenties. Large build."

Jill's elevator finally arrived and she punched the lobby button. As soon as she got to the lobby, the techie reported on the walkie-talkie, "I'm getting Berger's signal."

She answered as she ran toward the command van. "Where?"

"He's in one of the cars that just came out."

"Which one?"

"I can't tell. They're too close together."

"Townsend, get on the cars. Bernie, can you see anything?"

"Got 'em," said Bernie from the plane. "They're heading south on Avenue of the Stars. One is turning west on Olympic. The other's going down toward Pico. I'm gonna lose the helicopter if I don't get on it."

"Let the helicopter go. Stay with the cars."

Jill rushed inside the van, perspiring heavily from the run. "Follow the cars," she ordered the driver.

"Armstrong's still inside," he replied.

"Follow them!" The engine whined as the van squealed onto Avenue of the Stars. "Townsend, Larkin, have you still got the vehicles?"

"I'll take the one on Pico," said Townsend.

"I got Olympic," reported Larkin.

Jill barked at the techie. "Can you tell which car has Berger?"

"Not yet. When they separate a little more."

"Which one are we following?" asked the van driver.

On instinct, Jill said, "The Range Rover."

If there was any good news in this, it was that the operation was still intact. Since the men evaded the agents, they were probably unaware of the FBI's presence. So it was still possible to follow them to Combs. At least theoretically.

Jill watched the Range Rover drive leisurely below the speed limit, stopping at every light. Worried the van was too obvious a tail, she told the driver to hold back.

"I got a closer visual at the traffic light," said Townsend.

"The female driver is one of the goons with a wig. And he's not a particularly attractive drag queen."

"Both cars just turned on Bundy," Bernie reported. "I'll bet the caravan's headed to Santa Monica Airport. I can't get any closer without entering the airport's traffic control pattern, so you guys better take it. I see two private jets with engines fired on the tarmac. If I had to bet, they're gonna shuffle your people in a game of two-plane monte."

Jill turned to the driver. "Get us there ahead of them. Is there a place we can observe the jets?"

He stepped hard on the accelerator. "I'll cut down Gateway, so we're on a different route. There's a high spot where they park the private planes, though we'll be visible to them."

"We have to risk it." She turned to the techie. "Call the Bureau office and have them contact the airport tower. Tell them we need info about the private jets immediately."

"I'm just a radio guy. That's—"

"Armstrong's not here, so you're elected."

"I don't know how—"

"You pick up the phone, you dial the damn number, and you ask the question. Got it?"

The techie grumbled but picked up the phone.

Jill spoke into the radio. "Townsend? Larkin? What have you got?"

"Airport's the place. They're heading right for it."

The techie handed Jill the phone. "They want you."

She grabbed it out of his hands and recognized the voice of Kenny Stern of the Bureau office. "The jets' flight plans show Canada and Colorado. They're owned by a local leasing company, and leased to two different corporations. Cessna Citations. Very fast planes. We can't scramble anything fast enough to chase them in the next few minutes."

The van came to a rough stop and rocked in place. Jill

grabbed a pair of binoculars and jumped out onto the tarmac, among dozens of parked single-engine planes. Below
her were the two jets, barely visible in the low light. She
stayed in what were hopefully shadows and switched to a
night-vision scope. The scene appeared in a surrealistic
green. Two cars opened their doors simultaneously, and
four people rushed from each car. She tried to see if any
of them were limping, yet couldn't tell. Two people from
each car were tied up with sacks over their heads, and
they stumbled as they were being rushed toward the planes.
In less than fifteen seconds the groups were inside the
planes and the doors closed. The jets' engines screamed
as they both taxied toward the runway.

The techie called from the van. "I'm hooked into the
tower. They want to know if they should hold the planes."

Jill's thoughts raced. A few moments ago, she'd been
hopeful she was on her way to Combs. Now, Berger's
transmitter would be useless once they took off, and there
was no way to follow him without it. Any jets she could
get in the air would be at least a half hour behind, and
even assuming they could track them on radar, she couldn't
intercept before they landed and got the hostages into
ground transportation. If she stopped the planes, that guar-
anteed Berger's and Kelly's safety, yet there was no way
to find Combs. And the Thanksgiving plans go forward.
She knew Berger wouldn't want her to stop things. If
Rover—the system to track the chemicals—was working,
and if the chemicals were at the same place as Combs,
things could be okay. If Rover wasn't working . . .

Her primary concern had to be the safety of her people. This was all getting too dangerous.

"Hold the planes," said Jill.

"Hold the planes," repeated the techie to the tower.

The roar of a jet's engines told her they weren't listening.

"Hold them, dammit!" she shouted.

"The first one is taking off without authorization," said the techie. "The tower's yelling at them, because they almost hit a Piper Cherokee."

Jill looked through the binoculars and watched the jet disappear. Then she looked back and saw the other jet about to do the same.

She threw the night-vision goggles against the tarmac, shattering them into shards and metal parts.

CHAPTER 43

Even though Berger was blindfolded, it was obvious from the engine roar and angle of ascent that he was on an airplane. His hands were tied behind him with some kind of plastic that cut into his wrists. He shifted his weight several times, unsuccessfully trying to get his arms into a comfortable position.

The black cloth bag was still over his head. The fabric clung to his nostrils every time he inhaled, and each exhale filled the bag with warm air that condensed into perspiration. Several times he called out, "Hey!" Either they were ignoring him, or the engines were drowning out his shouts.

The fact that they hadn't yet killed him probably meant they weren't going to. At least right away. Why go to this much trouble to move somebody around if all you want to do is throw them in a Dumpster? He hoped Kelly was okay.

"I can't breathe," he yelled out.

No answer. He tried screaming at a shrill pitch that hopefully cut through the engines. He was rewarded with a slap across the face that knocked the side of his head into something solid. Probably the window of the plane, since the surface was cold and smooth. He rested his throbbing face against it.

Jill's comment that they might torture him crept up like a Ninja. Maybe they kept him alive to find out what the FBI knew. Berger had a low pain tolerance—"You're a complete wuss," as his mother used to put it—and he wasn't sure he could take any torture. He should have asked for a cyanide pill or whatever the modern-day equivalent was. Why put himself through agony when he'd be gone in a few days anyway?

"Slice him open," came a deep voice. Another voice laughed.

Berger froze. He felt a fist grab his shirt and throw him roughly onto the floor. His head scraped against the seats as he fell. Then he felt the icy edge of something cutting into his navel. A sharp pain shot through his abdomen as his skin parted like ripping fabric. Next the unmistakable feel of his innards spilling out, and warm liquid gushing from his body. Screaming in terror, he rolled onto his stomach as if that might hold them in.

That was when he realized he was still sitting up.

It had been another hallucination. The voices in his head. He felt the relief of waking from a nightmare, yet his body continued to shudder.

The hood was now soaked and clinging to his face, like shrinkwrap being heated to encase a package. It was becoming difficult to breathe, and his throat was closing.

He thought of his mother, lying in a casket near his father. He hadn't even gone to her funeral. He thought of Linda, strangled and discarded. Of Max, scared and alone. Or dead. Of Jill, rejected and hurt. Of the tortures that lay ahead.

*   *   *

Combs paced back and forth along the asphalt runway, which was lit only by the yellow-orange flames of round smudge pots. The dark Montana sky, far from city lights, was a black velvet canopy speckled with countless stars. Combs hadn't noticed any of them.

He lit a cigarette and took a deep drag. Then he pulled up the sheepskin collar of his rough suede coat, and thrust his hands into the pockets while he continued pacing in the icy night.

Bringing Berger and Kelly here was a calculated risk, yet he had to take it. Kelly would live or die, depending on Combs's mood at the time. But his plans for Berger were delicious. The joy of personally squashing an insect that had been droning around his head.

Combs looked up at the sound of an approaching plane. When he could see the red and green wingtip lights, he gave a nod to the four men standing nearby. They moved to their positions along the runway and picked up the bags of dirt.

The plane's tires squealed as the jet touched down with the nose inclined so steeply that the tail nearly scraped the runway. Several hundred yards later, it gently rocked forward and reversed engines to slow its speed. The four men ran behind, throwing dirt on the smudge pots to darken the runway and assure that no one following could see where to land.

When the plane came to a halt, the engines whined down to silence. The door opened and a stairway dropped to the runway. Combs pulled on a black ski mask.

The men inside were forcing Berger and Kelly down the jet's stairway. It was an awkward exercise, since they had cloth bags over their heads.

"Get them in the Jeep," said Combs. He turned to the

four men. "Cover the jet with camouflage and stay here. If anyone else tries to land, blow them up."

Berger was forced onto some kind of hard chair. His wrists were cut free and the returning circulation made his hands tingle. A few seconds later, he felt his arms and legs being tied to the chair with a softer binding. Then the bag was pulled roughly off his head.

The light assaulted his eyes and he reflexively blinked them shut. When he tentatively squinted to get his bearings, Berger saw he was in a small living room with knotty pine paneling. It had a woven-rag rug, lamp shades decorated with drawings of dogs, and floral curtains on the windows. All in all, the place looked like an Ethan Allen furniture showroom, which was hardly what Berger had expected. Welcome to our Early American Torture Center.

Berger's legs and wrists were bound with a white cotton rope. He tugged, yet there was no give. The feeling was already starting to drain from his hands and feet.

Next to Berger was Kelly, also tied to a chair. His face was sweaty, and Berger figured he'd also been bagged. Behind them were several large men, all wearing knit caps pulled down over their faces, with crudely cut eye and mouth holes, giving them the look of grotesque jack-o'-lanterns. Berger flashed on the image of a skier in one of his hallucinations, and he realized he'd seen it in this setting. Or someplace like this. His legs trembled, and he felt his bladder losing control.

A thin man, wearing a black ski mask, entered the room and studied Berger and Kelly. From the deference in the others' eyes, this had to be Combs. Berger noticed that Combs was holding something in his hand. A metal pole with straps, ending in a shoe that dangled on a swivel.

Kelly's prosthetic leg.

"Why are you treating me like this?" demanded Kelly. "I delivered Berger to you. I assume your goons told you that I've got a reporter on standby if I'm not back in a few hours. Why are you fucking with me?"

"We know you're working with the FBI," said Combs. He played with the leg.

"Bullshit."

"How does it feel to be without your leg? Can't run. Can't stand for more than a few seconds. How's it feel?"

"I take my leg off every night, so if that's supposed to intimidate me, you're on the wrong track. I kept my end of the bargain, Combs. Why are you doing this?"

"Do you think we're stupid, Mr. Kelly? We know Berger was in a safe house. You couldn't have gotten to him without the FBI helping you."

Berger looked at Kelly. How did Combs know about the safe house? More importantly, how was Kelly going to get out of this one?

Kelly blinked rapidly a few times, then spoke calmly. "Of course the FBI gave him to me. How else could I deliver him to you? I was using them to get the goods. I knew you'd evade their tail. If you'd treated me better, I'd have told your Nazis that he's wearing a transmitting device, and I'd have shown you how to remove it before you left Los Angeles."

Combs's eyes widened. Kelly was smiling. Berger was terrified. What the hell was Kelly doing?

"He couldn't be wearing a device. We checked him," said one of the goons behind Berger.

"Here's the deal," said Kelly. "I'll show you the device. If it's where I say it is, you let me out of here with my money. If it isn't, you can kill me."

Combs looked back and forth between Kelly and Berger. He twirled the leg like a pinwheel.

"Show me," he said with a slight smirk.

"Do we have a deal?"

"Sure. Why not."

"It's implanted under his skin. On his left thigh, about six inches below his pelvis."

"You sonofabitch!" yelled Berger, trying to stand up. He only succeeded in cutting the bindings into his arms and legs. "You're a . . . a . . . fucking traitor!"

Kelly laughed.

"And you're a fool, Berger," Combs said with a chuckle. "You could have profited from this, just like Mr. Kelly. Although I guess that doesn't matter to someone whose brain is turning into jelly."

The goons were now laughing as well. One of them took out a large knife with a deerfoot handle and sliced up Berger's pant leg. The fabric ripped with a sickening sound.

The man roughly poked Berger's thigh. "There's a fresh wound here," he said.

"Cut out the skin around it," said Kelly. "The device is in a little pocket."

Berger's leg exploded in pain as the man cut open the skin and peeled it back. Blood spilled over his leg, and he screamed loudly. Two men grabbed him from behind and held him down.

"Here's something," said the man. He threw the bloody device to Combs, who studied it. He looked up first at Kelly, then at Berger. Combs dropped the device on the floor and crushed it with his heel. Berger felt his hopes deflate as the transmitter was ground into pieces.

"Cut Mr. Kelly loose," said Combs. The man used the bloody knife to cut through Kelly's bindings. Kelly rubbed his wrists vigorously.

"I misjudged you, Kelly," said Combs. "You're a smart

man. I could use you." He threw over the prosthetic leg, which Kelly began to strap onto a misshapen stump.

"I'm flattered, but I'm strictly freelance. Just give me the money and a ride home. And quickly, if you don't want to be tomorrow's headlines."

Combs went into the other room and came back with a tan canvas suitcase. Kelly opened it and thumbed through the bills.

"Beta and Omega here will take you to the plane," said Combs.

Berger watched the exchange, helpless. He couldn't break the restraints, and in any event, he couldn't take the four linebackers standing around him. He would have settled for snapping Kelly's neck like a dry branch. Instead, he sat there impotently, strapped to a chair with his leg bleeding onto the floor.

CHAPTER 44

They untied Berger and jerked him into a standing position. Then they stripped off his clothes. He tried to fight when they got to his underwear, but a blow against the cut on his thigh collapsed his leg. They pulled off his underpants while Berger lay on the floor, like a mother undressing a child on the bed. The cold room, and his own humiliation, raised gooseflesh over his entire body.

The men retied him to the chair, then lifted the chair and carried him through a doorway. He was now in a larger, stark white room. His chair sat on a highly polished white tile floor, lit by fluorescent lights overhead. There were no windows. And no sounds.

Several minutes later, they brought in six other people. Three were placed behind him, and three by his side. The ones Berger could see were an old man, who looked to be in his seventies, an attractive Latina with raven hair that hung to her waist, and a balding Asian man with rimless glasses. All of them were nude and tied to chairs; all slack-jawed, not reacting to their surroundings. They appeared to be hypnotized, or more likely drugged. Berger moved his attention from one to the other, yet none of them seemed to notice him. He was ashamed to find himself glancing at their nakedness, and forced himself to look away.

Combs came into the room and approached Berger. "Does the room look familiar, Mr. Berger?"

"No. Should it?"

"Well, yes and no. You've been here before. Just before the EXC explosion. But you don't remember. You were one of our best subjects, Mr. Berger. I'm actually glad to have you back for some reprogramming."

"What is all this? Where are my clothes?"

"You're naked because it makes you feel more vulnerable. Works, doesn't it?"

A large man rubbed a swab of cotton in the crook of Berger's arm. Berger tried to pull away, yet was tied too tightly to move. The cold sting of evaporating alcohol was followed by the sharp stab of a hypodermic needle.

"We're giving you Neo-Ketamine. It will make you very suggestible, just like the others. Too bad you won't remember the show. It's really quite impressive. Last time, your girlfriend Linda was one of the stars."

Berger had the feeling he knew something about this. Buried deep below his conscious level of thought. He didn't want it dredged to the surface.

"The way we program people to destroy themselves," explained Combs, "is by creating a strong enough motivation. Most people have something they're willing to die for, given the right set of beliefs. With you, it was to avenge Linda's murder. You watched a man in an EXC outfit strangle her. She fought hard. One of the toughest."

Berger's eyes teared, though he thankfully didn't re-

member Linda's death. How could he live with the fact
that she'd died for the sole crime of dating him?

Berger spat at Combs, whose obsidian eyes flared.
Combs's body tensed, though he quickly checked himself. He spoke softly. "I kept you alive, Mr. Berger, because I'm going to let you go tomorrow. Back to that
pretty little FBI agent Landis who's been protecting you.
The two of you can have a warm, lovey reunion before
you flip the switch that blows you both away."

"Fuck you," yelled Berger. "I won't do it."

"Oh, you'll do it all right. When the Neo-Ketamine
takes over, you'll have no choice. Feel the drug? It starts
out as a tingle. First in your extremities, then working
inward. Very pleasant, actually. Relaxing. Just go with it,
and watch while we program the others."

Berger tried to wrestle free, yet could only rock the
chair a tiny bit from side to side. Large hands on his
shoulders clamped him down. He gave up the effort and
dropped his head back. Combs was right. He was starting to feel numb in his hands and feet, as if they were
falling asleep. He also thought his heartbeat was slowing, although he wasn't sure if that was his imagination.

"You won't believe how simple this is," Combs said
with a wink as he walked away from Berger.

Two of the masked men pushed the older man's chair
forward. His face was thin and sunken, and his spotted
skin sagged off his bony arms and legs. The man's mouth
hung open, as though his muscles were totally relaxed.

Two more men brought in an elderly woman in a
ripped, flowered dress. Her hair was half in a bun, and
half loosely tangled. The man in the chair straightened
his head in recognition. Berger noticed that he and the
woman wore the same gold wedding ring with a single

diamond. She looked at the man in the chair, her eyes pleading.

"Help me, Lenny!" she slurred. Combs's men kept a firm grip on her arms, as if holding up a drunk.

"Cynthia!" The husband suddenly came to life and tried to free himself, yet he seemed to be moving in slow motion. He twisted his wrists against the restraints, bruising his aged skin. Within moments, one wrist began to bleed.

Lenny's mouth tried to form words, yet he seemed unable.

"Help me!" she moaned.

Another masked man, wearing a black shirt with the white letters "JFK," entered the room. He held a black handgun with a long barrel, which he pointed directly at the woman's face. Lenny struggled so hard that he and the chair fell sideways. One of the men caught him, and Combs spoke loudly into Lenny's ear.

"The man with the gun runs JFK Airport, Mr. Seal. He's been after Cynthia for months. Stop him! He's crazy. He's going to hurt her."

Seal continued to struggle, managing to buck his chair forward a few inches. He tried to say something, but all that came out was a pathetic wail. His eyes overflowed with tears as he shook his head, *No, no!*

The JFK man put the gun into the woman's mouth. Her screaming stopped and her eyes widened in terror. Cynthia struggled to pull free, yet was too small and drugged for the men who held her. A plastic tarp crackled as one of the masked men laid it out behind her on the white tile floor.

"Help her, Mr. Seal. You can save her if you really want to. You're the only one who can rescue her. Get him, Mr. Seal. Hurry. There's no time."

"Cynthia!" Then a guttural groan that sounded like "Let her go" erupted from deep inside Lenny.

"Combs!" shouted Berger. "Stop this. You're a fucking sadist."

"Hurry, Lenny," said Combs, ignoring Berger.

"No!" yelled Berger, holding the "o" as long as his throat allowed. His shout ended abruptly with the gunshot.

The noise reverberated loudly in Berger's ears as he watched the back of the woman's head explode in a spray of crimson, bone, and gray. Then a horrid silence before she slumped to the floor. Berger's eyes went to Lenny, who was throwing up on himself while sobbing horribly. The other people in the chairs seemed oblivious.

Two men wrapped Cynthia in the plastic and began mopping up the spray that overshot the tarp. Berger felt as if he were going to retch, and he turned his head to the side. His body heaved, and his mouth filled with the rancid taste of bile.

"Mr. Seal, you didn't stop him," said Combs softly.

Seal gurgled incoherently.

"I can help you," Combs continued.

The other masked men gathered around Seal and spoke in a jumbled chorus.

"Yeah. We'll all help you, Mr. Seal."

"That was awful."

"He can't do that to her."

"He can't do that to you."

"We're with you, Mr. Seal. Just tell us what to do."

"Make him pay."

Combs waved them into silence and spoke to Seal. "The day before Thanksgiving, at noon, this man will be at JFK Airport near your house in Flushing. I'll show you where to go. We'll give you a special vest to wear that day. With it, you can destroy him."

Combs draped a thick, pleated gray vest over Seal's bony shoulders.

"Feel it? It's hard and strong. It will protect you. And see this? Just push this button and you avenge Cynthia's death. You couldn't help her this time, but you can have the last word. Nod if you want her killer to pay."

Seal nodded.

The chorus began again.

"That's the spirit."

"Way to go, Mr. Seal."

"We're proud of you."

"We'll be right there with you."

Combs spoke more forcefully. "Now, Mr. Seal, you're going to forget everything you've seen tonight. When you see the JFK sign at noon on Wednesday, but not before, you will remember your rage. Your helplessness. You'll know deep in your subconscious that Cynthia was killed by this man, and this is how you're getting even. But consciously, you'll only feel anger. And the reflex to push the button.

"Forget everything else, Mr. Seal. What you'll remember about this weekend was that you spent it skating. And it was beautiful. Blue skies, clear crisp air, and smooth ice. See yourself gliding, Mr. Seal? Long, clean strokes. Skating better than when you were eighteen years old. Happy children following you for the candies. Giggling because you're so kind to them. See yourself warming your hands by the fire afterward. Going home for a wonderful night's sleep."

Seal's face had relaxed and he actually seemed to be smiling, like a child falling asleep to a bedtime story. Berger wondered if Combs could really make that horrid memory vanish so simply. Then he remembered that was obviously what Combs had done to him.

Berger had been so enraptured in the display that he didn't realize his body was now numb. He felt almost as if his head were attached to an inanimate object, and wondered if that's how it was to be paralyzed.

Seal now dozed peacefully, and the men slid his chair back in line with the others. Then they pushed forward the Latina with raven hair. And spread out a fresh plastic tarp.

Kelly whistled as he walked through a wooded area with the two escorts. He wasn't crazy about the way they kept watching him, and wanted this over as quickly as possible. The bag of money, which had seemed light at first, was now wearing into the palm of his right hand. He shifted it to the left.

In his peripheral vision, Kelly watched the woods carefully, hopefully without alerting the guards to what he was doing. Finally, he spotted the red flash of light. It lasted only a millisecond, yet it sent his heart pounding. He took a breath, as if he were going to dive into a swimming pool, then dropped flat on his face in the dirt.

The two guards stopped abruptly in their tracks.

"Get up," one yelled, just as the bullet ripped into his chest. When the other turned to look, a second bullet took him down. Seconds later, a squad of ten commandos flooded the path.

"You all right, Mr. Kelly?" asked a young man whose face was blackened with charcoal stripes.

"Now I am. The cabin's back there about a half mile. They've got Berger and a group of others. Give me a piece of paper and I'll draw you a layout of what I saw.

I think there's a perimeter alarm, because one of these guys radioed back that they were outside it."

A rugged man in his thirties addressed the troops. "If there's an alarm and we can't avoid it, we'll have to move in very fast. Higgins, your men take the back and sides. Clark, Gibson, in the front with me. Mr. Kelly, behind that clump of trees is a Jeep. Have a seat and wait for us."

"Can't I help? I was in the infantry and—"

"Sorry, sir, no civilians. Gentlemen, on my signal."

The man held up his hand until he had the troop's full attention. Then he pointed and they moved stealthily forward, like a silent snake crawling over the landscape.

Berger closed his eyes, trying to tune out the horrific tableau in front of him. He hadn't watched anything since they spread the second trap. The screams of the raven-haired woman pierced his attempted hibernation. Then a school bell.

School bell?

The room was immediately silent, save the whimpering of the young woman.

"Perimeter alarm!" came a voice.

"We have visitors," barked Combs. "Defensive positions."

Combs smashed Berger on the side of his face with a gun butt, knocking him and the chair over. He landed hard on his side, sending a flash of pain through his arm. Then Combs shoved the gun against Berger's left eye and said, "Whoever's out there won't be any help to you."

Suddenly there was a bright flash, as if a lightning bolt had struck the house. It was followed immediately by an explosion. The concussion threw Combs off balance, and his gunshot hit the floor near Berger's head, spraying him with splinters of tile. Berger's first thought was that they'd been bombed, yet nothing seemed damaged. He assumed it was a concussion grenade, even though he'd never seen one. A moment of silence followed the blast, after which everyone began to scream, including Combs's men.

Berger wrenched his neck up and saw that everyone was on the floor, excepting the old man, whose chair was somehow still upright. Combs's men got up simultaneously, as if on cue, and there was a scramble of legs around Berger's face. Then the crashing of window glass, another flash of light and explosion.

All the activity had loosened Berger's bindings enough for him to start wiggling. There was only a small amount of play, and his limbs weren't functioning very well, yet he felt like the ropes were getting looser. After several minutes, one of his hands slipped free and he began to work his other bindings loose. He saw one of Combs's men taking off his clothes, and lying on the floor to look like a victim. Smart, he thought. Except that I see you, you bastard.

Berger got free and pulled himself upright with great effort. His body was leaden, sluggish, and he could hardly keep his balance. No longer conscious that he was nude, he was driven only by the desire to get Combs. Berger could see that Combs wasn't in the room, and that there were only two exit doors. He looked back and forth between them, chose the door on the left, and opened it slowly.

It led to a dark room. Berger poked his head in cautiously. In the low light, he couldn't see anything. Just as he was about to leave and check the other door, he heard a squeak. His ears perked. It had come from the room.

Berger fumbled for a wall switch and couldn't find one. He opened the door wide, hoping to draw in as much light as possible, then stepped slowly inside. His bare skin bristled and his hands were ice. He knew he was a sitting target in the backlight, yet he didn't have a choice.

There were no more sounds. Opening the door had added only a small amount of illumination, and his eyes were still not adjusted. Berger worried that Combs was already gone, and that he was wasting time looking here. He also worried that Combs might still be here, waiting to finish the job he'd started with the gun.

Berger took a tentative step forward. His body was propelled by the adrenaline he could literally feel coursing through him, and he tasted its metallic bitterness in his mouth. Another step and he saw it. A trapdoor in the floor, slowly closing. A hand lowering it quietly. That had been the squeak.

Berger moved toward the trapdoor as quickly as his body would cooperate, then stomped it closed with his bare foot, smashing the hand between it and the floor. A feral scream came from below, and Berger grabbed hold of the exposed hand. He then kicked the trapdoor open and dug his fingernails into the hand. Even though the room was still in shadows, he felt certain it was Combs. Berger had to hold him long enough for whoever set off the concussion bombs to arrive. He knew he couldn't beat up Combs even in his prime, much less in this drugged state. But hopefully he could hang on.

Berger's hands were sweating, lubricating his tenuous hold. Combs suddenly jerked with such intensity that he almost slipped free. Berger tightened his grip, then used a hand-over-hand technique to work down to Combs's wrist, where he got a better hold. He had to hang on.

There was no choice. Berger yelled to keep his muscles tense.

Berger's grip was now solid, even though his muscles ached from the strain. He braced his feet against the trap-door and leaned back, hoping to use his body weight as a counterbalance. He was holding steady. A standoff. Nothing wrong with a standoff. Where the hell was the cavalry?

Almost imperceptibly, Berger felt the tide changing. He realized he was being pulled forward, toward the hole. The trapdoor cut into the soles of his bare feet, and he struggled to hang on. He was now having to lean forward, and he felt his lower back straining to stay firm.

Berger dug his fingers into Combs's flesh. A few more moments of struggle and Combs's arm was moving toward him again. He managed to lean back, adding his body weight into the surreal tug-of-war. Yes! Combs's arm was clearly starting to yield. A few more pulls and he'd have him.

Then all the resistance stopped.

Berger tumbled backward, surprised by the sudden capitulation. His head hit the floor and stung in a burst of pain. He realized that Combs had sprung out of the hole to throw him off balance.

Within seconds, Combs was on top of Berger. He kneed him in his exposed testicles, which sent an excruciating pain through his groin. Then he began to smash Berger's face with his fists.

Berger's slowed reactions couldn't even deflect the blows. Combs now straddled him, and Berger couldn't free his pinned arms. He felt his nose shatter with one of the punches, and a gush of blood flowed over his upper lip into his mouth. He tried unsuccessfully to spit out the salty, viscous liquid.

Combs grabbed Berger's ears and used them to smash his head repeatedly against the floor.

"You fucking idiot," yelled Combs. "Picking a fight in your condition? You can't resist my suggestions. All I have to do is tell you that you're helpless."

Berger hadn't thought of that.

"Your entire body is paralyzed," said Combs. "You can't move."

The words were familiar. Like the hypnosis. And the statements connected directly into his subconscious. Berger felt his body going limp. He tried to move his arms and legs, yet couldn't. They were immobilized, and now even breathing was a strain. He had no feeling in his body, as though he were anesthetized. He couldn't even twist his facial muscles in panic.

Combs stood up and laughed a quick snort. Then he stomped Berger in the face with the heel of his boot. Berger heard the sound of his jaw breaking, and knew his face was collapsing. His body was growing distant, as if it were disconnected, and he teetered on the edge of unconsciousness. Gurgling with blood that now flooded his throat, he couldn't even bring up a gag reflex to cough it out. The only mercy was that he was feeling no pain. He closed his eyes and thought of Jill. Loving and warm. Nude and embracing him. Covering her midriff with her blouse.

Suddenly he was aware of cold metal being shoved into his mouth, cracking against his teeth. He tried to open his eyes and found that one of them was already swollen shut. With the other, he saw Combs's finger on the trigger of a gun in Berger's mouth.

"Too bad you can't even say goodbye," hissed Combs.

Not like this, thought Berger. Not here at the mercy of this asshole. Even if he had only a few more hours with Jill, he wanted them. Berger's anger ignited like a flame in his abdomen, then erupted through his entire body. Warming him, and returning feeling.

He remembered what Durham had said when he hypnotized him: "I don't hypnotize you. You hypnotize yourself." And he remembered how he'd used self-suggestion to soothe his leg pain after the shooting. Why couldn't he override Combs's suggestions with his own?

He ordered his fingers to move.

Nothing.

The gun barrel twisted deeper into Berger's mouth, scraping the back of his throat.

Concentrate! Move your fingers.

Nothing.

Move, for God's sake!

Almost imperceptibly, his index finger twitched. Or at least he thought it did.

He wasn't sure how much control he really had. Whatever he could muster would have to do. He'd have the element of surprise, if nothing else.

The sound of the gun's hammer cocking blasted into Berger's ears. He told himself he was strong and powerful. That Combs was light and weak. Berger summoned all of his strength and made his move.

He knew the first thing was to get the friggin' gun out of his mouth. So he quickly brought his left hand across, shoving Combs's wrist and the weapon to the side. The sudden movement took Combs off guard, and the barrel ripped the side of Berger's cheek. But he got the damn thing out of his mouth before Combs could fire. The bullet smashed into the floor about an inch from Berger's ear. He felt as if his eardrum had burst, and a loud ringing continued in his head. Forcing himself past it, he bit

Combs's hand until he let go of the gun. When he did, Berger swatted it away.

Combs grabbed his hand in pain, which distracted him enough for Berger to get up. He kicked Combs in the groin, doubling him over. Then he used both fists to bring them up into Combs's face, throwing Combs onto his back on the floor.

You are strong. You are powerful. Combs is weak.

Berger quickly straddled Combs and started punching him in the face. When Combs tried to fight back, Berger grabbed the top of his ski mask and began smashing Combs's head into the floor. Again and again. Harder and harder. Berger yelled with each slam, like a karate master breaking a board. The blood from Berger's face splattered onto Combs with each exertion. Combs's head made a cracking sound with each blow, and his skull felt as though it were softening in Berger's hands. Berger certainly hoped so.

A few more blows and Combs went limp. Berger moved up and put his knee on Combs's windpipe, then leaned all of his weight onto the man's neck. Berger willed his weight to be heavier, hoping he could crush this animal.

A light went on in the room, and Berger could now see that the exposed part of Combs's face was blue. He dug his knee in harder. Just a few more minutes . . .

A pair of hands pulled Berger off. Berger turned on his attacker in rage, throwing wild punches. A young commando in khakis easily parried the blows, sending Berger into a spin. Another commando took hold of Berger's arms. Berger started back toward Combs, and the first man put his hand against Berger's chest. With a gentle voice, he said, "It's okay, sir. We've got him."

Berger looked down at Combs. The young commando

put two fingers against the artery on Combs's neck. He
looked up and nodded that Combs was alive.

The survival instinct that had carried Berger this far
was quickly draining, and he fought against passing out.
He was now aware of pain in almost every part of his
body, and his legs were rubbery. Still, he held on, worried that losing consciousness would use up his last few
hours of coherence.

The commando pulled off Combs's mask. Just as
Berger collapsed into blackness, he saw that Combs was
Chuck Durham, the cult specialist.

CHAPTER 45

Berger had once read an article that suggested people could die and not know it. While everyone around you mourned, you would think you're continuing life as usual: waking up, getting dressed, going to the office, making love to the missus. All in some other plane of existence.

Right now, things were so blurred that Berger worried he was in that other plane. He couldn't remember what had happened. He didn't know where he was. He couldn't open his eyes, although he was in a light so bright that it permeated his lids.

He was aware of the cool softness of sheets against his skin, and assumed he was in a bed. A quiet breeze blew across his face, and he was lulled by the sound of birds chirping nearby. Hopefully it was a weekend, so he didn't have to get up early. He was so tired. Maybe a little later . . .

When Berger next awoke, it was dark. For the first time, he was able to open his eyes. As he blinked to clear the accumulated gunk, he tried to focus on his surroundings. In the dim light, it looked like he was in his boyhood bedroom. There was a plastic airplane hanging on nylon fishing line, twisting slowly in the heated air from a ceiling duct. There were posters of Apple Computers and chess tournaments on the walls. A collection of seashells and a purple lava lamp. All exactly like his room in high school.

Berger's pulse suddenly raced. Maybe he was in some other plane of existence. Back in his childhood.

No way. He didn't really believe that crap about life going on after death.

He reached up and felt his face. The heavy bandages certainly seemed real enough. So did the aches throughout his body. Hopefully you got rid of those when you "passed on," so he must be alive. Berger fumbled for a bedside light and couldn't find anything that felt like one. With great effort, he rolled his head to the side and saw the figure of someone sleeping in a chair next to his bed. Just an outline in the shadows.

"Hello," he said. Talking burned his raw throat.

A quiet snore.

"Who's there?" he asked, a little louder.

Nothing.

"*Hello,*" pretty loudly. The body stirred and sat up.

"Marvin?"

His body chilled. It was his mother's voice, calling his father. Both of whom were dead. The paradox short-circuited his brain, and he hesitated to acknowledge her. This was scaring the shit out of him.

"Marvin?" she repeated.

"Mom?" he blurted involuntarily.

The figure leapt out of the chair and turned on the light, searing his eyes. "Johnny! Thank God!"

It was his mother. And now she was hugging him so strongly that it felt like his ribs were close to snapping.

"Mom? I thought you were . . . gone."

She let go and straightened up. "Gone? Where?"

"I mean, they told me you were killed in the gas station explosion."

"Who told you that?"

Berger suddenly remembered. The FBI agent in the hospital. Of course. It was one of Combs's men. He'd told him Bert was dead just to throw Berger off guard.

The realization erupted into a broad smile across his face. He reached up to hug his mother with the little strength he had in his arms. She more than made up for his grip with a bear hug that suspended his breath. Her tears mixed with his in pools on their faces, muffling the repeated "I love you."

They held each other for several minutes without speaking. Berger didn't let go as he asked, "What about Raoul?"

She broke their embrace and stepped back, never taking her eyes off him. "Raoul and I got some burns and bruises, but otherwise we're fine. I needed a few skin grafts, so now I can scratch my ass and my neck at the same time. Fortunately, skin's something I got plenty of."

"You're awake!" came a woman's voice from the door.

Berger painfully turned his head to see an angelic figure standing in the light. "Jill? What are you doing here?"

Bert answered, "This sweet young lady has been here every evening for the last week."

"I've been here a week?"

"Yes," said Jill. "You were in the hospital for ten days before that."

"It's been over two weeks?" asked Berger. After a few moments, he added, "But what about my mental breakdown? Isn't it, like . . . overdue?"

Jill explained that Mirage had found a promising antidote just before the project shut down. Although Combs denied it, and there was nothing in the papers Kelly shredded, one of Combs's men said they'd been experimenting with lithium. For some of the subjects, lithium eliminated the psychosis.

"How long will the lithium work?"

"I guess we're going to find out."

Berger lay his head back on the pillow, which suddenly felt rough and jagged. "Did you catch Kelly?"

"Catch him?"

"Yeah. He sold me out and ran off with the money."

"No, no. He only pretended to sell you out, so he could get outside and give the commandos a map of the cabin."

"You planned that whole thing? He told them to cut my goddamn leg open. How could you hold that back from me?"

"Sorry. But after your performance as a telephone company employee, we thought your reactions would be better if you didn't know."

"Thanks for the vote of confidence," he said sourly. After a respectable sulk period, he said, "Although you probably made the right call."

"Sorry."

Jill went on to tell him there had been a break in the sunspots that allowed Rover to pick up a signal from the Neo-Ketamine bottles. Based on the original tracking, they knew that Combs's operation was in Montana, but not exactly where. So the FBI had assembled a commando team in Billings, then moved them by helicopter when they got the exact location.

"What if they'd taken the chemicals out of the bottles?"

"Then we wouldn't be having this conversation."

A long silence. "How badly did I hurt Combs?"

"Only a few bruises. You have a ways to go before you get your Rambo license. But you held him there, and now he's singing like a bird. Federal prison seemed like a Hawaiian vacation compared to what he thought the Serbians would do to him."

"Serbians?"

"A dissident group of Serbians, still pissed about America's meddling in Kosovo, were behind all this. They're led by a terrorist called Charlie, and he's the one who selected you."

"Charlie picked *me*? Why me?"

"Apparently you had a run-in with him in college. He was deported because of it."

Of course. Karla's brother. The man who interrupted Berger's first sexual experience. He was Charlie? Berger shuddered, realizing he was lucky to have survived the incident in college.

Jill continued. "It turns out that Charlie's parents were U.S. spies in the former Soviet Union. They'd gone into hiding because an American leak compromised them, and they jumped to the top ten on the KGB list. Charlie and his sister came to the U.S. under phony names to stay out of sight, but his deportation was in the public records and blew his cover. The Russians simply followed him, and a few years later, it led to his parents. No one has seen them since. And you can understand that all this didn't leave Charlie with a very good taste for the United States."

Berger was definitely lucky to be alive. "So what was this all about?"

"Combs assembled enough subjects to blow up six major U.S. airports on the day before Thanksgiving, one of the busiest travel days of the year. All synchronized at the same time. If he'd succeeded, he would have certainly created the atmosphere of terror he'd promised the Serbs. And established his reputation as the producer of future events."

Bert exhaled. "My lord."

"By the way," said Jill, "the Military Records people in Salt Lake City were impressed with your hacking skills."

"How'd they know? There shouldn't have been a trail."

"You left a few pieces of wire when you cut off a jack, so they knew someone had been there. But they assumed you didn't get into the system, since there was no trail in the computer."

"What tipped them off?"

"Yesterday, they finally decided to give us the Mirage records. When I told them not to bother, they put two and two together and wanted to know how we did it. I denied everything, of course, but they didn't believe me. They said, 'Just tell your computer gnome that we'd like to hire him or her to rework our security system.'"

"Sure. They can be the first client of my new consulting firm. I think I'll call it Lithium Industries."

Jill put her fingers over her mouth as she laughed in a light, singing melody. He savored her smile, her soft eyes and molasses hair.

"There's someone else who's been waiting for you," said Bert.

She whistled loudly and Max came lumbering in. When he saw Berger, he practically lathered himself with excitement. Bert scooped him up and put him on the bed, where he promptly stuck his nose under Berger's hand to be petted.

"Where was he?"

"He got picked up on a street in Venice. Your vet's name was on his collar, and the pound called her. She had my name as a backup."

Berger held out his hand for Jill, and she came up to the bed. Max started growling, and Berger pushed Max to the other side. "Sorry. He's a bit territorial."

Max nosed under the covers and burrowed down to

Berger's feet, still growling. Jill interlaced her fingers with Berger's, and the touch of her skin was electric.

"You came here every night?" he asked.

She turned a reddish blush. "Well, yes."

Bert came over and leaned close to Berger's ear, then whispered loud enough for Jill to hear. "You should marry this one."

Acknowledgments

I'd like to thank the following people for their generous help:

Shana, Danny, David, Josh, and Jordan, for allowing me the time and space to disappear and write, and for always being there with your love.

Mort Janklow and Eric Simonoff, for your encouragement and salesmanship.

Larry Kirshbaum, for continuing to believe.

Sara Ann Freed, for your fine editorial eye.

The women and men of the Los Angeles Federal Bureau of Investigation, for your insights into the Agency's workings.

Special Agent Scott Sweetow, Bureau of Alcohol, Tobacco and Firearms, for your expertise on explosives.

The late Dr. Jolly West, for sharing your vast knowledge of cult techniques and mind control.

Dr. Alan Konheim, for the crash course in cryptography.

Joel Zucker, for a primer on computer hacking.

Michael Lea, for the computer techniques.

Bea Shaw and Danny Passman, for your editorial help.

Chuck Phillips, for insights into the Arizona desert.

Drs. Ed and Riva Ritvo, for the medical and scientific info.

Heidi Rummel, for connecting me with the Feds.

Kim Mitchell, for always making me look good.

And of course Max, the Jack Russell Terrorist.

Beautiful businesswoman Lisa Cleary's life is being shattered by recurring psychic images of terrified women . . . mutilations . . . murder . . .

Then Lisa discovers her "hallucinations" describe actual serial killings. The crime scenes. The locations of weapons. And murders not yet committed . . .

Lisa's waking nightmares are growing more frightening, more precise, leading ever closer to a killer . . . and to secrets beyond all visions, beyond even the darkest dreams . . .

THE VISIONARY
(0-446-60-831-9)
by Don Passman

"A TENSE THRILLER . . . A SURPRISING GRAND FINALE AND A SATISFYINGLY LOGICAL CONCLUSION."
—*Midwest Book Review*

AVAILABLE AT BOOKSTORES EVERYWHERE
FROM WARNER BOOKS